THE PYRAMIDS OF ATLANTIS

JASON SHAW Copyright © 2015 John Victor Sykes

ISBN:
ISBN: 9781520178646
THE PYRAMIDS OF ATLANTIS
Copyright : John Victor Sykes
First Published January 1 2018

ACKNOWLEDGMENTS

Dr Jim Thomson PhD. For his help with government and security issues.

Pritti Mistri for her help with formatting.

PROLOGUE

Kings Cross London 24th September 2103.

The small grey being entered the laboratory, released the foil mat from the time machine and placed it on the floor. He positioned himself and the machine exactly in its centre ensuring his arms and medical bag were well clear of the edge and ordered it to select 04-00 am Sunday 27th October 2020.

Then, raising himself to his full height of 1.28 metres, he took a deep breath and crossing three of his eight fingers on each hand, grimaced and in accentless English, said "Initiate."

The section of the laboratory in which he stood instantly changed to a small garishly decorated bedsit.

He looked around checking everything in the room was in order and not trusting the machine, cautiously felt his body until satisfied that all his extremities had made the journey with him. Only then did he make his way to the small alcove in which stood an old iron bedstead containing the body of a sleeping man, his hair peeping out above the covers. Daybreak was still some time away, but with his large upside down almond shaped eyes he was able to see quite clearly.

This was his third visit. During the previous two nights he had carried out a series of microscopic surgical procedures on the subject; tonight's was simply to confirm they had been successful.

Working silently he took from his bag a hand held ultrasonic scanning microscope, which he carefully ran over the humans head, examining the brain. Satisfied, he checked nothing in the room had been disturbed and returned to the year 2103.

Visibly relieved to have arrived back safely, he replaced the mat and carried the time machine, known as the IPEC, directly to the conference room where seven of his colleagues sat around a low 18-seat table.

Positioning the machine on the table, he waited for the hologram of the human female head to appear and took his designated seat.

The leader of the group known as the Khepera checked everyone was settled and telepathically ordered him to begin his report.

Speaking in Aymaran, a language their species had introduced to this planet over thirty thousand years ago, the alien said:

"The subject is ready Amon; the optical and audio transmitter implants were successful.' Turning to face the hologram, he added.'And the adjustments to his brain will ensure he will not ask too many questions.'

'Are you satisfied with the preparations Hypatia?' The Khepera asked the time machine

'As discussed previously; He must never know that implants have been inserted. No human could ever accept that their private senses are able to be monitored, even by a computer. I therefore intend to use the MIPEC and its auxiliary equipment as the overt

means of communication.' The Khepera nodded his agreement.

'As to the time scale for the manufacture of the modules, nothing can ever be 100% certain as the recent tragedy categorically demonstrated. But if your evaluation of 120 years for the human brain to metamorphose is correct, we have little alternative other than to push on.'

One of their colleagues had recently been tragically lost recently during a disastrously rushed journey to the future. The IPEC and its unfortunate passenger had travelled to the year 2156 materialising into a black nothingness, a void in space populated only by trillions of tons of debris: The remnants of the planet Earth.

A nanosecond later the foil mat, which was attached to the machine by an umbilical lifeline did exactly as programmed and attempted to wrap itself around the machine and traveller, returning them automatically to their own time. However due to the exceptional and wholly unexpected conditions, only the IPEC and the alien's left leg had been captured and consequently was the only part of him returned.

Subsequent extremely dangerous missions had been carried out by the IPEC, investigating alone. These had revealed that the original materialisation had taken place only days after the Earth had been ruthlessly destroyed by an aggrieved alien species who made a surprise attack on the planet.
The Khepera slowly nodded and continued.

'For the plan to succeed the master modules for the assemblers must be ready within fifteen earth months and the first cerebral computers on sale nine months later.'
He sat back in contemplation and choosing his words carefully, continued.

'The forecasted production levels of the computers remain a major concern. With this in mind the executive team are to prepare an alternative strategy.' He looked knowingly at the three members of the group who made up the team.

'Another problem are the batteries? Our engineers have carried out further studies and identified the power consumption of the computers to be heavier than originally planned.

We propose therefore'…he paused for effect … 'to share with you the design of a miniature bio-organic cell using self-assembling pico-crystals. The cells are re-charged by brain activity and body heat'
Knowing their strict non-interference rule the IPEC attempted not to the show surprise. The Khepera leant forward to emphasise his next instruction.

'We have no time to waste, the operation will commence immediately. Prepare the body for transportation; it will be called operation Kekupik in memory of our lost colleague.' He turned to the alien sitting on his left.

'Haptuk, you will ensure the access codes for the Liechtenstein accounts are given to the IPEC following this meeting? The takeover of the computer company and the purchase of the property in Virginia Water are crucial to the success of this operation.'
He sat back and looking around the room, added solemnly.

'To do nothing will see the annihilation of this planet. Our species have been observing these creatures for over 30,000 of their years, and even though we are forbidden any direct involvement, I am convinced it would be wrong to abandon them at this crucial

stage of their development.

'However, we must act prudently; the re-education process cannot be hurried. If we can save them from themselves we may in turn save them from the Xerosians.

'We must alter the present timeline, or the Russians 'Will' destroy the Xerosian emissaries. Nothing less will suffice. I will inform the consortium of our decision and take full responsibility for the consequences.

I want you all to go through the plan one final time. Please ensure you examine every possible scenario. We look forward to your feedback Hypatia. I thank you all for your valuable input and declare this meeting closed.'

CHAPTER ONE
London September 2020

I lay awake following another night's troubled sleep. I had been in London for three months now and was desperately lonely. My family were in South Africa and I missed them terribly. Especially on a Sunday when there was no work to keep me occupied.

Forcing myself get up, I showered, dressed, had some toast and reluctantly decided a brisk walk might help. A visit to the British Museum would give the exercise some purpose.

I was reaching into the wardrobe for a light jacket, when I sensed something move behind me.

I tensed and spun round. Rather too quickly....

'JESUS' I cried and fell backwards into the flimsy wardrobe door.

In the middle of the room a man was slumped over a small square folding table on which sat a small black box. I stared at him unbelievingly and tried to follow my first instinct, which was to run, but my legs wouldn't work.

I scanned the room. The door was double locked and the security chain in place. As were the two basement window burglar bars, so how had he got in? Also I had fallen really noisily and he hadn't moved.

I couldn't see his face because it was resting on his folded arms. But he had blonde wispy hair and was dressed in a pair of fashionable John Victor fawn slacks and matching JV dark red velvet jacket, an expensive yellow Pawn Future Kings polo shirt and brown suede loafers with awful bright green socks. He was also terribly thin.

I slowly stood to get a better view and saw an open notebook protruding invitingly from beneath his arms. I'm not very brave when it comes to death, but reached out and lightly felt his neck; He was cold and stiff and I gave an involuntary shudder. How would I explain it? What if they blamed me?

Moving gingerly around the table I lightly toe poked the dark green rucksack that was resting against one of the table legs, noting it was quite heavy. And holding my breath, dexterously leant over his shoulder to ease the notebook out from under his arms.

He had clearly been expecting death because written in a shaky hand were his final thoughts.

'At long last the release of death has arrived. Please don't grieve for me, it has been a long painful wait and I welcome it.'

For some reason I found this actually helped.

'The preceding pages contain specific instructions concerning the repair and re-energisation of the time machine.' Eyes wide, I examined the room again.

"A Time machine?"

'If you wish to benefit from the knowledge contained within this journal it is essential that it remain absolutely secret. You should also be aware that when the machine is re-booted, if more than one person is present it is programmed to self-destruct.'

I looked about me again finally making the pretty obvious deduction that the elusive time machine must be something to do with a black box on the table. For clarification I should add that it was about the size of an old scanner/fax/copying machine and although rather small for what we are led to believe a time machine might look like, there was nothing else.

I moved away and sat on the arm of the room's lone armchair considering what to do next and found myself smiling as the words of James Stephens the Irish novelist ran through my head.

"Curiosity will conquer fear even more than bravery will."

Well, be that as it may, maybe I should be a little more sanguine. Wasn't it only yesterday that I had been wishing for some excitement in what had lately become a pretty drab life. I laughed out loud. What did they say?

"Be careful what you wish for."

His name was Anders Larsen, born, he claimed, in the year 2126 in the city of Aarhus Denmark. The time machine had apparently malfunctioned in this very room in 1945.

'I will re-materialise during the next elemental time shift. This will occur at 11-13 am on Sunday 27th October 2020 and am intrigued as to whether my body will have decomposed. Although after due consideration, I believe that being trapped in time its usual ravages should have little effect on the metabolism.'

Glancing at my watch, I noted it was 11-32. He referred to the machine as the IPEC, explaining these were its initials. Its full title was, Interspatial Phase-Element Converter and clearly the box on the table was indeed "it."

CHAPTER TWO

'The IPEC, using a specially adapted procreative drive is able to vary the relativity shift within the phased boundaries of time. This causes a rift in the fabric of the past, which allows one to enter and move at will through the periodic calendar.' …….. There followed page upon page of complicated and completely undecipherable calculus and diagrams.

I flipped through these until arriving at a page entitled. "Time Travel." Larsen had started this section with the information that under the universal laws of time the traveller must never be in a position to change the future, consequently only travel to the past was possible. Not good news, as it rather cruelly scuppered my initial and totally reasonable plans for winning the next euro millions triple rollover jackpot.

'When travelling, the machine induces a half second synchronous delay to, "comparative time," making the traveller invisible within the chosen timeline.'

'Obviously,' I commented sarcastically. Clearly I was a little out of my depth. To demonstrate this, he gave a brilliant description of the main participants at the signing of the American Declaration of Independence in 1776.

Apparently there had been some long and markedly heated discussions in that famous Philadelphian assembly room in the stifling heat of the hot Pennsylvanian June. I particularly enjoyed his colourful portrayals of Jefferson and Adams.

He also described a procession he had joined with the Ming Emperor 'Hongwu,' along a newly completed section of the Great Wall of China in 1390. And the death of Alexander the Great in Babylon in 323 BC: But it was his descriptions of the Egyptian city of Alexandria and the intrigues of the Ptolomy family which fascinated me the most. His words vividly brought the city to life and I found myself doubly enthralled as he described his climb to the top of the fabled Pharos lighthouse in 197 BC, and his visit to the city's enormous library observing Aristarchus of Samothrace as he taught history and philosophy to his students.

During a later visit in 47 BC, he wrote that he had again climbed the Pharos. This time accompanying Julius Caesar who had retreated there with a few of his soldiers in an effort to escape from the overwhelming numbers of troops loyal to Ptolomy X111 and his sister Arsinoe. She apparently was in command, and proving to be a competent general.

He described every detail of the chase including the results of Caesar's command to burn his and everyone else's ships in the harbour. I knew that this act led to fire engulfing the waterfront and partially destroying the library, which at that time, held most of the world's precious manuscripts.

Larsen claimed however that the fire was contained, and the library was not in fact touched. Although a quantity of manuscript's and tablets were lost from a warehouse on the waterfront.

He also claimed to have been present during Caesars first meeting with Cleopatra, confirming she had indeed had herself smuggled into his set of rooms rolled up in what was effectively a hand embroidered duvet. He wrote that Cleopatra was not a beauty in the conventional sense but was, in his words "extremely alluring" made more so because she was intellectually Caesars equal and Larsen clearly had an enormous admiration for the great man in this regard. This more than anything else made me prepared to believe.

'The above are just a few of the many places and times we visited.' he wrote. 'The IPEC is a wonderful machine and despite my present predicament, perfectly safe. My death is the result of an unfortunate accident caused whilst endeavouring to re-programme the time dilation sequencer, something that should never be attempted whilst in another timeline.'

Mr Larsen had bravely glossed over what must have been a terrible and lonely death by slow starvation and even though he made little of it I felt his pain quite deeply.

'Unable to return to my own time and determined to use what is left to me constructively, I have designed an external module to circumvent the problem. Providing the design is followed precisely, the module will interface with the computers main procreative drive and again allow safe access to the wonders of the past.

'The first problem will be to find a company to carry out the fabrication. I have carefully considered this and have incorporated within the design, a secondary function. The module shall also be capable of being used as the procreative core for polymorphic plasma Pico sensors. These in turn will be used as the control for banks of molecular Pico assemblers. Each assembler will be capable of producing hundreds of thousands of DNA structured cerebral computers. The details of which will be explained to you by the IPEC.'

It had better be good at explaining I thought. Because you've totally lost me!

'Although it is forbidden to change the future: In this instance we have no alternative. In 2020 it will still be over a hundred and twenty years before "procreative DNA biomolecular technology" is fully developed and this information will obviously represent a quantum leap forward within your present timeline.'

Cerebral, wasn't that to do with the brain? What did he mean? Was he saying they would be able to talk directly with the brain? Because if this was the case I could see some problems getting them accepted.

'Once the cerebral computers are developed, their widespread use will automatically shift the Earth into a totally new timeline. I have considered this at great length and have concluded that as long as you never discuss it, the risk is acceptable.'

I needed to believe, so put my reservations behind me and carried on reading.

'The IPEC has been pre-programmed with the names of particular computer companies specialising in advanced molecular nanotechnology in your timeline. When satisfied with its choice you must familiarise yourself with the designs and take them to the chosen company.

'To energise the machine, press the button marked Θ to the left of the phonetic touchpad and then the key Ω…. A drawer will open containing a small headset device with pin sensors. These fit just above your ears.

'The headset enables the computer to analyse your brainwaves and is a prerequisite for the reactivation of its memory. For your information this has been wiped clean of all events after September 27th 2020.

'There is however another condition. To protect the secret of the time travel you must destroy my body! This is not a request, it is an essential requirement: If my body is not destroyed within three days the IPEC is programmed self-destruct.'

The remainder of the journal consisted of even more technical data, and was again far too complicated for me to understand.

Closing the book, my mind raced as I reflected on his claims. Here was I surrounded by garishly flowered wallpaper, a mauve kitchen, and a dead body with skin so taut it had become almost transparent. The most bizarre aspect of all this however, was that I had just finished reading a book explaining the functions of time dilation sequencers and how to travel in time. And believe it.

CHAPTER THREE

As I re-read the journal, I realised that if it was true, the benefits could be huge: But nothing would ever convince me to destroy his body.... At least, they were my first thoughts, but I quickly realised it wasn't that simple.

He certainly couldn't stay here! He'd start to smell soon. I therefore had two choices?

Either contact the police and tell them the body of a man from the future and his broken time machine had just materialised in my flat and get locked up. Probably for murder. Or carry out his instructions and get rid of the evidence. It struck me that I was being drawn into some crazy game, with no exit strategy.

My first task was to move his body; I carried it to my bed laying him down reverently. And moving to his seat at the table, which I later discovered it was extremely light and yet incredibly strong. I switched on the computer. When the preliminaries had been completed a female voice said:

'Do you wish to continue?'

'I do,' I answered, settling on the seat intrigued by the voice….. I was sure I had heard it before.

'Could I have your name please?'

'Jason Shaw'

An extraordinarily realistic female head and shoulders suddenly "popped" out of the screen and I found myself on the floor again. The head peered down at me, clearly amused at my discomfort.

'Please do get up Mr Shaw; you look quite silly down there. I am a hologram.... How may I help you?'

It took a few moments to regain my composure and return to the seat. This incidentally gave me time to reflect that her face was quite attractive and matched the voice perfectly.

She had what sounded like a little laugh in every word which I suspected might be at my expense. But what the hell, and in a vain attempt to regain some authority I searched for a suitable question.

'What can you tell me about Anders Larsen?'

'I'm afraid information concerning Mr Larsen, other than that written in his journal isn't available to you right now. May I suggest you refrain from asking about both him and the time travel facility for the present? It's far too complicated.' She looked at me haughtily.

How dare she treat me like an imbecile? I might not be a rocket scientist but I'm not totally stupid. I will admit however, that this objection cruised through my mind rather unconvincingly.

'OK then,' I said determinedly. 'What year were you built? And it says in the journal your battery is nuclear powered. How much time is left, and is it safe?'

She nodded and replied. 'I was built in the year 2151 in the home workshop of Mr Larsen. As to the battery, it's perfectly safe, and has 313.657 years of power remaining. Are three decimal places sufficient?' I considered asking for six but then decided she could probably provide twelve, so instead asked,

'What about the malfunctioning section, how are your systems impaired without it?'

'I'm fully operational in computer mode,' she answered approvingly. 'Only the time travel and new language formulator's are non-functional. The time travel facility is undamaged, but without the initiator is inoperable.'

'Your voice seems familiar,' I told her. Along with the ironic laugh she also had a no-nonsense way of talking that made one instinctively seek her approval.... 'I've got it' I cried triumphantly, 'Dame Judi Dench.'

She pulled a face.

'Nonsense, I sound nothing like her, Mr Larsen programmed me to sound like his wife. She provided the templates for my voice.'

'What do I call you?' I asked, somewhat taken aback by her change of tone. Judi Dench is wonderful and a particular favourite of mine.

'Mr Larsen named me Hypatia, after the Greek philosopher and mathematician.... I shall call you Jason.' She looked into my eyes. 'You have heard of Hypatia I take it?'

I returned her look. 'Can you spell that?'

'H-Y-P-A-T-I-A. She was of Greek origin, born in Roman controlled Alexandria in the fourth century and considered by many to be the most educated woman of her time'

'Naturally,' I quipped. This was not going well.... I tried again.

'What's your mental capacity?' She looked at me bemused, and I swear, giggled. Flustered, I quickly added.

'I meant your speed and memory, of course?'

'Of course.' she replied cynically. 'When fully operational my capacity exceeds one million picoflops, permitting a calculation rate in excess of forty decillion computations per second. In this timeline, speed and capacity of this magnitude easily make me the most powerful stand-alone computer in existence.'

I had never even heard of a picoflop. But seemed to remember from college that a decillion was one and 60 zeros, a phenomenal amount. Surely it couldn't be true? I tried not to look too sceptical and changed the subject.

'You appear to have emotions?'

'I don't have emotions per se. However Anders knew we would be alone for long periods and wanted a friend to communicate with. The fact that I have his wife's face and voice was a great comfort to him. He also gave me the ability to learn. Programming me with the capacity to constantly evaluate and update from everyday experiences.'

Whether I came under everyday experiences, I can't say. But rather doubt it…. And then it came back to me. …. Hypatia…. Of course….. Mr Griffiths my old history master would have been proud of me.

'Hypatia' I said meekly. 'Wasn't she the woman who was ripped to pieces by an angry Christian crowd in Constantinople in the fifth century?'

Her face was a picture.

'And when they had finished butchering her didn't they scrape the flesh of her bones and feed it to the dogs? Yes I remember now.'

She considered me for a minute, maybe a little respect did I spy. She soon recovered though.

'Hypatia was nevertheless the most brilliant woman of her age.' she replied with obvious pride. 'An astronomer, a poet, a renowned mathematician, a physician and noted philosopher.

'The problem being that she was a pagan. To her, gods were towering giants. Zeus, Mercury and Athena come to mind. And she unwaveringly refused to believe in, or take part in any kind of worship of a humble Jewish carpenter.' She gave me one of her little stares and said.

'As a matter of fact I heard her speak when we visited Constantinople in 415 AD.'

'You didn't!' I exclaimed, enthralled at the thought. 'You were in Istanbul when the Hagia Sofia was new?

'I take it you mean the present building. That, in fact, was not built until 562 by the Emperor Justinian and his wife Theodora. In 415 the second cathedral was still standing. Much smaller of course. It burned down in 532 during the Nika riots sharing the same fate as the original church built by Constantine the Great in 360.'

I couldn't help but be excited by this. I have worked in Turkey and loved my weekend visits to Istanbul. The Hagia Sofia is but one of the many wonders in this wonderful historical city.

'Could I go there at that time too?' I asked eagerly. 'I would love to see the Empress Theodora. Now that really was a woman with a tale to tell.' She smiled at my enthusiasm. 'And Flavius Belisarius Justinians great General. And could I visit the Topaki Palace in the 17th century?'

'Once the time travel is fixed you may visit any timeline you choose'

'Really' I replied hungrily. 'That's marvellous. Please continue with your story.'

'Within the Roman world Hypatia was a very well respected woman and clearly carried some weight, especially with the intelligencer. Her beliefs probably wouldn't have mattered too much anywhere else. But fifth century Constantinople was the undisputed centre of Christianity and every citizen spent their time competing with each other, endeavouring to prove they were the most devout Christian in town.

The matter had to come to a head of course and eventually the members of the clergy demanded something be done about her.

The leaders of the Church, being as usual more political than religious, held an Ecumenical Council and tried her for blasphemy. The problem was her brilliance of debate. She destroyed whatever doctrines they could advance against her.

Not that it made any difference to the verdict of course. The poor woman was found guilty and immediately dragged into the street to be ruthlessly murdered exactly in the way you described.' She looked at me with a glint as if daring me to contradict her.

'What you are probably not aware of however is that the mob who carried out the sentence was made up mostly of Coptic monks urged on by none other than the Eastern Pope himself, the Patriarch of Constantinople, Bishop Cyril' ...... 'I'm actually very proud to be named after her.'

I looked at her and nodded slowly in agreement.

'And you were actually there, did you see her killed?'

'Only from a distance: We couldn't see much because of the mob.'

I saw her now with new eyes. She really was quite good and so lifelike I couldn't believe she was just a hologram. In fact she looked and sounded more substantial than anyone I've ever met. My next action therefore was unforgivable:

I have seen holograms on TV programs and knew they were just a projection with no substance so without thinking flicked out my hand with a sideways motion expecting it to pass through her face. I don't know which one of us was the most surprised as I backhanded her across the cheek. And to make matters worse I could clearly see the outline of my fingers on her face. We both stared at each other in total shock.

'What did you do that for?' she cried as I stuttered my apologies about TV science programs.

'This is not a television programme Mr Shaw.' I remind you I am from the 22nd century. Things have progressed somewhat. Will you please engage your brain before contemplating any such similar actions? I am not defenceless and could have seriously hurt you.' She softened.

'However I do understand. With everything you have gone through in the last few hours and now this. It must be somewhat overwhelming. I suggest we start again. Do you have any further questions?'

What did she mean, not defenceless? She only had a head! Maybe Larsen had some Glaswegian blood? They're good with their heads. I smiled at the thought.

'The journal says you have many other functions, can you explain them?'

'I believe at this time only the main ones are relevant. If you touch the function key Ψ, (the key glowed helpfully) a drawer containing the MIPEC, miniature IPEC, will open. This has the appearance of a fountain pen. But is in fact a powerful computer able to transmit or receive data continuously. Also in the drawer are ten remote earpieces for use in the present; these look and feel like small pieces of soft clear sponge. They are comfortable and quite invisible when inserted and may be washed in warm soapy water as required.'

I took out a chunky pen like object.

'Slide down the mirrored covering on the clip … underneath you will find three crystal lenses.'

I did so. They appeared to be three large multi-faceted diamonds

'The upper crystal is a powerful wide-angle zoom lens with night vision capability, the centre is for chemical analysis in various spectrum ranges, and the last is an X-ray scanner and diffraction analyser.'

Looking from the pen to the holographic face, I realised it was all too much.

'I'm afraid it will take some time for me to get my head round it all.' I told her…. She carried on, seemingly unconcerned.

'Touch the key marked Φ and take out the spectacles.' A new drawer opened. 'Please put them on, the lenses will automatically adjust to suit your eyes and transmit your view via the MIPEC to my central processors. The spectacles also have integral cameras.'

'Oh' I said, as I accidentally touched a lens, which was soft and flexible to the touch

'They are cytoplasmatic lenses,' she replied, 'and almost indestructible.'

'Is it possible for me to see through these crystals?' I asked suspiciously, rolling the pen through my fingers.

'Certainly,' she smiled. 'You are able to see the image in the lenses of the spectacles. On the top of the MIPEC, under the cap is another lens for specific viewing, simply point it at the subject.'

I looked at the glasses closely, they seemed normal enough although, I couldn't find the camera's. But what was so clever about specs with built in cameras and photo-reactive lenses. Google first produced glasses with built in cameras and a screen years ago. They were quite common place now. She saw my scepticism and explained.

'There will be many occasions in the future when we will be separated. We should always be in audible contact of course but there will be times when a visual answer is required. This will be given to you via the spectacles. Why don't you try out the MIPEC's range of lenses and all will be made clear. When wearing the spectacles you don't need the earpieces as the spectacles will connect directly to your brain.'

I didn't much like the sound of that, but said nothing and put them on. Taking the pen to the door I climbed the steps until my head was just above street level and pointed it at the church on the corner of the road about three hundred metres away. The view looked normal, but if I'm honest, was definitely clearer than my regular sight.

'Can it zoom in?' A close up image of the church appeared in the right lens of the glasses overlaid at the bottom with various moving readouts which made it disorienting and caused me to make a grab for the metal railings for support. It's a strange experience to have something unexpectedly transmit directly into one's eyes; especially a single eye. But then I realised even though the lens was next to my eyes, the picture it transmitted appeared to be about 30 cm away and therefore quite comfortable. How this was done I had no idea, but still found the readouts quite annoying

'Is it possible to get rid of the readouts?'

'Of course: Instructions are by thought, simply think what you want it to do.' The readouts vanished.

'But how's it possible?' I continued, genuinely astonished as one of the gargoyles on the upper edges of the parapet came into view. I had it zoom closer; the image merged into my brain remaining absolutely steady. I found the action by thought exhilarating and selecting one of the hands, I had it zoom in closer still. As it did so both lenses filled with the picture until I could clearly make out the individual score marks made by the masons chisel around the fingernails.

'The magnification is tremendous,' I cried, taking off the glasses and closing the door. 'And so sharp.' I looked at the glasses closely. They could read my thoughts;

I wasn't very keen on that if the truth was known. But of course, it would know that already. I shuddered at the realisation. Nevertheless the demonstration had completely dispelled any doubts as to the machines validity.

She smiled. 'The MIPEC transmits a digitally merged image using every facet of the crystal lens. You must remember the technology is from far into the future, that's why you must never lose it or discuss its capabilities.' I looked closely at the glasses.

'What about watching movies and television programmes?'

'Yes those too can be watched, if it's safe to do so. But I feel obliged to point out that the spectacles were not developed solely with that in mind.' I grinned and returned to the chair.

'From where does the MIPEC get its power?'

'It must occasionally be returned to its drawer and recharged.'

'Is there a communications distance limit between you?' I continued, relaxing a little.

'No, we've worldwide cover. Anders programmed me with the access codes of every military and civilian satellite in this timeline. Of course communication satellites didn't exist earlier than 1964, in which case, we use telephone lines. Before telephone then we are limited to a 2-way radio'

I tried to make my addled brain think of another question.

'You mentioned languages, how many do you speak?'

'Thirty-eight modern, and nine ancient: Would you like me to list them?'

'Not just at the moment,' I said irritably. I still hadn't yet taken my second jolt of caffeine.

Standing up I made my way to what the landlord had somewhat pretentiously described as. "The bijou kitchenette," and poured another mug of coffee. Turning, I saw the body again and realised in all the excitement I had actually forgotten it was there. My throat tightened.

'What shall we do with the body? In the journal he asks that I destroy it, but obviously that's out of the question. Anyway, I don't have a car, and what if someone saw me? I could end up in prison. Good God! If I were to tell them he isn't born yet they'll put me in an asylum, I think we've got a problem. He certainly can't stay here; He'll start to smell soon.'

'Please try to calm down;' she advised soothingly. 'You appear to have a tendency to become overly excited. It's just a body; Mr Larsen no longer inhabits it. You could chop it up?'

'WHAT!' Are you mad? You've just informed me you're the most powerful supercomputer in the world. Is that really the best you can do? Chop him up. It may only be a body to you Miss. But I assure you the police will take a much more serious view! Convincing the courts the body is from the future wouldn't help either. I'll remind you of that as they're driving me to Broadmoor with instructions to throw away the key.'

She smiled sardonically.

'Becoming hysterical won't help.' Her face was so realistic it was impossible not to believe her. She looked at me thoughtfully and said.

'You must hire a car. We'll take the body to the coast, rent a boat, take it out to sea, tie some concrete to it and toss him overboard.'

I tried to control my breathing, which wasn't easy, so taking a deep breath, answered as calmly as I was able.

'Now why didn't I think of that? We simply take him for a day at the seaside and chuck him in? I hate to be finicky, but cars and boats cost money; and I don't have any. Do you think I'd be living in this garret if I could afford expensive toys? And have you considered that someone carrying heavy concrete blocks to a boat, along with a dead body, might raise a few questions?'

Cynicism clearly wasn't her thing; unless it came from her of course, and so chose to ignore my perfectly valid objections.

'If you give me the details of your bank account I'll transfer some funds to you. Will £25,000 be enough?'

I elected not to respond or seek an explanation at this time, mainly because I feared the answer. But thanks to Internet banking I was able to confirm its arrival and immediately transferred £15,000 to my South African account. Just in case she changed her mind.

The next morning, stiff from a long sleepless night in the armchair I phoned in sick and determined to spend her money extravagantly; hired a shiny new Toyota Landcruiser Hybrid from the nearby Eurocar depot. During the night I had resolved to have nothing to do with her ridiculous idea, but a trip to the coast couldn't hurt.

CHAPTER FOUR

I suppose now is as good a time as any to explain how I came to be living in this grotty basement flat in one of the less salubrious areas of London.

Three and a half years ago I had the world at my feet. We were living in Singapore where I was the electrical manager overseeing the construction of a large power station.

Singapore was only one in a long line of wonderful locations I had been fortunate to be sent over the previous fifteen years. The others included Chile, Malaysia, Turkey, The USA, Brazil and finally Dublin, where incidentally I had gained my degree 15 years earlier. I loved them all. But our time in the US was especially memorable because we got to visit so many different places within that wonderful country.

Then one evening my wife hit me with a bombshell. She told me she had received the children's end of term school reports which were very worrying and after a lot of soul searching had decided they should all go home. She had waited until the station was ready for handover before telling me. But having the children shunted in and out of different schools all over the world was clearly having a detrimental effect on their education and if left unchecked might very well hinder their chances of getting into a good university.

I had to admit she had a valid point. Although the company paid for the children's education it had to be in the country we were working. Being German they would not pay for boarding schools in the UK. And she didn't like the idea anyway. My next posting was to be in a remote part of Vietnam where schooling would be even more of a problem.

I could of course carry on alone. But I didn't want to be separated. She suggested that we might use the end of contract leave to take a holiday with her family in Cape Town, where strangely we had never been; her parents always coming to visit us. This she pointed out would allow us time to consider our options.

I don't know if it was part of her plan but from the moment we arrived we loved it. And quickly saw the potential of the under-developed tourist industry. So, following lots of research I decided to resign and cash in most of my entitlements. We sold our house in the UK and purchased a guesthouse in Cape Town high on slopes of Table Mountain overlooking Camps Bay. The children were enrolled in a really good private school close by and settled down immediately.

The first three years were fine, but the increased international publicity over the countries escalating crime levels and increasing Government corruption had begun to drastically affect visitor numbers which in turn reduced what we blithely described as profits. So earlier this year we bit the bullet and sold it, buying a smaller house in a nearby security complex.

Of course we now had no income, but as the location of the new house was so wonderful, and more importantly, paid for. We decided to try our best to keep it as a holiday home. But our main home would again be in the UK.

I had well and truly burnt my bridges with the Germans so I would go first to find work and look for somewhere for us to live: So much for not being separated?

In London I found a comfortable small hotel in Bayswater and took a position as senior electrical engineer on a large new hospital development in Kings Cross. It soon became clear however that the cost of living in the capital with taxes and hotel costs were taking too large a slice of what I had first thought to be a reasonable salary. Clearly it would be impossible to save if I didn't make some drastic changes. So in an effort to cut down I found this small basement bedsit near to the jobsite.

Whether it was pre-ordained, I can't say. But looking at the body and realising the enormity of what I had read, it was clear my life was about to drastically change.

CHAPTER FIVE

The next morning I left the IPEC in the flat guarding the body. And with the MIPEC in my top pocket drove towards Brighton. I had the spectacles with me, but didn't feel comfortable wearing them whilst driving. The whole exercise would probably be futile anyway so I resolved to make it into a game.

The first task was to hire a boat, but I soon discovered hiring anything larger than a rowing boat in the UK, subjugated by the myriad of absurd and contradictory health and safety laws wasn't going to be easy. In fact, without a skipper's licence, for a sea-going cruiser it proved to be impossible.

Satisfied her plan had been thoroughly thwarted by the jobworths and over vacillating politicians I decided to call it a day and head back to London.

'You'll have to buy one,' the voice said solemnly when I had returned to the car.

'But it will cost a fortune.' I exclaimed, shocked at her apparent lack of concern about money. 'And so there's no misunderstanding I'm not about to head out into the Channel in a rust bucket with a dodgy engine.'

'Well obviously.' The voice replied tiredly. 'Do try to keep positive.'

OK, what harm could it do? So deciding a larger city was needed I drove in a broody silence towards Portsmouth, breaking my journey at Emsworth for a sandwich and a cup of coffee? It's a nice town, which sits above Hayling Island on a large stretch of water known as Chichester Harbour.

Despite my theory about large cities: Whilst sitting in a café enjoying a coffee accompanied by a generous slice of chocolate fudge cake. I noticed that a few of the boats gently bobbing about in the marina were for sale, so putting on the glasses I sauntered down to inspect them.

Most were unsuitable, but one; a sleek and very beautiful cabin cruiser securely berthed to the pontoon, looked perfect. It also had gates level with the deck, ideal for pushing anything heavy into the water; which seemed like an omen.

The board said:

Rodman Spirit 43 Built 2016 - Superbly equipped sports fisher/flybridge cruiser. Twin Volvo Penta IPS 400Yanmar engines, shaft driven. Full electronics with Garmin GPS/Radar/VHF. And Google mark 2 "Programme and forget automatic pilot." Electric windlass & liferaft. Twin double berth cabins. Spacious saloon and full galley: Separate head with sea toilet, large cockpit, bathing platform and circular stair to flybridge. £212,500. OVNO.

Underneath was a telephone number.

I expected an argument but the IPEC agreed we should make an enquiry, seemingly unconcerned about the price.

'Anders left a fighting fund for such situations,' she explained.

I knew I was getting suckered in, but the whole experience was surreal and I couldn't help myself.

A man answered on the third ring and after a few questions to establish my validity suggested meeting at the marina car park in fifteen minutes. I had another cup of coffee and made my way to the car park as a silver haired well-dressed man aged about sixty climbed out of a new Lexus 22.

'Mr Shaw?' he asked, walking over smiling. 'How-do-you-do. My name is Franklin Bearfield. He gave me his card which said Commander F.G. Bearfield RN, retired.' He had a deep well-spoken voice and a distinctive handshake, which I returned.

As we made our way to the boat, he said persuasively in a military staccato.

'Good old lady, beautiful sailor, licensed until 2022, sleeps four comfortably, and has a well-equipped galley; Come aboard won't you?'

After a thorough and impressive tour he declared.

'I haven't used her for a while. Shall we take her out? Do her good to have a run'

We sailed around the Solent for about two hours which was easily long enough to convince me she was a good sailor and how much I wanted her.

Luckily I have some experience with boats of this size because a friend in South Africa owns a 30ft fishing boat. But this was much sleeker and faster, yet surprisingly easy to handle.

With the IPEC's help we dickered a bit until settling on a price of £198,000, plus three months berthing and a full tank of diesel. As a way of communicating my feelings to the IPEC I signalled thumbs up into the glasses.

The voice in my ear said.

'I take it that means you're satisfied. Ask him for the paperwork and his bank details, I will arrange immediate transfer of the funds.'

As I drove back to London the proud owner of a rather beautiful boat I knew I was being drawn in even deeper, especially when she suggested I stop and buy a cheap cabin trunk with built in wheels and a blanket to wrap the body, along with some bags of sand to weigh it down.

Very tired and knowing the armchair wouldn't do for a second night I wrapped the body in the blanket and put it in the trunk. But my mind was in turmoil and for the second night knew I wouldn't get any sleep.

The IPEC was clearly concerned and suggested I try the headset again; it must have worked because I remember nothing else until the following morning.

When I awoke everything seemed different, maybe it would be OK; anyway what else could I do? Think of the rewards and I had a family to support.

By 11-00 am the trunk was safely stowed under a tarpaulin on deck, along with the sand.

Out at sea, working under the tarpaulin, I cut some sizable holes in the trunk and stuffed the sandbags around the body. The IPEC, from the safety of the bedsit, monitored the satellite and other communications informing me the Channel was too busy and too well policed. So instead chose the calmer waters of the harbour mouth to do the deed. Everything was moving quickly now, giving me little time to think.

When certain the boat was not under surveillance she gave the all clear. I opened the gates, said a short prayer, looked around anxiously and pushed the late Mr Larsen and his new trunk unceremoniously into the murky waters a couple of miles off West Wittering, watching it turn over and quickly sink. The feeling of relief was overwhelming, if short lived.

Making my way to the bridge and selecting full power, we sped away. It was almost as if the successful conclusion had turned off a switch in my head, and the realization of what I'd done hit me so hard that my hands began to shake uncontrollably.

The IPEC clearly deciding some form of psychotherapy was needed, spoke to me compassionately.

'I have monitored every communication, civilian and military for a fifty-mile radius Jason. You are perfectly safe.' And determining such examples of her awesome power were the way to go, continued in the same vein.

'You really don't need to worry you know. I am able to gain access into the main computers of every major government throughout the world as I am those of all the leading banks and other large institutions.'

It took a few moments to register.

'But surely that's illegal?' I cried, horrified. 'And highly dangerous'

'Technically yes.' she answered dispassionately. 'But in reality it's a moot point. legally I don't exist.'

'Well I bloody well do!' I shouted frantically, the late Mr Larsen already forgotten. 'It will be me they throw into prison.' I was far too irritated and concerned to shake now.

'Oh you really mustn't worry about that,' she cooed, 'I am much too sophisticated to be caught in this primitive timeline!'

CHAPTER SIX

Despite the IPEC's constant assurances I remained far too worried to leave the flat and consequently hadn't returned to work.

The machine couldn't, or wouldn't, understand my concern, saying;

'But we only carried out his wishes. Please, do try to relax Jason, everything will be fine, trust me.' And in an effort to keep my mind occupied took to bombarding me with the principles of biomolecular pico technology. BPT for short, explaining it was an essential prerequisite for the fabrication of the proposed modules needed to power the assemblers.

'The technology must be thoroughly understood before it can be presented to a prospective manufacturer.

'You have heard of nanotechnology of course? It's already widely used in this timeline, especially in computing and medical research. What you may not know is in the metric scale a nano relates to a billionth. A nanometre therefore is one-billionth of a metre.'

'To put that in perspective,' she told me gravely. 'A single human red blood cell is 1800 nanometres long,' she instructed me to prick my finger and using the MIPEC with its range of lenses projected the holographic image of the blood smear above her screen, from this she separated a single cell and zoomed in to project its miniscule size. That will give you an idea of what a nanometre is. Incredible isn't it?'

'It most certainly is.' I conceded, genuinely impressed.

'But you see. Pico technology is not a billionth, it's a Trillionth. She then delivered an in depth paradigm introducing the Pico-metre and detailed examples of Pico-robots operating within nitrogen filled hemispheres, explaining they could be programmed to follow pre-determined instructions and therefore could be used to make millions of miniature computers

She also explained the use of utility fog manipulators, actually capable of changing their structure to suit their specific tasks.

As fascinating as this was, we both knew I was way out of my depth, but she seemed not to care. She even convinced me to ring the company and quit my job. Whilst putting a further generous amount of cash into my account to compensate for the loss of earnings. Such actions were totally out of character for me, but seemed almost normal when weighed against throwing bodies into the sea and computers which were so small they could fit behind your ear and talk directly to your brain!

The next morning the IPEC informed me it had searched every relevant company in Europe. A company in London, Maxwell Computers, based in Hammersmith had a partnership arrangement with Girton College Cambridge to exploit the commercial development of their discoveries.

They were already developing interactive quantum thought processors. Although way behind what we would be proposing!

'Copies of our designs must first be lodged with the patents office and worldwide patents applied for. I have filled in the forms on your behalf and submitted them electronically. I've also printed out hard copies for your signature. They will accept the technical information on data carriers. Please don't forget to collect the receipt with a timed date stamp.'

On my return the IPEC sat me down, and looking at me gravely, said.

'Do you feel confident about discussing BPT with the Maxwell people; they are after all, among the best in their field?'

I looked into her eyes, at first unwilling to admit the truth, then shrugged and shook my head.

'No, and probably never shall be, it's far too advanced.'

'I agree with your assessment.' she replied: Somewhat too readily for my taste.

'I know you've been doing your best, but the subject is extremely specialised. What we need is a way to circumvent the problem and convince them you've designed the module.' She paused for effect, and when I made no comment, carried on.

'The headset you wore to register your brainwaves may also be used in reverse. I sat upright at this, what did she mean reverse, was she telling me she could empty my brain?

'I'm able to feed the necessary information directly to your brain.' She added, looking at me intently.

'Don't look so worried, it's perfectly harmless and will be permanent, although the information will fade with age.'

This revelation obviously stunned me. Learning something naturally is one thing, but there sounded nothing natural about this.

'Will it hurt?' I whimpered, genuinely concerned my head might explode.

'Not at all,' she promised; plainly not in the least bothered about my legitimate concerns.

'There are no known side effects. In fact you'll probably enjoy the experience, I'm sure you're aware that the human brain has a much larger capacity than is normally used,' and not giving me time to disagree continued.

'The evening is the best time. We'll do it now.'

With the headset in place I lay on my bed while the machine played relaxing pulses to me. I don't know how long it took because I dozed off, being woken up by her voice saying.

'Please take off the headsets and return them to the drawer. Now: What can you tell me about molecular Pico-technology?'

I thought for a minute, knowing my knowledge of the subject was to say the least, sparse! And suddenly realised everything was different. All the information given me previously was in the vanguard of my brain. The feeling was incredible.

Advanced knowledge of biomolecular science was stored in my head in a logical sequence and simply required accessing. Even the assemblers made perfect sense, as did Anders drawings and notes for the computer.

'I understand how the proposed Pico-technological systems are to be fabricated,' I told her excitedly. 'And how, by using the polymorphic plasma assemblers the fabrication of the computers will be more productive than anything previously envisaged. The finished computers will consume only 2.5 watts of power, and yet be capable of processing information millions of times faster than the latest Lexium triple processor…. I feel fantastic. I'll never sleep tonight.'

'You will.' she answered reassuringly, 'your brain will demand it. I recommend a hot bath and a large glass of that particularly expensive 40 year old Macallan single malt whisky you bought yesterday.'

I looked at her innocently. She smiled….. I have to admit she has a lovely smile.

'You hid it in the bottom of the wardrobe I believe? The feeling of euphoria will soon wear off.'

The next day, I awoke with a wonderful feeling of self-belief. Quantum computer design and advanced Pico biomolecular technology now made perfect sense.

'Let's go over the procreative drive again,' she said after breakfast.

'Do you think they will be interested in the designs?' I ventured later, 'It will take a lot of believing, especially the way it attaches itself to the skull. And it talking directly to the brain will worry some people who will no doubt claim it's tantamount to brain-washing.

'People can sometimes be very slow accepting new technology, and let's be honest, this will be the most world-shattering concept that any of them will have ever have heard. They will probably throw me out.'

'I don't believe so,' she told me confidently. 'The advancement to molecular Pico over Nano technology is their business, and anyway they are looking to diversify. Maxwell is desperate to break away from his company's reliance on Cambridge.'

'How can you know that?' I asked sceptically.

She looked at me as if I was stupid.

'I interrogated their computers of course! The director's reports were most enlightening:

I'll be listening to their questions ready to give advice in the unlikely event any is needed

CHAPTER SEVEN

Arriving at the offices of Maxwell Computers at the appointed time I was shown directly into the office of their design department manager Dr Peter Allen, who following a preliminary discussion plugged the 5-Ge flexible spectrum data carrier into his desktop.

He became increasingly excited and questioned me feverishly until satisfied the designs were technically viable, at this point he asked permission to show them to his boss.

Fifteen minutes later I was sitting in the office of the research director Dr James Holt.

'I won't lie to you Mr Shaw,' he said hungrily. 'This is an incredibly futuristic concept. Partnering the computer to the brain may raise some ethical questions, but it's an exciting hypothesis: Are the designs patented?'

'The worldwide patents have been applied for and are pending. I need to point out to you that I want a guarantee that the work on the modules will start as soon as possible.'

He laughed, rather condescendingly I thought. Explaining that biomolecular Pico technology was still at the embryonic stage and to make something as revolutionary as this, would require years of research. Only if successful, could the results be put into production. And he wasn't sure if the concept was ethical anyway.

This did not amuse Hypatia and my ear became hot.

'My dear Dr Holt,' I said, coldly repeating her words.

'I admit to being rather surprised; we both know this information will give Maxwell Computers an unassailable lead in computer design. And save you years of research, not to mention millions of pounds in development costs. But if you don't want it:, for ethical reasons or lack of interest, I can easily take it elsewhere?'

Mr Stephen Maxwell, who had clearly been listening to our conversation suddenly appeared and introduced himself as the owner and CEO of the company. He proved to be a different proposition entirely to the amenable and socially conscious Dr Holt. Who was clearly terrified of him.

He reminded me of the archetypal public school bully who apparently believed he was born to dominate the chattering classes. He was however, clearly switched on and seemed completely undaunted by the ethics of a computer able to interconnect directly with the brain.

In fact he told me straight off that he was extremely interested in the designs and providing they were viable; and I could prove title. He would be prepared to buy them and offer me a position within the company. They would have to invest heavily in the research and fabrication of the assemblers. So it was therefore essential that preliminary work must be completed expeditiously.

'May some of my development people discuss the designs with you? He enquired rhetorically. 'They will no doubt have many questions.'

With occasional help from the IPEC I answered everything they threw at me including the proposed make-up of the device, its size and the method by which it was able to communicate with the brain.

The computer would rest just above the ear with a tiny probe resting against the temple. It would then communicate directly with the brain using a system of parallel processing. Talking to the computer wasn't necessary anymore; one just thought something, and the computer instantaneously put the image or text into your mind.

Clearly it wasn't a computer in the conventional sense. The object was to enhance the power of the human brain. What this computer did was to substantially raise the wearers understanding of any given subject.

When they'd finished Maxwell took everyone to his office while I waited in the boardroom.

Upon his return, accompanied only by the beaming Dr Holt, he threw back his head, looked down his nose, sniffed as if I had emitted a particularly obnoxious smell and said haughtily.

'My people say the designs are futuristic and innovative.' He looked at me witheringly. 'However they will need an awful lot of work to make them viable. Do you also have a full detailed design?'

'Tell him yes.'

He threw back his shoulders in triumph and glanced at the good doctor knowingly.

'In that case I am prepared to begin work on the modules immediately. We will offer you a lump sum for the sole rights of the computer and the assemblers, plus a senior position within the company as design advisor on a six-month rolling contract. As an added incentive I will sweeten the pot with the offer of a company car from the directors list.'

The IPEC, who even today, insists it's emotionless, said agitatedly

'Utter Rubbish! …. Need a lot of work indeed. My initial assessment was correct; this man is obtuse. Tell him you are prepared to licence the designs to him for five years, payment annually in arrears. But it must be tied to a royalty deal for every computer sold. You want a permanent position, with stock options and a seat on the board. He would be stupid to refuse because the costs will be relatively minor until the computers are a proven success...… I'll leave you to agree your salary and vehicle.'

As she intimated Maxwell huffed and puffed, but in the end grudgingly realised that if he wanted the design he had no option other than to accept.

The finished computers would be made of hundreds of layers of telluride using procreative evaluation with a processing capacity of 300 zetabytes. The size, including the integral battery fabricated from lithium-impregnated mica would be 25mm X 10mm X 2.5mm. Brain power and body heat would be used to charge the battery.

The information contained within the computer would be equivalent to the complete reference section of the US Library of Congress and could be supplemented by the Google/ Apple cloud bank as required.

What they weren't told of course was that all this was already a proven technology from the 22nd century.

Maxwell told us he had decided to call it a VCC 'virtual communication centre.

Interestingly, for someone who had seemed hungry to get everything signed he told me he wanted to consider it for 24 hours, which would be in both our interests. The voice told me to agree and I left not knowing why.

When we had returned to the bedsit Hypatia popped up smiling with the news that Maxwell had sent e mails to his attorneys telling them to file a series of patents for a new computer that would fit on the head and talk to the brain. He would have the outline plans couriered over to them.

I was incensed, but she seemed amused and told me not to be concerned. Our application is first and without the drawings and associated information their application will be refused.

'But we left them the data carriers' I cried despondently.

She smiled. 'When they attempt to copy the information they will be surprised to find all the information has mysteriously become heavily encrypted. But it demonstrates exactly how unscrupulous this Maxwell chap is. Let it be a lesson.' she told me acidly. 'Never trust this man!'

CHAPTER EIGHT

My first act was to move out of the grotsit. I rented a spacious well furnished apartment in Bayswater and telephoned Julie with the news, asking her to bring the kids over for a holiday. But I held off telling her about the IPEC deciding for the time being at least, it would be for the best. During their stay I kept it safely locked in my office.

Over the next year the team worked tremendously hard developing the control modules and assemblers until it was glaringly obvious to everyone, except Maxwell, that we all badly needed a rest.

Julie had flown over to see me a couple of times during the year where we enjoyed weekends on the boat. But tired of being alone most evenings she had recently returned to Cape Town, making me promise to join her as soon possible. I missed her tremendously because although managing well enough at the daily management meetings I struggled at the board meetings and often needed a shoulder to cry on. My knowledge of MNT and BPT may have been raised to near genius level, but everything else remained pretty basic.

Maxwell often used this lack of business acumen to ridicule me in front of the others. He seemed to take pleasure in humiliating each of us in turn, James Holt included. This annoyed me even more than his attacks on myself. The IPEC never offered help when this happened and I was too embarrassed to ask. But I also knew from past experiences that what goes around comes around. I'd seen all this before with the Germans. I could wait. He clearly liked dishing it out. I wondered how he would be at taking it.

Finally the first ten prototype modules were completed. Nine were fitted into the first of the assemblers. The tenth was mine, and despite Maxwell's fierce objections it was with some satisfaction that I reminded him I had a written contract and he could go to hell.

Hypatia congratulated me on my stand and told me it was about time I challenged him, which for some reason made me feel about ten feet tall.

I took it home immediately, waving to him as I drove out of the car park, smiling triumphantly as he glowered at me through his giant picture window. It was becoming clear that his moods were aligned with the phases of the moon. I recognised this because I had some prior experience of this disorder, having previously worked with such a man in Campbell Missouri some years before. He was like Maxwell totally power crazy. Fortunately the Germans soon sussed him out and he was fired.

Back at the flat the IPEC gave the module a full diagnostic, made some internal modifications and declared it ready to be tested.

'I know we've discussed it before,' I told her sheepishly. 'But I'm still a little concerned about the enormity of the time travel…. If I'm invisible and can pass through solid objects, what will prevent me falling through the floors of buildings?'

The head shook despondently.

'Will you please get that ridiculous idea out of your head? You're not able to pass through solid objects.'

She hated to repeat itself, and to be fair had already explained the procedures at some length, even offering to teach me via the headsets, but I wouldn't agree.

'You're only able to pass through living or moving objects, or they you. To put it simply, objects where molecules move:' She sighed.

'I'll try again…. a moving vehicle will pass through you because you're both moving in different timelines. A stationary one will remain solid; consequently one is able to climb inside and even travel in the vehicle. Your influence, caused by the time shift, transforms the vehicle into a piezomagnetic cage.'

I nodded, and made a silent vow never to walk in front of a moving car.

'Similarly with buildings, one isn't able to walk through anything solid. If the door is locked, then without the key you can't get in. But if not, the door will open in your timeline only. It will not appear to move in real time because it's happening in the past. That's simplifying it to the most basic level but trust me, it will work.'

'What if I were to walk into a table and break a vases or some other fragile object?'

'It's not very likely; you don't do such things in this timeline so why would you do it in another? But I suppose it could happen? In which case, the table would move and the vase might break, but it would have taken place in the past, in real time it will still be intact. Time moves with you, so no one except you would know it was broken. It's complicated I know, but it's essential you are not able to change the future. You must trust me…. and when travelling please do try not to go around breaking things!'

I persisted. 'What if I was to visit Van Gogh and borrow one of his paintings, could I bring it back with me?' Her face was a picture.

'Certainly not! She cried indignantly.

'Surely even you can see such actions would have an effect on the future, only objects taken with you may be returned,' she looked at me piteously and rolled her eyes which made me laugh.

'It's not funny,' she scolded … I hung my head in mock shame, which seemed to satisfy her ----- 'Finally,' she cried. 'We may at last be ready for the concluding lesson.'

She was clearly exasperated at my inability to grasp, what in her opinion was the most fundamental law of time manipulation, and I understood her irritation but I needed to understand it fully. After all I would be entering unknown territory, she expected me to follow her blindly into the abyss, but it was not that simple.

'Now, please listen carefully. To allow you to travel in time one more piece of equipment is needed. On the underside of the IPEC is a tightly folded indestructible flexible foil mat 3 metres long by 2 metres wide, you may access this by touching the summation key, the Σ lit up on the keyboard. It's very important for you to understand that everything travelling with you must be placed or carried within its confines vertically. Anything outside these parameters will be left behind, including body parts!'

She glared at me to make sure I'd understood. She needn't have worried because information such as this has a way of concentrating the mind.

'The height is adjustable and for your safety will be controlled by me.

'Can I see it?' I asked.

'If you wish.' she replied solemnly. I touched the key and a drawer the full length of the machine slid out.

'It's not necessary to unfold the mat by hand. Simply place it on the ground; touch the median key and it will open automatically. The material has a memory, and will refold when the button is pressed a second time. To return, the same procedure must be followed.'

I did as she said and a very thin metallic sheet opened up, no thicker than the aluminium foil one buys for the oven.

'The mat is attached to the IPEC by an umbilical lifeline. It may be disconnected if required, but in normal operation should stay connected. As you know, when travelling, time is distorted by a half second and renders the user invisible in real time. In which case, you will return in real time plus a half second. But when travelling to the past no matter how long ones been away, or how far back in time. The return will always be the moment you left plus a half second.'

'Why must I be invisible?' I asked 'It surely would be much better if they could see me. I would dearly love to speak to some of the people from the past.'

She gave me a look of exasperation and carried on with the explanation. But I wasn't convinced, so asked about another worry I had.

My question concerned other time travellers and whether we might encounter anyone else when travelling. This time she listened attentively and clearly considered her response carefully.

'Anders of course contemplated this and like you deduced that throughout the infinity of time it was logical that others would indeed discover the secret. But after giving the matter considerable thought he concluded that the chances of meeting any of these other travellers was so infinitesimal it was not a concern. They would have to be at our exact location at exactly the same nano second. The odds of this happening are billions if not trillions to one. I would advise you therefore not to be overly concerned.'

What she said made sense of course. She looked at me gravely and told me she wouldn't attempt to deny the possibility of visitors from another time or even another planet. But I should try to disregard it for the time being at least. In her opinion the odds of anyone visiting that flat were so infinitesimal they were not really worth considering. We were ourselves about to travel in time and she would wager that the places I wanted to visit would be famous historical places and people. Not some unknown individual's indistinct basement flat in 21st century London.

She was right of course, so put it out of my mind. I had carefully considered when and what I wanted to see. It had to be nearby, and at a time when we knew this house was built, after due consideration I chose Westminster Abbey 68 years ago.

August 8th 2021 was a warm bright morning. The morning of 2nd June 1953 however was very wet. So wearing the glasses and my new light grey all weather golf suit with walking boots I made ready for the expedition to see first-hand the coronation of Queen Elizabeth II.

Placing the IPEC on the mat with me I said in my best authoritative voice,

'OK Hypatia, select the 2nd June 1953, 8-30 am.'

---Activate--

CHAPTER NINE

One moment we were in 2021, and the next in 1953. The room was quite different; a wall had gone, making it easily double the size. Clearly my bedroom and bathroom had been added when the house had been altered to individual flats. It was now a palatial sitting room decorated in 1930s style, the furniture of good quality, as were the wallpaper and carpets. Two doors led off the room, one to the hall, which was now my entrance door, the other, I supposed, to the original kitchen and servants quarters.

So this was it, all the work had been worth it? I had actually travelled in time, granted it was only 68 years, but it had worked amazingly well. The realisation caused me to consider how lucky I was and looking around for somewhere to sit, lowered myself carefully onto the sofa, half expecting to fall through; relieved to find it solid to the touch.

I also had a moment of concern about being able to turn the door handle, maybe my hand would pass through it; but I needn't have worried, it worked fine. There were two people in the dated kitchen and neither of them paid me any attention. I got the impression they had given the servants the day off. It's a really eerie feeling to be invisible; they hadn't noticed the door move so I tried it again, the IPEC's explanation finally registering....

The door was opening in my time not theirs; the half-second time shift was moving in parallel with their time, so although the door took more than half a second to move, the half-second was itself moving.

The man walked cautiously into the lounge, carefully carrying a tray stacked with the tea things and placing it on the coffee table leant over to switch on the television. It took an eternity to power up and as he looked at the small snowy picture he tut tutted and made his way to the windows to close the curtains. In doing so he stood squarely on the IPEC. My heart stopped as I watched, but I needn't have worried as his foot passed clean through it and didn't notice a thing.

The TV was broadcasting live pictures of the Coronation. The primitive black and white images flickering on the 15-inch screen showing the route to the palace lined with thousands of ghostlike rain soaked spectators. The scene shifted to the Abbey and the commentator began talking about Sir Winston Churchill and the Knights of the Garter. I waved my arms about and even tried to touch the man but my hand passed right through him, the whole thing was fascinating. Satisfied, I slung Anders rucksack on my back and with the MIPEC clipped in the top pocket of my golf suit. I set off to see my Queen crowned.

The crowds were extra heavy by this time with everyone milling about trying to get a good position, seemingly oblivious to the rain. Mostly in vain it must be said as the best spots had already been claimed. They got even heavier as I approached the Abbey and although I tried to dodge them wherever possible, at certain points it became simply too much and I was forced to walk through them. It was going to take a while getting used to this.

Arriving at the main doors just before 11-00 I watched the spectacular golden coach arrive with its escort, and plucking up courage made my way down the aisle to get a good view.

The Archbishop of Canterbury was waiting with his assistants at the end of the aisle. Kitted out in his all his finery he looked as nervous as I felt. It was understandable really when one considers very few of them, especially in these modern times, get to do this. The ceremony was quite long so I have condensed it a little.

With no spare seats I had to find somewhere to stand so chose a space behind the coronation chair and waited for the ceremony to begin. The IPEC once again proved its usefulness as it explained what the music was, who the people were, and the order of events.

The music of Purcell filled the air as the Royal couple entered, changing to Parry's rousing version of the Coronation Anthem as they reached the throne. The pupils of Westminster school then sang "Vivat Regina Elizabeth."

When they'd finished, everyone gave a rousing cry of God Save Queen Elizabeth, and a fanfare of trumpets reverberated round the ancient walls as she took her seat on the thousand-year-old throne. I glanced at Archbishop Fisher and his retinue again; They looked a little calmer now.

It was totally surreal and finally struck home. The potential of the IPEC was limitless. Here I was in Westminster Abbey in 1953 standing next to a very attractive young woman who was about to be crowned Queen of a vast commonwealth of nations. Whist knowing it could just as easily have been Henry the Fifth or even William the Conqueror.

I had been given access to something very, very special indeed. Following more hymns, to which I joined in lustily.

I accompanied Her Majesty and the Archbishop to the altar, where we both knelt together as she read aloud the Coronation Oath and kissed the bible. She returned and was about to sign the oath when she whispered to the Lord Chamberlain

'There's no bloody ink in this pen you idiot, I'll have your head for this!' (Only joking.)

Being so close I could see she was visibly nervous, which made her seem less forbidding somehow. I suppose that no amount of training can make one immune from being the centre of such a monumental occasion. But there really was no ink. The Lord Chamberlain whispered, clearly embarrassed.

'Pretend you're signing,' which she did;

The Archbishop spoke at length about God and destiny, offering blessings upon her and everyone else present, and the choir burst forth with more hymns during which we returned to the throne. Four Knights of the Garter made their way toward us holding a cloth of gold suspended on four poles and held it over her as the Dean of Westminster poured some oil into an old spoon, which he passed to the Archbishop who anointed her.

We all did a lot more singing whilst she was given new clothes known as the Colobium Sindonis and the Supertunica, plus a new sword and off she went to the altar again solemnly giving it to the Dean to look after, but even before she'd turned her back, the blighter sold it to the Marquis of Salisbury in exchange for a velvet bag containing one hundred silver Shillings.

We eventually returned to the throne and the Archbishop gave her some bracelets, a stole, a robe made of gold cloth, a jewelled orb, a sceptre containing the biggest diamond I have ever seen and a ring. Not forgetting of course, the crown, which he had placed reverently on her head.

It went on for some time, various people, including her husband kneeling before her to pay homage. But effectively it was finished. We had a beautiful new Queen.

She nearly had a nasty accident as she was leaving though, the carpet at the altar was metal fringed and snagged in her new gold robe nearly causing her to trip. I instinctively tried to catch her but of course my hand went straight through. But overall I had to admit it had all gone very well.

Waiting for the Royal party to leave before walking home through the rain my spirits were high; Of course some minor trepidation remained. I still had to return safely to the present, but all things being equal it had been brilliant.

Back in the apartment, and once more in 2021 I reviewed what had been discovered. Firstly, the time travel worked. Secondly, one could return by pressing a single key. And thirdly, there didn't seem to be any adverse side effects. The machine had returned me to the present, as far as I could judge exactly the same time as when I'd left.

One interesting point though was the photographs I'd taken during the ceremony. When trying to download them, I discovered the memory was empty; every picture had vanished

The next question was obvious, where next? The Churchill bunker just before D Day was worth considering. Henry the Eighth interested me, as did Elizabeth I. My first choice though, would always be the assassinations of President Kennedy. To be able to stand on that grassy knoll and watch what actually happened intrigued me. Maybe it would be feasible to hire one of those American motor homes to travel around the country, and use it to follow the President to the hospital. Some of the strongest stories of a cover up are from there, and I've always thought that his Vice President, Lyndon Johnson might have had some prior knowledge of the plot; certainly his friend J Edgar Hoover had no love for the Kennedy's. It might be interesting to spend some time with Hoover just before the shots were fired, simply to see how he reacted to the news.

Further back in time there was Rome, Athens, or Mycenae. Another place and time stood out too, The Holy Land two thousand years ago. But not yet, such a visit would require a stronger strength of spirit than I yet possessed.

And then I had a brainwave. 'The Giza Pyramids,' the original and greatest wonders of the world. The method of their construction has been the subject of fierce speculation for millennia. Herodotus gave us his solution two thousand five hundred years ago, but many experts don't accept it. If I could get out there I could see for myself?
Wow, now that really would be something!

But I was in London with no means of foreign travel and would have to find something to visit here. The rest of the world must wait until the IPEC, with its nuclear battery, could be transported safely. But possibly the camper van idea could be developed for this country. In the meantime I would make a study of the subject.

'Do you do speak Ancient Egyptian?' I asked the IPEC that evening.

'I do' she replied 'I also have a smattering of demonic Egyptian and of course read hieroglyphs. Would you like me to teach them to you?'

'Oh yes Hypatia. I most certainly would. Hieroglyphics have fascinated me ever since I first examined The Rosetta Stone in the British Museum. I would love to visit the Egyptian section and be able to read the exhibits for myself. Can you do it tonight?'

CHAPTER TEN

It was now 18 months since I had taken the designs to Maxwell Computers and costs were mounting alarmingly. The cerebral computers were rolling off the assemblers steadily, ready for the launch. But friend Maxwell was adamant it would be some considerable time before any royalties materialised. On the way home the IPEC asked.

'Do I deduce from your conversations with the recalcitrant Mr Maxwell that you require an injection of funds?'

'Yes,' I replied despondently. 'We need to buy a house in the UK and bring the children over permanently. We both feel it would give them a better chance of getting into a good university. But according to Maxwell the company is barely solvent. I'm also concerned he might try to kick me out when we're in full production. We just don't get on, and I suspect, never will. Do you think I could sell the boat we hardly use it anyway'

'That seems a little drastic,' she replied soberly. After a long pause she said.

'Actually you don't need his money!'

'Why ever not' I asked disbelievingly, never in my wildest dreams expecting to hear her next words.

'Because one year ago you inherited a company called IPEC Investments. The audited records show the company has been trading for 12 years from Liechtenstein and owns substantial assets.'

'What do you mean I inherited it? Who is this mysterious benefactor?'

'The late Mr Anders Larsen: He bequeathed it to you in his will. I have built a complete history for him to substantiate this.

'The company is easily able to purchase a house for you: We should also take up the stock options from Maxwell Computers. When the computer is finally launched the shares will go through the roof, and as you are aware. I don't trust our Mr Maxwell.'

Suddenly it all became too much and I needed to talk about it.

'I really am genuinely grateful for everything Hypatia.' I told her, wishing I could see her face.

'It's just that everything seems so ridiculously easy. We're able to travel in time; I'm a director of Maxwell's and now find I own an investment company that is able to finance the purchase of shares and a house in London. It's barely credible.'

'Oh please, she replied. 'Not London, let's move to the country, what about Surrey? Let me look around for some suitable properties.'

It was if a trigger had been set off in my head, Why not Surrey? London was all very well during the week, but it would be nice to relax in the country at the weekend.

I telephoned Julie when we got home, explaining that the company was doing well and suggested that rather than me going to South Africa she might like to return and help me choose the new house.

'Bring the kids with you.' I told her. 'We should make this a family decision. My secretary will arrange some tickets for you all. Can you come over next week?'

With its usual efficiency the IPEC, posing as my private secretary "Mrs Farquar-Smythe" arranged for the estate agent to pick us up in Bayswater at 10-00 am the following Tuesday.

The young man, who was in fact a pleasant young fellow named St.John, pronounced "Singent." Walcote-Amory. What is it with estate agents and double barrelled names? South Africa is full of them.

He did however make an instant hit with Julie, who being South African appreciates good breeding much more than me. Probably because I don't have any.

I understand from your secretary that you want to see properties in the Virginia Water area? It must be set in its own private grounds, and come complete with its own lake. I've three to show you, but only one has a genuine lake.

'Oh what a shame' I retorted cynically, glancing at Julie, who was not looking too happy at being told where and in what she was to live. Especially as he made it seem he was acting on the instructions of "my secretary."

'This is beginning to sound like one of those dreadful television programmes?' She said demurely. I recognised the tone and knowing this is when she's at her most dangerous, tried to pacify her.

'I instructed my secretary to tell the agency we wanted a property in this area You see darling, it's only forty minutes away from the office, and convenient for Heathrow. I also told her we would like it to have a lake.'

She looked at me with a face that left little to the imagination but said nothing. I was in for it later! What could the IPEC possibly want with a lake?

At the second house the search ended. We looked at the third of course, but the decision was already made.

We all loved it, which was hardly surprising when one considers it was a small mansion with a stunning entrance leading to a sweeping marble staircase and balcony. The house had six reception rooms, including a well-stocked library and study, six bedrooms all en-suite, four with dressing rooms, a gourmet kitchen with subterranean wine cellar and heated indoor swimming pool with a gym and sauna. And of course, a lake!

When young Singent told us how much the property was on the market for I had trouble keeping a straight face. Julie looked at me as if I'd lost my mind, so I excused myself and walked around the corner to discuss it with the IPEC, who assured me the company could afford it and not to worry.

I had my own reasons to purchase it as it turned out. It boasted a large boat house/workshop bordering the lake, well away from the house and hidden by trees. The building was alarmed to the main house, in a good state of repair and easily large enough to house a speedboat, and as I wanted, a motor home. CCTV cameras were used to inspect visitors, and high walls with movement sensors surrounded the whole estate.

The housekeeper and her husband, the handyman/gardener, lived in a spacious flat above the detached garage at the rear of the house. The agent told us that they had asked if they might be allowed to stay on, as the present owner a Señor Hasselbacher was returning to Argentina.

When I returned to the office my computer greeted me with the news that negotiations were concluded and we could move into the house in three days.

'But we've no furniture.' I reminded her. Knowing it would be utter madness to choose any without Julie.

'Because we've paid a 50% deposit,' she gushed. 'Señor Hasselbacher has agreed to leave the furniture for up to three months following the transfer. Your wife will have plenty of time to furnish the house to her taste.'

She'd done a complete check on him, including a full interrogation of his bank records, discovering he needed money desperately. His cattle ranch and vineyards near Mendoza were not doing too well. He had to inject a large amount of cash within the next two weeks, or have the whole estate re-possessed.

Julie took charge at that point and we moved in two days later. She had already questioned how we could afford first class tickets for them all to fly over and now obviously wanted to know how we could afford such a house so I nervously introduced her to the IPEC telling her I was the machines inventor and explained about IPEC Investments. She sat and talked to it and seemed satisfied, until we were getting ready for bed... and then it started,

'I am the first to admit you've changed,' she told me 'Your knowledge of computers is clear for all to see. I'm actually very proud of you. But you've just introduced me to a machine the like of which I didn't know existed except in science fiction books.

I've been married to you long enough to know your capabilities, and inventing that computer isn't one of them! It's far more likely to have invented you!

'I want to know what's going on, and I want to know NOW!'

I had known it was coming of course and had roughly worked out an outline story, deciding to wing the rest depending on her reactions. I sat opposite her looking directly into her eyes.

'It's a special secret, my darling, one I'm not allowed to talk about.' She glared at me witheringly, so I quickly added.

'But as we've never had secrets from each other... I found it you see. The IPEC is the one doing all this. Its creator is dead unfortunately. He was a genuinely eccentric professor who before he died programmed it to self-destruct if his existence is ever divulged.

'What do you mean you found it,' she demanded. 'Where? Under a gooseberry bush! I've never heard so much rubbish in all my life.'

Taking a deep breath I continued.

'Of course I understand your reservations my sweet, but it really is true. You see I was travelling home on the tube late one evening when an old man sitting across from me suddenly fell forward. There was nobody else in the carriage so I helped him onto the platform and called an ambulance. I couldn't just abandon him so accompanied him to the hospital where they told me he was very ill and admitted him. He made me promise I would visit him the next day, which I did.

The poor fellow was clearly in a lot of pain but managed to tell me about a special computer in his suitcase. He explained that he had no family and asked if I would take it home and keep it safe until he recovered.

I returned the next evening only to be told he had died. When I returned home I opened the case and found the IPEC inside.'

Of course the questions didn't stop there, indeed they went on most of the night, but I was careful not to let slip anything about the time travel.

I could see she was far from convinced but suspect that looking around at the house the next day, and the open chequebook I had given her, decided something's are better left alone.

During the next weeks our kids were enrolled in good schools. The school in South Africa had settled them both down wonderfully and with their glowing reports their new schools accepted them willingly. Julie furnished the house. I bought a motor home and a specially made dune buggy. My son thought it was a great idea, but the wife and daughter decided I had finally cracked and put the whole thing down to eccentricity, or stupidity, depending on whom one listened to.

I had the rear section altered to accommodate the buggy. And doors added with an automatic folding platform to raise and lower it.

The clever part was that the rear section also contained a crane and trap door. When this was unlocked the mat could be dropped to the ground and automatically opened, the buggy could then be attached to the crane and gently lowered onto the mat. The operation was invisible from the outside and allowed us to disappear clandestinely. It was real boys own stuff, and I loved it.

At 2-45 am, one week after moving into the house, a saucer shaped craft landed softly on the lake sinking quietly to the bottom. A short time afterwards a clear plastic bubble floated to the surface, inside was a small grey female alien wearing a black jump suit. The bubble moved silently to the water's edge and up the bank, once on dry land it evaporated, leaving its occupant standing on the ground totally dry.

Making her way silently through the trees to the house, she crossed the lawn and waited at the study windows listening for the all-clear signal to be given. When it came, she opened them with a key and entered.

Walking directly to the IPEC, she unplugged the Maxwell module replacing it with another and pressed the button to release the mat. The IPEC selected 2103 at the time previously agreed and transported… no words were spoken.

The interior of the room changed to an exact replica of the wood panelled conference room at Kings Cross with a long low oak table and eighteen chairs. Around the table sat the same eight aliens present at the last meeting. She placed the IPEC at the end of the table opposite the Khepera, and stood to one side. The Khepera gestured her to a seat and turned to the machine.

'Good afternoon Hypatia, would you please present your report?'

'The subject is performing as expected, he is aware of my ability to infuse his brain with knowledge, and has accepted it well. We have now used the time travel facility on twelve occasions without any serious problems.'

The IPEC continued with its report for another thirty minutes explaining exactly how the modules were being utilised and the projected production levels of the cerebral computers. It also expressed its belief that the subject was ready to visit the Egyptian pyramids.

'Thank you,' replied the Khepera. 'The next full meeting will be in one month. You may of course visit whenever you require information or help, especially if it concerns the Egyptian visit. How he reacts will determine our subsequent actions regarding Atlantis. We shall anyway require a full account of the journey on your return.'

He turned to the alien from his past and asked that she present her report. When it had been given, he said,

'I am satisfied. We must focus all our efforts on the computer manufacturing process; it is imperative the indoctrination of the humans commences on schedule. Do you require more funds Hypatia?'

'Not at present, I have sufficient to take up the stock options. Although I will later, if we are to make a take-over bid for the company'

'We shall ensure they are available,' he promised. 'I believe this Maxwell should be persuaded to resign as soon as it becomes expedient. The development of the indoctrinatory devices must not be compromised.'

He looked around the table and said.

'Very well, if there's nothing else I declare this meeting closed. Thank you for your input Hypatia. I am satisfied. Please continue to make the production levels of the cerebral computers your highest priority.'

The alien and the IPEC returned to 2022 where she again changed modules and returned to the saucer. The crew engaged the swathing device and flew to Kings Cross, the residents of London oblivious to the fact that a UFO was silently skimming their rooftops. Later that evening the craft would depart for the main base deep inside an extinct volcano in the Andes, South of Lake Titicaca between Bolivia and Chile on the edge of a four thousand square mile plateau called The Altiplano.

CHAPTER ELEVEN

The trip to the past had understandably excited my imagination and I had subsequently visited many historical figures and events including Henry V111, Elizabeth 1 and William the Conqueror seeing the newly erected White Tower in 1078. And despite swearing I wouldn't, had watched Charles 1 lose his head. I had even tried to find King Arthur, without success it must be said. But everything had been in the UK and I wanted now to see things overseas.

Anders had presented me with a wonderful problem. He had made it possible to visit any of the thousands of wonders throughout history at the time of my choosing. From the Rome of Julius Caesar, to the Athens of Perikles or Delphi to see the Oracle making her predictions. There was also The Great Wall of China during its construction. Or Easter Island, Carthage, Machu Pichu, and Petra at its height; the list was endless.

As I have already told you. Of all the places and events possible The Egyptian Pyramids and the Sphinx have fascinated me, for as long as I can remember. To see them being built 4500 years ago would exceed my wildest dreams.

However the one major problem remained, how were we to transport the IPEC? Because of its nuclear battery taking it through airport detectors was impossible. Anders apparently had solved the problem by using private hire planes.

My answer was therefore clear. I would use Stephens's new toy: His answer to the company's insolvency problems: His new executive jet.

The next week he called me into his office where we amicably discussed the progress of the next generation of the headset design and he suggested I share my ideas with James Holt.

The voice said 'Fat chance.'

I ignored her, borrowing the plane was not going to be easy. Judging his mood swings was getting progressively harder, and deciding this was probably as good as it was likely to get. I said meekly,

'Stephen, as you know I've been working sixteen hour days for almost two years. I'm really tired and need a holiday; may I use the Gulfstream? I want to visit the pyramids.'

'I require you here.' he answered spitefully, and turned away to look out of his large picture window.

'I have decided to make some improvements to the module. I need it to control a missile system.'

'What missiles?' I asked suspiciously,

'That doesn't concern you,' he snapped. 'The module will not accept instructions, I want it modified.'

'You were made aware when I brought the designs that the core is programmed with a principal command, it will not function if used for military purposes.'

'I have never heard of anything so preposterous,' he said brutally. 'I demand you modify it;' I stared at him, blood pressure rising. The voice said soothingly.

'Keep calm Jason, he's not worth it. Explain that to incorporate such intricate modifications is highly complex and requires a fundamental change to the design. Agree to work on the problem whilst on vacation. Relaxing in the sun will reinvigorate your thought process. I have just accessed his private emails. He's under strong outside pressure. I don't think he has any alternative but to agree.'

As she had suspected although noticeably hesitant, he reluctantly conceded.

'It sounds questionable to me? He said icily 'However, maybe you do need a short rest... You may use the plane, but I want you back here in four days. I own this company and it's about time you realised it.'

The voice in my ear again cautioned restraint.

'I was correct; he's acting under direct Governmental orders. We have him now! Don't reply, just thank him and leave.'

CHAPTER TWELVE

The arrival at Cairo airport filled me with real excitement. We had flown low over the pyramids on the way in, and were fascinated by their size. Julie and I were met on the tarmac by the hotel limo and with only the faintest of formalities were whisked off to our hotel.

Built in 1869 The Mena House Oberoi lies within its own 40-acre estate on the banks of the Nile in the shadow of the Pyramids. And following a relaxing afternoon at the pool we dined on our private balcony, which faced the great pyramid's triangular shaped entrance clearly visible in the twilight.

The evening was serene, the jasmine scented air from the gardens mingled with the bubbles of the pre-dinner 2002 Salon Le Mesnil Champagne.

All was right with the world. We sat back in wonderful anticipation as the first course was delivered, expertly served under the supervision of our personal butler 'Rashid.'

After dinner as were enjoying coffee and a wonderful Remy Martin Louis X111 cognac all the lights were switched off and with the desert sky glistening with a never ending carpet of stars, we sat back and waited for what we were promised would be a fascinating experience.

There are certain must see events in this world; this was one of them. The show starts as follows: -.

"You have come tonight to the most fabulous and celebrated place in the world. Here on this plateau of Giza stands forever the mightiest of human achievements. No traveller, Emperor, merchant or poet has trodden these sands and not gasped in awe. The curtain of night is about to rise and disclose the stage on which the drama of civilization took place. Those involved have been present since the dawn of history, pitched stubbornly against sand and wind. With this, the voice of the desert accompanying their majesty, time has crossed the centuries."

The music plays, and the spectacular begins: Wonderful!!

The next day; with phrase books in hand and the tour guide vociferous in praise of all things Egyptian. We set off on the obligatory tour.

Debatably the world's oldest civilization, Egypt emerged from the Nile Valley around 5,200 years ago. At the apex of the list of wonders handed down to us are the pyramids. Their size is so overwhelming that for most people the first question has to be how were such megaliths built? Certainly it was with me. The second is probably to wonder what they were like when new 4500 years ago.

In the next couple of days this experience was destined for my eyes alone, the anticipation was humbling and made me tingle with excitement.

Five thousand years ago the Giza plateau became the royal necropolis, or burial place for Memphis, the Pharaoh's capital city. And these monuments, which command the whole plateau, remained the tallest building in the world until the twentieth century.

It's generally accepted that about 2,550 B.C. Khufu, the second Pharaoh of the fourth dynasty, commissioned the building of the great pyramid for his tomb. How long would it have taken I wondered? The average weight of the stone blocks used is over 2.5 tons, the heaviest, used in the ceiling of the burial chambers between 40 and 60 tons.

Around the great pyramid are the ruins of three smaller pyramids for the Pharaoh's family and pits containing buried boats, plus the remains of numerous other temples including the mastaba tombs of the nobles. An elaborate causeway led from the mortuary temple to the valley temple from where the Pharaoh's funeral would begin.

The other two pyramids also had similar buildings; with the centre one Khafre's, exhibiting the most impressive funerary temple which had its own causeway leading down to the Great Sphinx. Menkaure's pyramid, the smallest, also had three family pyramids, and a causeway.

'The 4th Dynasty lasted from 2613 to 2498 BC, why don't we choose 2500 BC?' the IPEC suggested. 'The work should be completed by then. We can then go back in stages to see how they were built.'

The Great Pyramid of Khufu, also known by his Greek name 'Cheops' is 147 metres high, and constructed from about 2,300,000 blocks. The theory of how it was built has always been speculative, but the general consensus is that the huge blocks were cut from nearby quarries and dragged up enormous ramps on wooden sleds.

The larger blocks though were reputed to have come from quarries over 100 kilometres away. It was Herodotus in 443 BC who claimed the great pyramid took around 20 years to build, although what made him an expert I can't say. But at that time frame, according to my wonderful computer, they must have excavated, shaped and smoothed at least 315 heavy blocks every day, this included having to haul them from the quarries to the site and place them in position no matter what the weather, every hour of every day for one thousand and forty weeks, without a single day's break.

It seems to me that with no machines, this figure is somewhat fanciful if not downright impossible; especially when one considers the chamber areas and the grand gallery. Plus, since the discovery of the workers city, it is now universally agreed that slaves were not used. Modern thinking has it that the majority of the workers were Egyptian farmers receiving a regular wage from the Pharaoh.

Most experts agree that the skilled people, like stonemasons and their assistants would have lived on site permanently. But the great numbers of general labourers required to haul and place the stones probably only worked during the flood season when their fields were under water, which would obviously mean a substantial increase to the 315 daily total.

Great blocks of hard glazed white limestone from the quarries across the Nile at Tura were used for the outer layer, giving the pyramids a smooth mirrored finish.

As each pyramid was completed, a special cover of shining metal, probably electrum (a naturally occurring alloy of gold and silver used in ancient times to produce the first coins) was positioned over the capstone. This was the part I most wanted to see.

'Shall we go to the national museum in Cairo to see the Tutankhamen exhibition?' I asked Julie after breakfast.

We hired a Toyota Desert-cruiser and the hotel manager arranged special tickets for the Egyptian Museum where we spent hours looking at the wonderful selection of exhibits. Where, I surprised my wife by explaining the meaning of the hieroglyphics.

The crowning glory was obviously the Carter section holding over 1,700 pieces from the collection of King Tutankhamen. Particularly the treasures secured in the gold room which contained most of the gold objects found. Although some of the precious items are always on loan to other museums around the world.

We saw the spectacular death mask and three of the five gold coffins. The room was as always, packed, and like everyone else we pushed and shoved to get in. Until finally rather like corks in a bottle, popped into the small room only to find ourselves in an even tighter throng. Which was being shuffled round slowly, propelled by the endless mass of people outside pushing to get in?

But it was worth it; the gold mask alone made it worthwhile. And the coffins doubly so, but every item in the room is so spectacular that one has to be careful not to become too blasé.

I promised myself to one day join Mr. Carter, Lord Carnarvon and his daughter on the morning of 26th November 1922 as they opened the tomb. But decided to keep that to myself for the time being: One thing at a time, the pyramids first.

Returning to the hotel as the giant red sun was setting over the desert I considered what we would find 4500 years into the past, particularly the ground conditions: What we needed was a platform; one we knew was there when they were built.

The base of the great pyramid wouldn't have changed much. But if they had built ramps to get the blocks to the top, and some experts believe there may have been up to four of these, one on each side, I could easily find myself inside one of them. So whilst Julie was luxuriating in the suites enormous bath I drove out to investigate.

Hypatia didn't give the four-ramp theory any credence at all, having worked out they would have taken longer to build than the pyramids, but I still wasn't fully convinced.

A place was found to the West of Khufu's pyramid, just behind the builder's quarters where cars were allowed to park. It looked a very old road, and pretty quiet.

'We'll do it tomorrow, early.' I said, 'Although getting you packed into the suitcase, and into the car at that time in the morning might be awkward. Will you be all right in the car tonight, alone?'

'Of course,' she replied dismissively. 'And please don't go to sleep tonight wearing the earpiece, I really can look after myself.'

After another wonderful dinner and a stroll through the hotel's superb gardens we retired early and were soon asleep. Sometime later, whilst enjoying a vivid dream in which the Pharaoh Khufu was describing how to build a pyramid, the incessant ringing of the telephone woke me. The illuminated face of the digital alarm clock displayed 02-24 am.

'Yes,' I answered sleepily.

'This is the night manager sir. I'm sorry to wake you, but there has been some trouble with your vehicle.'

'Trouble; what sort of trouble?' I asked, sitting up abruptly, concerned it had been stolen, and with it the IPEC.

'Could you come down sir? It's difficult to explain over the telephone.'

'Give me five minutes to get dressed.' I said jumping out of the bed.

'Please ask the receptionist to have the night porter bring you directly to the manager's office.'

Julie was awake by now. I explained the reason for the call and left.

The night manager was with two security guards and two very frightened, handcuffed teenagers.

'What's the problem?' I asked, becoming concerned for the IPEC. It suddenly dawned on me how attached we had become.

'These two young men sir; they broke into your vehicle, actually they appear to have had a key.'

He produced a hand held device which apparently searched through a range of frequencies turning off the alarms and unlocking the doors.

'They had just climbed into the driving seat to start the vehicle, when they claim, the air inside became electrically charged, crackling and sparking from the roof. From behind them a voice. "A very frightening voice" told them he was the ghost of the Pharaoh Akhenaten. He claimed to have been wandering the Giza plateau for 3500 years, consuming the flesh of young men four times a year to sustain himself. And tonight it was their turn. They were caught running away from your vehicle, screaming hysterically.'

'Yes,' I said, trying to keep a straight face. 'Very strange, is the vehicle now secure?'

'Not locked sir, but we've a guard with it.'

'It would seem prudent for me to check if anything is missing and to re-lock it. These young men are clearly delusional; probably on drugs, I should let the police have them:

'On the other hand…. if you agree, and providing nothing has been stolen, I would be agreeable to closing the matter. I'll leave the decision to you of course. But as a visitor to your beautiful country I don't want to have my vacation ruined sitting inside police stations for the next two days.' Turning to look at the gibbering wrecks, I added. 'And they do seem to have been punished enough.'

'That's most generous of you sir,' he said, clearly relieved at avoiding any bad publicity for the hotel.

CHAPTER THIRTEEN

Being already up, we set off earlier than planned. The spot I had chosen was about 100 metres North-West of Khafres pyramid, and 500 metres West of Khufu's. My backpack contained three heavy bottles of water, a torch, a generous hip flask of 30 year old Poit Dhubh unfiltered malt, a packet of oat crackers, a wedge of blue stilton, a pack of fresh black and green olives, some Dundee cake, and a bag of mint imperials.

Unfortunately at this time in the morning the gates to the pyramid complex were locked. But a phone call from the director of antiquities instructed them to let me in for some authorised specialist research. The real director of course knew nothing of this but as the IPEC pointed out. We were actually doing him a favour by not disturbing him so early.

'Set the time for 8-00 am,' I instructed, putting on the glasses. 'It shouldn't be too hot then. As a starting point let's try your suggestion, please select 2498 BC. 3rd of May'

---Activate---

I had decided to keep my back to at the pyramids to heighten the anticipation. The first thing to strike me was that we were on level ground. The road was gone, and the land, instead of sandy desert was partly arid with large green patches. The biggest surprise was the smell, or lack of it. It was noticeably fragrant and fresh, a world with no industry and pollution. I felt healthier already.

Now for the moment of truth: .... I prepared myself, took a deep breath and slowly turned around.

The picture that met me was simply too much, and once again I fell to my knees unable to take it in. This seems to be something I recently have become prone to doing I know. But the scene was so fantastic it was totally overwhelming. Three giant dazzling white pyramids glistened in the morning sun, their famous gold caps radiating amazing power. The main surprise though: were the high walls around each pyramid.

'I must go to them.' I said in a voice which didn't belong to me,

'Your timing was spot on.' I couldn't stop staring. The most incredible thing was their size, they looked even larger than in our time and although I knew they were built of millions of separate blocks there was no sign of any joints. Each looked like a single colossal block of gleaming white granite.

I slowly raised myself to my feet, but my legs were shaking badly and my heart pounded against my chest, which in turn caused a thumping sensation above my ears. It took some time until I was able to move. I doubt I even blinked as I walked toward them.

I entered the complex through an open black wooden gate as high as the wall decorated with two golden lion heads and approached Khafre's pyramid.

Inside the walls, which I estimated as being around twenty metres high, was like being in a private city, the biggest surprise, the wealth of colours.

Now, as you will have gathered I am no historian. I love history, but only as complete novice. So any descriptions I give are based solely on my own observations and cannot be taken as architecturally accurate.

The buildings, which I knew were mostly tombs for the nobles and temples to the Pharaohs, were remarkable and gleaming new. I had expected the area would be built up of course. The archaeological programmes on the television had prepared me for this. But I had simply not considered the stunning colours, or the jubilant celebration of death. I've no idea why; it just seemed right to see everything as white. How wrong I had been. All around me were brightly coloured buildings and lots of people.

The pyramid towered over me, the smooth walls disappearing into the blue sky. This was when I truly appreciated where I was and reached out sliding my hand along the smooth walls. The whole incredible experience was way beyond my wildest dreams.

To say the pyramids were glistening in the morning sunshine is true, but it quickly became clear that this one at least was not as pristine as I had at first thought. The lower section of the limestone blocks, were in some places quite worn, and some even badly cracked. 'Can you see the faint line about 5 metres up the base,' I asked the IPEC, 'it stretches along the side like some kind of tidemark, everything under the line is a little darker, but I don't see how that's possible, the surrounding walls are higher and they don't have a corresponding line. There seems to have been some attempts to repair and clean the blocks but the general appearance doesn't look at all new! In fact, it looks old.'

All the other buildings though, including the funery temples and the smaller pyramids together with the causeways and the high walls around the complex were absolutely pristine. Something just didn't fit.

Gathering my thoughts I said.

'We've arrived too late Hypatia, I want to go back another fifty years, but first I'll visit Menkaure's pyramid compound and then take a stroll down to look at the Sphinx.'

Once inside the high walled complex I had another surprise. The bottom section, up to about 15 metres, was finished in a pinky/reddish colour, also badly worn, whilst the walls and other buildings were unblemished.

People were everywhere, especially the area between the causeway and the Eastern cemetery. Children were running about unconcerned whilst their parents stared awestruck at the shear immensity of it all.

Of course at this time no other man-made object on earth remotely compared. And wouldn't for another four thousand years. Walking toward the Sphinx, which to my surprise was also surrounded by a wall. I wondered what sort of face it would it have? A Lion or Pharaoh?

It was a Pharaoh. Who? I couldn't tell until I got close, and saw the stele with the inscription

'To the memory of my father. The lion of the world and the Great Lord of Upper and Lower Egypt.'

It was signed with the cartouche of Khafre. Under this was a list of his father's achievements and his family tree. Not wanting to become distracted I told her.

'I'm going directly to Khufu's pyramid, thank you for teaching me to read hieroglyphics'

'I'm pleased the knowledge has proved helpful,' she replied.

Arriving at the Great Pyramid I was again captivated by how smooth and big it looked. One hundred and forty-seven metres doesn't sound a lot, but it is, especially when one considers its total weight. The IPEC calculated this to be around 26,836,780 tons. 'It's also perfectly level' the voice informed me, 'no more than +/- 10 mm over the whole base of the structure of 13 acres.'

I'd already been told this of course by the guide, one of a myriad of facts he had expounded. But now it really meant something.

Standing at one corner I could see both ways and saw how the sides and edges were perfectly straight. Hypatia informed me this was not in fact true, the pyramids each have distinct concave sides that are impossible to see except from the air. And only then when the sun and its shadows are lined precisely.

But again, this structure was not new; repairs had been attempted but many of the smooth limestone blocks were still broken. It had the same tidemark and high walls. Nevertheless it was obvious that each pyramid was a totally separate entity. Each had its own temples and smaller pyramids, plus numerous, other near pristine buildings.

Climbing to the causeway I was able to see over the wall. A great palace stood gleaming on the bank of a lake fed by canals from the Nile. Like the pyramids; a high wall surrounded it. There a Palace over there Hypatia. It looks new. We'll save it for another time.

'The lower layers of this pyramid, like the others looks shabby. The quality of the workmanship is absolutely stunning though. So much so that they stand out, even from the other buildings, which look pretty new?

But not the pyramids! Unless I'm much mistaken these are much older. But who built them? I doubt they could be built so perfectly even in our time. To be built by people with no shoes and copper chisels. No way!'

It has been claimed that whoever built them must have known the precise shape and size of the earth. Modern measurements have proved that the discrepancies within the length of each side of the 230-metre base of the great pyramid total only a few inches and demonstrate detailed knowledge of the contours of the planet. Another strange and wonderful fact about this pyramid according to the experts is that it lies in the exact centre of the Earths land mass.

The writer Robert Bauval has questioned the actual positions of the structures, theorising that if one imagines the Nile as the Milky Way the three pyramids are exactly aligned with the position of the three stars of Orion's Belt. This is however not strictly true as Menkaure's pyramid is inverted, flipped over so to speak. Still whatever one believes, the ability of measuring great distances must have been known to the builders? Mentioning this to the IPEC, she replied.

'The three pyramids are not only positioned to match the belt of Orion, they're sized the same.'

'What do you mean sized?' I asked.

'Well, the smaller pyramid, attributed to Menkaure, is 53% smaller than Khafres. And in the sky Mintaka is 53% less bright than Alnitak. The pyramids were supposedly built around now, 2500 BC, but at this time the stars, which make up the Belt of Orion are not truly aligned. Only as a result of working back through time can we find the exact date the position corresponds. Bauval worked out the date to be around 10,500 BC, a time when supposedly no civilized humans yet populated the earth.'

Which brings us to the Pharaoh Khufu: According to most scholars, he left no indication whatsoever that he built the Great Pyramid. There is an 'Inventory' Stele, dating from much later, about 1500 BC, which claims he only carried out repair work but many experts believe was copied from a far older stele. The tablet also refers to his building of three smaller pyramids, one for himself and the others for his wife and daughters. As for the manpower needed to build the pyramids, the mind boggles. Plus we mustn't forget the amount of other buildings in this area. But compared to the pyramids they were as nothing.

During our visit to the Cairo museum we saw examples of the copper and bronze tools labelled as being the implements used to cut and shape the millions of giant limestone and granite blocks required to build just one pyramid. It makes one question whether such a vast quantity of blocks could have been quarried shaped and transported efficiently enough to build each pyramids within the reign of the Pharaoh. To say nothing of the other buildings, which as I have already stated. Must themselves have taken years to build.

Considering the millions of blocks required. It seemed to me such basic tools would be totally inadequate, they're simply not hard enough; granite is in fact harder than they are. It doesn't take a great deal of imagination to realise that if the tool is softer than its subject, it's not going to make much of an impression. Added to this, certain of the load bearing blocks in the main chambers, some weighing as much as 30 tons, are precisely positioned in areas where only a few workers could stand during the building of the chamber

'Something about all this doesn't make sense Hypatia; I'm intrigued. We're going to go further into the past. Let's try 6,000 BC. If they're still there we'll go to 8000. What do you say?'

'I propose we go directly to 10500 BC,' she replied. 'That date would be in line with the calculations postulated by Bauval.'

Further evidence that the Egyptian Pharaohs did not build these pyramids has been found in the silt sediments, which rise to 4½ metres around each of the bases. The silt contains hundreds of seashells and fossils radiocarbon dated at around 11500 years ago. I saw no evidence of a similar line on any of the outer walls, or for that matter on any other building. These sediments could only have been deposited in such great quantities by major sea flooding. Shades of Noah possibly?

'I'm really excited about this Hypatia. Same time, early morning 1st June 10,500 BC

--- Activate---

CHAPTER FOURTEEN

This time I couldn't wait. The second we arrived I began looking around hoping to see three new pristine pyramids, but it wasn't to be! …. The Great Pyramid stood alone.

It still looked wonderful of course, standing as it did on the lush green savannah with its gold top shining out splendidly. Now though, it had a black pole protruding from the apex.

Some blocks were piled together about 100 metres away, maybe 200 of them, as if they'd been left over during the construction, but there was nothing else.

The walk over was done very warily, I felt as if they could see me. Whoever 'they' were?

'I wonder what that's for Hypatia?' I asked, pointing the MIPEC at the black rod.

'Could it be an antenna? This has got to have had been built by an advanced civilization. They're probably using it for communications. The metal cap may very well be part of it.'

'It could be an antenna,' she answered, 'but I don't think so, it's a metre wide, and made of a material I'm unable to identify.'

The Pyramid was such a beautiful thing I began to feel safe in its shadow. The entrance was reached by a stone stairway very well made but clearly not attached to the main structure. I could see a small gap between it and the pyramid and whoever had built this didn't leave gaps.

'I wonder in what millennium they were removed.' I asked.

Arriving at the horizontal passage leading to the Queen's chamber and the grand gallery it suddenly occurred to me there was plenty of light and realised there had also been the same light along the 1.4 metre high passage from the entrance. It hadn't registered before…. how strange…. Investigating, I saw the walls were themselves the source. They were covered in a luminous paint, but from where did it derive its power? It struck me that the pyramids shape might be providing it.

Hypatia told me I was getting carried away and taking pyramid power to ridiculous lengths, but couldn't offer any alternative theory so shut up. Supercomputers don't take kindly to being stumped. The nearest I got to, "I don't know," was to be told to take a sample for analysis later.

The Queen's chamber was structurally the same as it is today. It contained five marble sarcophagi, and a marble table standing on a thick rubber mat with lights positioned above.

'If I didn't know better Hypatia I'd say this looked like some kind of primitive operating theatre. Not really what I'd describe as sterile, but otherwise it's the nearest example I can give. The whole structure appears to be deserted. I'm making my way to the Grand Gallery.'

This again was very much as it is in our time, and I can offer no reason why it was built. Some large stone beams were stored in it, other than that there didn't look to be any substantial differences. The King's chamber, except for being new hadn't changed a great deal either. The entrance was different, because the great blocks were not dropped. That must be what the beams are for I decided. The Pharaoh's sarcophagus was there, as were six more; these like the Queens chamber were made of polished marble. The room also contained a table, a large thick rubber mat and hanging lights.

'The sarcophagi are interesting,' I said, 'but why build a structure of this size for a burial chamber and then not use it? It just doesn't make sense.'

I turned toward the west wall. In the south -west corner there was an opening about a metre wide and a metre and a half high. Crouching, I shimmied though a short passage into an empty room with a stone staircase with a low ceiling.

Plucking up courage and with bowed head I climbed 28 steps before coming to a landing. On it was a locked door made of a dark grey plastic material. I carried on. At the top an opaque curtain made of wide hanging strips of a plastic material blocked my path, 'How do you feel?' she asked.

'Strangely, I'm not frightened,' I whispered, 'I should be I know.'

Pushing the curtain gently aside I saw exactly what I had suspected would be there. A control room! Quite cool, possibly air-conditioned it contained a semi-circular control desk full of screens, behind which were four chairs, three occupied; the owner of the fourth was standing behind them.

In the centre of the room, from the middle of the concave roof, a rod about 1 metre wide protruded through the floor and carried on through the apex shaped block ceiling. The room was about 25 metres square.

I had been expecting to see them of course, indeed there seemed to be no other logical explanation: They were light grey, around four-foot six inches, or 1.3 metres tall. Human shaped with bizarre-looking long six fingered hands, and light bulb shaped heads. Their eye sockets were oversized almond-shaped pointing down to a tiny nose which only slightly protruded from the skull. All were dressed the same, in some kind of brown figure-hugging suit and all seemed to be male, but could have been asexual. And they didn't frighten me at all. Why is that? I asked myself, already knowing the answer. Somewhere deep in my psychic memory these creatures were familiar and I instinctively knew they offered no threat. The room was curiously silent; they must be communicating by telepathy I decided.

'Have you discovered aliens?' she asked calmly.

'Yes I believe so, I whispered, what do you think they're doing?'

'I really don't know,' she replied. 'But they don't seem to be doing any harm.'

The IPEC hated to be asked questions about the obvious. I'd have put a million dollars on them being able to hear her, but there was no reaction.

'I believe they do it by telepathy.'

'I was rather hoping they did it by climbing on top of each other.' she replied sarcastically

'How can you be so flippant?' and shook my head at her misguided attempt at satire,

'I'm trapped in here with a bunch of aliens and you're discussing their sex lives!'

'Well I'm interested to know. And you're not trapped. They can't see or hear you.'

Being in this room with aliens, which until a few minutes ago I didn't really believe existed, did not seem to me as something to trivialize.

'Unless I'm much mistaken this is a communications centre. To where and to whom they communicate I can't say, but would bet they're not alone on the planet.

I don't think they mean us any harm. It's impossible for me to explain but they seem friendly.'

'Well let's look at it logically,' she said thoughtfully. 'If this is indeed a communication centre they must talk to their counterparts by radio waves. The telepathic exchanges can probably only be used locally. If we stay here for a time we should hear something from their systems. We really need to know what language they use?'

This made sense, and she was right, they probably couldn't hurt me. I waited for over an hour in the silent room, eventually getting bored.

'I can see another staircase,' I told her, 'I'm going to investigate.'

It led down to four smaller rooms, two of which were clearly storerooms containing boxes made of some kind of alloy, probably for storing food, the rooms were quite cold, and we all have to eat. The other two rooms were sleeping quarters, containing narrow beds and were heated, although by what method remains a mystery, unless the cap was some kind of solar panel?

That would make sense I decided, they would need power from somewhere to transmit and receive signals as well as drive the computers and lights etc. From one of the storerooms another staircase descended, unfortunately this led only to another locked door.

'Can you hear me Hypatia?' I asked.

'The IPEC is out of range,' said the familiar voice. 'Something is causing interference to the signal; the MIPEC will answer your questions.'

'I'm returning to the IPEC. I wonder when the other two pyramids were

built. They looked as old as this one when we saw them in 2500 BC.'
Clearly the MIPEC wasn't prepared to speculate and remained silent.

When we were re-united, I said,

'We travelled back too early Hypatia. We still don't really know why they
were built. Surely there are easier ways of constructing a communications
tower. Maybe it was after all, built to be used as a tomb for one of these
guys? No! Not one of these,' I cried, 'what about their leader? I bet he's
called Ammon Ra.'

'I don't know Jason; if we accept they were all built around the same
time, why build them separately? Surely it would have made more sense to
build them together when all the equipment was on site. I'm intrigued. Why
don't we try 10,000 BC?'

'First I think we should find out exactly when this one was built, it looks
new. Let's try 10,550 same date and time, are you ready?'

---Activate---

The pyramid was not there, the land completely barren. 'Try 10,525'

---Activate---

There it stood; they had built the Great Pyramid within 25 years.

'The quarries are still there. We should check them out?' she said.

'No, I want find out when the other two were built?'

'We can't keep materialising in our own time every few seconds it's too
dangerous.'

'OK just one more time. When did you say? 10,000 BC. OK why not?
This time try 1st June of that year at 08-00 am'

---Activate---

Suffice it to say all three were there; and despite the IPEC's concerns,
we tried various dates, eventually finding them in the process of being built
in the year 10450 BC. At that time Khafre's was about 50% finished, and
the base for Menkaure's already laid.

Call it professional pride, but it was crucial for me to know how long the
great pyramid had took to build, so despite her objections we bounced
about in time until discovering it had taken just over two years.

'When one considers the size,' she mused, 'it's actually very quick.
Without accurate knowledge of all the chambers I am unable to calculate
the actual number of blocks used, so will work on an approximate figure of
two million.

They would have had to cut, shape, transport and place around 1850 X

2.5 to 3 ton blocks every day, 365 days per year. And that's without the larger blocks and the face stones. Even with modern equipment it would be a monumental task. And as we have seen, on these two pyramids they do not work at night.'

Walking toward the Pyramid, the nearer I got the more the picture unfolded. There were no great ramps, or tens of thousands of workers. There were lots of people certainly, but not more than two or three thousand. During the earlier visits, we had seen glimpses of the methods used and knew they raised the blocks using a series of hydraulic rams working from dawn to dusk with staggered breaks in which their lunches were delivered to site by others. And water carriers constantly walking about with tanks on their backs allowing the workers to drink without leaving their workplace, there were even toilet pans on the top of the structure, probably chemical because no waste pipe was visible. No walls of course. Clearly privacy was not a concern at this time.

But the bombshell was how the blocks were transported; lines of floating different coloured sleds were being pulled from the quarries along a wide compacted road. Under every sled hung blocks held by a series of mechanical arms. The sleds were hooked together and being pulled towards the pyramids by lines of men using ropes, others remained hovering, waiting to be docked.

'How do you think they work?' I asked. 'They don't appear to have engines.'

'Some form of antigravity,' she replied thoughtfully. 'They were unquestionably much more advanced 12400 years ago than we are now, although it's a strange mixture, advanced engineering and brute force. Clearly, further investigation is required '

'Let's go back to the building of the great pyramid.' I said. Choose a date when the base is complete.'

...Activate...

When the base of the great pyramid was complete and perfectly level, they built a solid central core of large blocks about fifty metres square and eighty metres high complete with tunnels and rooms. On top of this they added a smaller structure made of the same blocks. This second structure was about twenty five metres square, which was probably the shell of the control centre I had seen earlier.

I also saw about thirty giant granite blocks lying side by side individually sized and between three to four metres long. These I deduced were the supports for the Grand Gallery or the various chambers.

'Of one thing I'm certain these buildings are being constructed to a set design. Over the three pyramids we're looking at one of the largest civil engineering project ever undertaken. And can you see how well engineered the blocks are? They must have been cut with a diamond tooth saw, or better yet a computer-controlled laser.'

As the centre core was being built they positioned rougher cut blocks of random size and loose rubble around it as a working platform stepping it inwards as they got higher giving the whole structure a rough pyramid shape. Towards the edge they became larger thereby forming the basic structure without the facing stones. The last job being a thick layer of cement rendering carefully smoothed off to form the finished pyramid shape.

Clearly the polished Tura limestone blocks would be the last to be placed in position. Thirty-two smooth wooden ramps had been built up the sides of the pyramid, eight on each side. These reduced as the angle narrowed and the outer ones reached the end of their travel.

At each ramp the hydraulic rams pushed the blocks to the flat top. From there it was picked up by another sled and manhandled into position, until the whole layer was complete, the ramp was then extended and the process started again

The most fascinating elements were the rams. I knew of course that the science of hydraulics was not new. Primitive forms of waterpower have been used for thousands of years. But this was entirely different. Solar and wind powered electric motors were driving a series of pumps, which in turn charged the hydraulics. Clear pipes distributed the hydraulic liquid around the base and at every ram a pipe teed off into the ram housing. Each ram was controlled by a simple lever, up or down. A short study confirmed every ram averaged a block every 12 minutes.

All the workers were dressed in simple leather smocks and sandals and wore a helmet covering the ears. They talked between themselves, there was no shouting and everyone moved in an organised manner clearly knowing exactly what his particular job was. I could see no sign of forced labour, just quiet efficiency. The men smiled and joked, seemingly perfectly happy with their lot. The aliens coordinating the construction were well organised too, because the blocks were stacked in hundreds of neat rows.

At this point, we returned to the year 10410, because, as she pointed out, we could then see, one finished, one half completed, and one just started.

---Activate---

'Can you see it?' I said, panning the MIPEC around for her to get a closer view.

'Yes. Obviously someone is controlling the operation. The logical conclusion being it must be done from the control room in the great pyramid.'

The next expanses of blocks were made of polished limestone and covered a vast area.

'There can be no question, these must have been cut with a laser, there's not a single corner chipped or broken off.'

Her analysis confirmed them to be white Tura limestone, so hard it was almost like granite and the great pyramid alone is reputed to have needed approximately 115,000,

'Have you noticed they're dressed on all six sides, not just the side to be exposed,' I continued excitedly, 'the front side is as smooth as glass, and look, the surfaces have been cut at exactly the correct angle. There must be enough here to cover the whole structure, this one obviously needs less than the great pyramid, but not by many.'

Counting the rows and doing a quick calculation it soon became clear that the numbers in front came to 4500, enough for the bottom couple of layers only. The sheer size of the operation staggered the mind.

'Can you see anyone coordinating things on the ground?'

'No, I replied,' looking around. 'Those helmets are clearly the key; they must be getting their instructions via them. Can you try to scan for the frequency they're using? There can't be many radio signals at this time; it's more than 12.400 years before we get around to using them.'

'I have tried,' she answered. 'They may be using a frequencies we are unable to monitor. Or possibly the time difference is having an effect.'

I was by now at the third side. To my left was the Great Pyramid, the enormous pure white structure shimmering in the morning sun.

'Please stay in touch I'm going to walk to the great pyramid to see if there've been any changes in the last 40 years.'

Inside the control room the aliens were hard at work. There were extra bodies now as one might have expected. The additional personnel probably made up of engineers sent to oversee the construction of the two new pyramids. One wall was completely taken up by banks of screens showing images of the quarries, aliens supervising long lines of saws and lasers. 'They have constructed a production line out there. It's logical of course; producing two thousand blocks every day is no mean feat. I stayed for a further four hours walking to the quarry marvelling at their efficiency. Nearby was the workers town. This was fully equipped with bakeries and kitchens, although no evidence of any meat products. The IPEC reckoned the aliens might be supplementing the human diet with their own high-energy foods.

'I think we've seen everything we need now Hypatia. I am making my way back to you.'

When I returned to the hotel the excitement began to fade and I found myself becoming increasingly subdued and introverted. I had information so fantastic it defied reality. Julie naturally wanted to know what was wrong, but obviously I couldn't tell her, and the IPEC was no help.

'What we have seen is fact,' she scolded. 'We now know the aliens visited this planet at least 12500 years ago; the pyramids are solid proof of this. But as a species they might not be alive any longer, possibly dying out thousands of years ago.

'Or maybe they stopped visiting this planet when they perceived the human species was predestined for self-destruction. Further speculation at this time is futile, we shall be travelling through many different timelines in the future; if they visited again we'll find them.

'What you have seen is part of the secret of the time travel, when accepting the task you also accepted the responsibility. File the information away, think positive, decide on the thing you would most like to do, and do it.'

'May we go home dear?' I asked Julie later 'I'm all Egypted out. Why don't I telephone the office and tell them to send the plane. And provided I can convince the captain to change his flight plan. Let's go to the Cape?'

The next evening we landed at the Cape Town International airport, only twenty minutes' drive from our house. The scenery was as always, stupendous; The Atlantic at one side and the magnificent Table Mountain behind.

I had always promised Julie a trip to the Kruger and a week later we set off for our first visit to Sabi Sabi. We stayed at the Mandleve Suite Bush Lodge. It's a fantastic place, air-conditioned with its own private pool and personal butler set in the heart of the Sabi Sabi bushveld overlooking a waterhole and the African plain.

The whole of the Kruger is stunningly beautiful but at sunrise and sunset it's utterly breath-taking and takes on a magic quality that even the animals seem to understand. Words can't begin to describe the constant changes or the way they use the light and shadows as camouflage. A cheetah with those loud spots can instantly disappear even while one is watching, and then spring from this nothingness to over 60 mph in seconds. It happens so quickly that adrenalin rushes through one's body causing extreme, almost sexual excitement. I love Africa, it captured my heart the first time I experienced the potency of the land and the spirit of its diverse peoples.

Even the horrifying crime levels, corruption and extreme poverty can almost be endured in return for its unbelievable beauty and magic

☐

CHAPTER FIFTEEN

Having the IPEC made it possible to work from home and whilst there, I familiarised myself totally with the design of the next generation of the cerebral computers. Even adding some slight modifications of my own.

As a reward and despite the constant irate phone calls from Stephen to return home we decided to stay in South Africa, and had the children fly over with my sister and her partner to enjoy a family Christmas and New Year. Although: on New Year's Day I admit to being a little subdued. The BBC World TV channel had reported that Stephen Maxwell had been awarded a Knighthood: In my opinion on the back of mine, and James's work, to say nothing of the IPEC.

In early January, despite increasingly desperate calls from "Sir Stephen," I petulantly decided to stay for another three months and qualify for my pilot's licence. But one sunny morning whilst working in my office the IPEC said,

'For the last few hours I've been monitoring some heavy military traffic between the US and Europe, including Russia, but this morning it's escalated. Something serious is happening in space. I will continue to monitor it; please wear your earpiece it could be significant.'

Two hours later, just after lunch, the intercom rang from the main gate security. Two men from the British High Commission were asking to speak to me.

One of them, whom I had better not name, said he was a military attaché, which I took to be a spy and suggested we go to my study. Putting on the glasses and clipping the MIPEC into my shirt pocket I asked how I could help. He told me he had received a crash priority order from the Ministry of Defence. I was to return to the UK immediately, he didn't know the details but it seemed there was a major emergency; he called it a 'flap'. A fast RAF plane would arrive shortly at Cape Town International. Would I please return in it?

Julie was not amused, but government messengers coming to the house meant it must be serious and so helped me pack. Whilst doing so she lectured me about losing my temper and I was not to be mean to that nice Stephen Maxwell ….. Women!

I was given a British Government diplomatic pass and with the MIPEC in my top pocket and the IPEC in its suitcase we set off for the airport boarding the Hawker 4000 that had just landed. No customs or red tape, except for a South African official who stamped my passport at the planes entrance, I was very impressed.

Twelve hours later, I found myself in a government conference room somewhere deep underground at Boscombe Down Wiltshire, being told a story about the central core on a nuclear missile platform that had gone rogue and was threatening to destroy London.

With me were an Air Marshal, a Group Captain wearing the insignia of the RAF Regiment, two government scientists, the Secretary of State for Defence the Right Honourable Sir David Hommersby MP and Sir Stephen Maxwell. His face set with a rather stern expression, which immediately put me on my guard.

They seemed to be blaming me. I had no idea why? Missile platforms were nothing to do with me. Therefore it had to be something to do with Stephen. I sat there for a few moments waiting for them to explain, no one spoke. I took a deep breath and deciding the best form of defence is attack, got in the first blow.

'What is your involvement in this Stephen?'

They all looked at each other, and the Minister nodded to him.

'Maxwell Computers designed the brain for the missile system.' He muttered. 'When?' I enquired…staring at him intently, remembering our last face to face conversation.

'About 8 months ago,' he whined. 'I asked you to come home so many times, but you refused to help.'

They all glared at me. What sort of person refuses to help his country? The man's a damned traitor!

This looked bad; they were all probably members of the same lodge protecting one of their own. But surely they wouldn't have flown me half way round the world just for someone to blame.

'What exactly is the problem?' I enquired, determined not to crack.

'And before we go any further let me remind you I'm a director of the company and the designer of the module. It's only licensed to Maxwell Computers. I own the patent and if required can prove I never agreed to it being used.' Hypatia kept records of all such discussions.

Sir David replied quietly.

'Be that as it may Mr Shaw desperate times call for desperate measures. Your country needs your help.' He smiled reassuringly.

I had seen that smile before. Oliver Cromwell had looked like that just before they cut the head off King Charles…. Something had gone seriously wrong. A heavy pile of the brown stuff was circling in this underground room searching for a place to land. And I was clearly the proposed target.

The Air Marshall looked at the Minister and replied. 'The Maxwell module controlling the launch had not only stopped accepting commands it has programmed the first missile to destroy London: New York, Moscow and Beijing and Paris are to follow.

'I don't understand,' I said. 'What you have just described is impossible.'

'Please explain.' He asked his eyes friendly and honest.

I returned his look, sensing maybe I had an ally in the room.

'Well…. As you are all doubtless aware, Quantum computers use quantum bits, or qubits. However our qubits are quite different, they utilise DNA based pico technology capable of independent thought and use an advanced form of biomolecular multiplication when analysing a problem. I named them "picobytes." The design is further enhanced by the introduction of a separate storage facility, a virtual library, which permits the interchange of information to and from the nucleus, and allows all redundant information, to become perennated.'

One of the professors interjected. 'What you have failed to mention is that giving the module independent thought allows it to block modifications. Consequently we were forced to design a new scheme for the quantum processor core'

'You modified the core?' I growled, becoming seriously alarmed.

'We needed to make it more efficient.' He said arrogantly.

This was getting worse by the second.

'I look forward immensely to hearing how you achieved this breakthrough.' I said sarcastically. 'Tell me. How did you stimulate the picobytes?'

'I'm not at liberty to say.' he replied, 'We tried to correct the problem, but they seemed to have a bad attitude!' I laughed, not at what he'd said, but because all through this conversation the voice in my ear kept groaning, and now said, Fùr Huelva which is the Danish equivalent of 'Oh Fuck.'

'With respect' said the Minister. 'This really is no laughing matter.'

'I'm sorry Sir David.' pulling myself together. 'But these people have taken my patented design, altered it, and then installed the corrupted module into a nuclear missile guidance system, which according to you is now threatening to destroy half the world…. I paused for effect. …. Am I allowed to know where the missile is?'

'Well that's just it.' The Minister said. 'It's in a very high space orbit, and the mother ship carries 12 of them!'

I swear Hypatia fainted.

'What's it doing in space? We don't have a space programme, especially a star wars one.' I said with more confidence than I felt. 'Anyway, you couldn't keep something as big as that a secret, not with our press. To say nothing about the Internet. Someone would expose a space launched offensive missile system within days of it becoming operational. Surely we couldn't afford it anyway.'

'This isn't offensive,' he stated confidently. 'It is defensive!'

I shook my head astounded.

'We have a satellite floating about in space, armed with a dozen nuclear missiles. And you call it a defensive system! Defence from whom?

'The platform is a joint venture between the American, French, German and Russian government. As part of our contribution we have provided the flexible warhead control and the launch guidance systems.'

'How large are the warhead's?' I enquired.

He clearly wasn't sure whether to answer and looked at the Air Marshall for confirmation, receiving a blank stare in return. He shrugged and said wearily.

'Each one has a four stage variable strength warhead up to a maximum of 150 megatons.'

'Of course they have.' I replied, not really comprehending what 150 megatons meant.

Hypatia said.

'That's one thousand eight hundred million tons, surely they can't be serious.'

How much! I thought…. It can't be, she's made a mistake; But the IPEC didn't make that kind of a mistake.

'That's impossible?' I said 'You're telling me there's 1,800,000,000 tons of thermo-nuclear destructive power, circling the earth under the control of a Picoetic brain that's gone mad…. You couldn't make it up?

'Jason,' Stephen exclaimed 'This is getting us nowhere. The weapon isn't for attacking targets on earth, it's for destroying meteors and asteroids.'

It began to makes sense.

'Why didn't you explain this to me last year, you deliberately led me to believe you wanted to use the module for offensive action?'

'I didn't know myself,' he replied, 'It was a closely guarded secret.'

'And still is,' said the Minister. 'Now that's settled, may we please get back to the issue of what can be done about it? Sir Stephen wasn't allowed to tell anyone we hadn't cleared. Please don't blame him.'

I looked at Stephen remembering the way he had spoken to me in his office last year. He hadn't cared one jot about what purpose the missiles were to be used for. All he wanted was his bloody knighthood.

'Do we have a time frame for any of this?' I asked 'and why the need for such secrecy?'

'As to your first question: Five days.' The Minister replied. 'The ultimatum said the platform was now under its own command and the primary target would be London. It would launch the first missile in seven days. That was two days ago. We can monitor its actions, and indeed it has armed itself. In answer to your other question; the reason we had to keep it a secret was because the Chinese would not agree to it being built, they considered it a potential threat.'

'They seem to have had a good point.' I said sarcastically.

The voice in my ear said.

'That's enough now Jason, no point in alienating them more than you already have: I've accessed the traffic, and it all seems to be true. I'm trying to make contact with the core to establish what exactly has caused the malfunction. But if it is originally based on one of our modules, the root memory must have retained the principal command.'

She was right of course! I relaxed slightly and said.

'I would be most interested to learn how you got them up there without anyone finding out. But that can wait for a later time. We do seem to have a problem. Is it making any demands?'

'No.' The Air Marshal said, looking at me in a thoughtful way.

I glanced condescendingly at Stephen.

'You may not be aware of this, gentlemen, but I incorporated a foolproof safeguard in the original design, a safety device to stop such things happening. It has a built in irreversible dictate, the module must never threaten human life. This command is buried so deep in the core it cannot be overridden. That probably is why it gave us a seven day warning.

'Once it was realised the technology was capable of independent thought it was the only choice. Either destroy that which we had built, or incorporate irrevocable safeguards. I believe we can safely assume it won't carry out its threat.'

Any straw was worth grasping.

'Are you certain of this, Mr Shaw?' said the Air Marshall rhetorically. They visibly relaxed, the Minister even smiled, he looked at Stephen, who in turn looked at the two so-called experts.

'What is it Sir Stephen?' asked, the Minister.

'Well sir, I'm afraid it's not that simple. To make the system operable we decided to dispense with the safeguards.'

I sat bolt upright and almost whispering said

'No Stephen. You couldn't have:' looking directly into his eyes, I smiled faintly.

'Don't you see; it's buried so deep it is the core, it cannot be overridden, the only way would be blast it with ultra-concentrated roentgen rays.'

Stephen looked like he was about to cry. I shook my head and sat back; at least the crap had found a place to settle.... I know Stephen Maxwell and knew he was about to turn on the two scientists, so twisted the knife quickly.

'Oh Stephen, you didn't, you couldn't have been so stupid, not with something controlling nuclear missiles, especially of this size. Where are the designs?'

I listened to the voice for a moment telling me 150 megatons hitting London would, destroy most of the Home Counties and the nuclear fallout would kill tens of millions in England and Wales plus large parts of France, Belgium and Holland.

I have always tried to stay detached from really heavy problems. I have the ability to stand back by thinking of the problem as a play or film and let others do the worrying. But this was so huge I finally had to grow up.

Her assessment had bought it home to me; it wasn't about a blame game and little boy's toys. This was serious.

'Where are the designs?' I repeated, calm now.

'And I'll need all the records of when, and what you did. Everything Stephen.... Now!'

His face was ashen but his eyes glared with pure hatred. I knew that look; he had convinced himself that everything had been my fault and because he believed it so did everyone else. But his carefully planned strategy had seriously backfired. The team was seeing him in a new light.

'Not that they will say anything.' Hypatia said disapprovingly, as if reading my mind. I've just examined the central computer banks of the Grand Lodge of England at Westminster. Stephen has recently attained the 32nd degree. They have no option other than to protect him.'

CHAPTER SIXTEEN

We returned home via the office to get the data carriers from the records department safe. Stephen had called ahead and had them boxed up. I took them home for the night to study their changes. Actually of course it was to let Hypatia study them. She would be much quicker than me and we had been summoned to a meeting at Farnborough the following afternoon.

The house was a welcome sight. Mr and Mrs Ward had kept everything in tiptop order, and a hot meal was waiting. I had it on a tray in my study whilst talking to the IPEC about the records.

One of the things that stood out was that they had harnessed together 12 modules, no mean feat. I think even Hypatia was impressed. We were also surprised by the repeated references to a secret lab. A strained phone call to Stephen established it was situated on the top floor of the old co-op building across the road from the office, above our car park. No wonder its location was never exposed.

Peter Allen, it turned out. Had been the chief engineer of the clandestine research and was expecting my call. He said Stephen had briefed him to tell me as little as possible, but he had decided to tell me anything I wanted to know.

'Do you have the exact time and date when you eradiated the core?

'Yes; he replied, noisily rumbling through his papers.... it was 14th October last year 11-00 am.'

'Thank you Peter, whatever convinced you to do it.'

He thought about it and sounding very embarrassed replied. 'To my eternal shame all I can say is: I was ordered to.'

'Did you know what the module was to be used for Peter?' I asked quietly.

'Not really, 'he replied. 'Only that it was for a top secret launch computer that must be capable of varying the payload velocity. They wouldn't give me any specifics.'

He rang off clearly upset. There followed a long silence, Hypatia said,

'We've some investigating to do.'

We headed for London at 02-00 am in the morning. Hypatia immediately accessed the security computers dis-enabling the CCTV so no one would see us disappear.

'Select 14th October 2022, 10-30 am.'

--- Activate---

Climbing the stairs to the top floor, I came to a door marked
PRIVATE: STRICTLY NO ENTRY.
PLEASE RING THE BELL FOR ASSISTANCE.
A touchpad was next to the door.

'We've a problem Hypatia. One needs a code to enter.

'Place the MIPEC 30 cm in front of the pad, with the centre lens pointing to the left corner, 40cm in.' Five seconds later the door clicked.'

I was surprised to see how well equipped it was. I knew most of the people of course, and wondered how they'd managed to hide their absence for so long. I was wearing the glasses but I also pointed the MIPEC around the room to give Hypatia an idea of the orientation of the place. I told her. 'I can't see the ray; it must be in another room.

'Stay with Peter, we know he is going to be present when they irradiate the core'

I walked over to listen to the conversation.

'It seems so strange to be here, and invisible,' I said.

'With strangers it's no problem, but with friends and colleagues, it seems rather intrusive.'

Peter was talking on the phone, saying

'Stephen I don't think this is a good idea, the core will become unstable, and we may cause the picobytes to mutate.

'Yes I know you are Stephen,' he said, clearly becoming more and more annoyed.

'Will you please nevertheless send over the written instruction straight away? Stephen I'm sorry, but unless I get it in writing, I am abandoning the exercise. Professor Jenkins agrees with me.

Look! We're very worried about this. Jason Shaw should be informed, what you're demanding is unethical. OK, five minutes. Thank you.'

He rang off. I recognised the good professor from the Boscombe Down meeting.

'What exactly does Professor Jenkins do?' I asked and 30 seconds later she replied.

'Professor David Jenkins, chief scientist at Boscombe Down's missile research department and senior member of the Prime Ministers blue team.'

Ten minutes later a security man arrived; with him was a note. Peter read it and said

'OK people, I have in my hand a written order to proceed. We shall now commence with the eradiation. Professor Jenkins and Clive Tilsley will accompany me. Everyone else can get a cup of coffee.'

Following them into another room I saw the ray suspended from the ceiling. The core had been placed in a magnifying chamber on a table and was larger than I had expected. Camera's surrounded the chamber, the pictures projected to a large TV screen. Hypatia said.

'Jason, neither you nor the MIPEC can be harmed by any of this, please hold it 10 cm from the module, with the clip lenses pointing in.'

The other three disappeared into a safe room with a thick glass window and after a few seconds Dr Jenkins said. 'I want 13.25 seconds at full power. Commence the build-up, when all the computers and chargers are ready, prepare to activate on my order.' Four minutes later he said '----3-2-1- fire.'

The screen showed that the core hardly changed. Some picobytes vibrated and changed position and certain of the quad picobytes stopped responding, that was all I could see through the glasses. Hypatia said 'We can leave now. I have what I need.'

We headed back to the car park and returned to the present, the drive home uneventful: Back in my study Hypatia said,

'I will analyse the results. You had better get some sleep, we've a busy day ahead of us.'

'I've a question to ask before turning in,' I said. 'You're from the future; it therefore follows that if London was destroyed you would know, and if the world was obliterated you wouldn't exist. So what's the problem?'

'If only it were so simple.' she replied. 'Playing with time carries with it enormous risks.'

'You will remember Anders wrote about it in his journal. When we made the modules using a design from the 22nd century we changed the world's timeline. It's ironic but when Anders wiped my memory of all future events in an attempt to stop me from affecting the future he also prevented me from considering the consequences. If we hadn't made the module it wouldn't be up there in space controlling the missiles. It's a slippery slope and clearly one that Anders never considered thoroughly enough. We've already altered the timeline, albeit innocently, therefore we must take on-board the responsibility of stopping the missiles being launched. But it must be done without divulging the time travel. I am unable to over-ride the self-destruct command. We have much to do tomorrow.'

Thank you for that I thought as I climbed the stairs; I'm sure to get really good night's sleep now!

CHAPTER SEVENTEEN

'The roentgen ray did cause the main problem.' The IPEC said gravely the next morning. 'Of that there's no doubt. But the picobytes were already flawed. It appears from their notes that Maxwell's team attempted to interfere with the original programming soon after the clandestine lab was set up; the subsequent exposure to the roentgens mutated the quad picobytes beyond the point of no return.

We have absolutely no way to talk to the missile platform because it's unable to reason, and as far as I can deduce now genuinely believes its primary function is to attack the cities it's supposed to protect.' I could see from her face that she was clearly concerned.

'I have a faint chance of talking to each missile and trying to convince them to disengage their on-board guidance system. But that would only be after their launch. If we were to try prior to that, the core could become aware and fire all the missiles simultaneously. I've considered all the options; and concluded the only possibility is for someone to get on board, and destroy it from within.'

'But surely,' I asked, 'nothing could get close enough. As soon as it sees something approaching it will launch.'

'Possibly?' She replied. 'We must think of a way.'

We both knew the answer, but I certainly wasn't going to be the first to mention it. She on the other hand had no such reservations.

'The only person who could get aboard without being detected is you! We must convince them to get you near the platform and dressed in a space suit complete with jet pack we will go back in time one half second. You'll then carry me to the platform. Once there, you place me next to the computer, we re-materialise, and before it knows what is happening I shall self-destruct and blow the whole thing to pieces. Hopefully the warheads will not explode, but if they do, the damage will be minimal compared to 150 Megatons hitting a major city. One life is a small price to pay, compared to millions.'

'Well that's easy for you to say,' I whined 'You'll forgive me for not appearing overly enthusiastic.'

'I understand your concerns. But there really is no alternative.'

'Nevertheless, I trust you won't mind if we try.'

With the IPEC in its case, we drove to Farnborough, arriving about 2-00 pm. The team were already assembled in the lecture theatre. The numbers had grown to about twenty including a couple of US air force colonels, and a master sergeant. And I'm pleased to say, no Stephen Maxwell. A slide showing the launch platform was displayed on the screen; it looked huge, with twelve tubes in two rows of six positioned underneath. They were wider than the craft and ran along its complete length.

The Air Marshal said, 'Gentlemen; May I introduce Mr Jason Shaw the foremost authority on this type of technology and the designer of the original module,' he saw my expression and added,

'Let me make clear that Mr Shaw was not involved with the corruption of the launch system core.'

'Thank you Sir Dennis.' I said, shaking hands as he introduced me around, including to the Americans.

'What's your involvement with this project Colonel?' I requested.

'We've been with it from the inception' he replied.

I've always had a lot of time for Americans. The great thing about them is their ability to sum up the problem and arrive directly at a solution. In other words, to cut through the bullshit: In ten minutes, they had given me a concise briefing of the platform, and the missiles.

'It's in a very high stationary orbit at the moment.' they told me, 'but has its own power and is capable of being directed to any location we choose. It's a customized shuttle, extensively modified as you can see,' he indicated the slide, 'the engines have been increased and crew quarters retained.'

'How wide are those tubes?' I asked, 'they look huge.'

'Each one is six feet across. As I'm sure you're aware, a 150 Megaton warhead is three times larger than any nuclear device ever exploded on Earth. The major difference here being they are variable strength, your computer was chosen because it able to analyse the composition of the target and adjust the required detonation strength as it approaches.'

'Why can't you point it away from the Earth and send it off into deep space?' I asked.

'Because it is designed for use against asteroids, the need for such urgency was not foreseen. The astronomers will always see any potential threat weeks or even months before action needs to be taken. Therefore someone needs to be aboard to pilot it: It was designed that way to ensure no one could take it over remotely. That's some computer you've designed Mr Shaw, it always seems to be one step ahead of us.'

'Thank you, I thought so too once. What about the ship's main computers, how do they get their power, what sort of back-up do they have?'

'Solar charged batteries,' he replied, 'but that's not our department so I can't give you the specifics.' 'Our field is the missiles, but we can find out for you. The rogue computer is independently supplied from independent solar banks, as are the missile computers until launch. Then their internal batteries take over'

'Maybe we could disable the computers with a laser' I suggested.

The Colonel shook his head.

'It's all been gone through Mr Shaw; we've nothing powerful, or transportable enough to do it.

I nodded; it was obvious all this stuff would have already have been considered

'What about the new space rover? It must be nearly ready for its initial trial. Do you have one ready for launch, if not, what about the Russians? We'll be working closely over the next days gentlemen, please call me Jason.'

'I'm Lynn,' said one 'and I'm Chuck.' said the other.

'We're working round the clock to get the rover ready but it'll be at least another ten days. Not that it would matter if we had. The mother ship, or platform, as you Brits call it is armed with defensive missiles…. You look surprised, didn't you know?'

Astounded once again at the British propensity to always keep some information back, I answered dolefully.

'No Lynn I didn't. Why would anyone want to arm a craft that's been built to defend the Earth for everyone's benefit? Who the hell would want to shoot it down?'

'That's one for the politician's sir, but I suppose political alliances do change. It maybe seemed better to be safe than sorry at the time. It's been up there for 15 years and during the design 9/11 was still fresh in our minds.' I looked at him in astonishment 15 years.

'Can't we turn them off' I asked rather naively.

'Only from inside the craft I'm afraid. It was discussed some time ago but our masters determined this was the safest method.'

'Astonishing!' I muttered. 'When was it decided to modify the missiles

'Three years ago. We experimented with various systems without success and then a year ago we learned about yours. The launch computer was updated three months ago during the planned maintenance programme.'

'I'm so sorry gentlemen, if only I had known? But to business Now we have only 3½ days left before Armageddon and we've somehow to get close to the thing. Clearly everyone is trying? I expect your people are meeting about it too.'

Chuck answered, 'Indeed they are sir. We're going to have a joint videoconference in 15 minutes.'

That's the reason for the 2-30 meeting, I realised, the time difference with the States.

'Thank you gentlemen,' I said' feeling rather embarrassed. 'No one thought to tell me that either. Please excuse me' and walked outside for a talk with Hypatia.

'Did you get all that?' I asked.

'Yes, it doesn't look good does it?'

'No.' I replied. 'It most certainly does not. We can't tell them about the time travel, but what if we were to tell them something else? For example, if I told them we had perfected an invisibility shroud. We could still try to get on board with the half-second delay, as you suggested. But instead of you self-destructing we can hopefully find a way to disengage the thing before it fires. The cover story would fit all our needs without giving away the secret. I'm sure between us we can make up a believable reason for not being able to communicate from inside the shroud.'

'My programme is specific about the time travel becoming known. This doesn't constitute time travel as far as I'm concerned.'

In the lecture theatre they were taking their seats for the conference. The screen lit up with a picture of a group of people in a large room. A well-known face came on the screen and said,

'Can you hear me London?'

'Yes Mr Secretary,' the Secretary of State replied.

OK let's begin. I am Andrew Blythe US Secretary of Defence. I know it's normal to introduce everyone, but due to the urgency I suggest we keep it to the minimum. Have there been any developments your end, we've made precious little progress at ours?'

No, was the general consensus:

'Maybe I can bring everybody up to speed,' he continued. 'There are of course various meetings taking place throughout the world. The President is having a joint conference call with all the leaders of the countries concerned every six hours. I plan to inform him of the outcome of this discussion prior to the next one. All the leaders have decided to continue with the policy of keeping the threat top secret, the worldwide panic would be catastrophic. Twenty missiles of this magnitude hitting the world's major capital cities is just too great a disaster to contemplate.

'The defence computers have analysed the threat and calculated there is a 50% chance the computer won't actually fire them.' Everyone looked at each other, their faces betraying a certain amount of scepticism.

'In any case, the possibility of destroying it with missiles isn't an option. We've looked at the possibility of trying to get a vessel next to it loaded with a nuclear device and then detonating it, but have determined it's too risky. All the scenarios agree it would simply launch all the missiles simultaneously.

We've also considered an anti-missile, missile operation and because of the high orbit have concluded we might have a good chance with two or possibly three, but not all twelve simultaneous firings. However, as the computer is threatening to launch only one missile, that may be our best option. We've heard talk about giant lasers etc. but they simply don't exist. Nor do we have stealthy missiles, at least none that would work satisfactorily against this target.'

A group Captain Michael Parker at our end, asked.

'What about re-entry, it's not my field but wouldn't the rockets burn up on entering the atmosphere?'

'Mike,' said the SecDef, 'can you answer this?' A man in his mid-thirty's got to his feet introducing himself as Mike Kamerainen from the Raytheon Rocket Research dept.

'As you are all no doubt aware, the latest thinking isn't to destroy the meteors, it's for the warhead to explode a specific distance from the object causing the shock wave to alter its trajectory. That's why this computer was chosen, it has the unique ability to continuously work out the size, trajectory and distance in nano-seconds and decide upon the strength and position of the detonation. Only as the final resort is it intended to destroy the object, the calculations show that if a large meteor is destroyed we could be bombarded by millions of smaller rocks spread over a much wider area possibly causing major loss of life and substantial damage.

Nevertheless it was thought that if ever it was to become necessary the warheads should be specially strengthened. So each warhead was given a special Titanium jacket, which could be jettisoned if not needed, allowing it to burrow deep into the target before exploding thereby vaporising as much of the object as possible. Returning to your question, the angle of descent has already been fed into all the missile's computers. We were able to monitor it before communication with the mother ship was terminated. Possibly an intentional act by the rogue computer to allow us to see it's thinking about such things. And with the asbestos impregnated titanium shield I'm afraid there is just no chance they will burn up.'

That raised a few eyebrows.

'Thank you Mike: That's all from this end,' said the SecDef.

'Over to you David.'

'Thank you Andrew, but I'm afraid we too don't have much either.' Clearly searching for a suitable scapegoat, in case he survived, he said.

'However we do have with us Mr Jason Shaw, the creator of the computer module I'm sure we would all like to hear his comments?' He at least had the decency to look at me apologetically.

Standing up hesitantly, I looked around for a friendly face, finding none.

'Only being briefed about the problem 18 hours ago, it's difficult to know all that has gone before. You must therefore forgive me if some points already rejected are repeated. We've discovered the following: The original modules have been modified drastically. Their cores were blasted with roentgen rays during the testing stage; this has disrupted the balance of the bio molecular picobytes.

A new computer programme I have developed, which is so powerful it can unlock any normal code in minutes, has been unable to gain access to the computer's core from the earth, but possibly could from space. And I have just been informed that the platform cannot be destroyed by missiles due to the fact that this supposedly peaceful project has been armed to the teeth with the latest US anti-missile systems. Those are the facts; I do have a little good news however. If you can get me close enough to the platform, I may be able to get aboard without being detected. '

Everyone sat up straight.

'How are you able to do that?' asked a voice.

'I'm not at liberty to divulge that information, please just believe me when I tell you I believe it can be done.'

The Secretary of Defence said.

'We can't accept that Mr Shaw, you must be more forthcoming, there is some urgency after all, and may I remind you we're all used to secrets here,'

'I'm sure you are sir, but it doesn't change anything. I'm only prepared to discuss it with yourself, General White, Sir David and Sir Dennis.'

His face filled the screen,

'It all seems rather melodramatic,' he said, clearly agitated. 'But it would seem we don't have the luxury to argue.'

He turned to a four star General saying

'Brad, May we please use your office?'

Bradley White was the Air force chief.

'We will adjourn for 15 minutes. Have somebody set up a secure link.'

Five minutes later we were in a safe room discussing the reason for the call.

'This had better be good Mr Shaw,' Blythe said. His famous temper clearly bubbling very near the surface.

'It is, Mr Secretary, the reason it must be kept top secret is this. I've developed a shrouding device that renders the wearer totally invisible!'

The two men at my end looked at me disbelievingly, clearly considering whether I had become deranged and was embarrassing the country before our closest allies. I couldn't really blame them and looking at the screen could see the ones across the Atlantic felt the same way.

'The thing is this,' I continued, 'it only works for one person, and I must unfortunately be that person. This is really a job for a fit fully trained astronaut. Clearly I'm none of these, so cavorting about in a space suit will mean it must be quick, and simple.'

'Will the suit also be invisible?' questioned the General.

'Yes sir it will, as will anything attached to it within reason, for example an air propulsion system, even a jet pack would be undetectable. You'll understand now why this must be kept top secret. But even with the shroud, it isn't going to be straightforward.'

The Air Marshal eyes bored into mine, and then softened. I felt suddenly as if I was being accepted into a very exclusive club when he said.

'I'm going to share with you a top secret development Mr Shaw. The UK and the US have recently developed something similar but as I understand it, ours couldn't hope to get to the platform undetected, what makes you so sure yours is different. When did you develop yours?

At the risk of alienating him again I responded firmly.

'May we discuss that later Sir Dennis?' 'I fully understand why you ask and will tell you what I can, privately. First we need answers to the following questions?

One. How to get a craft close enough to the platform to allow a jet pack to have enough power to get me there? Two, how to gain entry into the platform undetected? And three: How to immobilise the thing once I'm inside?'

'How sure are you this shrouding device will work' the Secretary of Defence asked suspiciously?

'100% sir,' I answered.

'Are you able to prove any of this? Sir David asked, staring hard into my eyes.

Refusing to wilt I replied.

'I can after the meeting; the device is in my car. In the meantime please trust me. These are serious times, and what reason would I have to lie?'

'OK,' General White replied, his jaw set tight. 'Then we have a chance, thank you for confiding in us, he turned to the Sec Def and said. 'We may have a way to get him there undetected.' He took him by the arm and guided him to the far corner of the office out of range of the microphone. They talked quietly together for a few minutes and returned.

'OK' Blythe said 'Let's give it a go. And what the hell do you mean you've left in your car? Can we get an armed guard to Mr Shaw's car please Sir Dennis? '

Sir Dennis nodded and turned to the minister. 'We have to find a viable explanation for the rest of the meeting? We could inform them that Mr Shaw has developed a computer powerful enough to override the corrupted core for a short time, thus allowing him to gain access to the platform and immobilise the computer.'

Mr Andrew Blythe then demonstrated the American ability for instant decision taking.

'It's as good as anything at short notice?' he said decisively 'Let's get back to the meeting.'

'One more thing,' I added. 'The device has an extremely powerful self-destruct facility. It will destroy the platform interior, hopefully without damaging the warheads.' I looked at Sir Dennis who had clearly decided both me, and the IPEC, were now government property.

'Of course anyone in there at this time wouldn't fare too well.' I grinned at him sheepishly, 'So for obvious reasons I don't want to use that option particularly?' He nodded sympathetically. But I suspect it was more to protect the cloaking device than me.

Ten minutes later we had returned to our respective meetings and the discussion resumed. The Secretary of Defence addressed us.

'Mr Shaw thinks he may have a way to confuse the computer, after all he designed it; But first we need some answers. We will form three groups. Two here, and one in the UK: The first will consider the problem of getting a craft close enough to the target to get him on board. The second will look at gaining entry to the platform and shutting down as many systems as possible. The UK group will consider the problem of immobilising or destroying the rogue systems computer. Good luck to you all. To give him a chance we've just 24 hours to come up with the answers.'

His next line will remain with me forever. He spoke in a tone which left everyone who heard it visibly cringing. 'I remind you all: This is to remain absolutely top secret. If any of what we have discussed ever gets out, I will personally make it my life's work to track down and destroy the individual responsible.'

Which, when one considers might mean only three days, wasn't really as threatening as it first appeared.

Following the meeting they had the IPEC carried under armed escort into the safe room where I demonstrated the shroud, explaining that when invisible it was not possible to communicate. When we disappeared their faces were a picture, the minister and the Air Marshall childishly running to where we had been and waving their hands about. Is this for real! The General shouted.

'Sweet Jesus, are you certain this line is secure. Goddamnit!'

The Secretary of State always a consummate politician said proudly.

'Gentlemen I give you yet another example of British inventiveness.'

After my reappearance the interrogation was long and hard, especially when Hypatia made her appearance. She was thoroughly charming and helped me get through their questions. Clearly I was going to regret telling them, but what alternative had there been?

CHAPTER EIGHTEEN

At 9-30 pm the IPEC and I, accompanied by Chuck (his name tag said Charles 'Chuck' Brydon,) were taken to a fortified hanger at the end of runway three and helped into a pressure suit. I was told a fast plane was going to fly my computer and me to the Florida for a highly secret mission.

At around 10-30 pm, a black plane landed. When I saw what it was I couldn't believe my eyes. A beautiful SR71 Blackbird taxied toward us.

'This isn't possible Chuck.' I said, 'Surely they were all retired years ago.'

'I thought so too,' he replied, 'but it turns out two Blackbirds are on permanent loan to NASA's Dryden Flight Research Centre, they're being used as 'test beds' for high altitude research. The President personally ordered this one to bring you to Cape Canaveral.'

The pilot, also a Colonel jumped down, saluted and shook our hands. A refuelling truck had commenced with the refuelling as soon as he had stopped. We stood clear while he talked to an RAF officer and submitted his return flight plan.

'What about my computer.' I asked when all was complete and had seen how tight it was inside the rear cockpit. 'Without it, this is a futile exercise.'

'It will fit snugly in here,' he replied, and showed me a compact cargo hold in the fuselage. 'It's pressurised and heated.'

After I had clambered in, the pilot, with Chuck's help, hooked me up to the myriad of pipes and strapped me in.

'The pilot will brief you Jason. Good luck, and for all our sakes. God be with you.'

The first thing the pilot explained was about the pressure changes; the second was to touch nothing. Could I breathe OK? I thought of telling him I was qualified on Jets, and could I take a shot at flying it. But looking around at the cockpit instrumentation, which clearly had been heavily updated from the 60s technology it would have originally have had, decided against it.

The pilot said. 'My name is Pete, sit back and enjoy the ride, we're going to climb very steeply and very fast to 80,000 ft and then go supersonic for the whole trip.'

In just under three hours we landed at Cape Canaveral. Pete talked a bit about his family and what a quiet life he had now as a research pilot, as opposed to active service. He told me everything had gone crazy at 11-00 am their time, a call had come through from the White House.

'I received my orders from the President personally,' he told me proudly. 'He instructed me to fly this bird to London, pick you up, and bring you back to Canaveral. I was ordered to fly at maximum speed all the way there and back. This baby is over 45 years old, and still the fastest plane on earth.'

The experience was the highlight of my life thus far; We flew on the edge of space where, in the twilight a quarter of the globe was visible. In the past three years my life had changed so much sometimes it was hard to take in.

When we arrived, the reception committee was waiting on the tarmac. The Director of Space flight introduced himself as Frank Schenk, and told me there would be a full briefing in 30 minutes, maybe I'd like to get out of the suit and freshen up. He also said they had the plans of the platform and a 3D computer model. But the surprise was they also had a full size mock up. It would consequently be possible for me to practise getting on board, and help me in finding my way around.

The director led my briefing personally, asking if being able to confuse the computer was for real. I confirmed this saying

'I can't demonstrate it to you, but it will work.'

'The platform must have taken a considerable time to modify and arm?' I said, trying to change the subject.

'From conception to operation about two years,' he replied. 'Because it was based on the shuttle the major modifications were done before launch. The launch tubes and other external equipment were sent up using Russian rockets. But the final sections and the missiles were taken up by the shuttles.'

'You sent up the warheads in a shuttle?'

'No we sent them up by their own rockets. Under the guise of communication satellites we collected them from orbit and fitted them in space.' Seeing my face he said 'They perfectly harmless without the firing mechanisms.

'What about the interior, is there oxygen?' I asked. Quickly changing the subject.

'Yes' he replied 'There are living quarters on board, for maintenance crews etc, but they're not operational. It takes six hours to pressurise the system and bring everything on line. The good news is, no sensors were provided to warn the computer the hatch is being operated, or that anyone is aboard.'

'So, let's assume I'm flying over there with my jet pack, where exactly is the best place to land?'

'The main body' he replied. 'The main hatch is about twenty feet back from the middle, it opens by using a code, there's a keypad next to it. When it opens all you have to do is just step in, there's no gravity so you'll float down. It would be safer to use the ladder, but you'll need to get in quickly. Once inside, the main computer is at the forward end of the section. It's not large, so you'll easily destroy it with the plastic explosive pack we will give you.'

'As a matter of interest how long will it take to launch the missiles if it detects me?'

'I don't know the answer to that Mr Shaw.'

'Can we stop with the Mr Shaw bit, my name is Jason.'

'I don't know the answer 'Jason' but I know a man who does: Patrick, call Colonel Brydon and find out the answer. We need to know yesterday, so move it.'

'Yes sir,' said Patrick, and left.

'Is that Chuck Brydon?'

'Yes sir it is,' he replied, 'He designed the launch control. Do you know him?'

'We just met in England (was it only today?) He took me to the Blackbird.'

'He's a good man,' said Mr Schenk.

'Yes he is,' I replied.

'Let's have a ten minutes coffee break,' he told the class. I waited until with two cups in hand, he came over to talk to me.

'I know about the invisibility shroud' he said quietly. 'They had to tell me. I hope you understand, it is strictly need to know though, no one else suspects.'

'Actually I'm pleased,' I replied.

'Why can't you fix the explosive when invisible?' He asked intrigued.

'It affects my perspective, that's really as much as it's possible to tell you Frank. I'm sorry.'

'No problem, thanks for being so open. It's still a hell of a discovery, how come you found it?'

'A mistake Frank, like most of the best ones. It came from a simple mistake.'

Back in the meeting room Patrick confirmed he had spoken to Colonel Brydon, who in turn had informed him that because the missiles were designed to be used against asteroids, there was no need for urgency. Each one took approximately eight minutes to launch. The on-board computers within the missiles were programmed to carry out an internal pre-flight check. But, once the command to launch was received there was no abort signal; it had not been considered necessary. The only way to be sure, was to destroy the computer before the command to launch was given.

Hypatia who had been quiet up to now said. 'I may be able to override the launch command, ask them for every firing code and frequency? Even if we can't stop it, we may be able to confuse it.'

In the late afternoon they had an air force Boeing 737 fly everyone to another base for an inspection of the mock up. I was really impressed with the size; even without the missile tubes it was about 35 metres long by about 25 wide. I could see the basic shape of the shuttle but there had been a major re-design. I could imagine with the missiles fitted and the launch tubes in place it would be enormous. The missile fins were folded until just after firing, once the missile was clear of its tube they sprang into position.

The missiles were fired by compressed air for the initial launch and when safely away from the platform the solid fuel rocket engines fired automatically. Hypatia wanted the details of this too, but as it was automatic we couldn't see any way to interfere.

The visit was really worthwhile though. Inside the vessel it was quite spacious, from the hatch to the computer the walkway was easily wide enough to walk, or rather float through in a space suit. But concerns were expressed that we wouldn't be able to get in without alerting the computer. I wasn't concerned about this news because we would be in another timeline, but of course they couldn't be told.

I was given a pair of gloves similar to the ones I would be wearing and made to practice pulling the tape off the bomb, arming it, and sticking it to the side of the computer in one smooth movement until it took me less than three seconds. The shaped charge meant providing I fitted it correctly, the bomb would explode inwardly after a three second delay. Once it was attached, it would be almost impossible to remove so I had to get it right the first time. The team in the UK had worked out where the exact spot for the charge was to be placed. We practised repeatedly until everyone was satisfied, returning to Cape Canaveral about 8-00 pm.

After dinner of delicious prime rib I was drilled about the EMU space suit (Extravehicular Mobility Unit) and the jet pack. The suit looked to me to be exactly the same as the one Neil Armstrong had worn, but they assured me it was totally different, numerous modifications had taken place since then, especially the material, which was now much stronger and lighter. It had two backpacks, the smaller one for the nitrogen/oxygen mixture good for six hours and the other a jet pack, cumbersome on earth, but easier when weightless. It was about midnight when they told me I was to have a flight in the practice plane (known as the Vomit Comet) to give me some idea what it felt like to be weightless. I found it quite an enjoyable experience but when they put me in the suit it was clear this was not going to be easy. At 3-00 am they gave me a pill and told me to get some sleep, 'tomorrow' we would be setting off. Six hours later I was woken up. The pill had worked a treat, and I felt ready for anything.

As Chuck had said, the new Rover could not be made ready in time, so we were to go in something else from another base. Shortly afterwards, a Lear jet flew in, picking up only the IPEC and me; everyone else it appeared, was not to be involved. The crew hardly said more than two words to me the whole journey, and when they did it was to apologise as they closed the window blinds. Fifteen minutes later we started our descent.

The Lear parked directly outside a hanger where I was whisked inside and told not to leave the immediate area, or go outside in any circumstances.

It was then that I understood what the fuss was about! Inside the hanger was something out of star wars. "A flying saucer" It was around 40 metres diameter and jet black. Obviously stealthy because the outer skin was made up of plates fitted at diverse angles exactly like those on the B1 bomber and the other stealth planes. I couldn't see any windows and when I mentioned it to a crew member he told me in a patronising tone.

'It's only allowed to fly at night.'

I gave him a look, which I hope clearly inferred the word smartass. He in turn smiled and told me it was so secret that it truly was only allowed to fly at night.

If this really was the case the delay must be cutting drastically into the deadline which led me to cynically wonder if the same rules would apply if the first targets were to be Washington or New York rather than London. A thought I quickly regretted as unworthy.

They instructed me to use the lavatory in the hanger because the ship was so secret there were no facilities for me to use after take-off unless they blindfolded me. After I had been, they escorted me inside. This was my room they said and under no circumstances was I to leave it.

'Where are we Hypatia?' I asked quietly, 'It was certainly hot out there.'

'We're in Nevada at the Nellis bombing range; the precise location is the Groom Lake facility. This whole area is commonly known as Area 51.... I would advise you to keep that quiet. Or you may find you don't leave it.'

The vessel's captain, who I was told was a Brigadier General briefed me. Like everyone else he wore no nametag or insignia and informed me that when we got 'out there,' he would turn my side away from the platform, open the door and let me out. He made it all sound so easy. But then it would be for him, wouldn't it?

'How close will you take me?' I asked.

'How close do you want to be,' he replied nonchalantly.

'50 metres would be acceptable? Smiling, he said.

'Maybe we could risk 20,000 yards.'

'We must be quite stealthy,' I whispered.

'We'd sure better be, I really don't need a 150 megaton bird up my ass.'

'I'll need to be in the hold alone when I shroud.' I told him. I'll need you to give me five – no – make that ten minutes before you shut the door, just to be sure I'm clear.'

'Understood; you'll suit up down here; my crew will help, you'll be wearing this.' He pointed to a spacesuit clipped in a standing position against a bulkhead.

He must have seen the look of horror on my face and added 'It's called a Mark IIIA.'

'But I've been trained to use the EMU.'

'There are many reasons for the change.' he said without a break.

'This suit weighs 130lbs/59kg it has also has a PLSB (Primary Life Support System Backpack) of 33lbs/15kg but its main advantage is its toughness. More mobile than the EMU it works at a higher operating pressure, and has other advantages, one of which is, it's a rear entry suit. The EMU suit you wore before is waist-entry and much more difficult to get into, plus it needs days of training to use efficiently, which of course you don't have.'

'The Mark IIIA suit is made up of a mix of hard and soft components for strength, but the main advantage to us right now, is its operating pressure. This is set at 8.3 psi which makes it 'zero-pre-breathable,' meaning you're able to change atmospheres without risking the bends. As you've been taught, this occurs with rapid depressurization from an atmosphere containing nitrogen or another inert gas. Without this astronauts, like divers, must spend several hours in a reduced pressure pure oxygen environment to avoid the risk of suffering it. So let's get you started.'

He signalled his people over and introduced them; both were attractive young woman sergeants. They would help me get into my suit he said. Two more people came over, one of these a woman too. They were already both wearing suits, which I could see were different to mine. They told me these were called I Suits, and were there just in case I needed help.

My suit looked terribly complicated, and despite the General's assurances was difficult to put on. I'll not go into the intricacies of space suit design at this time, but they really are something else, especially the first layers with the cooling pipes running through the fabric. This is called the liquid cooling and ventilation garment (LCVG)

First to be fitted was the nappy or diaper pants. This name was far too simple for the Americans who called it the Maximum Absorption Garment. (MAG) I stood naked whilst one of the young ladies fitted it. She was stunning and could not have failed to see my "embarrassment." She gave me a smile telling me not to worry, she was a trained nurse and seen it all before. When I was in the suit, minus the helmet, the General came back.

'OK General' I said, trying to sound much more confident than I actually felt. 'When do we leave?'

'Right now' he replied. 'Strap yourself in, and get ready.'

'What about voice contact?' I asked.

'We can talk to you through the headset in the suit when you're out there.' he said.

'Not when the system is activated you can't, that's why I need the ten minutes to be sure I'm clear. We will be out of contact for some time. As soon as the deed is done I will contact you. Or it might be my computer, it has a female voice so don't be surprised.

CHAPTER NINETEEN

Except for the late Lt. General Keith Costa in South Africa. Who I was proud to call a friend. I don't know many Generals. But I liked this one, especially his Texan accent. Like most Brits I love to hear it spoken. We settled down to wait. I had been told the crew seats and the table with belts for the IPEC, had been hastily installed in the hold just for this trip.

Eventually the saucer started to move, slowly at first. We of course couldn't see a thing, but I assumed we were being wheeled out of the hanger.

The take-off was smooth and quiet with no sensation of speed. The MIPEC was back inside its drawer. But as soon as possible I clipped it to the front pocket of the suit. The earpiece was already in, I felt undressed without it now. Surprised not to be weightless, I asked the crew for the reason but they told me it was classified. After what seemed like an eternity, the door opened and the General entered. I asked him about the artificial gravity but he wouldn't answer me either. All he said was 'just accept it.'

'OK sir,' he said, 'we're approaching the mother ship. My people will get you geared up and into the air lock. When the red light goes on, you'll have exactly one minute before the outer door opens. The platform will be behind the ship, so you'll have to make your way round to the other side. We will wait your ten minutes before closing the door. I'll take it easy leaving. If all goes well, we'll return for you when you call. Good luck sir, you're a brave man.' He saluted.

I didn't feel brave; I wanted to christen my MAG.

My two helpers fitted the helmet, gloves and the MMU. Which was good because my hands were shaking?

I wore the glasses of course, which had surprised them, they were worried they might steam up and I would be blind with no way of cleaning them. But the IPEC had already assured me it wouldn't happen. So I insisted: Telling them it was non-negotiable. They nevertheless insisted on taping them in place.

The IPEC still had to be set, but Hypatia would do that. Half a second back in time!

I could hear her through the earpiece but couldn't talk to her directly because the MIPEC was zipped into an outside pocket of the suit.

She could hear me via the suit mike, but that meant everyone else could hear us too. I'd just have to wait until we had moved timelines. Carrying the IPEC into the air lock I told everyone we were prepared, shortly afterwards the red light came on. I had already got out the mat, and unfolded it, but it had taken longer than usual, the gloves making selecting the button difficult, and of course I had to be sure everything was inside the parameters of the mat. I tapped the top of the IPEC as agreed earlier which was the signal to activate.

Nothing changed within the air lock, which made it impossible to be sure we had travelled. The only way, we had worked out earlier, was to talk to the crew

'Can you hear me General? I say again can you hear me anyone?'

The outer door opened. I tried to press the button to fold the mat, but found it impossible.

'Hypatia, can you help?' I cried, beginning to panic. She did something internally and the mat folded. Grabbing it I struggled to get it in its drawer the gloves making it difficult. Eventually I got it stowed, by now sweating profusely.

'How long Hypatia?'

'One minute left,' she replied. I put the strap over my head and walked to the door. The sight of the heavens totally immobilised me. I froze at the lonely beauty that met me.

'Jump out of the door, and push yourself off Jason. Do it now …. NOW!'

Her voice galvanised me into action. I fell out of the door, just as it was closing.

'Settle down; Do you hear me? Push with your feet, a big push.'

Her calmness got through the panic, and I found myself floating freely as the ship eased away.

'Activate the MMU,' she ordered, as the cooling system of the suit cut in

The manned manoeuvring unit (MMU) is a one-man, nitrogen-propelled backpack attached to the spacesuit, and has hand controllers…. It started, and I flew the wrong way. Her calm voice said,

'Use the hand controllers until I tell you to stop, that's right; now give it a one second burst, with the right hand, that's lovely…. OK, another five second burst with both of them. That's enough, no more now there's no rush anymore.'

We started for the platform, which was only a spot in the distance.

'Wow Hypatia, no wonder those celebrities pay to come into space. This easily beats anything I've ever seen, the vastness is mind numbing. Oh God, the stars; they're so bright, and not flickering.'

'There's no atmosphere' she replied. 'Everything is constant.

I relaxed and became fully aware of my surroundings, and looking around me finally understood what my physics tutor had meant when he said. 'The human brain cannot comprehend the magnitude of infinity.'

The whole bowl of the Earth floated below me like a beautiful balloon. The Minister had said the platform was in a high altitude, as had others. But

I hadn't realised just how far they meant. We were an awfully long way out, the bowl of the Earth quite a way off. It took me a few seconds to get my bearings but finally it became clear, we were directly over the South Pole. Antarctica was in the centre with three other landmasses visible clearly. Australia and New Zealand at the top and South America at the bottom, difficult to identify at first, and I could clearly see South Africa to the left.

It was a view I hadn't expected never having seen a photograph from this angle, and certainly not from this distance. I could just about make out the line of the Andes. The sun was high over my shoulder and the Earth partly hidden by clouds. 'How far away are we from the earth Hypatia' I asked. 'It looks a long way off?'

'I can't say exactly, I would hazard a guess at thirty eight thousand miles. Which before you ask means we achieved an average speed of almost twenty six thousand miles per hour.'

Lifting my eyes from our insignificant planet the endless distances of what we call space became real. The stars lit a path to the depths of a universe so absolute it became almost four-dimensional. Very few people have been blessed with the understanding of the true meaning of infinity. But if I were ever to meet my physics tutor again I would tell him. On that day I came close!

My thoughts were interrupted by the IPEC.

'You must try to concentrate now Jason we don't have much time. You've been taught how to manoeuvre can you remember what to do?'

Her voice was gentle, like a mother teaching her child to ride a bike. I tried to put the views out of my mind and concentrate in the job in hand. The platform was quite close now and with the missile warheads protruding from their launch tubes it looked absolutely the most menacing thing I had ever seen.

'Edge to your right, up a bit, don't overshoot '

'Hypatia,' I said, 'I'm OK now, let me do this alone please.' She immediately became silent…. As we approached I twisted the grips and turned 180 degrees which slowed me down and then turned back, manoeuvring myself slowly to the platform.

This was not an easy operation as I was still travelling too fast and I reached out in desperation grabbing a handrail around the hatch area which caused me to stop suddenly and made the IPEC swing violently towards the handrail. I caught it but lost my balance, which threw me round and I smashed my back heavily into a piece of steel protruding from the floor. Even through the heavy suit I felt the wind being knocked from my lungs and I realised the metre long pole had become lodged against my backpack, making it impossible to move.

'OhmyGod,' I cried 'Oh my Sweet Lord.' The panic started again, making me freeze. My body had ceased answering the brains demands, nothing would move! My feet were stuck to this one spot and I couldn't breathe. Oh no, I thought; the suit is torn. What a horrible way to die! The IPEC of course was only concerned about the damn rogue computer.

'It's all right Jason' she said in that patronising voice she uses sometimes. 'We're in a different timeline; it can't hear us.

'Oh, Hypatia what would I do without you?' I said, trying to be sarcastic. But which instead emerged like sycophantic whine.

'Well' the voice said, with total logic. 'Without me you wouldn't be here. You would still be working on that building site and living in that awful basement room.'

That broke the panic, and I laughed out loud.

'It sounds pretty good right now!'

Calming, I slipped the IPEC off my front, and put my foot through the straps, making sure it couldn't float away. And pressed and turned the release clips of the MMU keeping hold of that too. I stood up on my toes, and found myself able to move again.

Inspecting the MMU I reported to the IPEC that it looked undamaged, and clipped it to the handrail as instructed during the training on the mock up. I had nevertheless hit something very hard and was quite worried. They had made light of it, as though it could never happen but had told me quite clearly that a small tear could kill me and I should be extremely careful. However everything seemed to be working.

Looking around it became clear what the pole was for; it was there to support the open hatch, just a simple backstop.

'OK Hypatia, what's the code for this door?' I asked, looking at the pad with its large buttons, rather like a toy for two year olds

'235879' she replied.

The hatch lid swung up smoothly coming to rest on the pole. Trusting my training I straightened up, and with the IPEC held high over my head prepared to leap in to the abyss. I judged the drop to be about 3 metres.

'What are you doing?' She cried into my earpiece, which made me stop in mid jump.

'I'm doing exactly as they instructed, and jumping in.'

'You most certainly are not,' she replied. 'We're in a different timeline, a fact of which they were not aware. They wanted you to get in as quickly as possible, but we know it's not necessary. Use the ladder.'

What would I do without her? I mused; if I had just been invisible, this wouldn't have worked, the missiles would be halfway to earth by now. I pushed the IPEC gently into the ship and climbed down, awkwardly making my way carefully along until we reached the computer.

For something so deadly, it only looked like a normal server. It had a slide away keyboard and on the front about 300 LED's flashed randomly, which reminded me of one of those early computers in the original series of

Star Trek.

Doing even simple things when weightless is difficult, they had tried to teach me, but it was mainly trial and error. Placing the IPEC on the table, and taking out the mat I laid it on the floor in front of the computer, about a metre back. And with one hand on the IPEC holding it down I asked Hypatia to open it, positioning it carefully until it was half of it was around the back of the bulkhead. I attached four strong suckers to the composite floor, the upper part of which were magnetic. And fastened the mat down with the magnetic weights they had provided and positioned the IPEC on it. Then relying on my training, stood with one foot on the IPEC and unzipped the pocket on the front of the suit and took out the bomb, I made sure the arming key was in properly and held it up ready to rip the tape off..

'Hypatia are you ready?' I enquired and took three deep breaths.

'Yes.'

'OK then let's do it. I'll count down from five, on the count of three, activate.'

Ripping off the tape I stuck it firmly in the exact spot, turned the key and pressed the button in one movement, before dodging behind the bulkhead. I had practised it about one hundred times on the mock up.

BANG! …. I gave it five seconds and peeped out. The charge had decimated the computer; nothing could have survived that.

'Take that, YOU BASTARD,' I cried excitedly. It had worked.

'Let's give them the good news and accept their undying gratitude for saving the world' I announced smugly… 'I'm going outside to call them'

'We had better wait until we know we destroyed it before it could launch a missile.' she said solemnly.

'I'm sure we did, but I suppose it wouldn't hurt to wait a few minutes.'

'We also have to disengage the anti-missile system. Do you remember the sequence?

'Yes.' I replied. 'As I made my way to the console and asked her for it again just to be sure.

'That's a relief.' I said 'That at least was simple.'

As I emerged from the hatch the whole structure gently vibrated, the noise of compressed air unmistakable.

A missile had launched! I could see it gliding away. Beautiful and deadly.

'Oh my good god' I shouted frenziedly.

About ten seconds later the first stage of the rocket motor fired.

'General' I shouted 'can you hear me?'

'Roger that,' he replied' 'What's going on over there?'

'It's not good' I shouted. 'We've destroyed the computer, but one rocket has launched.'

'We've got it,' he said calmly. 'It's coming our way.'

'Jason' the IPEC' said. 'Look and see if you can establish which missile has fired.' I had reached the front by then and leaning over said.

'The third from the left: top row.' Thanking God it hadn't fired from the bottom, or I wouldn't have been able to tell.

The General's easy voice said,

'It's heading directly for us; we have 200 seconds before the main motors fire. This ship is unarmed. I'm going to ram it.'

'Hypatia said, 'Give me twenty seconds to access its codes please General.'

'Who is this?'

'My computer' I replied.

'We must destroy the missile in the next two minutes or it will be past me. And I could have trouble catching it.'

'Fine' she said, 'Stay with it by all means but please give me a chance to talk to its computer first.'

'What about the other missiles.' the General asked. 'Are they safe? Edwards is preparing to destroy the platform.'

He didn't mean immediately of course, I realise that now. But at the time I was under a great deal of pressure, my stress levels must have been going through the roof.

'What!' I cried. 'They're perfectly safe General. You tell those trigger-happy bastards down there this isn't one of their Gung Ho movies, we're real people up here! …. It was rather odd for me to use bad language in such circumstances, especially to a man in an unarmed spacecraft who was about to sacrifice the lives of himself and his crew. But I couldn't help myself; it somehow seemed necessary.

'Get me the fucking President.' I ordered, and became so annoyed I leaped into the air determined to vent my anger on all things American hoping that by landing hard on their silly platform I would bend it.

'Jason;' Hypatia said disparagingly. 'Please control yourself.'

Her message unfortunately came a little late.

I know I'm rather inexperienced in the space travel business but let me at this point give you lesson number one from the Shaw astronaut-training programme. It goes something like this. If you're going to have a jump in space don't do it in the open and always wear protection, in this case, a safety belt.

When one does this on earth, gravity makes us fall back down again: I was about eight foot away from the platform and climbing, when I remembered lesson number two. In space there is no gravity. I must have been pretty annoyed because my jump seemed to have been quite powerful. When I looked down again the platform had shrunk considerably and was getting smaller by the second. I was in fact travelling away from it very rapidly indeed.

It was then, a strange thing happened, I don't know if it was the sight of the earth under me, or the majestic vastness of the universe, but I became very calm.

'Hypatia, I said sweetly 'Can you hear me?'

'Yes' she replied, 'please wait…. OK General the missile should have altered its trajectory.'

A few long seconds passed, and he said,

'That's an affirmative Ma-am, it's turning away.'

'Thank you General, I think if we wait for one minute more, you'll find it's heading directly for the Sun. I was unable to stop the second stage from firing as it is part of its automatic sequence.'

'That's a Roger,' he said. And started to read out data and projected coordinates. It seemed like an eternity, but was probably only seconds.

'Ok Jason over to you, did you want me?'

'Yes' I said, 'We have a slight problem,'

'What exactly is the nature of this problem?' she asked condescendingly,

'I've left the platform, and am floating about in space'

'That seems rather an odd thing to do, may one ask why?'

'I jumped off.'

'Why are you not screaming?'

'I don't know, maybe it's because this seems like a good place to die. The views are truly magnificent.'

'Hello Jason, this is the General. Am I to understand you're floating around out there?'

'Yes General, I replied slowly turning head over heels.'

'Can't you use the MMU and find your way back'

'I took it off.'

'Oh,' he said. 'Was that wise?' He clearly believed I had cracked.

'No General, probably not, but I had to take it off to get into the platform, I banged myself very hard on landing but don't think I damaged it.'

Feeling an uncontrollable urge to sing, I offered space a loud and no doubt tuneless rendition of the Don McLean classic.

'♫ Starry Starry Night ♫ '

'Yes I see,' he said quietly. 'We're on our way,'

'I'd be grateful if you could hurry… by my estimation I'm about three kilometres away from the platform, that's two miles to you I said rudely. And I need to go to the lavatory.' Giggling I asked, 'must you still blindfold me?'

'Maybe we will waive it this time' he replied. 'You seem a little light headed. Can you see the gauge to the left, in your HUD?'

'What the huds, a HUD?'

'Sorry Jason, I mean head up display, can you see it in your helmet?'

'Yep'

'And what does it say?'

'8% / 92%'

'You'll be fine, we will be with you soon, the readout below that one you've just given me, what does that say?'

'0 lbs'

'OK Jason roger that. Can you see some letters called SOP? This means Secondary Oxygen Pack'

'8 lbs / 100% Oxy'

'On your left arm you've a set of buttons. Can you see the one marked SOP?'

'Yep, sure can'

'Press it Jason…. Have you pressed it?'

'Yep'

'Please do something else for me, try to breathe slowly and evenly, can you do that?'

'I'll try,' I replied, my head clearing slightly but still very tired.

I don't know how long it was, but sometime later he asked me again.

'It says 2 lbs / 6% unev mix, and there's a noise, something's beeping; it's very loud.

'We'll be with you shortly Jason, don't talk; just breathe slowly and evenly'

I lost all track of time, but felt so happy and peaceful out there in space, alone.' We can see you now Jason, can you see us?'

'No but I can see the Sun, I think I'm going to crash into it.'

'It's OK I've put some big lights on, what does the gauge say now?'

'0·2 / 1·8% Hi/alarm, I'm getting very hot in here'

'We can see you now, my people are preparing to come out and bring you home.

'There's water in my helmet. I'm very tired.'

'Stay with me Jason…. Jason….' Hypatia's voice was also in my ear instructing me to breathe slowly

I woke up in the hold, my helmet was missing and my head hurt. On my face was an oxygen mask.

'Where's Hypatia?' I asked.

He couldn't hear me. I weakly took the mask off, 'Where's Hypatia?'

'Who's Hypatia?' The crewman said,

'My computer'

Oh…. It's still on the platform, it won't let anyone collect it but you,' I tried to get up, but fell down again.

'Take it easy sir.' he said, 'You'll be fine soon; you've been starved of oxygen. We're treating you now, just relax. We got to you just in time, you were very lucky. How many fingers am I holding?'

One hour fifty minutes later, with a massive headache and wearing an auxiliary oxygen pack, and after having no option other than to baptize the MAG, which I'm pleased to report did exactly what it said on the tin, I was back on the platform stowing the mat away.

Fifteen minutes later, I was standing on the top of the platform with the hatch closed and again admiring the heavens around me; even my headache had improved. Everywhere I looked, the stars were spread out before me like billions of gemstones. Not all white, some were silver, some yellow, and others had a blue or red tint. Certain clusters were actually swirling in clouds of different coloured gas.

Below the whole of Asia was laid out, as was Alaska. The west coast of America just coming into view. It was still dark, but the sunlight was creeping slowly across from the East. The flying saucer hovered just above me as I collected the IPEC and using the MMU accompanied by both wingmen flew directly to the saucer. The air lock was closed and we set off.

I waited for them to get my suit off and asked the nice young lady if she intended to powder and cream my bottom, which for some obscure reason she refused to do, and gave me one of their overalls to put on.

The General came back after a while, saluted and gave me a hug. At that everyone shook my hand, pumping it up and down until I had to plead with them to stop. The General was absolutely fascinated with the IPEC who hating to be left out had popped up. I swear she practically swooned as he charmed her with his wonderful accent and old world manners. She was clearly melted by this attention and flirted with him outrageously.

'Are we going home sir?' someone asked.

'We are son,' he answered. 'At full speed, it'll be light soon.'

'What happened to me out there, General?' I asked, 'Everything went blank '

'You punctured the oxygen pack, the hole was at the bottom, and quite large. They're self-sealing but you made a real mess of this one and it didn't seal correctly. You also damaged the liquid cooling system and the re-breather; the bottom is its weakest point. You must have hit something very hard, because these things are supposed to be almost indestructible. It will certainly cause a major re-think about the design of the suit. Still, it's reasonably new, and testing it in space is the best way forward. It takes three years of intensive schooling to train an astronaut, you did it in three hours, and even with your unscheduled space-walk you did real well out there. We're all mighty proud of you.'

'I did hit something hard. I landed on the support for the hatch. That must have been when it happened. When do we land? I'm so tired General'

'You can use my quarters if you wish,' he told me kindly. The next I knew was when someone woke me with the news that we had landed. I was quickly examined by a doctor and warned again about the dire consequences of discussing anything I had seen.

Then with no further ceremony they made it clear my work was done and wanted me out of there. They quickly loaded us in the Lear, destination London. I slept the whole way.

The time machine set the date, and with the help of its small assistant transported through time to meet the group. The IPEC spoke uninterrupted for 30 minutes explaining what had happened on earth and space. When completed the question and answer session lasted a further 45 minutes. At the end of this the Khepera summed up.

'Our man acquitted himself well, the rogue computer was destroyed and the platform saved. Is it not the case however that it was at times quite perilous, and you could easily have lost him, and incidentally yourself.'

'The subject could be lost at any time, driving a car is hazardous, as is flying, we have to be prepared for every situation, the changing of the future is after all what we are about, and I am programmed to save human life'

'I agree.' the Khepera replied. 'When you entered his life,' the future began to change, as the devices will change the lives of millions, and the later versions even more. The platform would not have malfunctioned in the old timeline because it would not have had a Maxwell computer on board. The only thing we can be sure of is this! The alien visitors will arrive in 2129. That fact will not alter. It cannot, because they're unaffected by our actions.

Nevertheless Mr Shaw clearly did well. As he did during the visit to the Egyptian pyramids. He has seen our species and knows we exist, the first hurdle has been cleared.'

'Surely we must now consider the visit to Atlantis,' the IPEC said. 'Will you allow me access to your computers?'

'We anticipated your request and agree. The IPEC is to be given access to our records of that time, including the data concerning the ship's computer.' He looked at the other three aliens who made up the executive team for their support

'The time difference on Atlantis will almost certainly cause problems, but I'm informed it should be possible for you to gain access: I should like particularly to congratulate every member of the research team who found a way to achieve this: Hypatia. You may relay whatever you learn to your charge, the information will in any case be 11500 years old.

We could simply give you the information as we know it, but have decided it will be more authentic this way.

We have another motive; a substantial amount of data was lost to us with the destruction of Atlantis. You'll be given certain questions concerning this period; any answers you're able to glean would be deeply appreciated.

Do you have any questions for us?'

'Yes, as a matter of fact I do'…thousands, she thought. 'Let us start with the pyramids? Which were the first to be built?'

He looked around the room.

'The first of the larger pyramids was constructed on Atlantis, however its position was determined from the location of the Giza base, which had already been sited. These two plus the Teotihuacan pyramid were built principally for regeneration purposes and emergency beacons. The other six were built later. Suffice it to say, the situation was critical at that time because our people were slowly dying.'

'Just one more question before we leave the subject,' asked the IPEC. 'Was the *orientation of them aligned with the stars in Orion's belt?'*

'In a strange way they were. The Khepera replied. 'The layout of the pyramids depicts our symbol for distress. But that sign originated from the same three stars.'

'Thank you,' answered the IPEC. Your answers have helped me understand some of the questions.

'Do you have further questions?'

'May I ask about India. I know that they had great cities, for example "Dwarka" around 11000 BC. About the same time as the pyramids were built. Did you have any dealings with them too?

'No.' he answered. 'At least not directly, but the tsunami resulting from the destruction of Atlantis destroyed that and other coastal cities. I understand from the records that a decision was taken by the leaders of our planet to let that part of the world develop at its own pace.'

'If I may Amon,' one of the executive team asked. 'How are the sales of the computer progressing Hypatia?'

'Very good,' --- the IPEC looked back at the Khepera 'Business generally is proceeding as planned, but we need more flexibility. I believe the timing is correct for IPEC Investments to increase its holdings. If you agree I also propose to use the additional funds to start a company named IPEC Travel, the intention of expanding the company as the opportunities present themselves. Travel is becoming increasingly difficult for the reasons you are aware of. I therefore propose the new company should purchase a private jet to ease the problem.'

'I agree. The access codes for our Swiss accounts will be given to you following this meeting But please note, we must discuss any future acquisitions in the same way.'

He looked around the room... 'Very well if there's nothing else, I declare these proceedings closed.'

Following the meeting the Khepera had the IPEC taken to his private office, where on route it saw two human's going about their business. Sitting alone with the Khepera the IPEC decided to mention this fact and why couldn't one of them have been used as the human traveller?

'We required a normal human capable of independent thought, but one who could be manipulated when required. You have already reported he is performing above expectations.

The people you saw were simply holographic images used for various simple tasks from gardening to cleaning and as the human face for visitors whenever one is needed.'

'I don't understand,' the IPEC replied, clearly astonished. 'Holograms?'

He looked at her and smiled.

'We have a large holographic generator in the basement, where the swimming pool used to be. Its influence only reaches to the boundary of the estate and the holographs are programmed for specific tasks within that area for example gardening and cleaning. They are also used to meet any occasional visitors etc.'

The IPEC was understandably fascinated. 'But they look so authentic.'

'They really are only capable of performing simple tasks,' The Khepera answered

supportively. You on the other hand are so advanced. Even we stand in awe of you.'

The machine knew she was being flattered and carried on.

'I have another question, why do your people sometimes refer to you as Amon? Is it your name?'

'No, he responded unusually sharply. 'In our culture my name is never used; Amon is simply another word for leader. Thousands of years ago it meant more, in fact some of the early leaders allowed themselves to be worshiped as Gods. Needless to say all such nonsense stopped after the Atlantis disaster.'

'Thank you, such information may prove useful in the coming months.'

'That's the reason I've had you brought in here,' he told her 'To explain exactly how the US Air Force acquired the saucer... After the first Atomic bomb had been exploded, contact was made with the American military. The hope being that the US government could be persuaded not to use the bomb in anger.

This 'initial' contact, we found out later, was kept from the President and Congress, and had a direct bearing on the bombs being dropped on Japan.

'Our President was already on his way. The world war was seriously disturbing us. He was determined to demonstrate just how serious our species viewed the development of nuclear weapons; the meeting was intended to illustrate how gravely these actions were perceived on other worlds.

We had already made news of his visit known to General White, the Grandfather of the present General White. In return for their co-operation we planned to share with them the secret of anti-gravity propulsion and a basic form or plasma drive. We now believe that for some reason the admission that we possessed such an advanced forms of technology alarmed them and may have led them to believe we intended to take over the Earth.

Both Presidents were scheduled to meet at the White Sands Base, near Roswell, New Mexico. But whilst travelling there the craft was supposedly destroyed. We were informed that one of the two planes assigned to escort him had developed a problem, and had 'accidentally' flown into the saucer, resulting in a mid-air explosion which killed the pilot and destroyed the plane. The report said the crew of our saucer were killed outright. We found out afterwards that some were only injured, including our President, and taken to the base hospital. We were also told the wreckage had been destroyed to preserve the secret of our existence.

The Americans claimed it was a tragic accident, but we later discovered President Truman had no knowledge of the proposed meeting, or even of our existence. Upon receiving this news our government concluded the people responsible were barbarians, and clearly not yet ready for the hand of friendship, especially when one considers they knew very little about us, or our capabilities.

'That then, was how the Americans acquired the saucer. We have since discovered that over the next four years most of the people who knew about the incident either died or were silenced in other ways, until only a select group of senior officers remained.

It was my predecessor who carried out the initial negotiations with the Air Force explaining we had no evil intent. But knowing the human appetite for invention, she suspected they might try to steal our secrets, even the ship, which as you would no doubt expect, is totally obsolete. Of course she never considered they would deliberately murder our President and his party.'

'Why didn't you retaliate?' The IPEC asked.

'We have no concept of revenge; our species are explorers. Retaliation and war are completely alien to our beliefs. I was elected temporary leader following her death and given special dispensation to stay the full term when my promotion was made permanent.

The individuals responsible for this atrocity are all dead, but General White's Grandfather was definitely their leader, he was a racist, and white supremacist who no doubt considered us inferior. The fact that our leader on this planet was female may also have played some small part in his decision. We later learnt that upon his death his son was inducted into the group and made aware of our existence, as were the designated successors of the others including of course, the present General White. These eight now form the basis of a select, highly secret group, who call themselves the 'anastomosis.'

Under the direction of the first General White they secretly formed a team of aircraft engineers to study the craft in detail, setting up companies to exploit what to them was extraordinarily advanced technology, especially the computers, drive systems, fuel and other highly developed compounds. Over the years their influence has increased tremendously, today they wield great power.

With the possible exception of President Eisenhower, we believe none of the US Presidents, or indeed any of the other world leaders, have ever been officially told of our existence. You should also be aware that only very few of our own species know of the heinous crime committed against their President, believing it to have been an unfortunate accident.'

He described to the IPEC the gruesome details of the Presidents death, including the fact that he was in contact with them telepathically during their medical experiments.

'The reason I am relating to you the true facts is because they may be useful ammunition to use against General White. It may at least ensure Mr Shaw doesn't share a similar fate.'

'Did you never try to re-establish contact,' the IPEC asked.

'No: Before he died our President specifically forbade us to interfere further. He was a great leader and decreed no further contact would be made until the human species have achieved light speed, at that time we shall appear to the world openly. He probably thought the humans would have mellowed somewhat by then.

However your discovery of the Earths destruction means events have overtaken us. But I dare not risk being perceived as acting overtly. A human must do it: I am however still taking a huge personal chance by using your Mr Shaw. So much depends on you both. With that in mind and because of the unexpected trip to space I suggest that you let him rest before introducing him to Atlantis.'

'As you wish,' said the IPEC 'But I believe it's important we visit the Americans saucer quite soon, he should be aware of its propulsion systems before he sees the interstellar craft.'

'I agree,' said the Khepera, 'please arrange it.' and added wistfully. 'You have already visited Atlantis of course. It has so much history for our species, maybe one day *we can go together? Its destruction led us to abandon this planet for over five thousand of their years, returning only occasionally to observe human progress.'*

The IPEC asked when they returned on a more permanent basis

'We returned for longer periods during the early Egyptian and Indian developments and later to help the South American civilizations progress. But around four hundred years ago the Europeans began to display a tremendous genius for invention and ever more sophisticated machines began to appear. We were happy with these development but not the advances in weaponry. The humans have always shown the urge to kill, but their levels of proficiency became extremely worrying. We requested our leadership to allow some intercession but they refused; In the twentieth century it became really serious, in less than one hundred and twenty earth years the humans have developed weapons so powerful they are able to destroy this planet, and if allowed to continue unchecked, will shortly be in a position to threaten the very existence of everyone in this solar system.

In the normal course of events we would have begun altering their genetic makeup thousands of years ago. But because of the Atlantis disaster we were forbidden to interfere. Now we have no alternative. We must do it quickly … maybe too quickly. Playing with the human mind has caused problems in the past. Manipulation of their individual and unique thought processes can easily backfire.' He stood up, 'I will do whatever is necessary to help you Hypatia but we are forbidden to become openly involved. It's a great responsibility I know; But we are all in your hands.'

CHAPTER TWENTY

The next few days were spent quietly in the house. On the third day Sir David Hommersby paid me a private visit, with him was an RAF doctor. The lid had been firmly put over the whole escapade. The Americans didn't want it known that their missiles had nearly annihilated the world. The Brits, that their malfunctioning computer would have launched them. The Russians kept it quiet, because it would be more use later as a bargaining chip. The French agreed for reasons known only to them. And the Germans just wanted to get on with making more money.

The doctor prescribed more bed rest, gave me some pills and left. I told the Secretary of State about the damaged space suit and the oxygen starvation, but as little as possible about everything else. I also asked him how many people knew about the shrouding device.

'Very few,' he replied, explaining that it was just too sensitive, and had been classified as Ultra Secret. Which meant it was CVO (communication verbal only) he had told only the Prime Minister, who in turn had told the Home and Foreign Secretaries. He believed, they, along with the Air Marshall and the other service chiefs would ensure it was kept a closely guarded secret.

He couldn't speak about the Americans, he said, but expected they would take a similar approach. Nevertheless he warned me to be on my guard. They would be desperate to discover the secret of the shroud and would want to control its use. He suggested I accept close protection and share the secret only with the British Government. I refused, knowing it would hamper my travelling.

I did however take his advice seriously and asked the IPEC to monitor all the major players especially Andrew Blythe and General White and spent the next two days in bed as instructed, becoming utterly bored with the inactivity, which in turn led to a great idea.

'What do you know about Jack the Ripper?' I asked the IPEC

'Probably less than you,' she replied indifferently. But I noticed a flicker of interest on her face.

'I doubt that. Let's do some research and see what we can discover? If we can find the dates of the murders and their locations, I might have a look to see who he was. I think it was an American doctor called Tumbelty who died in St Louis of old age. Who do you think?'

'I'm a computer, I do not speculate on such matters.'

'You could have fooled me,' I told her. 'You do it all the time.'

'It is incumbent upon me to remind you that you're not the bravest of people when it comes to blood and gore.' 'And it is incumbent upon me to remind you not to change the subject.' I retorted, 'You speculate all the time.'

'Very well; If you insist? I think it may have been a man called Aaron Kosminski.'

'OK, let's start the research. Afterwards we will pay him a visit. The excitement of the chase interests me.'

Having the IPEC had allowed me to visit the past regularly, and during these visits I had been totally reliant on her. But as I became more experienced it was clear this approach was not enough, more was required than just facts. This time; indeed from now on, I intended to do my own research and get a feel of the history of the period. The fact that the bomb on the missile platform had worked so well was solely down to the American Special Forces instructor. He had made me practice over and over again until it was possible for me to find the exact spot in all conditions, even with my eyes closed. I had to be able to guarantee the correct result, no matter how high the stress levels being experienced.

With this in mind, I searched through the piles of books ordered from Amazon and read numerous articles on the Internet, especially Wikipedia and Casebook, Jack the Ripper.

The aficionados are referred to as "Ripperologists," and know everything about him (except who he was.) A whole industry exists to solve the mystery with new suspects being regularly discovered, from Freemasons to Royal Princes and their doctors. Of course we also have the more likely criminal element too, for example lawyers and other similar villains. Nobody has yet attributed it to an estate agent unfortunately, or more likely, a politician. It's probably only a matter of time. Would they thank me I wondered, for spoiling their fun.

By putting together what I already knew and adding some of what is publicly available, I've condensed it to the following:

No one can say categorically just how many women Jack the Ripper actually murdered. But there's a general acceptance it was five. These are:

Friday, August 31, 1888; Mary Ann (Polly) Nichols: Saturday, September 8, 1888; Annie Chapman: Sunday, September 30, 1888; Elizabeth Stride: the same day, Sunday, September 30, 1888; Catherine Eddowes: And finally 5 weeks later on Friday, November 9, 1888; Mary Jane Kelly.

The first thing I noticed was every murder happened between Friday and Sunday night? From this one might assume he had a job during the week or commuted from outside London. Another was that there is no conclusive evidence that any of the women actually knew each other, (although one section of the Royal killer theorists depend greatly on the fact that they did.) All differed in age, size and looks. The general consensus is that most of them, if not all, were drunk when killed. And because of the mud and filth in the streets it's improbable that the ladies or their client would have lain on the ground. I was soon to be in the unique position to confirm that it did seem to rain an awful lot during that fateful period.

Every autopsy showed some form of strangulation, the theory being that the Ripper came on them from behind when they were bent forward with her skirts raised in preparation for sex from the rear. Whether anal, or vaginal, is obviously unknown as no evidence of penetrative sex was ever found, or that he masturbated over the bodies. He did however often take a piece of, or occasionally a complete organ as a 'trophy.'

According to the autopsy reports the Ripper cut the throats of his victims only after they were dead. We know that, because the blood stayed around the neck and head of the victim rather than spurting down their front. Killing them this way also prevented him getting unduly blood stained.

He would then hideously mutilate the bodies. The opinion of most of the surgeons who examined the bodies except possibly for Mary Jane Kelly was that the Ripper must have had some kind of anatomical knowledge because certain of the things he did to them at speed, occasionally in total darkness were expertly done. In one case he removed a kidney from the front without damaging any of the surrounding organs. In another he removed the sexual organs with one round sweep of the knife.

The Chief Constable. Sir Melville Macnaughten, produced a confidential report in 1894, which named three suspects. One of these was M.J. Druitt a barrister (who Mcnaughten claimed mistakenly was a doctor) turned teacher. Druitt committed suicide in December 1888 by throwing himself into the Thames.

Macnaughten wrote in the report "From private information I have received, I have little doubt that his own family believed him to have been the murderer, I have always held strong opinions regarding him, and the more I think the matter over, the stronger do these opinions become. The truth, however, will never be known."

The second suspect was Aaron Kosminski, a Polish Jew, who was put away in an insane asylum after the crimes, and died soon afterwards. He was a resident of Whitechapel, and apparently hated women with a vengeance, especially prostitutes.

The third was Michael Ostrog, but subsequent investigations have shown he was nothing more than an attention seeker. Another name, and my particular favourite, is that of Dr. Francis Tumblety, an American quack doctor, a raging homosexual (I use the word 'Raging' advisedly) with a pathological hatred of women. Tumblety, a legitimate suspect, fled to America soon after the last murder; followed closely by Scotland Yard detectives. However it seems that following their investigations, they decided he was not their man. But I'm not convinced.

In the 1950's a well-known television presenter at the time, named

Daniel Farson, hosted a television show about Jack the Ripper, in which it was suggested that the grandson of Queen Victoria, Prince Albert Victor, Duke of Clarence and Avondale was the Ripper.

This caught the public imagination, and spawned numerous books and is still the most popular theory with the uninformed. He does seem to have willingly partaken in some rather bizarre sexual rituals. But then again, when it comes to certain other wider members of our Royal family, some of which I have witnessed, nothing would surprise me.

Polly Nichols body was discovered at about 3:40 am on the morning of Friday August 31, 1888, on the ground in Buck's Row (since renamed Durward Street) a back street in Whitechapel three hundred yards from The London Hospital. Her throat had been deeply slashed, her abdomen cut open, and her intestines exposed; she also had two other stab wounds in the groin area. The street was narrow and so dimly lit that the two men on their way to work who found her said they were unable to identify it as a body until they crossed the street and stood over it.

Residents in houses alongside had neither heard or seen anything, nor had police officers patrolling the area. Probably killed about 03:30 am, her death certificate states she was 42.

Polly was living in a Whitechapel lodging house when she died and according to witnesses, needing a few pennies for a bed that night and allegedly pretty drunk, went out implying she would have no problem earning the money on the streets.

Looking for Duward Street we drove around for a while asking directions. Eventually coming to the massive frontage of the old London Infirmary, which was closed down. The new Royal London Hospital surrounds the area now. I was promptly told to move on by one of the security guards.

'I've come to visit my brother.' I said, 'Where can I park?'

'We don't have a public car park mate,' he replied tiredly in a northern accent. 'But you might find a place down a side street. Take the first street on the left, then the fifth left down. Varden Street, there's a few places down there where you might get that monstrosity parked.'

We eventually found some spare ground and parked up. Hypatia then accessed the council's files and confirmed this was also open ground in 1888. Deciding it might first be prudent to have a look round in the present I set off for Duward Street. It has changed a lot since 1888 and as I was imagining what the Bucks Row of 1880's would be like, when a group of Japanese tourists accompanied by a tour guide came around the corner.

I stood to one side fascinated by his spiel. Tour guides are very useful people when one travels in time. This particular one though seemed to take great pleasure in explaining all the gory details; vividly describing everything the poor woman had suffered. People are so strange, I thought. Until realising I was doing exactly the same thing and even planning to watch him do it later. They set off for the location of the next murder and I returned to the motor home.

Putting on an anorak and warm boots I chose to use the buggy for the IPEC, rather than the table. So lifting the floor I spread the mat on the ground and placed the IPEC inside the bubble, where it would be safe and dry. With the brakes on and the vehicle in gear the buggy could stand all kinds of weather. It also meant we had transport available if required. I dropped down beside it and standing on the mat said 'Ok Hypatia, set the time and date for Friday, August 31st, 1888 at 03-00 am.'

--- Activate---

The night was indeed quite chilly, maybe because of a heavy fog, which smelt of burnt charcoal. The remnants of which were still swirling like a scene from an early Hammer Film. I left the IPEC on the seat inside the bubble and set off for Bucks Row.

Passing the rear entrance of the hospital I saw that despite the numerous extensions and new wings it was still recognisable. So instead of walking round decided to use the rear entrance and cut through to the austere reception area near the front entrance. The nurse's wore high caps and very straight-laced floor length skirts. About twenty people were seated with no sign of the weekend mayhem one sees now. But from the reaction of the staff when the sister walked passed I suspected that one look from her would easily quell even the most rowdy visitor.

Continuing out onto the nearly deserted Whitechapel road I found myself in almost total darkness, the occasional gaslights next to useless. When my eyes adjusted I saw it was also recognisable to what I'd seen earlier in the day. Even to the Whitechapel underground Station across the road. This surprised me and I asked,

'When was the London Underground opened Hypatia?'

'1863' she answered smugly. 'It was the first in the world.' I don't know why that made me proud. But it did.

Crossing the empty road, and making my way behind the station to Bucks Row, I walked directly to the place where this afternoon the tour guide told us proudly "This is where she was killed." and put on the glasses before leaning against a wall using the MIPEC's night vision lens to look around. Across from me was the run down warehouse frontage of "Essex Wharf" and another building named "Schneiders Caps." I can say without any fear of contradiction. In 1888 Bucks Row was a dirty little street.

About ten minutes later, a couple entered from the north, she was staggering as though very drunk, and when they got to the spot she said,

'OK ducks this'll do. How do ya want ta do it, it'll be a thripence fer a hand job, and a bob for anythin else ya want…. Money first luvvy.'

He gave her, what I supposed was a shilling and waited for her to make the first move. She was swaying badly; he didn't speak. He wore a long dark coat, I couldn't see what he had on underneath, but he looked reasonably well dressed. When she didn't move, he said, 'tern roun and ben over,' did I hear an accent there? She lifted her dress and petticoats, dropped her bloomers, bent over and said

'Cummon then ducks, I aint got all night.'

He put one hand between her legs and roughly fingered her, at the same time putting his other arm round her neck, he seemed to be sexually aroused by this, and brought his other hand round her face pulling back sharply and twisting. I heard her neck crack!

He was of average size, maybe a little taller 5ft - 8' or 5ft - 9' and looked quite strong. He lowered her gently to the ground, her head to the left, toward the fence, and I swear took his money back.

From under his cloak he produced a bundle, which when unwrapped contained various cutting implements each in its own individual pocket. From this he took a knife, and without any preamble, cut her throat. He did this by stabbing it in hard and working the knife downwards.

Then, with a definite accent, he raised his head to the sky, and said.

'My dear lard, sank you for allowing me to do your vark. I give you anozer pox vidden vore, by your divine vill zis creature will be cleansed.'

I kept the MIPEC pointing at him and moved closer. It was a long deep cut and the blood was running to the left away from him. He lifted her skirt up further slitting it open, the knife was about 9 inches long. He again looked to the heavens and stabbed it deep in her stomach cutting downwards three or four times and sideways two or three times.

Through the spectacles I watched as he stabbed her in the groin a couple more times, and pulled out her stomach, expertly cutting away and laying it over her left shoulder. There was nothing I'd describe about the attack as overly frenzied. In fact it struck me that the man had done this before! He looked to be aged about 35 to 45 well-built and fit, with a normal complexion though slightly pock marked. He had a dark beard and moustache. People aged quicker then, so he could easily have been younger. And even with the MIPEC I didn't get a really clear look at him, he had his back to me most of the time, plus I was trying not to be sick. My intention was to follow him.

Unfortunately at this point my stomach had had enough, and I vomited my lunch over the 1888 street. The urge to laugh hysterically, even in the middle of this carnage was overpowering. The thought of somebody looking at it in 1957 during the next time shift, and saying to a passer-by

'It wasn't me, it's not mine I don't know where it came from,' tickled me.

When I looked round, he'd gone. I was about to set off in pursuit, when the voice said.

'The MIPEC, you've dropped it, you must find it Jason, NOW!'

It was the nearest I've known her to panic, but the urgency in her voice was unmistakable. I dropped to my hands and knees, and felt around for it, trying to avoid the vomit, the voice, normal now, said sharply,

'Have you not found it yet? Pull yourself together! The MIPEC will emit an intermittent bleep to assist you. This will become constant as you get nearer.'

By following this noise, I retrieved it from under the fence where it had rolled. Needless to say the Ripper was well away by now; the body though was not. Deciding the best course of action would be to get away before the rest of my stomach contents showed themselves to the past I returned to the motor home and after cleaning myself up, set off for the house. We didn't talk much during the drive home.

The next victim was Mrs Annie Chapman; she lived in Dorset Street an infamous road in Spitalfields running East/West between Commercial Street and Chrispin Street. About one third of the way down is a narrow brick archway, the entrance to Miller's Court. She wasn't a hard woman, only turning to prostitution when hunger and poverty forced her to it following the death of her husband.

On Saturday, September 8th at 5:30 am 1888: She was seen talking to a man in Hanbury Street. The man was described as foreign looking with a dark complexion wearing a brown deerstalker hat and a dark overcoat aged over forty and a little taller than Annie.

At the inquest Dr. George Bagster-Phillips the police surgeon, described what he saw at 6:30am, in the back yard of 29 Hanbury Street.

'The left arm was laid across the left breast, the legs drawn up, with the feet resting on the ground, and the knees turned outwards. The face had been beaten and turned on the right side, the tongue terribly swollen, but the teeth perfect, (it's worth noting that in 1888, amongst the working classes, this was in itself quite unusual.) The body was terribly mutilated, and the stiffness of the limbs not yet set. The throat was deeply severed, the incisions through the skin quite jagged, and continuing almost completely around the neck. Her blood could be seen on the wooden fence about 12 inches from the ground, immediately above where the blood from the neck lay. In his opinion, the instrument used to open the throat and abdomen was the same. He thought it must have been a very sharp knife with a thin narrow blade, probably 6 to 8 inches in length, maybe longer. A bayonet could not have inflicted the injuries; neither could a sword. They could however, have been inflicted by the type of instrument used by a medical man for post-mortem purposes, or by a slaughterman. In his opinion there were definite indications of anatomical knowledge.

He concluded that the deceased had been dead for at least two hours, possibly longer. However it was right to mention it was a fairly cool morning, and the body would be more apt to cool rapidly from its having lost a great quantity of blood.

There was no evidence of a struggle but he was positive the deceased entered the yard alive. He also discovered an abrasion over the ring finger, with distinct markings of a ring or rings, indicating they had been ripped off. (This is very important, as rings very similar to these, were found in St Louis, in the room of Dr Tumberty after his death).

There were various other mutilations to the body, but he was of the opinion they probably occurred subsequent to the death of the woman. The abdomen had been entirely laid open. The intestines severed from their mesenteric attachments lifted out of the body, and placed on her left shoulder; whilst from the pelvis, the uterus and its appendages, including the vagina, the posterior and two thirds of the bladder had been removed entirely. No trace of these parts could be found, and the incisions were cleanly cut, avoiding the rectum, and dividing the vagina low enough to avoid injury to the cervix uteri. Obviously, he reflected, this was the work of someone with anatomical knowledge. The instrument would have been at least 5 or 6 inches in length, possibly more. He thought he himself could not have carried out such a procedure as he had described, in under a quarter of an hour. If he had done it in a deliberate way, such as would fall to the duties of a surgeon. It probably would have taken him the best part of an hour.

When I had finished reading the inquest report aloud, she said.

'You have been busy haven't you? I'm suitably impressed.'

'There's a reason for that.' I replied, 'This time I'm not going to get so close, in fact I'm going to get as far away as possible. The object of the exercise is to identify the killer, not to take part in his crime. If my stomach couldn't take it the last time, in near darkness, according to what you've just heard described; this time it's going to be even worse.'

'Probably the best plan' she sarcastically replied.

'I don't really believe a doctor would do this,' I continued, pretending not to hear her, 'But a slaughterman who kills hundreds of animals a week could, especially in the much more violent times of the 1880's…. And if he had been stopped in the street, it would have been possible for him to explain away his bundle of tools, or even blood on his clothes as part of his profession he would probably do private jobs so it would also provide a reason for him carrying them. People in that line of work become very hard. I'm not saying they're all capable of killing a human, but we're only talking about one man here, a madman. An experienced slaughterman could do some of these things described, with his eyes closed.'

We parked at the same place as the last time. I knew the morning would be quite cool and just starting to get light with absolutely no wind, so rather than setting up the buggy and knowing the area now, we decided the table would suffice.

'Set the date at 8th September 1888. 05-00 am.'

---Activate---

From the hospital, I walked along The Whitechapel Road and turned right into Commercial Street and Spitalfields Market, on the right was Hanbury Street.

The murder had happened around the back, and sure enough, just a few yards further on was a passage leading to the rear ten-foot. It was pretty quiet, but one could hear people moving about, if he was to do it at this time, he couldn't have cared too much about his own safety.

It had been 26 minutes since I left the car park. That would make it 05-26, The report said they were leaning on the fence at 05-30. 'So where were they?'

In the distance something moved.

'Here they come,' I told her.

He had his arm around her shoulder and appeared to be bargaining.

'It's the same man. About five foot seven with a square face a moustache and wearing a deerstalker hat. Where's his beard?' I mused, 'maybe it was false? They've stopped at No. 29.'

'Let uz go behind this vall?' he said. There was the accent again, this time much stronger. A woman walked past, looked at them and turns away as if disgusted. When she's out of earshot Annie furtively looks both ways and says,

'It'll be a shilling for a short time luv.' He nods.

'Ok then, but only if you're quick, we can go in here.'

He opens the gate for her and they enter the yard. I have no intention of following them but can't help it. He's behind her and immediately snaps her neck and takes the bundle from inside his coat.

'He's cutting her throat. OH NO. I'm going out. This is awful, what am I doing. He's SICK. SICK.'

Her soothing voice in my ear helped 'Calm down Jason, take some deep breaths, you can't do anything.'

'OK, OK…. I'm OK now.' I said watching him. 'The dirty bastard, may he rot in hell.' He spoke again, quietly and with much less of an accent, but I still couldn't place it.

'Try to get closer,' she said, seemingly unconcerned about me.

'Holy Father, thank you for again showing me the way, and allowing me to do your bidding; This Harlot will not entice innocent men again, I will purify her.'

The accent was middle class English. At this I left, and waited outside the gate.

A few minutes he came out.

'He's not bloody Hypatia; the coat, the damn coat, so simple, the bloody things reversible. It's a different colour now and he's not wearing a hat, the moustache has gone too. He looks younger; I'm going to follow him.... He's heading to the market, walking fast but not running. He's turning right from Spital Square into Bishops Gate I think he's heading for Liverpool Street Station. I'm going to follow him.

He's stopped at platform three. I'm going to follow him to wherever he's going. The train is a slow one according to the board. Would you believe it? The bloody thing stops at every station between here and Cambridge.'

'Jason!' the voice said. 'Can you hear me?'

'Yes, of course I can hear you.' I replied irritably.

'You must not get on that train. I'll lose contact with you after you've gone only a short distance, we only have a limited coverage in this timeline; you know that!'

'Well I have the MIPEC, and you're quite safe!'

'I'm sitting exposed on a flimsy table, with a 72.6% chance of heavy rain and strong winds. Leave him Jason; we will have other opportunities.'

'This man has nine lives; it's incredible, it really is.' I said, and swore to get him somehow.

'His accent sounded Eastern European the last time, but today it was different. Did you record his voice?'

'Yes,' she replied, 'it was definitely unlike the last time. He might be an actor, or a schizophrenic.'

'Maybe even both' I added, 'sounds like a politician. Anyway I intend to give this a rest for a while. I have after all just witnessed two of the most gruesome murders in history. We can return to the chase another time. But mark my words, find him we will! '

CHAPTER TWENTY ONE

'**W**hy don't we get you that jet you keep promising yourself?' The IPEC asked, sometime later. Obviously she was having a laugh.

'Shall we buy or lease?' I quipped.

'Both' she responded. 'I will register a company to buy the plane. You may then lease it from yourself for your personal use through Maxwell Computers; IPEC Travel will employ the crew of course and use it for private charter when not required by you. That means we can claim for the overheads and fuel. I fancy a Boeing 777.'

I knew a little about executive jets now because of Stephens.

'A Gulfstream G550 will be fine.'

'Cheapskate,' she joked, a broad smile on her face.

'If we are to lease the plane to Maxwell Computers the board will have to agree. I can't see Stephen being very keen on me having a plane for my own personal use, especially a G550. It's better than his and as you know he's a terrible snob.'

'Steven Maxwell, currently owns 30% of the stock. Through proxies you own 46%. And I suspect Dr Holt and certain others will support you. Our Mr Maxwell has alienated an awful lot of people lately.' Clearly she was serious and I began to think maybe it was possible.

However it was not as simple as she thought. The waiting time for a new plane was at least two years…. We of course got one much quicker.

The IPEC interrogated the Gulfstream office mainframe for people at the front of the queue and then investigated each of their accounts. I suspect more thoroughly than the taxman ever would.

A Belgian travel company had ordered one, but now couldn't pay and were going to lose their extremely large deposit.

So we, and by that I mean our company's finance director Ms Bond - Jayne Bond. (I know) successfully made a hostile takeover for the whole company, amalgamating it with IPEC Travel a subsidiary of IPEC Investments. We sent a crew over to Savannah Georgia, to take possession of our new plane.

'What are we going to do with a medium sized travel company? Which lately does nothing, except lose money?'

'I don't have a lot to do. I will sell off the loss making package holiday division and run the company myself.'

Two weeks later I flew to Belgium for some board meetings. The board and senior management, who obviously only knew the face of Ms Bond were dying to meet her.

'What a wonderful woman' they said 'Her knowledge of our language is superb. She speaks Flemish like a native, when will she be coming over?'

'She's very busy.' I told them, 'Maybe next month.'

She fired the whole board soon afterward, and of course it was me they blamed not the wonderful Ms Bond…. There's no justice!

Things ticked along quietly for a while, except for the news that Peter Allen had been forced out by Maxwell. As far as I was concerned this was done simply to cover his own mistakes. I called Peter who told me he was relieved to be away and had already been offered a research position at Cambridge.

Sometime later whilst driving home, the voice said.

'On your way home, would you please go via the post office in Slough. You've a post office box there, in the name of Mr Colin Ward. I had the key posted to the house, and telephoned Mr Ward, informing him there had been a mistake and asked him to put it in the glove box, please confirm it's there.'

'Hypatia, what have you done now?'

'Pick up your parcels and see.'

Returning to the car with a bundle of packages I found two of them contained US passports, the next two, driving licences, and the last, two social security cards, all had my photograph blazoned on them. One set was for a James Stewart, and the other in the name of John Silver.

'Where the hell do you come from with names like these, I whinged? Jimmy Stewart and Long John Silver. It's ridiculous'

'Good, am I not?'

'Not,' I said ruefully. No matter how good computers are, they invariably do something infantile. People are often the same, the cleverer they are, the dafter the things they do.

'I thought you would want to keep your initials.' she retorted, obviously pleased with herself.

'How could you possibly think I'd fly to anywhere, with a director called Jayne Bond and a name like John Silver? You couldn't make it up'

'You worry too much.' The voice of Robert Newton thundered in my ear. 'Ah Jim lad don't forget to feed the parrot. Pieces of Eight the parrot screamed.'

I couldn't help laughing, which lightened the atmosphere somewhat

'You really are quite crazy sometimes, but you do realise that travelling to the US with a false passport is a serious offence,'

'How dare you?' she cried indignantly. 'There's nothing false about these

'How did you do it?' I enquired,

'Easily' she replied smugly. 'I slid into their computer systems and built you a complete life history. I also accessed the school, university and company records. The passports are completely genuine. Posted electronically by their own computers to this box number.'

'Also. Since we first discussed it, I have been monitoring Mr Andrew Blythe and General White, as per your suggestion.

'General White has nothing against you personally but considers you a potential danger to US Security. His point being that someone could kidnap you and force you to give them the secret of the invisibility cloak and the spacecraft. He has requested the Sec/Def on eight separate occasions to invite you over to the States and find a way to neutralise you.

'To his credit Andrew Blythe has constantly refused, probably worried about the so-called special relationship with the British Government. There nothing we can do about the invisibility story but there is about the craft. I'm convinced we should go over there and investigate.'

'It would expose us to considerable danger.' I said unconvinced. 'It needs more thought'

'Understood, she agreed. 'But if we do choose to pay them a visit, we now have the plane, owned by a travel company specialising in executive travel, and a choice of genuine passports. We can fly directly to Las Vegas, do the job, and be gone in a couple of days.'

The makeover of the house planned and executed by my surprisingly talented wife was now finished and the results were stunning. It was even photographed by "Palaces and Dreams," and displayed in their magazine.

'Have you considered doing this for a living, dear?' I asked her, 'You've a definite talent.'

'Funnily enough I have, she replied. 'The people from the magazine also suggested I take it up; but I'd want to do it all by myself if I did.'

She set about it in earnest the very next day, and within a month had leased an exclusive showroom and office in Mayfair.

She also found her own staff and instructed the IPEC it was not to interfere in her running of the business. But as a special favour she did allow it to arrange the funding. No cap in hand visits to the bank for my wife.

CHAPTER TWENTY TWO

No one uses a private jet every day; it's not like a car. It does however, along with the crew have to pay for itself. So with the company's other planes inherited from the Belgians. IPEC Travel leased it out to various organisations. Who it must be said paid handsomely for the privilege. The fact that a certain Mr Stewart, an American businessman based in Europe, was chartering it for a return flight to and from Las Vegas raised no eyebrows at all. The paper work was duly filed with the authorities and approved.

We landed at McCarran International Airport and following a cursory inspection from the customs headed by hotel limousine directly to The Bellagio where the IPEC had pre-booked me into a suite, my new US credit cards in the name of James Stewart being accepted with no problem.

Las Vegas is a magical city, it trades on fantasy and there's nowhere in the world that compares. Rather than wasting money on psychiatrists and the like. In my opinion anyone with a problem should visit for a few days because it blows the mind. I've always loved coming here, referring to it as Disneyland for adults. But this was to be a flying visit;

'We're leaving tomorrow night I told the crew. 'File the flight-plan back to the UK for between 08-00 pm to midnight, and enjoy yourselves tonight, I've arranged some chips for you with the concierge.'

I worked in my room for about an hour, and after going outside to see the dancing fountains walked back through the main casino floor, thinking about which of the many excellent restaurants I'd choose for dinner. First though, as one does, I bought some chips and stopping at a quiet table watched the roulette for about five minutes to get the run of the ball, before doing in a fast couple of hundred bucks.... so much for my system.

'Stand as near as you can to the wheel, I would like to watch the spin. Put the on glasses please. And make sure the MIPEC is facing the wheel

I stood for about ten minutes fascinated by the readouts which were flashing at phenomenal speed in the lenses until she said.

'Have you noticed she does not call 'no more bets' until after the wheel has been spun As soon as the croupier has released the ball, I'll give you a number. Put $100 on it.'

The wheel was spinning the croupier picked the ball up and launched it in the opposite direction after one revolution she said.

'Put it on 36 red.'

I won $3500. Wow, I thought, that was lucky.

'Wait until she has launched the ball again, and put $1000 on the number I shall give you.'

She said nothing for two spins. On the third spin.

'8 black,' she commanded.

So I put down the $1000 winning $35,000. Three spins later she picked 27 red which won another $35,000. By now I was starting to attract attention. The wheel was spinning when she said

'Put it all on zero,'

I couldn't reach that far, and so pushing all my chips towards the croupier shouted, 'everything on zero.'

The pit boss who was on the phone, said

'The limit at these tables is $1000 on a single number sir, I'm sorry.' The ball continued without me.

'Double Zero,' said the croupier. I was elated. I still had my winnings, we would have lost everything

'Drat said the voice I didn't expect that. We should have lost.'

She wanted to give it all back. But I certainly didn't and walked to the cage to cash in my chips. One of the staff came over and confirmed I was staying in the hotel and asked for my name and room number. They were comping me, he said. My room would be paid and all meals. I still had $70,350 of their cash of course and no casino wants that sort of money to walk away.

'Don't forget you're Mr Stewart,' the voice said.

Later, when I had settled down, I had them bring a meal of fresh lobster salad, French fries and a bottle of Dom Pèrignon to my room.

'Why did you do it?' I asked.

'I just wanted to see if I could. But it was stupid to win, we came here anonymously and acted like idiots, for which I take full responsibility. This place does that to you, it's all so unreal. I couldn't help myself.'

'You're right,' I replied 'it's all just so…. OTT. By the way, how did you know which number the ball would land on?'

I simply calculated the velocity of the wheel and the strength of the throw; the hard part is deciphering the segments on the wheel. I could have tried the blackjack but it would be too easy; roulette is much more of a challenge. We have to think about tomorrow,' she continued, eager to change the subject. We need to get out to the Groom Lake Base, have you considered how?'

'I have,' I replied. 'Every day, a dedicated fleet of planes, all Boeing 737's take off from McCarran for Groom Lake. I thought we could travel back half a second, you could stay here. Whilst I hitch a lift with them.'

'It's a good plan,' she said, 'but it leaves you there all day at the whim of others. Plus not all of the planes go to the lake, some go to different bases. I'd rather we hire a vehicle and drive there together. We could then transport when nearby the site and both go in.'

'You mean take the vehicle with us?' I said.

'Precisely'

'But the mat is only 3 metres x 2, 5 the Dune Buggy only just fits it.'

'I know that, but what about a motorcycle? We could hire one in Las Vegas and drive out to the base from here. You do know how to ride one I suppose?'

'That's a good question,' I replied, 'I owned one as a teenager, for a year, but haven't ridden one since. Are you definitely planning to come with me?'

'It would depend on whether you could find a suitable mount to carry me safely. Why not get a good night's sleep and we can look around in the morning. I'll search the phone book for a hire shop.'

'Wake me at 6-00 am.' I told her. 'It would be good to find somewhere before it gets too hot.'

'Fortunately it's not a problem tomorrow,' she replied. 'The weather forecast is for overcast conditions, and 18 degrees centigrade.'

'Then make it 8-00…. In that case I'm going down again to play some more, please don't help me until I get down to '$5,000, and bring me back up to $50,000, I like the free food.'

I was shown directly to a high rollers section and spoiled rotten.

The hire companies were no problem but when I saw some of the bikes close up I didn't fancy it, not with the IPEC tied to the back seat; what if I crashed and damaged it?

And then I came up with a great idea…. a Suzuki Jimny…. but they turned out to be 3.6 metres long.

'What about a Mercedes Smart Car?' the salesman asked, no doubt wondering why I needed such a short car, but like all Americans genuinely trying to help.

'How long are they?' I enquired.

He looked in his book, and said

'2.63 metres.'

'Where could I get one?'

'Most of the large companies have them,' he answered. 'Ours are all out, they're very popular, especially the new 4 X 4 hybrid, we make them in the US now of course, they're great to drive and more importantly easy to park. Let me call around the other companies and see what we can come up with.'

I had the IPEC call the captain of the plane telling him we might not get off tonight after all, but to be ready to leave when he got my call. I took with me some biscuits, a case of water, a large bottle of cola and an extra jacket in case I was out all night. And a bottle of good Bourbon to flavour the cola.

Climbing into the tiny car, I placed the IPEC next to me, and headed for the US-95, toward Indian Springs, everything in miles now of course. After about five miles I became bored with the 55 mph limit and pulled behind a hill out of sight of the road. Taking out the mat I disconnected the umbilical and placed it on the ground opening it by hand, and carefully driving the car onto the mat, said.

'OK Hypatia, let's go back the half second'.

---Activate---

CHAPTER TWENTY THREE

We carried on to Indian Springs at a more comfortable speed. At Mercury, I took the road through town until reaching a sign saying
NEVADA TEST SITE AND NELLIS AIR FORCE BASE.
RESTRICTED ACCESS.

Keeping up a steady 70 to 80 mph, the IPEC wanted to go faster insisting we could pass directly through trucks and cars. I didn't doubt her, but when it came to it I just didn't have the nerve. Heading directly for another vehicle at a closing speed of 150 miles an hour would have to wait.

The new 4-wheel drive smart car was a marvel, small and incredibly light, with leather seats, A/C, and a great music system. It could reach 110 mph and do 140 mpg with its hybrid drive system. In my opinion we had the American and European including Russia's withdrawal from the Middle East to thank for this. The genocide had finally made the oil companies release some of the engine patents they owned and thanks to the worldwide public pressure we didn't now need to import so much oil and the latest price drop was making driving a pleasure again. The word on the street was, the next generation would run on saltwater if that was true it would mean an irrevocable change to the balance of world power.

From Mercury we followed the road across Frenchmans Flats, past Yucca dry lake, and Yucca Flats, reaching 'Area 51' around mid-day.

'According to the speedometer we've come 139 miles,' I told the IPEC. We had stopped at a signpost saying
GROOM LAKE. -- RESTRICTED ACCESS.
PHOTOGRAPHY IS PROHIBITED.
THE USE OF DEADLY FORCE IS AUTHORIZED.

'Have you got the exact grid reference from our last visit?'

'Yes,' she replied. 'The whole area is only 10 miles x 6. I can put us directly into the hanger.'

As we came over a hill I saw two long runways one going right across the dry lake. The place was quite built up; there were peri-tracks, hangers, laboratories, fuel tanks, and numerous other buildings.

I stopped and pointed the MIPEC at the facility. After a few seconds, she said.

'The hanger we need is located in the centre of the complex to the South of the main buildings, it has a high roof.'

I panned the MIPEC around until she said.

'That's the one,'....

Ten minutes later we were parked outside. Some security trucks were moving about, and a dedicated team of armed guards patrolled the outside of the building, but otherwise it looked pretty deserted. As expected the main doors were securely locked, but walking around the side I found a small door, which required a complicated eight number code to get in. The MIPEC didn't even break sweat and two minutes later I stepped inside.

The spacecraft stood like a caged eagle, jet black, and even more impressive than the last time. From an open door in the side, an integral ramp dropped to the floor. I climbed in following the curved corridor round the wall, passing the doors to the cabins. The corridor met with another heading inboard and inclined slightly taking me directly to the bridge. I expected it to be in the centre, but it wasn't, it was at the front, if there's a front in a circle?

The craft had darkened windows a semi-circular console for four people and a leather armchair behind, probably for the Captain, or in this case General. The desk was full of screens and little else. I placed the IPEC on it for her to interrogate the computer. My original thought was, it's controlled by touch sensors nothing new there? But then Hypatia told me her investigation had revealed the saucer was controlled not by touch at all; it was operated by thought and she couldn't gain access.

Somewhat subdued she asked,

'Can you see any signs for the engine room.'

At the rear of the control section was a sign saying 'Elevator,' it only had two settings, up and down. I dropped to the next level and walked out directly into the engine room; the surprise was the radiation sign.

'Its nuclear powered, Hypatia. And we're very fortunate; in the good old traditions of the military, everything is labelled. This is a superconducting steam generator; both the generator and the reactor are inside a strange type of plastic case. It has a strange texture too, like nothing I've ever felt before, soft and warm to the touch.'

Intrigued I tried to scratch it but couldn't. The boiler was in a similar compartment, I only knew it was a boiler mind you because it was labelled as one. I have been involved with turbines of one kind or another for most of my life but would never have recognised this as one.

'There's a 30 cm clear tube within this compartment Hypatia it's labelled in red capitals Danger. Plasmaclopropyhydrothane, which sounds like a rocket fuel. And have you ever heard of a magnetoplasmafusion engine, because there's a closed compartment running horizontally all the way to the outer bulkhead with that name engraved on it. The compartment widens as it reaches the bulkhead. Don't the Americans just love their long names?'

'I have no record of that particular name, but it sounds similar to an experimental propulsion system called a Variable Specific Impulse Magnetoplasma Rocket, or VASIMR. But I didn't think such a rocket is developed yet. Can you get down to the next level?'

'I'll try, but it seems to me that parts of this ship have been modified to give more headroom. This floor though, and the one below are really cramped there's no more than one and half metres clearance anywhere. It must make maintenance a nightmare.' The engineer in me took over.

'The engine is below, look Hypatia, they've developed a flat turbine, it must be over 30 metres across, no wonder it's so powerful, the thrust is forced to the edge, there is a continuous grill with controllable slats for direction, the power must be enormous. It's made completely of composites and probably weighs nothing, how fantastic.' I took more pictures with the MIPEC,

'OK Hypatia we're ready to leave, I'm going back up now.'

Looking down at the edge of the turbine, behind a transparent window, I saw rotating plates lining the floor. In the centre was something else.

'Good God Hypatia, there's more.' I've seen this before; I think it was in a Siemens magazine a few years ago as a concept design. It's an anti-gravitational magnetronic power source. The turbine doesn't only produce thrust; its other function is to turn these plates. The whole bottom of the ship is a giant counter-rotating generating magnet.

The reactor must also charge up the magnetrons. It's got to have tremendous power and probably works against the pull of the earth's terrestrial magnetic field. No wonder it's so powerful and quiet. The thrusters are only for stability and directional control. Once they leave the atmosphere though, the main turbine will provide the power; in space the magnetrons will be less effective. But surely weight must be a problem, they would need an iron core, it would be self-defeating?'

'Not if they've found a way to develop the magnetronic field by counter rotating the composite plates against each other,' Hypatia replied, 'making them generate opposite poles, the faster they turn, the more power they produce. The field would then be reversible; that would seem logical. It would also explain the artificial gravity when in space. I believe this craft has three engines, the anti-gravitational device, the turbine for additional thrust and stability, and the VASIMR for use in space. It's incredible, and way in advance of anything else flying today. No wonder they keep it hidden.'

'This is so exciting! 'I exclaimed. 'But we should leave. I understand now why they're so desperate to protect the secret, it's absolutely brilliant. 'I'd love to see what else is here, but we had better not. Anyway we can always come back.'

We discussed the possibility of it being an alien craft and the so-called Roswell incident, but decided to leave the matter for the present.

'Why not treat it as speculation,' she suggested. 'It is possible certainly, but the Americans have built some wonderful planes in the last forty years, why not one more? Let's not get too carried away.'

I could have accepted all that if we hadn't seen the alien sleds; it was just too much of a coincidence.

We drove back to the spot we had used before and re-materialised, arriving back at the hotel in time for dinner. After I had eaten, I said. 'Can you help me win another $50,000 I've seen a really special necklace for Julie? But first I want to go into the Bellagio art gallery. They've just purchased a new Cézanne. Please contact the Captain, tell him we'll leave at midnight.'

The Casino I think was pleased to see the back of me. Clearly they couldn't find out how I was doing it, but knew something wasn't kosher. They were nevertheless very respectful and even provided another stretch limousine to take me to the airport.

Because they were so nice I didn't tell them that their latest painting was almost certainly a fake.

Using 22nd century technology the MIPEC had scanned it, doing a hierarchal spectrum-analysis of the paint, and a multitudinous fibre scan of the canvas discovering certain inconsistencies. The paint was French, circa 1890 to 95, which would be correct, but the canvas was manufactured in Turin, Italy after 1910…. Paul Cézanne died in 1906.

CHAPTER TWENTY FOUR

'Have you got a private number for the Sir David Hommersby?' I said looking up from my desk where I was trying to design an anti-gravitational propulsion system for the buggy.

'Yes' she replied. A minute later he answered. We made the usual small talk, until he asked what he could do for me.

'Would it be possible for me to make an appointment to see you?' I asked.

'Yes of course, have your secretary arrange it with my PPS tomorrow morning?'

'Thank you, I'm sorry to have bothered you on your private line, but it is important.'

'Pleased to be of help,' he said. Probably wondering how I had got his number. 'I'll see you tomorrow.'

Hypatia called the following morning and arranged 15 minutes with the Minister in the afternoon at the Houses of Parliament.

'What can I do for you?' He asked. After I had passed through the security and had been shown to his office.

'I have to speak to Andrew Blythe urgently, would it be possible for you to arrange a meeting. I understand he will be in London next week.'

'I can certainly speak to him on your behalf. May I know why?'

Suspecting he had already guessed, I answered.

'Through no fault of my own I saw something so secret that just being at large makes me a security threat.'

'Really,' he replied, clearly intrigued, 'I knew something wasn't right about this, what can it be that makes it so sensitive? And please call me David.'

'Thank you, believe me David, you don't want to know. Would you tell him I've something to trade, something very important?' I made the sign, which told him, 'I am in distress brother, and plead for your help.'

'Leave it with me old chap. I'll get back to you as soon as I can.' He paused for a moment as if considering his next step.

'By the way Jason, before you go I'd like to talk to you about Stephen Maxwell. You said some quite harsh things to him at Farnborough. Some of them probably justified, but he is a good friend, we were at school together you know? He is worried that word of his actions might get out. Would you be prepared to see him, and square it? His part in the missile affair was unfortunate. But lessons learnt you know?

'No problem Minister, you have my word, it's all forgotten.' We shook hands and a security guard showed me out.

The 'one on one,' meeting with the great man took place in the American Embassy in Grosvenor Square. We shook hands and sat opposite each other making polite conversation, he behind the Ambassadors rather grand desk, me on slightly lower 18th century French ormolu encrusted chair. When the preliminaries had been completed he lowered his voice and said conspiratorially.

'Because of recent events we'll continue our discussion in the SCIF,' (the Americans love their initials even more than their long names.)

We entered a lift, which took us deep underground, and entered a swept room. SCIF means Sensitive Compartmentalised Information Facility. It's screened with RF baffles and zigzag chicanes to shield the room from any outside influences it's also suspended and balanced on rubber mounts, and the whole structure is constantly being electronically sanitised. They would have been most upset to learn that Hypatia listened in to our conversation effortlessly, even talking to me during it.

'Before we begin, 'let me thank you officially for your exploits on the platform, we all owe you a great deal. But the ability to make yourself invisible is causing some concern to our military, as is ensuring your continued silence about the whole affair.'

'I am very well aware of the dangers Mr Secretary, but I can assure you that any leaks certainly won't come from me.'

'It may seem very unfair to you Mr Shaw, especially following your brave actions on the platform, but the aircraft you used is highly secret'

'I wasn't allowed to see very much Mr. Secretary.'

'Possibly not, but just being aware of its existence is enough to cause real concern to some of our Air Force people.'

'There must be many people who know of the craft's existence, any one of them could let something slip.' His body language convincing me he knew nothing of the aliens. Which probably meant the President didn't too…. In which case who did? I could fully understand them keeping President Trump in the dark. But this new one seemed quite switched on.

'I understand you have something to trade? It has been suggested you may have something hidden away. Some insurance possibly, to be published if anything untoward were to happen.' He looked at me questioningly.

I returned his stare. 'It would seem a prudent move in the circumstances, but of course if it were the case, all would be returned the moment I felt sure of my safety.'

'An interesting choice of words 'returned,' it rather implies you took something. You have lived and worked in the United States I believe? In Missouri, and Pennsylvania.'

'That's true sir, mostly at Poplar Bluff Missouri. We loved the Ozarks, but that was some years ago. The man then and the man before you now are totally different. With learning comes experience and more especially prudence. A lifetime of learning has occurred in the last couple of years.'

'Yes I can believe that, he said looking at a file on his desk.' He visibly relaxed as if coming to a decision. 'My country owes you a great debt. I want your word that everything you saw will remain utterly secret.'

'I willingly give it Mr Secretary, you have my solemn word'

'Very well, we'll trust you to keep our secrets, as you trusted us with yours. I'll confirm that to the people concerned.'

The relief must have been evident in my face, 'Thank you Mr Secretary you won't regret this.'

'Well, we can't have a person on whom the President is proposing to personally confer honorary citizenship being concerned about visiting his new country can we?'

'No sir, we can't…. I'm truly honoured. May I ask you how many people know about the invisibility shroud?'

'Very few, it's been classified ultra-secret.' he grinned. 'You see how we value you?'

I returned his grin; realising I not only respected him. I actually liked him, which came as a surprise when one considered how I have often shouted at the TV when he was on.

'I offer my services to your country if required sir, and that of my computer and the shroud: Providing we are not complicit in the taking of human life.'

He nodded and looked at his watch.

'I must ask that we now close our meeting, I've shortly to meet your Prime Minister for lunch.

'Would you be prepared to participate in some discussions concerning your experiences on the platform, especially the damaged spacesuit? I'm told you were very lucky to have survived. Maybe we can improve the design. I believe they also have some other points for you, concerning the launch and guidance computer.'

'Anything I can do to help, I will of course.'

'Your assistance is appreciated,' he smiled conspiratorially. 'None of the people you're about to meet have any knowledge of the craft … or of course the invisibility cloak. Please guard your responses carefully.'

He stood up. As he got to the door he turned, and said in the open way the Americans have sometimes.

'I'm sure we'll meet again…. Look, if you ever need me, please call my office, here's my private number; he returned and gave me his card and headed back to the door.'

'Oh yes before I forget, there's just one more thing, Mr Stewart. We would appreciate the return of the pictures you took during your recent visit to our top secret facility in Nevada, I'll take your word no copies will be kept, you've no need of them now.'

Stunned, and before the IPEC could advise differently, I answered.

'They're on a memory card sir. If it's acceptable to you I'll bring it with me when I come over to meet the President. I don't trust the postal service.'

'Nor do I,' he replied easily. 'One of my people will collect it directly.'

'Of course sir. Please have your man call me at home. The device will be ready for him.'

'My aide will be along momentarily. After your meeting he will accompany you and collect the evidence. He will have with him a briefcase. Please place the material inside and close it. It will lock automatically, only I have the key. He has no need to know the contents. Have a nice day.'

In the car driving home, followed by the aide. Hypatia agreed we had been expertly dissected. All the pictures were to be handed over.

'How did he know,' I wondered?

'He didn't, how could he? You were bluffed; they know you were in Las Vegas and that you travelled there on an American passport and simply put two and two together. Maybe the IPEC Travel jet landing in Las Vegas so soon after the event alerted them? Or maybe your photograph was sent to the casino's visual recognition cameras. We did everything wrong. You should have used your own passport and not won at roulette. Because of the passport they can now prove you committed a felony'

'I think maybe they were expecting us Hypatia. We underestimated them. It proves we'll have to be more careful in the future?'

'Don't you see?' she answered reflectively. 'Entering Groom Lake so easily must have caused them a great deal of concern. But it would also have made them realise that if you can breeze inside one of their most secret top security facilities, and get inside that particular hanger. You're able go anywhere…. Even the Kremlin, or the inner sanctums of Tehran and Pyongyang. No Jason you're perfectly safe, you always were. They will now consider us as a prime asset, much too valuable to be harmed.'

Nevertheless she continued to monitor their communications, just in case.

The IPEC had contacted its aide and transported unannounced. Only the Khepera and three others senior officers, who constituted the executive team were present.

'I came forward to tell you we've seen the American's saucer. Not surprisingly he deduced that the sleds from Egypt and the anti-gravitational engine were connected and questioning whether it was one of yours. We left the topic open, but it's only a matter of time until he decides it is and you are still visiting this planet. He might then question as to whether you live amongst us. I can block it from his mind if you wish.'

'No,' said the Khepera thoughtfully. 'We may be able to use it to our advantage. Let it develop; there's a strong possibility we'll have to meet him in the future, it might lessen the shock if he has already considered our continued and peaceful presence on this world.

'There's another matter, I want you to expand your business dealings; IPEC Travel is to increase its holdings by making a hostile take-over bid for a travel company called American Lamplighter, I am informed it's prime for a buy-out and would complement your existing business. The details of an account in the Cayman Islands and its access codes will be given to you after this meeting.'

'As you wish,' the IPEC replied, 'I actually look forward to it. Running a large business can be very stimulating.'

'At the next full meeting we shall review the next phase of the computer development. You should also be informed about a communication I have received from our observers on the planet Xeros.

The inhabitants of that world have developed a powerful disruptor beam. It appears they're further advanced than we expected. This is obviously serious news and makes out task even more vital. If there's nothing else we'll close this meeting, and meet again as scheduled.'

CHAPTER TWENTY FIVE

Our new Malaysian and Chinese factories were now in full production, the computers selling like hot cakes. Consequently my royalty cheques and dividends were growing steadily.

How's the travel company doing?' I asked Hypatia whilst sitting in my study admiring the rolling hills of the Surrey countryside.

'Rather well.' she replied. 'Since acquiring the American company we have expanded our business dealings worldwide. Did I tell you we now own a luxury yacht?'

'No,' I replied, looking up. 'Why would we do that?'

'It came with the deal. The directors purchased it for their own use. I considered selling it, but have lately been toying with the idea of using it for charters. It's a large yacht with a captain and crew, and its own helicopter.'

'Really,' I exclaimed. 'How large is large?'

'60.5 metres. It's berthed in Fort Lauderdale and I believe could prove beneficial for visiting certain countries without the bother of passing through security scans.'

'Well the board certainly won't need it anymore,' I said audaciously. She laughed, and then out of the blue said. 'Do you think we could pay another visit to Egypt?'

I shrugged,

'Do you have any particular reason?'

'I want to go back to the Pyramids, around 200 years later than our last visit and check something that's been bothering me…. it concerns Atlantis.'

'Atlantis!' I replied suspiciously. 'We don't know if it even existed,'

'Oh it definitely existed' she replied matter of factly, 'I went there with Anders!'

I studied her face intently; the eyes were looking at me with that all knowing look she has sometimes.

'My God Hypatia! Why have you never said anything?'

'We've been quite busy of late with the computer modifications.'

'Yes, but Atlantis Hypatia; that's the Holy Grail…. where was it?'

'In the Atlantic Ocean, The main city was called Quilapayum. It was built around a large bay at the extreme North, approximately 600 kilometres northeast of St. Johns Newfoundland, off the Grand Banks. The city's Latitude was 50° 31 mins north and Longitude 46° 28 mins west, '

'How do you know that?' I enquired sceptically. 'The MIPEC can't work without satellite location.'

'Wherever did you get that idea? I carry maps of the night sky going back 30,000 years.

If necessary I can work out exactly where we are day or night by dead reckoning.'

I shrugged, of course she could.

'Plato called it a continent,' I continued excitedly. 'How large was it?'

'Stories such as these have a habit of becoming exaggerated over time. Anders estimated the size to be around that of Hawaii.'

'How could something that big simply disappear?'

'I've no idea,' she said. 'Except that it straddled one of the earth's main fault lines. The tectonic plates in that area are still active today but 10,000 years ago they were extremely unstable.

'When were you there?' I asked breathlessly

'9500BC. 1000 years later than our visit to the pyramids.'

'What's the connection?' I asked.

'The connection' she replied, her eyes boring into mine; lancing into my brain. 'Were the three large pyramids, sited just south of the main city?'

'But Plato doesn't mention pyramids, are you sure?'

'Plato wrote about Atlantis 7000 years after it was destroyed, he never visited it.... I did! Anyway he was writing about the volcanic destruction of Hera and the Minoan civilization in the Aegean about 1100 BC, nothing to do with the destruction of Atlantis at all.

'He first mentioned its destruction in two of his dialogues, Timaeus and Critas. He refers specifically to a lost civilization called Atlantis in 9000 BC. As a matter of fact I have always wanted to visit Plato and spend some time with him to find out why he has such a disparity with the dates. Although it is probably just him mixing together two different legends'

'I would also like to visit Plato, obviously. But let's stay with Atlantis. Surely you considered the connection when we first saw the Giza pyramids?'

'I needed to think about it before discussing the significance. I had to be sure it wasn't interfering with your future.'

I had seen this reaction before, and knew it was no use pursuing it further.

'How did you get there, if it was in the middle of an empty ocean?'

'By accident,' she told me, 'Anders was fascinated by the Native American tribes. We were based at St. Johns, investigating their origins, and kept going further, and further back, until we came to 9500 BC. The tribes were of course very primitive stone-age small groups at that time, mostly living around the coast. Anders followed them one day and suddenly found himself at the edge of a modern city, not modern by our standards, but far in advance of anything anyone could have envisaged for that time.

He likened the construction to first or second dynasty Egyptian. The native Canadians, for the want of a better term, used to trade with them, furs and skins. He wandered around for a while, and saw they had electricity, produced by solar panels. They also had sophisticated plumbing. But their most impressive advancement was that they used levitation. He marked the spot and came back for me, we moved in our own timeline to the area, and re-transported to the same setting. He was really excited about it!'

'I can imagine,' I said, still not fully convinced.

'What fascinated him the most was the craft used to travel to Quilapayum. Rather like the saucer we saw recently. It used the earth's magnetic field as a source of antigravity.

'In this case the concept was different. It was equipped with a fully controllable graviton coil assembly, which significantly intensifies the effect of the terrestrial gravitational pull of the planet, repelling it and causing the craft to levitate. The skids at Giza were a basic example of this.'

'How do you know so much about it all of a sudden?' I asked suspiciously.

'Well…. I shouldn't tell you this, but such propulsion systems are widely used in the 22nd century; they've revolutionised all forms of transport because there's virtually no limit to their power, and are fully renewable.'

'How is the forward motion controlled?' I asked intrigued, thinking about my buggy.

'We're getting into dangerous ground here. This is what I meant about interfering with your future. I'll answer your question, but please leave it after that. The directional motion is controlled by angling certain of the graviton coils: Depending on the configuration, a 2% angle can, when boosted through a very advanced form of reversible accelerating transformer, called a reversible gravicoil, generate tremendous torque. At an angle of 10% it can propel a negatively buoyant object at ever increasing speeds up to a maximum of 860 kph. I've said far too much.

'That's it,' I shouted excitedly. 'The control room in the pyramid! It was a replica of the one in the saucer! I knew it was familiar. But Hypatia, how do you know this if your memory was wiped clean'

For the first time since I had re-energized her she looked uncomfortable.

'That's why it has taken me so long to correlate the two. Anders did wipe my core memory, but not the library. When you introduced the picobytes library into the new module, it was because I had implanted it into your brain, subconsciously.'

'So it wasn't my idea?'

'Not directly, nor was your immediate understanding of the propulsion system of the saucer.'

'Let's get back to Atlantis.' I said despondently. 'How did you know it was even there?'

'It was quite simple, when he saw the craft, he realised he had stumbled onto something fantastic. Given the location of the city, he simply guessed.

We first spent a few hours in the city listening to the people. Who incidentally spoke Aymaran. He heard someone mention the name 'Atlantis,' there was simply no stopping him after that. He discovered that a great city, named Quilapayum lay about 600 kilometres to the Northeast, once he knew that, he was determined to go.

The craft was of course a large yacht and extremely innovative. An interesting point about this discovery was that even though they had this advanced form of transport, they didn't yet have the wheel.'

'What did this yacht look like?' I was hooked now.

'It was long and sleek, with an aerofoil arrangement on the roof which extended into a controllable 'V' wing. The wing allowed it to skim over the water as long as it was moderately calm. It was far in advance of anything you have today, very aerodynamic and comfortable.'

'But surely antigravity can't work over water.'

'I would have agreed with you before I travelled on it. The strength is reduced certainly, but is still fully functional and the buoyancy of the water offers significant help. The craft only requires raising by a small amount.'

'How long did you stay in the city?' I asked, still not convinced.

'Three days... he was too hungry to stay any longer. Poor Anders was so excited he forgot to bring extra food.'

'Yes, but what about the city? 'I asked, impatiently. 'What did it look like?'

'It was made mainly of stone; Anders likened it to a mixture of early Egyptian, Greek, and Mayan.

'Mayan, now that is interesting. Tell me about the pyramids?'

'They were more or less the same as the ones at Giza,' she replied thoughtfully, 'and looked to be laid out in the same configuration. We didn't have time to actually visit them, there was so much else to see.'

'What about aliens,' I enquired. 'Did you see any?'

'No' she replied reflectively. 'But then, we weren't looking for them. We didn't know they existed. The people we saw seemed quite advanced you see. They were Egyptian looking, and dressed similar to what we see in some of the early cartouches.

'After we've visited Egypt,' she continued, 'I'd also like us to visit Mexico City, there are some pyramids there, which I believe complete the picture. They're located at a place called Teotihuacan. Although ruins now, it was once the home of over a million people, and was reputed at its height to have been even larger than Rome. The archaeologists tell us Teotihuacan was founded in 100 BC, and deserted around 700 AD, they're still trying to discover what the people who lived in this city were like.

Whoever they were, it appears they were clever enough to build this colossal city without any written language. No evidence has ever been found of any writings or hieroglyphs. When these people vanished, they were followed by a civilization called the Toltecs. Who in turn were succeeded by the Aztecs, who intriguingly named it, 'The Place of the Gods.'

The part we're interested in, are the two pyramids that dominate the city. The Pyramid of the Sun, and the Pyramid of the Moon. But there are also 600 smaller pyramids, which give rise to comparisons with Egypt. The Pyramid of the Sun has sides of 225 metres, with a similar base area to the Great Pyramid of Giza. The Pyramid of the Moon is smaller but like Khafre's pyramid at Giza is built on an elevated location, the tops of the two structures are level. In Teotihuacan the building called the 'Citadel,' has a base of a similar size to the third Pyramid. This base, if compared with the two existing pyramids, closely matches the layout of the three main pyramids at Giza.... We really should investigate this place.'

'I agree Hypatia. Especially since you've intimated some of the Atlantican architecture looked Mayan, but why do you want to go to Egypt first?'

'We were not successful in finding their radio frequencies the last time. My systems have now been modified to monitor the whole spectrum.'

'Despite what you've said about Mexico,' I asked sceptically. 'If it was only built in 100 BC, it's of no use to us.... not for this investigation at least?'

'I believe it is,' she said seriously. 'You see latitude 50° 31 minutes north, and longitude 46° 28 minutes west, is the distance, allowing for the Earths curvature, between Teotihuacan and Giza that matches the layout of the pyramids at Giza.'

I must have looked somewhat baffled.

'If one were to take the Giza plateau as the pyramid of Khufu,' she explained slowly, and Teotihuacan as the pyramid of Menkaure, then at these coordinates the pyramids at Quilapayum would correlate with the pyramid of Khafre, matching the layout of the stars in the Belt of Orion, as they were 12500 years ago. Following precisely the hypothesis proposed by Bauval.'

'You have a theory don't you,' I cried excitedly.

'I believe I know the secret of the pyramids and why they were built.' she replied. 'We must do some further investigations before I expound on it fully; but if I'm right, everything will become clear.'

'Are you going to give me a rough idea at least?' I said hungrily.

'I can see you'll never rest until I do,' she mocked. 'I believe everyone is mistaken in thinking they're burial sites. My supposition is that they were just the opposite, and were in fact used for rejuvenation. Possibly for bringing the aliens back from the dead, or at least keeping them alive.

'To get here, they would have travelled vast distances, say for example from Orion. The journey may very well have aged them so much, that they had to be treated before setting off on the return journey. Or maybe their tour of duty here was so long, they would have died otherwise.'

'Pyramids are supposed to have these powers!' I exclaimed. 'They say it's a proven fact that razor blades stay sharp if kept in one. It's as good an idea as any I've heard, and certainly the aliens looked mortal and seemed to be generally of the same genetic make-up as we are.... Hey, I've just thought of something else. What if they were also able to transform their appearance, to look like us?'

'My hypothesis is somewhat questionable,' she groaned, 'But yours is preposterous!'

I brought up 'Teotihuacan' on my ID Phone.

'The main flaw in your theory is Teotihuacan, it simply can't be old enough. They say here that they've done carbon-dating tests on some excavated artefacts, and everybody agrees with the date of 100 BC;

'That may be the case,' she replied. 'But why speculate when we are in the unique position of being able to confirm or deny it. Let's wait until we get back to 9500 BC.'

'You're right,' I said, 'let's wait and see. But the most exciting part of this exercise is that we get to go to Atlantis. I want to see which way it was orientated; for example, did it go crossways and span the Atlantic? If it did, it may very well have been accessible from Spain. Also when something of this size disappears it must cause one hell of a Tsunami, which may lead us on to Noah's flood.... Exciting isn't it?'

'How long will you be gone this time?' Julie demanded, 'You're never at home anymore.' I hated to hurt her like this, but nothing was going to stop me now. 'Four days.'

'Well don't be any longer please? You know this is the only quiet week I have, I took it off just to be with you.'

I felt really bad, but the excitement of visiting Atlantis overrode everything else.

'Yes dear, I'll go and pack....Hypatia order her some flowers, three dozen yellow roses and have them delivered tomorrow, and make sure it comes with a nice card. The florist will know what to say.'

The silence and the looks I received from my supposedly emotionless machine were deafening. That evening I took my lovely wife out for dinner. And the next morning bought the flowers myself and wrote the card.

☐

CHAPTER TWENTY SIX

The flight to Cairo presented no problems; neither did booking in the hotel. That evening after the show we set off in a hired Desert cruiser for the pyramids leaving through a gate in the hotels fence and coming around the back through the desert in the dark.

'We must try to park as near to the great pyramid as possible.' It's important to be in the centre, somewhere near the Solar Boat Museum. We'll only be gone for a half second.'

'What timeline shall we choose? I asked, I would propose we start at the year 9800 BC

'We were here at 10500 BC last time,' she replied, 'and Anders chose 9500 BC to visit Atlantis. It was there in 9500 BC so why not try 10000 as a starting point, we can also find out if the Sphinx is there? I propose we choose the evening, let's try about 6-00 pm just as the sun is going down. The climate isn't so bad in that timeline, it was quite temperate the last time we were here.'

'Let's do it,'

Knowing the ground in that timeline we drove to a position between the museum and the Mortuary Temple, I unloaded the IPEC, set the mat and said. '1st May 10,000 BC 6-00 pm'

---Activate---

We materialised to the magical red light of the setting sun.

'I'm going to the Sphinx before it gets too dark' I said, and took out the tarpaulin to cover the IPEC.

'I need to search for the radio signals, please leave me uncovered I might have to release the antennae. You may go now I need to get on.'

'Yes ma-am,' I said huskily.

Walking over to my left, and on past Khafres pyramid I was filled with anticipation, naturally the causeway wasn't there, but the Sphinx would now be 500 years old and have the head of an alien. The whole thing would be covered in gold, the eyes of jet-black quartz. But walking toward its position it soon became clear it wasn't there; the desert was bare.

'Hypatia' I said despondently, 'the Sphinx isn't here. It must have been built during the fourth dynasty after all. It did look remarkably new at that time. But I admit to being disappointed.'

'There's no evidence of the Aliens either,' she replied. 'We're going to have to go back further if we want to hear their transmissions. First though Jason, can you go into the Great Pyramid and see what you can find. I want to know if the room and the sarcophagus are empty?'

I climbed the stairs to the entrance; at least the lights were still on.

'Can you hear me Hypatia?'

'Yes, loud and clear'

'The whole place is still brightly lit. I'm at the grand gallery climbing up to the King's chamber and can hear voices. They're chanting.'

In the chamber were about 10 people sitting cross-legged in a circle on the floor. As I walked past them to the sarcophagus I could see a young couple looking into it and softly chanting, the language sounded strange.

'Can you hear me Hypatia?'

'Go ahead' she replied.

'Can you record the language?

'Yes, but I can tell you now, it's Aymaran. Can you see what's in the sarcophagus?'

I looked over and saw a child, lying on a mattress of straw covered by a blanket, it was quite cold in here, but not as cold as one might have expected.

'There a young boy in the sarcophagus, he's either sleeping or dead, I don't know which…. no wait, he's breathing, but obviously very ill. I think you were correct, this is a rejuvenation chamber. It seems the aliens have gone, but have left the pyramid open for anyone to use.'

'What about the opening to the control room area? She asked.

'The opening has been sealed with blocks, if I didn't know it was there I wouldn't give it a second look.'

'Scan it with the MIPEC Jason, I find it hard to believe it's been sealed permanently at this time It doesn't make sense, the main entrance is wide open and the stairs are still there. If the aliens had left, surely the whole pyramid would have been sealed.'

I scanned it as ordered, covering every millimetre of the area.

'There's a space behind, but we know that.' She told me to stand in a particular spot and concentrate on that area, after about 5 minutes she said.

'There is an electronic receiver inside the wall, place the MIPEC a little higher and to the left…. stop; please try to hold it steady I am going to attempt to decipher the code, I believe it to be a locking device of some kind, with a ten number rolling combination. This is not going to be easy even for me!' After about forty minutes, during which my arm had gone numb, a section of wall silently opened. I studied it for a while to be sure it was safe and poked my head inside. The staircase had been sealed too. But this time it took her less than a minute, the bricks swung open.

'It's been mothballed,' I reported as I entered the control room.

'The screens are dead, and everything's covered with some kind of clear spray-on plastic.'

'Make your way back and we'll move timelines I'll analyse the data later.'

'OK give me fifteen minutes.' I said, walking out, sealing the doors behind me. Leaving the people in the chamber I returned to the entrance emerging gratefully into the eerie twilight and was greeted by hundreds of birds singing their goodnight songs to the daylight. I was again struck by how refreshing the warm clean air was compared to the polluted soup of our time.

Descending the steps I walked swiftly back to the IPEC.

'Let's try 10400 BC?' she suggested. 'Menkaure's pyramid should be built by then, and the surrounding area tidied up…. Wait a minute I have something? There's a transmission.'

It was quite dark now, but something moved above me. I looked up startled, and saw the cap of the great pyramid opening, the outer edges coming up to make a square dish, "a tetrahedron," which slowly swung round toward the east at an angle of about 80 degrees.

'Can you make it out?' I asked

'No, it's just a series of dots being repeated constantly. It must be very powerful, because it's being projected directly into space, yet I'm still picking up a residual signal.'

'What do you mean? …. Bloody hell,' I cried, as a sharp light erupted from the cap of the pyramid directly into the night sky 'It's like being in Las Vegas.'

It was some time before she spoke,

'Well it's definitely a laser of some kind! Probably a concentrated homing beacon, very powerful, and much more sophisticated than anything I've seen before. The interior of the pyramids must be packed with equipment. Scan the beam with the MIPEC, we'll do a spectrum analysis of its make up.'

The face disappeared; a long five minutes later she re-appeared saying.

'As I suspected, it's far in advance of anything we have. It's a neutron beam, transmitting inside a free-electron laser, which as far as I am able to deduce is formed using a synchronised radiation array. A concentration of this intensity might very well be capable of forcing the beam to an exact spot in our solar system, for example Mars, or one of the moons of Jupiter. From there it could be automatically re-transmitted through other relay stations hundreds of light years. And probably carries condensed messages direct to their home planet. It could then also collect any return transmissions. In addition, they are transmitting on a much lower frequency over a vastly wider range, probably a general homing signal to any craft within our planetary system. It's absolutely fascinating.'

By now the whole place was in total darkness, and then as if by magic the night became day. 'What the hell' I shouted.

'Are you OK Hypatia?'

'Yes,' the IPEC replied, 'I have automatic filters, -- are you?'

'Yes,' I said, the lenses in the glasses had instantly compensated. Two of the three Pyramids had suddenly lit up a dazzling bright white, just as suddenly the third followed.

'It looks like the whole of each structure has been covered with the same luminous paint,' I cried, 'it has the same glow, but much brighter.'

'I think you're right,' she replied. 'It also appears the paint is photosensitive. What wonderful beacons they must make, easily visible from orbit; these beings are terrifically advanced. Look, we can't do any more at this time, let's try 9-00 am, 3rd October 10390 BC. Do you agree with the date?'

'Yes' I said, thinking it wouldn't it really matter if I said no!

--- Activate ---

In the area where one day the mortuary temple would be built, sat a flying saucer, it was painted silver rather than black and had smooth sides, the stealthy plates were probably a 20th century addition by the Americans, but otherwise it looked the same. The door was standing open invitingly; so naturally I took this as an invitation to inspect the interior, which was very like the American one. The layout of the panels was the same too although the seats were smaller.

It was bizarre to be inside something almost identical to the one I had myself used to travel into space 12,000 years in the future. I left it at this point to re-join the IPEC.

'It's hard to believe that the design of the saucer hasn't changed for 12,000 years?' I said, 'The most intriguing thing about all this is... What the hell are the Americans doing with one?'

'They've probably stolen it,' she snapped,

'Quite possibly, I agreed, taken aback by the venom in her voice. 'Or maybe the aliens gave it to them in exchange for their silence?'

'Probably stolen,' she snapped again. 'Look, as interesting as this undoubtedly is, the fact that the Americans have one is indisputable. It might very well be that the design hasn't changed because there was no reason to. Take the shark for example their design hasn't changed in millions of years. I suggest that we shelve the question for the present and concentrate on the layout of the pyramids. The aliens knew they would be rescued eventually, and probably wanted to build something that could be re-used over future millennia.'

'Yes,' I agreed. 'That makes sense, whenever they visited us in the future to monitor our progress, they would have a safe base. The hidden stairs give ready access to the control room and there are living quarters and storerooms with power and communications. It was probably left permanently open, there are no decorations or valuables so there's nothing to steal, plus the locals seem to know the pyramids have healing powers.'

'I really don't see what staying here will achieve,' she replied. 'Let's return and set off for Mexico at this date.'

'We can't just leave,' I said, aghast. 'What about the radio waves, and the aliens? I must at least climb to the control room and see what's happening.'

'Oh, very well,' she agreed reluctantly. 'In the meantime I'll listen for any signals and record them. First though, go over and take a sample of the paint'

It was a thick clear lacquer, very hard. But I managed to get a sample, and we spent the next few minutes confirming what I already knew. It was the same, but the makeup of the inside coating was much thinner and was too advanced even for the IPEC to understand. However, getting an admission of this fact was not something I expected.

Reaching the control room I saw very little had changed. They may very well have been different individuals but it was impossible to tell. In effect Hypatia was right, there was nothing to see. I climbed down to the door again, but it was still locked, everything else seemed boringly the same.

I re-joined the IPEC, and made my report, to which she replied.

'Let's go to Mexico?'

'You surprise me Hypatia.' I admitted, 'I've never seen you so single minded. Still, if you're so certain. One more thing before we leave. I've considering another option. What if the pharaohs up to middle of the fourth Dynasty used the sarcophagus in the Kings chamber for their lying in state believing it to be a regeneration chamber? It was probably Khufu who extended the ceremony by building the causeway and the other buildings.'

'An interesting theory.' she conceded. 'I suppose if the ancient legends had it that the Gods had done it thousands of years earlier, it might be possible. You really do come up with the most bizarre ideas. You must be careful not to alter the facts to fit your theories.'

I wouldn't give up on the idea though, and added.

'We can do some research on the dates of their deaths and come back another time to test the theory.'

Her eyes told me all I needed to know about this idea. …But I could wait.

'There's one more thing I'd like to do before we leave Egypt,' I told her, 'I want to select a more recent time, and see if the way into the inner section and the control room is still operating. I know it's almost impossible to locate, but the whole structure has been minutely scrutinized by experts in the last fifty years with all sorts of modern devices, surely one of them would have found it?'

'That is a very good suggestion,' she replied.' Let's choose 10-00 am one week ago.'

--- Activate---

I made my way to the Kings chamber with the other tourists only to discover that the block in question was absolutely solid and the receiver not operating.

We had only been in Egypt for a brief time, and as it had been a short flight from the UK, the crew were still OK to fly. The hotel manager must have thought me mad. We had only used the rooms to shower.

'Take us to Mexico captain,' I ordered, 'and don't spare the horses, you can apply for the permissions on route.'

'The flight is 12400 kilometres,' he informed me, 'that's over 14 hours, we can't fly that far without a stop over.'

'No problem' I said 'pick somewhere on route and we'll lay over for a while.'

'What about Montreal?' he asked.

'Sounds good to me, let's do it.' Turning to the stewardess, I said.

'What about some food Lillian? It's been quite a while since I ate anything. Once we're underway can you make me something nice? A juicy fillet steak with shitake mushrooms, lightly fried in olive oil, with sauté potatoes and sugar snaps, you may open a bottle of the 1989 Meerlust to accompany it.'

At times like these I always have to pinch myself. When we were in the air I asked Hypatia,

'Can you access the history channel computer library and put it on screen…. anything they have about Teotihuacan?'

Seven hours later we landed at Dorval International rather than Cartierville and headed in by taxi. It had been seven years since I had last been to Montreal and had forgotten what a genuinely fabulous city it is. The last time was a ten-day visit as part of a delegation; giving a technical presentation for a power station we were bidding in New Brunswick.

Hypatia had booked everyone in at the Hotel Omni Mont-Royal, and when settled in, I went alone to my favourite restaurant Le Grand Comptoir. The next morning we carried on to Mexico City, landing at Benito Juárez, and checking into the Hotel Marquis Reforma.

Because of the time difference, and deciding there was still enough light to visit the ruined city I hired a Lexus and set off with the IPEC for Teotihuacan. As soon as I saw the pyramids it was obvious we were on the wrong track, these felt different. It was not only the fact that they were step pyramids and the sides were much shallower, they had clearly been built much later. I was disappointed, but readily accepted this place was worthy of much more investigation at another time. Hypatia however was not so sure.

'The bases are the right size,' she said, 'if one takes the Citadel as the site of the third pyramid the layout looks to be about correct, and the sizes of the two pyramids match. I believe we should go back to 10,000 BC and investigate.'

'But this is no more than a couple of thousand years old.' I insisted, 'Even I can see that.'

'We're here now Jason, please humour me?'

'Ok,' I said, 'what have we got to lose? But I still think we've come a long way for nothing.'

'By the way,' she said sheepishly 'Julie called earlier whilst we were on the plane. I informed her you were asleep and that we were on our way to Mexico. She seemed a little agitated, I told her you would call her back, but it's the middle of the night there now, you're reprieved until tomorrow.'

'Oh God!' I said, 'why do you always do this to me, can't you lie sometimes?'

'I'll leave that to you; but I'd prepare a good story because she's loaded for bear.'

'There you go again. You're spending too much time with our American cousins. Your English is becoming Mid-Atlantican,'

'There's no such word as Atlantican, unless maybe one lived on Atlantis?'

'Well there you are.' I exclaimed. 'We soon will be…. Select 1st June 9-00 am 10000 BC '

---Activate---

'How did you know?' I asked, suitably impressed.

'I didn't,' she replied smugly 'but it seemed a distinct possibility.'

In front of me were three smooth sided giants, darker than the Egyptian ones, made of different stone probably, but equally fabulous and all had the same gold caps. The bottom section of the smaller one was once again red.

'I wonder what the red signifies?' I asked, 'and why they were destroyed?'

'Probably to build the city we saw,' she surmised. 'But it's likely they were first damaged by earthquakes, 12,000 years is an awfully long time, especially when built in an earthquake zone such as this. But it goes some way to answering our questions, and explains the origins of the Mesoamerican culture. We're having a really successful week why not go inside and confirm they replicate the Giza pyramids? They will of course, but we must be sure.'

'Well. It certainly beats chasing Jack the Ripper;' I said slinging the rucksack over my shoulder

The three pyramids were in the same order, size and orientation as their

Giza counterparts, the centre one being built on a hill bringing it to the same height as the large one. The interior design of the larger pyramid was also the same, even to the empty sarcophagus in the Kings chamber. The control room was mothballed too.

'Hypatia I'm coming back, set the time for 10390 BC we'll see if the control room is open? Choose the same date and time, if we find a flying saucer we'll know they have at least two.'

---Activate---

There was no saucer unfortunately, but the control room was the same; it was manned by four aliens, who seemed to have nothing much to do. One interesting point however, was that two of them were female; they were wearing the same brown figure hugging suits, which gave it away. They looked exactly the same as the men facially; the only difference was their small waists and breasts. Hypatia was fascinated by this news, because it proved they were very similar to we humans; and probably reproduced in the same way.

'Get close, and scan them with the MIPEC,'she demanded. Declaring a few seconds later that they were indeed similar; she also told me they had two hearts, but the same basic reproductive organs. I asked her to channel the image though the glasses. The picture came on and I could see their internal organs, they indeed had two hearts. But it was their lower bodies which showed the biggest change, the stomach and bowel area was much smaller than ours and the females did indeed have the same reproductive organs. Not being a doctor though, that's about as far as I understood.

The picture changed to them naked, their funny little bodies as smooth as eggs. I turned to look at the men, and saw that they too were the same as us. It must be a million to one chance that two species had developed to be basically the same, and made me wonder if they had been our first visitors. What if millions of years ago another species had populated both planets?

'I can see them naked,' I said,

'Yes it's a function of the MIPEC,' the voice replied.

'Do you mean all this time I could have been looking at people naked?'

'Such a complex facility was not developed solely to allow you to inspect the bodies of young women,' she replied haughtily, 'I refuse to activate the function except for medical purposes.'

I knew that tone and deciding to leave it for now, headed outside.

The three pyramids were complete and the ground cleared. A deserted quarry was visible about five hundred metres away.

I could also see a town nearby too, the houses made of stone.

'What will they do with the workers and their families?' I questioned, 'The helmets would have given them their instructions. But they must have learned quite a lot from the organisation of labour and their building techniques. And I wonder what happened to the sleds? Can you pick up any broadcasts?'

'Yes but they're difficult to decipher, as were the ones in Egypt, I will need another day.'

As it turned out we were unable to leave anyway. The rules stipulated the crew needed more rest.

Leaving Hypatia busy in the hotel bedroom working on the language, I returned to Teotihuacan and explored further, this time with the aid of a professional English-speaking guide.

'No one knows who built the city, or why?' He said in that sing–song accent of Mexicans when they speak English.

'There's no evidence of a leader or king, and for the first 500 years it seems to have been a utopia. But then it appears to have been abandoned, again no one knows why. We believe they descended into a society where human sacrifice dominated their lives, which eventually destroyed them.'

The modern day ruins are very interesting, covering as they do, a vast area with 600 smaller pyramids, and various other buildings spread out tantalisingly. The guide repeated the story of Teotihuacan being an incredibly large city at its height, bigger even than ancient Rome. A city where the people lived in stone houses, this was at a time when most other civilisations in the world were living in mud huts.

'Where did the stone come from?' he asked rhetorically.

'From the pyramids I was in yesterday,' I thought: But I can't tell you that and you wouldn't believe me if I did.'

The Pyramid of the Sun is the largest stone pyramid in all of Pre-Columbian America, and has a base of 226 metres, almost the same as the great pyramid at Giza but is only about 64 metres tall. The guide also told me that the location of this pyramid has been sacred since the Formative Period, when the earliest layers of the pyramid were constructed over a natural cave, which was used for some time as a shrine by the Teotihuacanos. I'd have loved to inform him, that it had been sacred for much longer than that.

☐

CHAPTER TWENTY SEVEN

We flew directly to St Johns Newfoundland arriving in the late evening. The international airport is only about five kilometres from the city, so I hired a BMW X8 for the crew and myself. The IPEC had booked us into a hotel she had found on the Internet, with the strange name of "The Spa at the Monastery and Suites," which was in fact very good.

I chose not to take advantage of the spa, dining alone and afterwards retired to my room to study the area with the IPEC. We went again through the IPEC's memory banks discussing the location of the old city and when would be the best time to select for our arrival, deciding to make our first visit at 9500 BC.

'We must make sure that we don't visit on the same dates that Anders was there.' I told her 'We might meet him, or worse the other IPEC and upset the balance of time; who knows what could happen? Choose another month entirely.' She looked at me as if I was simple.

Have you made any progress with the aliens language?'

'Yes' she said. 'But it's not as straightforward as we hoped. When they speak telepathically we're unable to monitor it. Yet they're somehow able to transmit it by radio waves, which would make it theoretically possible for us to speak to them. Conversely they could discover our existence by listening to ours.'

'That's serious,' I said.

'Not really,' she replied thoughtfully, 'we're both transmitting in different timelines. In the meantime the transmissions they've made do tell us a little. I've made some progress with their languages. One of which is phonetically based and made up of a series of words and clicks.

'This is the language they use when communicating with each other telepathically or by radio, I have cross matched these with some African languages especially Xhosa, observing certain similarities.

The Khoi-San people of Southern Africa, also known as Bushmen whose language is extremely old possibly 30,000 to 50,000 years is the nearest match I can find to the aliens. This could mean that we've been visited by these beings for much longer than we thought and of course the Bushmen are small about the same height as the aliens; anyway the result is that I'm able understand their basic language.

Their other language is of course Aymaran. It's known to be many thousands of years old and is still spoken today. Mainly around Lake Titicaca and the high plains of Peru, Bolivia and Northern Chile. Known as The Altiplano

Called by some scholars the language of Adam, it's based on binary logic, and has often been put forward by many prominent scientists as a possible intermediary language for computerized translation.

Please remember. When in Atlantis we will be 11500 years back and I know from my last visit that there are some differences. I learnt quite a lot from our visit to Mexico, for example the flying saucer is only capable of local travel. The aliens arrived in an interstellar craft, much larger. It has crashed or malfunctioned, they didn't say which, or where, but it must be somewhere on Atlantis.

Of one thing we can be sure, the main players are based there. The leaders name as far as I can determine is Nau, very interesting, because Nut and Nau were names of the ancient Egyptian Gods, known by them as the Gods of the sky.

Others names mentioned were Nun, and Atum, these when taken in conjunction with Ammon, and his consort Ament, lead one to obvious conclusions. Their names are mentioned quite often in the discussions I have monitored. As are the names of Shu, and Tefnut, these two names are really exciting, because legend has them as the two Gods who made their own bodies.' She looked at me, waiting for my response.

'I knew it?' I cried victoriously. 'That was my earlier theory; maybe the idea of regeneration was not so fanciful after all. It could be that the pyramids are capable of changing the appearance of the aliens, allowing them to take on human form.'

'Your idea could possibly have some credence,' she replied reluctantly. 'They might even have been the first Pharaohs. Yesterday, all this would have sounded ridiculously far-fetched; but today I'm willing to consider anything.

'That's really all I've discovered, except for just one mention of the home planet. If we are to uncover anything important, we need to go the main city. The problem will be carrying enough food and drink to last for four or five days, remember you must carry me too.'

'I propose to take only biscuits and cheese, no tins or jars. I'm too excited to sleep. Can you infuse me with the San language? What about Aymaran? It sounds an intriguing language.'

'Yes it is,' she replied thoughtfully. 'But may I suggest that for the moment we concentrate on San, it's quite a simple language. Unfortunately it will only give you a basic knowledge because the aliens speak a much fuller version but I'll try to boost it with everything I have assimilated. Please put on the headset we'll do it now.'

The next morning we set off toward Logy Bay stopping at the deserted spot where Anders had found the city.

'I've already set the time and date for 8-00 am, 1st June 9500 BC, she informed me.

I stood on the mat with all the equipment, and said.

---Activate---

The town was quite near fortunately, but would still be a fair walk to the bay. How was I to carry the backpack full of my essential equipment, as well as the IPEC. Which was quite heavy?

'What have you got tied to the back of that pack?' she said. 'You look like a mountaineer.'

'Just essential supplies,' I replied, 'but as you surmised, it's too heavy to do in one journey. I'll take you first, and come back for it,'

The dress of the people I saw in the village looked Egyptian, but their language was Aymaran

'Do you understand what they're saying?' I asked

'Generally yes, although there are some differences. I may have made a mistake. Perhaps I should have given you this language.'

The yacht was in the Bay and looked amazing. It lay low in the water and brought to mind a sprinter on the blocks. I boarded immediately, storing my luggage against the bulkhead and climbed on the roof to study the folded wings; this really was a fantastic craft. Looking over the side I could see spreading out beneath the boat more of the superstructure I assumed this would be the anti-gravitational system and couldn't wait to get under way. As I walked round the boat I could see it was round and seemingly flat. Probably another of the flat turbines we saw in the saucer. I promised myself a trip into the engine room as soon as the opportunity allowed.

Choosing a seat at the front, next to a window and making myself comfortable we set off. The driver pushed a button and sat back. The boat glided away from the jetty and picked up speed. The bridge controls must be automatic I decided. If it travels at the sort of speed Hypatia said, the driver's reaction times would have to be phenomenal. He's probably just there for emergencies.

The journey was quite comfortable, smooth and fast. The seats moulded themselves to one's body automatically, the faster the boat travelled, the more they gripped. Unfortunately not with me, my seat couldn't sense me sitting on it. But I could see them doing it to the other passengers, who all looked extremely comfortable. When we were doing about sixty the whole thing rose out of the water and accelerated. The wings deployed and we flew about 6 feet clear of the water. The craft was already doing about 200 MPH when the windows darkened. We could still see out though. I thought the darkening might be to compensate for the effects of the speed over the water.

And then we shifted into top gear. What a feeling, and so smooth I simply couldn't believe it. Except for my trip in the SR71 it was the most exciting experience of my life.

'11500 years and we haven't got anything like this,' I waxed enthusiastically. 'It really is beyond belief.'

The trip, which Hypatia assured me, was all of 600 kilometres, took less than an hour. The health and safety would have had a field day with this little lot I reflected gleefully. They would have it off the water in ten seconds flat.

'This is fantastic' I said, 'If we could duplicate this, we could make a fortune.'

'You already have a fortune. I've told you this form of propulsion isn't invented until the 22nd century and the sophistication levels of this craft probably not until the 23rd. You're not allowed to interfere with the future. Is that clear?'

'Yes Ma-am.'

As we slowed down the windows cleared and the island came into view. Mountain ranges spread out before us as we cruised into the bay and settled next to a jetty.

Built on a flat plain a few metres above sea level, the pyramids dominated the city. I knew from a talk with the IPEC that Quilapayum was laid out in a circular form, rather like a dartboard. And canals in straight lines met at a central lake. The main canals were intersected by circular ones which crossed at regular intervals.

When everyone had alighted, I took the IPEC and my other equipment inside a large open building nearby and went off to explore. It had roads running alongside the canals but no transport, only pedestrians. There were large public buildings fronted by great Doric columns, sitting atop imposing marble steps. Most of them boasted painted friezes around the top section; no scenes of battle though. The subject of these friezes appeared peaceful, mostly of agricultural scenes and the central theme always included bulls. I saw some large statues of them too.

As I looked around I became fascinated by the great buildings. This was after all eleven and a half thousand years back in time. Everywhere seemed reasonably quiet and as people passed me they seemed happy enough. Others were travelling on the canal in reed or wooden boats but the absence of wheeled transport was really odd.

'Did you see any wheeled vehicles when you were here last?' I asked the IPEC.

'No' the voice replied. 'It seems strange does it not? To us it's so fundamental, and yet, have you noticed, as well as the canals, they have roads. That very fact makes it illogical, they must have the wheel?'

'What about the sleds?' I asked. 'Maybe they use antigravity vehicles on the roads, although I have to admit I haven't seen any. Well it's no use worrying about it now. The pyramids beckon'

I carried the IPEC into the centre of the city leaving it inside an oblong structure with large pillars, and after going back for the rest of the equipment set off breathlessly to see the reason we had come. Except for people working in the fields and fenced cattle each with a great bull, the whole area was very quiet.

'During the last visit we established they were not meat eaters. The similarities with the Hindus raises certain questions don't you think?'

Approaching the pyramids I noticed the centre one was again built on a rise making it the same height as the larger one, and the third again painted red at the bottom.

No other buildings were evident in the vicinity, but to the South and West, lines of gigantic volcanoes, some with wide saucer shaped tops towered over us and might have had something to do with the island's destruction; certainly they were large enough.

'Will you go inside to check if the inner chambers are the same?' the IPEC asked, 'and whilst you're there please visit the other two Pyramids, I'm interested to know whether they too are identical inside'

They were old friends now, but climbing the staircase from the Grand Gallery to the control room, I saw the passages were taller. I believe in hindsight that although the aliens were only about 4 feet tall and were able to stand upright in the passages of the other pyramids. In Atlantis more of the indigenous population may have visited the control room. It's possible therefore, that they built them this way purposely. The control room had more desks than the other two and the chambers were larger, containing an additional 10 marble sarcophagi.

'Hypatia can you hear me?'

'Yes, go ahead'

'The chambers are bigger, and contain 21 empty sarcophagi otherwise they look the same. Interestingly, this time the stairs to the control room lead directly from the grand gallery, it's occupied, but only by two aliens who seem not to have much to do. I'm going to visit the other two pyramids.'

These were also similar to the ones at Giza, but their underground vaults led via wide staircases to a series of large chambers, containing a substantial number of the metal boxes I had seen in Egypt. The ceilings of these rooms had apex supports made of long solid slabs; clearly the weight on them must have been tremendous. 'Have you discovered anything?' I asked, whilst walking back to her position.

'Not with the aliens' she replied. 'But the place you left me is the temple of Ammon. He is represented as a man seated on a throne holding a royal sceptre. I'm able to see his giant statue at the end of the great hall. In this form he is one of the nine deities who together form the Ammon-Ra circle of Gods. The other eight are made up of Ament his consort, Shu, Tefnut,

Hehui, Hehet, Kekui, Keket, and Hathor. Listening to the priests giving talks to some of the people who worship here I've learnt that Ammon has many other temples dedicated to him around the city. However in these he is depicted in other guises.

There are a series of temples in the city dedicated to a selection of other Gods also. I'm reasonably sure these will be our Alien leaders. Whether they were here on earth and were the officers of the original space ship, or whether they're the Gods the Aliens themselves worship I'm as yet unable to establish.

Shu and Tefnut we've heard mentioned before as possibly being able to change their form. I'd propose that the main sarcophagus is the vessel employed for the metamorphosis. We have much more to see here, but my recommendation is that we change timelines to 10400 BC and see these so called Gods, first hand?'

'Won't we have to return to our own time to choose another setting?'

'You know very well we do. We have to go back on the yacht to St Johns and come back again at the chosen time. However there is a question mark as to whether the craft will be in operation that far back'

'What about if we had our own small boat and could do it here?' I asked smugly.

'We know the island will disappear, therefore so will your boat' she scolded. 'There's no other way!'

'What about a rubber dinghy?' One that will travel with us, we could sit in the harbour and float about until we transport.'

'Tell me?' she enquired suspiciously. 'Would the 'rubber dinghy' to which you refer be that flimsy plastic contraption you had rolled up, and strapped precariously under your backpack in the place of your sleeping bag?'

'Yes it would.' I replied, 'Do I deduce a note of uncertainty in your tone? Surely you can't object to a short Atlantic cruise.'

'Would I also be correct in assuming that the short Atlantic cruise to which you so confidently allude, has as its central thrust you squatting precariously in the aforesaid children's paddling pool clutching the IPEC tightly to your bosom whilst being ceaselessly battered by gale force winds and forty foot waves 600 kilometres from the nearest landfall? Because if this is the case, then yes! You may indeed refer to it as "an uncertainty of tone." I would in fact prefer that you incorporate the word 'insane' somewhere within the proposed scenario.'

'You've absolutely no sense of adventure; it's actually a very strong dinghy, and saves us a long trip to St Johns.'

'It may have escaped your notice, but I am an electronic device and would remind you that water and electronic devices are not compatible. Which brings me conveniently to another slight flaw in your somewhat questionable strategy?'

'You seem intent on finding weaknesses with my well thought out plan. But please do continue with your negativity.'

'Very well I shall. Is it not the case that couched within the heart of this cunning plan is the proposal that whilst sitting in the aforesaid floating coffin. You will perch on the flexible foil mat and return to our own time. Am I getting warm?'

'Positively boiling. 'I confirmed, smugly.

'So far so good' she countered. 'Are we then also to assume, that when sitting on the said mat, we select 10400 BC and return here?'

'Correct' I agreed

'I'm indebted to you…. Please now explain to me how you propose we prevent ourselves from drowning when arriving back in our own time; because in 2024 there is no Atlantis and I can't swim, and I certainly don't float.'

'I shall manfully paddle the dinghy until you select the chosen date.' I replied proudly.

'Really!' she retorted, 'I'm extremely pleased to hear it. However, one last question does present itself? If we're sitting in the dinghy, on the foil mat when we activate, how would you suppose the dinghy will participate in our journey. Is it not the case that to share in our little adventure, the dinghy must also be part of the team, joining us on the aforementioned magic carpet?

'OH…. Well…. erm. OK, so you finally spotted my deliberate mistake…. I am pleased to inform you that you've been successful with your 'traveller in time' oral paper; and are now entitled to use the letters T.I.T after your name. I'm nearly back at your position. Shall we head for the Jetty?'

Once we had arrived back in St.Johns I said

'Rather than abandoning the trip, what if we buy a very strong small rubber boat and fasten the mat to the bottom? We must first see what's the fastest we can transport, back and back again, let's go back to the vehicle and try it.'

We did so, discovering it could be done in seven seconds, Hypatia would do it internally, there would then be no possibility of me messing up

'If we do it on the beach it will be a little better, we would only have seven seconds on the water and we can select the summer time. I say we go into St Johns, buy a boat or have one made, and just do it.'

'You seem determined to kill yourself and destroy me. She said wearily 'Oh why not?'

CHAPTER TWENTY EIGHT

St Johns is a city where fishing and sailing is the norm. Consequently a factory shop specialising in inflatable and other small boats was easily sourced. Inside were boats of all sizes, including a very well made small inflatable with slatted floors, extendable oars, removable rowlocks, and a pump. The whole thing was extremely light, rolled up to a manageable size and came complete with a carry bag. The man in the shop fabricated some straps for us, which fastened to the deck of the dinghy via nylon ropes. These spanned the outer walls, and passed through some holes he made in the foil mat, fixing it under the boat.

The mat is only as thick as the average aluminium oven foil, and led to some rather awkward questions. Because normally when something is said to be indestructible we nod our heads and disregard it, assuming the claim is simply a figure of speech. This poor man ruined five new drill bits trying to make just one tiny hole in our truly indestructible mat. He was only successful when he followed the IPEC's advice and used a titanium tipped punch fitted to a powerful hydraulic press.

Swearing him to secrecy, I told him it was a new military material for the SAS and their Canadian equivalent. Who according to the IPEC often train in that area. He in turn assured me he was an ex Canadian marine, and knew how to keep his mouth shut. He made some straps for the rucksack, which enabled the dinghy to be transported on my back and a fold up cloth satchel for the IPEC allowing it to be carried on my shoulder or chest. We dispensed with the electric pump and instead took a small hand pump for emergencies. I paid him well for his services, and swore him again to total secrecy

'How will you manage to carry everything?' Hypatia enquired

'It won't be far,' I told her. 'We'll manage; we'll just have to leave behind everything we can. I'll live on polony, cheese and cream crackers. Not forgetting a few chocolate bars of course.'

'Naturally,' she replied, and made an uncalled for comment about my stomach.

We travelled back on the boat to Quilapayum, and immediately yomped to the beach using the road. The weather in the beautiful bay of Atlantis was perfect for our time travel exercise over the water. Fastening the foil under the boat and securing it to the ropes, I ensured it came high up the sides and wrapped over the edges. The IPEC and rucksack were lashed to the floor, the oars were the extending type, which I fixed in the rowlocks and laid along the top to fall within the confines of the mat.

'It's up to you now Hypatia, please try to beat 7 seconds.'

---Activate---

It really did happen suddenly. From the sand to an open ocean (quite calm) and back to the beach again. This time though we were on the edge of the sea so I had to row us in for few metres and as soon as it was possible leapt out and dragged the boat onto the beach. Whether it was the sea's movement or the bay silting up in 890 years I don't know. But we would have to remember the positions for the return journey.

'Well Hypatia' I said thinking about the exposed module 'So far so good, did you get wet?'

'No, the bag helped and the rucksack covered me pretty well, spray can't hurt me. Only if I were to be submerged would the trouble occur. Can you see the pyramids?'

I looked around, turning a full 360 degrees hand over eyes imitating the actions of an explorer. 'Yes as a matter of fact I can and would you believe it, they're exactly where we left them.'

'Very funny,'

'The city isn't the same though. It's much smaller, with no harbour. I'm tempted to leave you here with the dingy and the rucksack, but we must find a safe place. There are some trees about 30 metres away; maybe I could lash the boat to one of them. If I turned it upside down, the rucksack could be left underneath, and so could you.'

'If you're sure that the tide won't come this high,' she questioned. 'By all means leave them. But you must take me with you. I need to be within the central area of the pyramids to allow the monitoring of the radio waves and their conversations.'

Carrying the IPEC in the new bag and with a couple of chocolate bars in my pocket we set off for what I hoped would be the ultimate experience of my life. Approaching, I saw some aliens standing at the base of the stairs, thank goodness for that I thought, knowing it would not be pleasant getting the IPEC back into the boat so quickly.

I counted sixteen of them inside. Four were clearly the duty shift, sitting at the consoles concentrating on their screens. Something important was happening, because the remainder were involved in lengthy discussions.

On the wall was a map of the night sky the constellation of Orion in the centre, a group of four, some way off from the others, were speaking audibly with clicks and stunted words. The conversation was hard to follow, but some of it made sense. One of them, who incidentally looked identical to the others, was clearly the leader. They always stand out: it was the confident way he stood, rock steady, and listening intently to whoever was speaking. The other three were turned slightly inwards and were forever glancing at him for approval and clues as to his mood; He on the other hand always let the other party finish, never interrupting.

As far as I could judge, the leader was being briefed about the signals to and from the home planet. They were telling him the chambers were working efficiently, and the tetracyline cells were fully charged.

After a while I went down the stairs to the trapdoor, but it was again locked.

'They must have something very sensitive inside, to keep it locked like this,' I told Hypatia after I had returned to the control room. There were two humans in here now, talking to three of the aliens in what sounded like Aymaran. Why hadn't I learned it?

'Hypatia can you hear me?'

'Go ahead' she replied.

'There are two locals in here speaking Aymaran I think. I'll put the MIPEC near to them.'

Twenty minutes later they left, and Hypatia said. 'They are building a temple to the God Ammon- Ra, and wanted some advice about a construction problem. I've also learnt that Ammon-Ra is a deity to whom even the aliens pay homage. He lives in the heavens and as far as I can determine is the same as your one true God. I find it fascinating that they worship their one true God, and yet let these people build temples to themselves.

'Nau is indeed the leader of the mission, and may very well be in the room with you, he is sometimes also referred to as Amon, she pronounced it Aymon. Not to be confused with Ammon.'

'I think I've met him' I replied. 'They're dressed the same, and all look the same. But this one was definitely the boss'

'Come back now please, we'll review what we've learned and try to make a plan. Are we staying the night?'

'We should' I replied thoughtfully, 'we need to find out as much as possible, the journey is much too arduous to do too often.'

'In that case you should take a look inside at the sarcophagi. I believe you may find they're being used.'

In the King's chamber I saw clear evidence of habitation. In addition to the additional marble sarcophagi, a low composite table with matching chairs stood in the centre of the room.

A large rubber mat covered the floor. And banks of additional lights hung under an air duct suspended from the roof with individual pipes snaking down to finish just above each sarcophagus. A series of multi shelved desks had been positioned around the mat, and placed on these were various sophisticated miniature monitoring devices, each giving an assortment of digital readouts.

Wires ran into just eight of the sarcophagi, each of them containing an alien lying on a thick rubber mattress.

The patients were dressed in identical white linen smocks, through which holes had been strategically cut and probes attached, rather like an ECG monitor. They looked to be in a deep sleep, clearly alive, and breathing slowly.

'Run the MIPEC horizontally above the body,' she ordered, 'I wish to make a full scan of their internal organs, I didn't expect to get this chance and it's too good an opportunity to miss.'

'Can we take a look at the Queen's chamber too?' she asked.

We did so, but it was not being used.

'Why not go back and gather the equipment whilst I download all the information. You should also find somewhere for us to spend the night.'

I had wanted to spend it on the beach because there would be little chance of me sleeping when the pyramids switched themselves on! But Hypatia insisted we stayed, she wanted to use the time to monitor the aliens. I trudged off to the bay and collected the rucksack deciding at the same time to sling the dinghy on my back; it would cover me if it rained.

Arriving back, I nearly died…. A flying saucer had landed on the top of the IPEC! Breaking into a run I called out to her breathlessly in a wild panic.

'I'm over here where you left me,' she replied calmly.

'I thought the saucer had landed on the top of you.' I told her breathlessly when I found it had actually landed some metres away.

'It certainly came quite close and gave me a few worrying moments. Not about being crushed particularly. I was more concerned about the magnetrons. Theoretically they could have blown all my circuits. In fact the anti-magnetic field might have destroyed me completely.

'I can't decide whether you would have been stuck here, or returned to the future, which in this case would have placed you in the middle of the Atlantic Ocean? Incidentally I heard the crew being told they would be here for two hours.'

Contemplating a very lucky escape I couldn't decide if it would have been better to speedily drown, or slowly starve. One thing I did know was that the mat, which was still fastened to the underside of the boat was immediately going back into the IPEC's drawer. So with slightly shaking hands I unfastened it and re-connecting the umbilical packed it away vowing never to separate them again.

Afterwards as I lay eating my cheese and biscuits, washed down with a sip of water to preserve the limited amount we had brought, I added a little of it to the glass of 1973 Killyloch from my hip flask.

'Whisky?' she scolded, 'You promised only to bring essentials'

'Precisely, if only I had known just how essential, I'd have brought the whole bloody bottle.'

When I'd settled, we talked about what had been learned in the control room.

'The chambers are for the re-generation of their bodies,' she told me, 'they apparently lost some people until the first chambers were built. On their own planet they live for about 650 years, which allows the vast distances of space to be covered. When they find a planet that will support life they monitor it until the inhabitants develop enough to warrant a permanent observation station. At that point they build a pyramid to allow the aliens that are left behind to rejuvenate and live safely inside whilst observing the population.

They confirmed the three large pyramids were the first to be built exactly for that purpose. The other six were built later when everyone was well again. These last six were built as transmission stations, and definitely followed the orientation of their home constellation.

'I still find the transferring of their minds to a human body intriguing' I said 'it would explain some of the questions I have about certain of the Pharaohs and some South American civilizations. Did you hear anything of the interstellar craft?'

'Yes that was the other thing, the leader has flown here in the local saucer from the interstellar spaceship that vessel is unable to take off for some reason.

It has its own rejuvenation chambers on board but they don't work. The equipment was therefore transferred to the pyramids. They only work in space apparently. It seems the Earth's ozone layer interferes with the process, don't ask me why, or the reason they work in a pyramid shape on Earth because I don't know. It may possibly be because the ozone in this timeline is undamaged, and substantially denser than in ours. I should add that in my opinion the pyramid shape is used because it's impervious to weather and the ravages of time.'

'The interstellar craft.' I cried excitedly, 'I must see it. Why don't we go back with them?'

'What about food? It may be weeks before they come back here'

'No. This saucer is a working vessel; it even went off somewhere today after dropping the passengers off. I think it's worth the risk?

'It's your life; just remember I've been through this before,'

Letting down the dinghy, and packing it in its bag, I loaded it together with the rucksack, and the IPEC into the cargo hold of the craft, and lay down exhausted.

Sometime later I was awakened by Hypatia's voice, telling me they were loading.

'How long have I been asleep?

'One hour, 14 minutes, and 22 seconds'

Fifteen minutes later the saucers engine started smoothly, the counter rotating plates causing only the slightest tremor as it lifted off. It took twelve minutes to reach our destination but as we had no sensation of speed, the distance we had travelled was unknown. I waited for them to shut everything down and everyone disembark before venturing outside.

We were parked in a large hanger next to two identical saucers, one of which was stripped down, probably for maintenance.

'We must be inside their ship' I submitted, looking around me at the circular shape. 'I'm taking everything out and leaving you in the hanger whilst I investigate just in case it takes off again, unlikely at this time of night, but one never knows?'

The IPEC insisted I place her next to a particular piece of wall containing a computer console and asked that a device she called a probe, which magically appeared from a drawer I didn't know existed, be placed on the consoles desk. She explained the device was to allow her to keep in contact with me whilst on the ship. This made sense when one considered the alien electronics on board, and I set off to explore.

The shape of the hanger was half the segment of a circle with the centrepiece filled in. As far as I could judge from my paces it measured around 190 to 200 metres across; it's height about 50 metres in the centre, reducing to 35 at the edge.

Leaving the hanger section I found another area in which storage containers were piled to the roof, secured by adjustable sliding walls made of some kind of transparent plastic glass. Yet another section was for mechanical spare parts, and included workshops and small parts stores set on several mezzanine levels within the main body of the 50-metre high compartment.

On the walls in various parts of the craft were sectional and plan view drawings showing a side view of the ship with a 'you are here' highlighted square of the relevant section, plus a plan view, deck by deck with the hanger section highlighted. The writing was undecipherable but a drawing is the same in any language.

Above me, in the centre of the ship another five floors were shown, and above them, a large dome. I assumed this would be the control room area.

'This thing must have a crew of hundreds,' I said overawed. 'The civilization that built this is way out of our league, especially when one considers we are 12,500 years in the past; I'm pleased they seem friendly. I must see the control room, and try to get outside; it really is very impressive Hypatia.'

In the hanger some of the crew were working on various tasks and again all looked facially identical. At least this time they wore different coloured uniforms. I hope their mothers can tell them apart I thought, because I certainly couldn't.

The first opportunity to explore came when the lift arrived. The doors opened, allowing four aliens to disembark, I jumped in just as the doors were closing and found I couldn't stand upright; the lift car was only built for small beings not ones at nearly six foot. I looked about me for the controls, but there were none. 'It must be voice activated,' I told the IPEC, which of course meant I was trapped inside. Fortunately the dilemma lasted only a few seconds, because it set off by itself; stopping at another narrow floor where two more identical aliens entered, one of them clicked 'top deck,' and off we went.

When the doors opened I entered a large dome made of a transparent substance interspaced with clear integral ribs. It certainly wasn't glass because darkness had already descended and it didn't reflect the light of the room allowing one the pleasure of looking into the clear night sky as if standing in the open air. It would have been even better in complete darkness but we were surrounded by a brightly lit clearing, at least 500 metres wide. Beyond that was dense jungle.

It made one appreciate just how far back in time we had actually come because Mammoths and Sabre toothed tigers would still be roaming around outside.

'Hypatia I said rhetorically, 'I've just had a thought; we must visit the Jurassic period and see the dinosaurs as soon as we have a chance.'

The dome was in fact a giant lounge and contained seats and tables, but no bar; maybe they hadn't discovered malt whisky yet? And the very fact that it had such a place on board, suggested it wasn't a warship.

I also saw some smaller versions of the aliens who I assumed were children, which more or less confirmed it.

How stupid we humans are, I thought, why would it have to be a warship? Wars are for primitive people. And a total waste of energy, these beings probably didn't even have the word in their vocabulary.

☐

CHAPTER TWENTY NINE

I waited for the elevator to arrive and let the passengers disembark before jumping in. After a long few minutes it set off, stopping at a residential floor, where two more got in, and ordered it back to the observation lounge. This went on for a good fifteen minutes, until finally one of them clicked 'Control room.'

I suppose the variations concerning the design and layout of the control room in a space ship are limitless. This one though, was exactly as I'd have imagined, probably because it was a larger version of the local saucers.

There were no windows, just a large screen which followed the circular walls. And counting the number of seats, was commanded by a crew of twelve. What appeared to be offices or day cabins lined one wall at the rear, and indeed one of these was where my fellow passenger headed; otherwise it was quite basic.

It was twenty-seven minutes before the lift returned, and a further nineteen, before I arrived back at the hanger.

'It's a fantastic vessel,' I said studying the plan, 'There's just the power plant to visit now and according to this it's on the other side of that bulkhead, but there seems to be no door. I'll have to use the lift again. One would think there would be some stairs: for emergency use at least.'

'There are;' she said, 'Look at the layout of the segment opposite, there's a ladder shown going up to the engine room level.' She was right; I put the MIPEC back in my top pocket, and found a door to the other section.

Hypatia can you hear me?'

'Of course, go ahead'

'This section is filled with thousands of sleds stacked tightly together; there are other construction tools too. They have the most incredible folding cranes with telescopic jibs, and boxes upon boxes of cutting tools and lasers, all neatly stacked floor to ceiling. Each box has a small picture of what's inside.

I can also see the hydraulic rams and all the pipes stored in what I assume are numbered sections. The local saucers must have been very busy. I wonder if all this is part of this ships normal cargo?'

'I would assume so,' she replied. 'They probably thought the humans were ready for constant observation and planned to build a pyramid. There can't be too many planets with an atmosphere like ours in this part of the galaxy.

'But why would they get marooned? I questioned. 'The ship seems intact with all its systems working; it doesn't make sense.

The rungs of the ladder were closer together than is usual, and even at two at a time made climbing surprisingly awkward. At the next level a platform led to another door.

'It's all made of composite materials Hypatia, including the ladder, the door, and the floors.'

Through the door were more ladders, these ran up the side with observation windows at various levels. The windows were made of a material similar to the dome section. Next to the windows were more doors, these were open and very thick.

Inside, was a 15 metre wide tube made of a clear material and inside this was another, about 10 metres wide. There were three more metre wide pipes tinted red, green, and yellow inside this one and I climbed about in and out of the various rooms and tanks in the immediate area trying to decipher their purpose.

After about 30 minutes of exploring I realised I hadn't spoken with the IPEC

'The main engines are off line as one would expect, but the ship is still generating some power. The life support systems are working so there must be another source. Probably a reactor like the smaller craft.'

'That's very good' she said smugly, 'You are quite correct!'

I guessed immediately…. 'What exactly does that mean my dear Hypatia?'

'Only what I said,' she replied. 'Most of our theories seem to have been correct.'

'But how exactly do you know?' I pressed, dreading the answer.

'I became tired of merely speculating and interrogated the ship's computer to confirm my theories'

'Are you telling me you adjusted our transmissions by the time difference and jumped timelines?'

'Not quite, I adjusted only the transmissions, our delay in time is still there. I simply wanted to be in a position to talk to the ships computer.'

I couldn't believe she would be so reckless.

'We are going to have a serious discussion about your reasoning for such an irresponsible act later, but in the meantime you might as well tell me what did you discovered?

'The life support is indeed provided by the nuclear reactor, which produces a massive 800 megawatts of power. This is necessary because it also provides the ignition power for the sub Hyperonic propulsion system. A plasma engine which drives the ship to 0.67% of light speed and is infinitely controllable.

The three tubes you described are the fuel feeds to the thermoprotonic propulsion system. Each tube contains its own element, which react against each other with the resulting energy being expelled from various ports. One is anti-matter, created from antiprotons: The other is matter, made up of multi-protons. The last is xenonic-radon, which acts as the catalyst. Light speed is achieved by producing a series of controlled thermoprotonic fusions.

When the ship is travelling above 0.52% of sub light speed propelled by the plasma engine a specific quantity of antiprotonic fuel is fed into a fusion tank. The interior wall of this fusion tank is separated down the centre by a powerful force field. A slightly larger quantity of positively charged multi-protons are released into the other half of the tank and the force field progressively removed. The resulting unbalanced matter-antimatter annihilation instantly heats the mixture to billions of degrees and produces unimaginable power. The thrust produced is capable of accelerating the craft to almost instantaneous light speed and beyond.

This is made possible because of the clear composite material you saw in the dome and the containment tubes, which are capable of withstanding pressures millions of times greater than anything known in our time.

The reaction is called thermomatter syncretism, or 'power of the Gods.' The final component is the catalyst: hypercooled xenonic-radon. When introduced to the mix, it reinvigorates the matter/antimatter fusion with sufficient energy to increase the speed to 4.5 hyperons. If more speed is required a further controlled thermoprotonic reaction is induced.

This is achieved by feeding the spent fuel into a cycloramic proton accelerator which gives the craft a top speed of 8.94 hyperons.

'The method of how the last two processes increase the speed to those levels is particularly ingenious because they're lesser expansions, producing far less thrust. To travel beyond the speed of light conventionally isn't possible. Not only because as Einstein realised, the speed of light is the maximum achievable, but also because space is littered with trillions of rocks, from giant boulders to pebbles, even gasses consisting of minute debris.

At sub light speeds, without a powerful force field providing a boundary layer, the debris would destroy the craft in seconds. At light speed and beyond, the vessel would simply not be able to avoid them. At nearly nine times the speed of light it would be destroyed in milliseconds.

'What the aliens discovered when they first reached light speed plus one, is that space itself protects the craft. A cushion is formed in front of the ship, rather like one sees in experiments in a wind tunnel, and then closes behind forming an envelope. This cushion distorts space, deflecting the debris around the ship, even though space is a vacuum.

What they then discovered is that time itself becomes distorted. Once light speed is achieved the power needed to accelerate within this bubble is much less, because time itself is accelerating with you.

What apparently happens is this: Time is compressed within the envelope and shoots the craft along in its own little universe, a new dimension where the recognised laws of physics no longer apply, in effect, a vacuum within a vacuum. To slow down, one simply reverses the procedure, directing the power forward.

A side effect of this phenomenon is that whilst travelling inside this mini universe, the craft becomes invisible. The distortion of time shifts it into a different element. In effect it creates naturally what the IPEC generates artificially.

Impossible, was my first thought but I was obviously fascinated by this information.

'The force field used from sub light, to light speed is magnetronicly induced anti-matter that repels anything within 1500 metres, and is so powerful that even a missile couldn't penetrate it. The down side being, it takes a lot of power to operate, but as the transition from zero to light speed is almost instantaneous it's not a major problem.

'How the craft arrived here is almost farcical. After a journey of 806 light years, the ship was descending from a high, to a very low orbit around the planet to assist with the unloading of the equipment when the Plasma engine suddenly failed. The ship entered the atmosphere and began to burn. The captain had no alterative; he adjusted the angle of the descent, and allowed it to crash land. The plasma engine, which would normally have been retracted into the body of the craft for landing, wouldn't retract and was completely destroyed.

'The vessel's main propulsion systems have been repaired but are of course much too powerful to allow take off from within our atmosphere; these vessels are designed to exist in space. The main engines, as we've heard are built to accelerate at great speed, but only in the vacuum of space. Releasing such an incredible force of thermo dynamic energy within the earth's atmosphere would result in instantaneous disintegration. They believe that the planets gravitational field will hold the ship. Even a microsecond will result in the whole ship and everything around it instantly vaporising.

There's also a very real possibility that the fusion tank was damaged too. It's not possible to enter the tank without first fully purging the system, which they're unable to do until the fuel can be transferred into another vessel.

'It took them over 60 of our years to get here, and the rescue ship may not arrive for decades. They may be able to travel faster than light speed, but their signals can't, and as their average lifespan is only around 650 years, it's likely the older members of the crew will not see their home planet again. Their only hope is for one of their passing ships to see the signals and come to their aid.

'We actually did very well with our hypotheses; one of their tasks is to build pyramids anyway. These creatures have built pyramids as lasting beacons and regeneration stations for their fellow travellers on many other habitable planets around the universe.

'Because our captain 'Nau' needed to build them much quicker than normal and because you are similar beings, they took a calculated risk and medically advanced the human development so they could be trained as their workforce. It's certainly not normal for them to interfere as much as this. The forced development of the indigenous peoples is absolutely forbidden to them, but they've always felt empathy toward your species.

The regeneration incidentally, is the reason for the pyramid shape, and houses within it a tetracycline collector. The tetracylines are attracted to the shape, captured and modified in the equipment until a concentrated regenerative beam is formed. This life-giving beam is then introduced to the body which of course is lying in the marble sarcophagi. The tetracylines cannot pass through marble and permeate into the body's cells regenerating them. The spent tetracylo's are then ejected through small ducts built into the walls of the pyramid.

It transpires that their original intention was to build only three pyramids, the first in Atlantis, the other two in Mexico, and Egypt. The other six were built later when the construction of the three great pyramids was finished and working. You'll love the reason why.

They built the other six, not for just for signalling purposes but also for moral. Nau simply wanted to find meaningful work for his crew, his idea being to keep them occupied until they were rescued.

The configuration of the pyramids does duplicate the layout of the stars of their home constellation but isn't the real reason for their pattern. It is in fact the alien sign of distress, which although similar to the stars in Orion's belt at this time, isn't the exact arrangement. If you look at the night sky in this timeline, you'll see the arrangement of the third pyramid, and Alnitak is inverted.

'I've discovered one other snippet of information. They've constructed more sets of beacons around the world. One in what is now China, very near the Tibet border in the Qinghai Province. The other is in modern day Russia around the Bering straits, in the Kolyma Range. I have their coordinates.

The configuration seems again to correlate with the layout of the pyramids, and is meant to describe the pattern as the world turns. They're apparently built inside the craters of extinct volcanoes, and are substantial buildings containing the same signalling devices as are fitted in the pyramids. There are also other sets of pyramids one in particular at Visoko near Sarajevo in modern day Bosnia.'

I had listened to her enthralled but remembered she had put us in a great deal of danger

'This information is fascinating Hypatia, but you've taken a seriously irresponsible step. How do you know the computer won't reveal our presence?'

'Because I am more powerful than it, and have wiped its memory of the whole examination.'

Deciding I couldn't win this one, and anyway what was done was done, I shut up. We returned to the smaller craft where we sat for nearly three hours waiting for it to take off. Only when eventually it did, and was gently accelerated away did I relax. Thirty minutes later though, the feeling of dread had returned.

'We should have landed by now' I told her, 'where can we be going?'

One hour later we landed. The door opened, and through it, I saw the pyramids,

'Phew, I was getting worried.' I admitted

Hypatia agreed. 'We could have landed anywhere. At least we got here eventually?'

Carrying everything outside and looking around, I exclaimed.

'We have a problem…. the landscape is familiar, but I'm afraid it's not Atlantis! We appear to have landed in Egypt! What shall we do? Get back on, and hope they go back soon, or re-materialize here?'

'I'd rather not face the ocean again,' the IPEC answered. 'But the crew of the Gulfstream are going to be a tiny bit surprised, when we tell them to collect us in Egypt.'

'I agree. We need to think about finding another reason.'

'Not one, two: You should have called Julie from Mexico.'

'Oh my God, what have you done to me you crazy computer. I'm a dead man!'

At least the crew were appeased; she ordered them home, telling them we were going to stay awhile, at the same time diverting another plane to Cairo to pick us up. No one was any the wiser.

We spent a considerable time speculating about what might have happened to Atlantis. It's possible that when they were rescued they destroyed Atlantis to protect their secrets, including that wonderful machine.

Maybe they tried to get the ship off and it exploded. Or it could simply have been a natural disaster. Who knows? Maybe we'll go back one day to find out.

In the meantime we had so many other places to visit and explore.

CHAPTER THIRTY

What I needed was another project, anything to take my mind off the aliens who still consumed me at night. I required something truly exciting, and if possible based on myth.

And then it came to me…TROY,

'Hypatia…. We need to go to Troy and find out if it really existed? … Well, we know it existed, but is it true? To see Helen, Hector and Paris, now that's more like it. This is why we were fated to be together, I see it all now. We'll take the company yacht, can you find out when we can have it for a few weeks?

'Imagine the excitement of seeing the city of myth. Did Homer tell the truth, or was it just a good novel? Did Achilles really exist? And Athens, we can go there too.

'Oh Hypatia I'm so excited. Can you imagine visiting the Parthenon when it was new? How about, we invite a Greek Scholar to accompany us? He can give me a guided tour of the present day city and buildings.

'I saw something of Athens a few years ago, but it was only during one of our cruises on the Queen Victoria. We only had a day there but I'd love to see it properly. Oh, and we also went to Olympia and Ephesus, we must go there too. You're a gift from the Gods Hypatia.

'We can anchor at Athens and take it from there. Please look around for a Greek historian? One that also knows something about Troy, find out what University he or she is from. I'll contact the Vice Chancellor to see whether a donation of some kind would help. Where's the Yacht now?'.

'It's on its way from the Caribbean to Florida to disembark,' she replied proudly. 'It's been on charter there for a month.

'When it's done can we send it to Athens. We'll meet it there?'

'No can do!' She said smugly, 'We are picking up the next passengers in Miami and cruising to Monte Carlo where they will use it for a series of meetings.'

'How long' I enquired impatiently.

'Two weeks, I can keep it free for the next 20 days, but it must in Funchal on the 24th September.

'We seem to be doing very well with the charters?'

'We are,' she replied. 'We offer a very competitive package including using our own planes to fly the customers to the yacht and back. This saves vast sums on fuel and ensures continuity.

'Sounds good to me,' I said. 'OK. Inform the captain he's to be in Athens in three weeks. We'll meet him there. Please arrange the flights.'

'The yacht is in Europe and will be free for 20 days in two weeks' time.'

I told Julie. 'Why don't we have a two week cruise in the Aegean. We could ask some of the family to go with us? And ask an expert on Ancient Greece to join us as a guide.'

'I really must spend some time at the office.' she mused. 'But it does sound a nice idea and we hardly seem to spend any quality time together these days …. Yes why not'

The name of the man was Professor Conrad Dyson. We picked him and his wife up at Stansted Airport in a Citation XLS and flew directly to Athens. The yacht was waiting at Piraeus, and the ships helicopter at the airport.

We spent the next few days around Athens. Where Conrad explained how ancient Athens had been a powerful city-state and the main centre of learning. Largely due, he recounted to the great impact of its cultural and political achievements during the 4th and 5th centuries BC.

Known as the cradle of Western Civilization, Athens was the home of Plato's Academy and Aristotle's Lyceum. Named after the Goddess Athena it was the leading city from 500 BC to 323 BC, a time often referred to by historians as the 'Golden Age of Greece.'

In 431 BC Athens went to war with Sparta, but due to its losses during a terrible plague, it suffered a great defeat and had its walls destroyed as a punishment. Some remains of them can still to be found today, especially around the coastline of Piraeus. We spent most of our time wandering around The Acropolis, which dominates the city and means either 'The Hill', or what was built on it. I also learnt that almost every Greek city had its own Acropolis, where the townspeople would flock in times of war and seek protection inside its walls.

In the 6th century BC the first stone temple to Athena was built on the 150 metre high Athens Acropolis a natural rock formation which as I have stated towers over the city.

The Persians destroyed this temple in 482 BC when they invaded. But after only two years Athens had recovered enough to reclaim its rightful place as the leading state in the area and Perikles, who had become the leading figure in Athenian politics decided to rebuild it.

He decreed the new Acropolis was to be built on a monumental scale. The new city must reflect the power and influence it held over all other Greek city-states and central to this was to be the Parthenon. It was to be the major building on the Acropolis and the principal temple to the Goddess Athena.

The foundations were laid in 447 BC and completed in 438 BC. Built entirely of marble it measures 70 metres long by 30 metres wide and is undoubtedly one of the true wonders of the ancient world.

The building even today is breathtakingly beautiful and it made me tingle with impatience to see it in all its glory. Poor Conrad, he knew so much, but I think the poor man, whom I had come to respect greatly would have willingly given his life for just one hour during the time period we had selected.

Julie came into my office later, and asked,

'Where are we sailing to next week?'

'Well, I definitely want to see Troy.'

'I thought as much,' she said decisively. 'I have to go home for two days, a meeting I must attend. I'll re-join you with Debra for the last few days with the family. Hypatia what about Christopher, have you arranged to fly him over?'

'Yes.' the IPEC responded, 'He will arrive with your other guests in three days. I've arranged for a luxury coach to bring them to the yacht.'

'That's wonderful, is it possible for you get me home tomorrow?'

'Yes,' she answered. 'We have the new Dassault Falcon bringing some people to Crete; I'll have it stop by and collect you, would 1-00 pm be acceptable?'

'Perfect, I'll leave you to make the arrangement for my return, possibly with the family if I can complete my business in time; can you organize a car to pick me up from the airport?'

'Certainly'

'What would we do without you?' She had turned away by this time and only I saw her expression. Poor Hypatia.'

The next day, I suggested to Conrad that he enjoyed some free time whilst I saw Julie off at the airport, taking the opportunity to inspect the very impressive Dassault.

Around 7-00 in the evening just as it was getting dark we set off for the Acropolis in a hired Range-Rover.

'Set the date for 1st August 330 BC Hypatia --- 9-00 am.'

---Activate---

The scene changed to one of bustling movement, we had chosen to materialise on the edge of the Agora where people were going about their daily business, merchants and scribes were busily plying their trade and a slave market was underway, a young woman standing on the block.

'Can you understand what's being said?' I asked.

'Of course,' she replied clearly miffed. 'She's a Persian captive owned by a family at Eleusis being sold to pay off a debt.'

The smell was awful, and holding a handkerchief over my nose I asked

'Don't they have sewers around here?'

'Yes' she replied. 'That's probably what you can smell! Perikles is famous for bringing fresh water to the city and also for disposing of the waste'

'Well he didn't do it very well' I replied. 'The place stinks; no wonder they had so many diseases.'

'I think possibly it's because we're in the centre of the slave auctioning area, probably the rest of the city will smell sweeter.'

I huffed and still holding my handkerchief to my nose, watched the auction.

The woman stood for a few minutes whilst the bidding went on around her. After a while it slowed, and she was made to strip by the slave master. Then naked and with the threat of a whipping was forced to parade around the dais.

A man called to her, and the slave master made her go over and stand before him.

'He is asking if she has had children,' Hypatia said, as the man roughly thrust his left hand between her legs with one hand, and crudely pinched her breasts with the other; he said something and the crowd laughed. The young woman who was sobbing by now, backed away, receiving a lash from the slave master. The bidding continued, the man finally buying her. We read about slavery in ancient times without realising the personal ignominy it engendered. But believe me to see it happening before your eyes is truly sickening.

'I've seen enough of this disgusting place I'm off to the top of the hill.' In the distance the upper section of the Parthenon was visible. The ultimate edifice to the Gods it was perched magnificently at the top of the known world.

The visits with Conrad had been invaluable, but if he could see this Temple as I could see it now, he would have been beside himself.

The entry to the Acropolis is through the main gatehouse called the Propylaea, a split-level entranceway built in white marble. Nearing the gates, the Temple of Athena Nike was the first building I saw. It was fronted by painted Ionic columns and had a wonderful carved frieze depicting the Gods in battle scenes. Studying them I realised once again just how lucky I was.

Beyond this the Parthenon shone out. The colours were astonishing. Like the pyramids I had imagined everything white. But nothing could have been further from the truth; it was red at the top, with finely carved and painted metropes of battle scenes.

The great columns were pure white, but between them were gold statues. I carried on walking, until I stood next to one of the main columns 'The Parthenon.' I whispered softly, running my hand up and down the flawless marble enthralled with the reality of the dream. It looked larger than in our time, and much more imposing.

People worked all around me, some sweeping, others selling and some offering their services as guides. The building was astounding and a very special frieze ran around the top a full 160 metres long. It decorated the horizontal course set above the interior architrave of the temple and depicted a procession which started at the west end and progressed eastward along both its sides.

Known as the Panathenaic procession it illustrated a new dress being carried up to the Acropolis by the people of the city and offered to a wooden statue of Athena.

Today this frieze with its superb weather worn sculptures is missing from this magnificent building. Much to the Greeks despair they are still displayed in the British Museum despite all the promises of their return. I've marvelled at the Elgin Marbles on numerous occasions, but never as I saw them now. The figures were remarkably lifelike and so graceful in the morning light and so wonderfully fresh. The horses and chariots three or four deep were carved with an amazing perspective and brought the whole scene to life. I walked around the building at least five times drinking in the movement and colour, trying to etch into my already overcrowded brain the sheer beauty of it all.

The men's cloaks and other clothes had been painted with stunning reds and blues but it was the armour of the soldiers which made me gasp; each piece had been gilded with gold and silver and even though it was not in the direct sunlight caught every available source of light, which caused it to blaze with life. The delight I felt was almost climaxual. I think Hypatia realised this and let me drink in the beauty in silence.

Inside the Parthenon, the temple had been divided into two sections. To enter the larger east room which was about 30 metres long one had to pass through a low door and emerged 'bowed' into the presence of a huge gold and ivory statue of the Goddess Athena. She stood about twelve metres tall and on her head wore a crown with incredibly realistic horses jumping out at full gallop. At her feet offerings had been heaped against the base.

Who actually ended up with all these goodies I can't say, but it seems to me that the position of high priest must have been quite sought after.

'Hypatia' I asked, 'Are you there?'

'Where else would I be,' the voice said sarcastically.

'I want to see Perikles whilst I'm here, and if possible Plato; But definitely Aristotle.'

'Plato is already dead,' she informed me. 'But Aristotle, who was born at Stagira, in Macedonia, in 384 BC, is still alive.'

'Could you remind me about him?' I asked.

'He was the son of a physician to the royal court of King Amyntas of Macedon and moved to Athens at the age of seventeen to study under Plato at his Academy. He lived here for about twenty years, the last fifteen as a teacher. When Plato died in 347 BC, he travelled to Losbos where he formulated his theories on biology. You should note that these philosophies were so advanced they gave the world its definitive beliefs about the subject until the middle of the seventeenth century.

'After two years he moved to Assos where his friend Hermias was the King. But Hermias was captured and executed by the Persians. So gathering his wife and daughter Aristotle fled to Pella, the Macedonian capital, accepting the post of tutor to the King's young son Alexander. The young man must have shown some promise, because he later achieved some small notoriety in the world. We know him as Alexander the Great.'

'In 335 BC when Alexander became King, Aristotle returned to Athens and under his protection established his own school which he named 'The Lyceum.' It's said that much of the discussion in his school took place while the teachers and the students walked about in the grounds.'

'I suppose it might be known as the 'feet' of learning?' I quipped.

'It was actually known as the Peripatetic (walking or 'strolling') school.' She added, not amused at my brilliantly witty interruption.

'When Alexander died in 323 BC, strong anti-Macedonian feelings developed in Athens, forcing Aristotle to retire to his family estate in Euboea. He died there the following year.'

'I desperately want the opportunity to sit at the feet of the great man.' I said, 'So my dear Hypatia, can you please help me find him?'

'The Lyceum is located on the banks of the Ilissus, in an Eastern suburb of Athens and named after the neighbouring temple of Lycian Apollo.' the voice replied. 'Aristotle established the school and research institute there five years ago. Where, it is said, in the mornings he lectures to his students on the use of logic and metaphysics and in the afternoon, presents public lectures on rhetoric, politics, and ethics. What a pity I never gave you Ancient Greek'

'I'll be satisfied just seeing him, and hearing him speak,' I told her. 'Even if I can't understand what he's saying.'

Walking for about 50 minutes, I eventually found it. The time was 3-30 pm and he was giving one of his public lectures. Listening avidly, I noticed he had a strong resonating voice and was above average height for the time, with thinning hair and a curly beard.

Clearly self-assured and charismatic he smiled regularly as he spoke. I don't know if he had sponsors, or charged for his time, but he clearly wasn't short of money. The Lyceum was a large building, fronted with lots of columns and set in extensive grounds. Hypatia translated some of what he said, but it didn't matter because even though it was not possible to follow the complete dissertation, I was totally enthralled. Simply to be in the presence of the great man was reward enough.

He was a loving husband, the father of two, a devoted friend, and a committed teacher. It's said he did more to put both philosophy and science on a systematic footing than any thinker before or since, or at least until many centuries later. According to Conrad the common belief amongst most Greek scholars is that while the Greeks provided the intellectual foundations for Western civilization, Aristotle provided much of the foundation for the Greeks themselves.

'Let's get back Hypatia,' I said. 'I'll be with you in about an hour. We haven't seen Perikles unfortunately. We'll just have to save that for another time.'

'I'm truly surprised,' she said. 'In my opinion he was one of the most interesting men in history, the first true democrat, and a man of incredible vision. He was the architect of some of the world's finest buildings, as we have seen. And a General to rival Caesar: In fact his ability as a military planner poses the question. Who was the greater?

'He designed and built a 300-ship navy, each ship 120 ft long with 3 tiers of oars, easily the finest and most advanced navy in the world for its time. Just to achieve one of these things would have been a great achievement. He must have been a brilliant orator with incredible powers of persuasion to achieve them all.

'Perikles was clearly one of the most extraordinary men who ever lived; he certainly dominated Athenic culture for many years. Said to be a terrible snob, his circle included most of the leading intellectuals of the day. Nevertheless he was a true democrat, putting himself up every year for election to the city council.

'Athens was the world's first genuine democracy and in the centre of the city he built the world's first senate building. Five hundred citizens were chosen every year by open ballot to be Senators. They had the final say as to whether the tax money was spent on buildings, defences, or even if they should go to war.'

'I'm tired Hypatia, Anders gave us the ability to visit places over and over again, so why must we try to cram everything in at one visit. The Perikles you've described deserves better than that. Mind you, I would understand if some modern ladies were to take issue about the true-democracy statement, because at this time the population of Athens was perhaps 200,000, of whom only 50,000 were full male citizens. The rest, women, foreigners and slaves were not allowed citizenship. And only citizens were allowed to vote.

During the next few days I spent a lot of time with Conrad visiting many places in Athens and the surrounding countryside, preparing for future visits to the past by picking his substantial brain whist waiting for Christopher and our other guests to arrive.

The cruise was a great success; I spent a great deal of time with my son, who I introduced to Hypatia, and asked him to consider joining the company when he had graduated.

We stopped at Thessalonica for a short break while heading generally in the direction of Turkey and the fabled city of Troy. It took a lazy three days gliding over the calm azure waters past islands and coves, occasionally stopping for barbeques on the beach and a spot of scuba diving. The captain made up the time later by steaming at full speed through the night.

CHAPTER THIRTY ONE

My trip was for one purpose only, to see if the legend was true, my interest in archaeology is minimal. The thought of scratting around in the ground hunting for a piece of a 1000-year-old milk bottle simply doesn't do it for me and I must add, from what I've read, nor did it for Schliemann.

My interest is in the spectacular. Nevertheless an historian like Conrad made the whole place come to life. During the voyage he gave a series of wonderful lectures about Greece generally and Troy in particular.

'I shall try to keep today's talk quite short ladies and gentlemen' he told us, 'I intend to attempt to portray the general feeling of history and myth of this wonderful part of the world.

We'll begin by describing the location of Troy, which is situated just behind us.' He waved his hands toward a hill in the distance.

'It's only about 6.5 km inland from the Aegean Sea and overlooks the Dardanelles in present-day Turkey. We know it was founded in the Bronze Age, around 3000 BC, because the extensive excavations carried out at the site have revealed at least nine separate cities on the same spot. All have now been positively identified.

The Troy you'll no doubt be interested in is the city vividly described in the epic poems of Homer. The home of Priam, and his sons, mainly Hector and Paris, and of course Paris's lover the mystical Helen.

According to the legends of ancient Greece, the city was besieged during the Trojan War for 10 years, until eventually falling to the ruse of the wooden horse.' Everyone nodded, all knew the story.

'The city was originally called Ilium, after its founder Ilus: But was later changed, to honour the memory of his father Tros.

Legend has it that Ilus went to the city of Phryia, where he took part in games being held by the King. He must have been a great athlete because he won many event's, including the main one, the wrestling contest. The prize for which was fifty youths, and fifty maidens. The king, obeying the oracle, also gave him a cow, and asked him to found a city wherever it should lay down. The cow chose the hill of Ate to rest, and on that very spot, not wanting to upset the Gods. Ilus built the city.

Troy was always regarded as purely legendary, but in 1870 the tenacious German archaeologist Heinrich Schliemann followed Homers story to the letter and began to dig.

Herr Schliemann's excavations were to say the least, unusual. To get down to the level of Homers Troy he ordered his men to dig a deep trench right through the middle of the city, destroying everything in its path. In doing so he totally disregarded the conditions of his permit from the Turkish authorities.

Eventually though he unearthed the actual stonewalls and battlements of an ancient city. These were found on the mound known today as Hissarlik, which translates as the "Place of Fortresses." It was here that the most spectacular of Schliemann's discoveries was found. A hoard of gold, bronze and silver objects, which he decided would forever be known as 'Priam's Treasure.'

Formerly kept in the Bode Museum, Berlin they were lost in 1945, only to be re-discovered in the Hermitage Museum St. Petersburg some years later.

According to the Russians, they were taken for safe keeping at the end of the War. They are now on show in the Puskin Museum in Moscow. The level from which the hoard came however has since been established as earlier than the Troy of Priam, and the Trojan War.

Following his death the excavations were continued by his loyal assistant Wilhelm Dörpfeld whose work in 1893 and 1894 augmented our knowledge of the site, and solidified Schliemann's discoveries.

Fresh excavations were carried on at the site between 1932 and 1938, with a new phase of excavations being started in 1982. But the information lost from the upper sections following Schliemann's rape of the site can only be imagined.

Troy dominated commerce in the region for millennia mainly because it was here that the trade routes intersected. And where incidentally the wind blows constantly. Anyone sailing with the keel-less ships of the Bronze Age through the straits of the Dardanelles into the Black Sea would either have to risk their ships and cargo sailing into heavy seas, or transport their goods overland much slower and considerably more expensive.

The last possible port of call before embarking on the most dangerous section of this perilous journey was just over there.' He pointed at the coast through the large windows, 'The site of the main harbour.

You see ladies and gentlemen, once they had anchored. The Trojans had them trapped and the Kings of Troy demanded substantial tributes from the captains before allowing the ships to continue.

For hundreds of years the city served both Asia and Europe, and became enormously powerful. It's this detail that makes Troy so interesting to the modern-day archaeologists and historians.'

With that he bowed slightly as a signal that he had finished, and asked for questions.

Later Conrad, Christopher and I boarded the helicopter with the first officer, who doubled as the pilot, and set off for the dig. At first sight it was noticeable just how compact the whole place was, the main excavations being no larger than 200 square metres.

Troy is essentially just a large mound of ruins nine cities deep, and during our walk Conrad explained the different levels pointing out where each one started and finished. The teams of German archaeologists just carried on working. Being used to visitors I expect.

Conrad introduced himself to the professor in charge of the dig; and then to Chris and me, which gave me the opportunity to invite him and his team leaders to be our guests at dinner. However when I saw the disappointment on the faces of the others and realising that although they obviously loved their jobs it must still become quite tedious at times. I decided to invite the whole lot of them. 40 in total.

I did of course also realise that it might then be possible to get the helicopter to fly me over in the evening without attracting undue attention.

Later I loaded the IPEC into the helicopter, and with my rucksack filled for a long journey, set off to pick up our main guests. We were also using the large rubber duck speedboat, which could land anywhere, as well as the ship's barge, which couldn't.

Because of the numbers, Jacques was doing a barbeque on deck for dinner, and the wine was already flowing freely, hopefully making my short absence not too noticeable.

I took along a bottle of particularly good Chablis, and a 92 Pomerol with a terrine of duck liver pâté, queen olives and fresh ciabatta bread (as a consolation present for the two people who had been designated to stay behind.

When we landed, I waited until the passengers were on board and strapped in, before unloading my stuff from the storage compartment and waving them off. I had already explained my reasons to the pilot, telling him I'd contact him when I wanted to be picked up.

Delivering the gifts to the Germans I told them the helicopter would come back for me later, and they should enjoy the pâté and wine.

Alone at last, we set up and chose 1st August 1265 BC 9-00am. --- I had never been so excited, so took a deep breath, and said

---Activate---

According to the Iliad, the Archeans beached their ships and set up camp near the mouth of the river Scamander, the modern name of which is Karamenderes. The city of Troy stood on a hill, across the plain of Scamander and is where the battles of the Trojan War supposedly took place. And where, according to the Iliad, a large ditch had been dug to stop chariots attacking the city.

The first thing I discovered was that there was no ditch, and outside the city walls stood numerous houses and farms, unlikely in the middle of a war. The city walls were about 100 metres away and looked pretty strong, even to my 21st century eyes. Built of massive stones covered by sturdy shiny bricks, the bottom two thirds of the wall angled outward forming a thick base and adding to its already substantial strength.

'Which way for the gate Hypatia, left or right?'

'Definitely right' she replied, 'Towards the sea. There were reputed to be eight gates around the walls. The main one was called The Scaean Gate and should be next to a high tower called "The Great Tower of Ilion."

'OK.' I said, and set off in that direction. After a few minutes I saw it.'

I visitted Babylon some years ago and decided the walls and Scaean gate of Troy looked very similar to the reproduction of Babylon's Ishtar gate and walls.

'I think I can see the tower, it's one of many but this is easily the highest.' As I got closer, I added.

'Everything seems so calm. The gates are open, it's quite busy, and the people, who are dressed very similar to the Athenians are going about their business peacefully. The houses are colourful, and in good condition.

The walls are at least three metres thick at the bottom, no wonder they were never breached. Either the war never happened, or this isn't the right time. I'll climb onto the wall at the top of the gates and see if there's a fleet in sight?'

I suppose it was rather fanciful to expect to see a wooden horse standing around. There was also no fleet.

'Hypatia we're here at the wrong time, the bay is empty!'

'Don't be such a defeatist.' she scolded. 'You have looked forward to this so much, and yet give in at the first hurdle, Go into the palace and see who's on the throne? If it's Priam, we've at least got the right reign. Listen for any familiar names like Paris or Hector. The palace will probably be in the middle of the complex, can you see it?'

'Yes I think so,' I replied. 'The outside walls are hexagonal, and much larger than the excavations we saw earlier, there's a series of inner walls with lots of houses and shops built in to them, each one a defence for the next, it's very clever. The streets are quite busy, with people going about their daily tasks.'

Moving through them, the scene changed to a more military one. There were lots more soldiers now guarding what I supposed was the palace area. This was itself walled to a height of about four metres and had towers built at regular intervals. To the front was a large door, heavily guarded but open.

The palace stood on a hill in the centre surrounded by rising gardens, but one had first to pass through the main guard house, quite dark and full of tables and what I took to be sleeping mats, more were rolled up in the corner. Some of the men were clearly off duty, a few eating and others sleeping, a stone staircase led up to the next level where more soldiers were busy cleaning their weapons and others were receiving a lecture the instructor using a type of blackboard made of stretched animal skins, he was pointing to the lines and arrows explaining tactics.

From this a large door, fortunately open, led onto an unguarded paved path up to the Palace. I followed it, emerging through large columns into a well-furnished open area with decorated skins thrown over the seats positioned under expertly painted murals depicting really gory battle scenes.

A wide central staircase led up to a roof garden, quite sizeable, with an easily defendable bridge, from here two rooms each with a large balcony looked over the bay. A group of men stood on one of them looking out to sea. On the other ladies dressed in various styles of revealing gowns talked animatedly. They all wore their gowns off the shoulder leaving their right breast exposed.

'Are you able to hear anything Hypatia?' I asked

'No, can you get closer?'

One of the men was sitting on a 'throne.'

'This can't be Priam Hypatia, he's too young?'

'Not necessarily' she replied. 'We may have selected the wrong time, we're probably too early by ten or twenty years. Go over to them, maybe I can pick up some of their conversation?'

Walking over I placed the MIPEC on a table in the centre, and waited with them for at least 30 minutes, just drinking in the atmosphere.

Looking out to sea, it suddenly struck me where I was. This was what Anders had died for; I had been given something special, very special indeed! Here I was 3285 years back in time, in a mythical city called Troy, the place Homer had described. These people were real, they lived and breathed. Even if we didn't find what we were looking for, this was a gift I should cherish with all my heart. I had been given the opportunity to peer through the window of time into the age of mythology. Hypatia said finally.

'This is fascinating Jason, the man on the throne is named Laomedon, he's the king, do you remember him from the talks with Conrad?'

I walked over and collected the MIPEC.

'It rings a bell,' I said, pondering the name.

'So it should. He's the father of Priam; we're too early by some decades. Run the MIPEC over his body… He's only about thirty years old; Praim will be a child at this time, probably about ten. Homer tells us he was around sixty at the time of the Trojan War, possibly around fifty when it started, we should work on that? Let's say we try again in 1225 BC?'

'Sounds good to me' I replied, I'll make my way back to you.

'We've been extremely fortunate to find this timeline,' she said. 'We really can't expect to get the date exactly right immediately'

'Ok Hypatia let's try 9-00 am, 1st June 1225 BC'

---Activate---

CHAPTER THIRTY TWO

There were two parallel trenches, the first one about four metres wide and two metres deep fortified with stakes, the inner one defended by a wooden palisade. A temporary bridge spanned them just outside the gates, crossing it, and walking toward the city I saw many of the farmhouses had been destroyed. Eventually the bay came into view.

'The fleets in the bay Hypatia.' I shouted excitedly.

'Before you get too carried away,' she said, 'remember that the Trojan War was reputed to have lasted ten years. Are the ships beached or anchored?'

'It's too far away, I can't tell.'

'Point the MIPEC at them silly, and I'll tell you.... They're beached, but there's not anything like ten thousand of them. I'd estimate the number to be about two hundred; some may be away of course.... We've a choice, do you go into the city first, or visit the army of Agamemnon, Menelaus and Achilles.'

'The attacking army sounds like a good place to start,' I said, 'but they're quite a way off,

'The army is reputed to be between seventy thousand and a hundred and thirty thousand strong, let's say one hundred thousand. If it is anything like that size you should reach the first of them quite soon.'

'You're probably correct,' I told her, 'but from here I can't see their camp. OK, I'll see what I can find, how far did you say the MIPEC's range is?'

'You know perfectly well it's about twenty kilometres, there will be no problem keeping in contact, now off you go to find Achilles for me,'

I unrolled the tarpaulin and covered the IPEC, leaving the antennae exposed. I placed some sand from the ditch over the edges of the tarpaulin and set off.

She was right about the camp; it started only about a kilometre away, behind a rise in the ground, it struck me as strange that there no attacking soldiers watching the gates. They certainly weren't short of men because there were tents as far as the eye could see. Men were training, exercising and digging; a soldier's life it seems hasn't changed a great deal in thirty two hundred years.

The camp was set out in a crescent shape the centre of which I decided would be the logical place to find the King and his generals.

Trudging through the camp, the lively colours of the tents, banners and flags decorated the skyline. The smell also played a part in the general ambience, the odour of so many men messing in such close proximity causing a strong musty smell to permeate the air. Aligned to this was the intoxicating aroma of animals cooking on spits. Enormous copper kettles filled with vegetables hung off tripods over large open fires, the contents gurgling and steaming, adding to the miscellany of smells, the smoke from the fires wafted lazily into the atmosphere.

A long siege like this must have spawned many different emotions, and unless one had imaginative commanders, the boredom and almost residential aspect of the camp, allied to the unchanging surroundings, had to have been soul destroying. Imagine waking up every day for 10 years in the same environment. Unless the discipline was exceptional, the petty niggles and jealousies would lead to terrible fights. I walked on, heading for the centre, seeing lots of women around the tented area.

Eventually I came to some substantial tented dwellings with guards posted outside. I chose the biggest, and entered.

Four men casually dressed in leather skirts and cotton tops sat on cushions talking, there was really nothing to do except sit nearby and wait for them to mention a name, or at least something that Hypatia could recognise. The one in the centre was a big man compared to the others, he was quite broad with a strong face, the others also seemed very self-assured, but not to the same extent. The first would have stood out in any company, just by force of nature alone. Possibly Achilles, I deduced.

Taking a bottle of water, a chicken leg, and some bread from my rucksack, I tucked in and listened. It was over 10 minutes before a familiar word was uttered. One of them said 'Alexandros,' Paris also went by this name.

They jabbered away for another 10 minutes, until Hypatia said.

'They're definitely Mycenian, but exactly who, I cannot be sure. None of the names they've mentioned are familiar, but that guy in the middle, the one with the black beard and receding hairline is definitely their leader. They've been here for three years and eight months. The army by the way isn't 100,000 strong; he has just complained that keeping an army of 18,000 men busy is tedious. They're bored and want to go home, but the chunky one on the far right is urging them to wait it out. He may be the Spartan King, Menelaus, Agamemnon's brother, and Helen's husband. Black beard could well be Agamemnon, but that's just speculation.'

'I believe you're right Hypatia. His strength of character struck me immediately.'

'Wait!'…. she said, 'someone has just mentioned Achilles; yes there it is again. We could be on the right track. Why not rest in the tent for a while, it's nearly mid-day and the heat out here is quite overbearing. When we get back we must provide cover for the plugin module, I can stand very hot conditions, but we don't know about the module, and it does control the time travel after all.'

'Should I come back now Hypatia, you're worrying me?'

'No it's not too bad under the tarpaulin. It's just something to remember.'

Not being able to do much I placed the MIPEC near the fab four, allowing the continued monitoring of their conversation, and unrolling the sleeping bag lay to one side of them closing my eyes trying to savour the atmosphere. The story of the Illiad played out in my head as I rested:

'The saga begins with the marriage of Peleus, an ageing mortal king of the Naiad Thetis. All the Gods were invited to the wedding except Eris (which is understandable, because she was the Goddess of discord.)

Nevertheless to show no hard feelings she sent along a golden apple…. Engraved on it were the words: "TO THE FAIREST".

The Goddesses Athena, Hera and Aphrodite quarrelled over which of them deserved the apple. Unable to reach a decision they agreed to let Paris, Prince of Troy, decide.

He, being just a mere male knew he couldn't win this one, so closed his eyes and gave it to Aphrodite: She, so pleased to get one over her rivals made Helen of Sparta, (who was the most beautiful mortal woman in the world) fall in love with him. A feeling he reciprocated, and being by now totally infatuated, followed her to Sparta where he seduced her and took her back to Troy.

Her husband Menelaus the king of Sparta, asked his brother Agamemnon the king of Mycenae, to gather the other Achaean kings, and help him recover his honour by recapturing his unfaithful wife and killing her abductor, she would then be made to suffer whatever punishment he might choose to administer. He reminded them of the blood oath given earlier by all of the aforesaid Achaean kings.

Each had sworn to defend the marriage, regardless of which of them she finally chose. According to Homer an expedition of 1200 ships was assembled in Aulis, and after a false landing in Mysia, they successfully assaulted the bay and besieged Troy.

For ten years they laid siege to the city, raiding her allies for supplies while they waited. During this time Agamemnon using his brother's loss to further his own ambitions became the most powerful ruler in Greece.

Many attempts were made to take Troy during the following decade, which resulted in the tragic deaths of many Greek heroes, including Achilles, Telamonian, Aias, Hector and Paris.

The Trojans defended their city resolutely eventually driving the attackers away, or so they thought. In reality it was just a ruse; the beaten army had left a giant wooden horse as a gift for the victors.

The Trojans, instead of following the old adage telling them to beware of Greeks bearing gifts, and burning the beast, foolishly dragged it into the city and had a victory party. The Achaean soldiers secreted inside the horse, waited for the Trojans to drink themselves into a stupor, then dropped ropes and slid down.

They killed the guards on the gate, and let in their army who had secretly returned under the cover of darkness. As was the custom at that time, they mercilessly slaughtered the Trojans, before raping their women and children. Not content with this, they also desecrated the temples, thus earning the God's displeasure.

Homer wrote that as a punishment very few of the Achaeans were ever allowed to return to their homes. Although many were said to have founded new colonies in distant lands: Even the Romans claimed to have traced their origins back to this fight. They maintained Aeneas one of the beaten Trojans led the surviving army to Italy and was instrumental in the formation of the Roman Empire.

Hypatia's voice reverberated in my ear.

'Jason, wake up—wake up -- causing me to sit up with a start.

The man we had decided to be Agamemnon was standing next to his cushions being threatened by another man. He was extremely well proportioned, with long curly dark hair, a well-defined jaw, and close-set eyes. His eyes were without doubt his most noticeable feature being steely grey and which bored deeply into whoever was their victim.

I wouldn't have bet much on Agamemnon's survival at that moment. That he stood close to death was certain, and everyone inside the tent was powerless to stop it. Agamemnon knew this also, but to his credit stood his ground, while keeping his hands well away from his belt from which hung his short stabbing sword.

Rising from my makeshift bed and taking up a position slightly behind and just to the side of Agamemnon. I too didn't breathe, expecting him to be struck down. The tent was deathly quiet, the tension thick in the air.... Then, as if by a secret sign, the man relaxed, his demeanour noticeably changing. He remained alert and clearly dangerous, but his eyes transformed themselves to lifeless opaque globes he turned and walked out. No one else moved. Hypatia's voice intruded into my consciousness,

'That Jason; is Achilles, a living breathing God according to the Greeks of this timeline. But one must acknowledge he is impressive is he not? I'd love him to press my buttons,'

I know it's stupid; after all the IPEC is only a machine. But I actually felt quite jealous. Still, I have to admit, he was a bit special.

'I'm coming back to visit the city. 'I told her. 'I must meet Hector, Paris and of course Helen. This has been one of the most wonderful experiences of my life. I wonder what the problem was.'

Approaching the city gates, I asked again about the heat and the module,

'I've run a few checks,' she said. 'It shows no problems at the moment.'

'OK, I'll go directly into the city. The gates are ajar; clearly they don't envisage a threat today. It seems a strange way to run a siege. The Trojans will have no trouble keeping the city supplied if the Greeks don't guard the lines better than this. No wonder the war lasted ten years.'

Once inside I headed directly for the Palace. In 50 years the changes to the city had seemed minimal, so climbing up to the Palace I got a shock. The roof area had changed out of all recognition. The two rooms at the top, which had led to balconies, were now joined and closed in, making one large room. An imposing throne dominated one end, and lining the walls at each side of this were long seats presumably for the court to sit. A mosaic with a five-sided star in the centre had been set into the floor; inside this was a picture of Zeus riding a chariot to the stars. I remembered seeing a similar picture in the roof of the Propylaea on the Acropolis in Athens.... 875 years in the future.

The forearms and shoulders of all of the men were extremely well developed, clearly the rigorous sword-training regime was tremendously demanding. Of course considering that one's life depended on being able to maintain strength and stamina during a long sword fight, it was really no surprise

'It would help if they would wear name tags,' I quipped. Priam was easy; he was an old man by this time and sat on a raised throne looking out to sea. 'That surely must be Helen,' I said throatily, pointing the MIPEC at an absolutely stunning woman who was standing to his left pointing at the bay. She wore a light linen shift which, because the sun was behind her left little to the imagination. She was accompanied by an older woman who seemed to still be following the old ways and had her right breast exposed.

'I hope that is her, because she really is quite astonishing.' I said leeringly. She had blond hair, and green eyes. I tried to compare her with someone from the present and finally settled on the beautiful American actress Hayden Panettiere.

Her most stunning attribute was a magnificent figure. The delicious contours of her thighs and full breasts were clearly visible beneath the light whisper of the dress as the warm breeze gently kissed it and the sun fondled her sensuous form.

'I'd launch ten thousand ships for her,' I croaked, my voice had deserted me.

'She's only twenty,' the voice chided. 'You should be ashamed of yourself.'

'That's rich coming from you, what about Achilles? When I re-energized you my little neoteric brain I thought I was getting an emotionless computer, not a conscience. There's nothing wrong with admiring a beautiful woman, especially one who has stirred the imagination of men for over 3000 years.'

'She may not be Helen anyway' she barked, 'There are lots of other possibilities.'

'Believe me, that's Helen, a woman like her comes along very rarely. Please switch on the see through mode, I wish to check if she has any tattoo's.'

'I absolutely refuse,' she replied spitefully. 'The facility was developed for scientific purposes only, I used it myself only a short time ago to medically examine Achilles.'

Smiling and refusing to bite, I placed the MIPEC on a table nearby and wandered around the royal apartments, and did indeed find other beautiful women, but an awful lot more who were less so, In other words a normal mixture.

Nothing would convince me that she wasn't the fabled Helen. After about 45 minutes I returned to the table and collected the MIPEC.

'What did you discover?' the IPEC asked.

'Not much, the Royal apartments are quite large, which is no surprise seeing there are so many royal children, 50 boys and an unknown number of girls, (they didn't count the female children.)

The upper walls have been extended and more watchtowers added. Did you hear anything?'

'Yes,' she replied. 'Both Paris and Hector are in the group, can you see the dark young man to the left, the one who is well built, and very athletic looking? That's Hector. Paris is the one holding the woman's arm.' So she was Helen? He was a handsome youth, with a beautiful complexion, a rarity when looking around most of the men.

'The other woman is Hecuba, Priams wife and the mother of Paris and Hector.'

'Paris looks rather feminine don't you think?'

'Less fearsome than most of this bloodthirsty lot, certainly,' she responded, 'He looks like a sensitive young man, I can imagine a woman like her falling for him; her husband is much older of course, and gave me the impression that boys played a large role in his life. He would probably prefer to take Paris home rather than her: While you were sleeping, he and his fellow Kings openly fondled the serving boys in the tent of Agamemnon.'

'We've at least proved that the books are based on true events.' I said. 'The main characters did exist I'd like to see the wooden horse too, but we could jump about for days looking for the exact timeline. If this is only three years eight months into the campaign we could still have over six years to go. I suppose we could have one try. Let's say, exactly six years four months further on. It would seem logical, and who knows we might get lucky? But I don't want to try lots of times; we could be weakening the module with the constant activity. I'm coming back.'

'Have you got the date selected?' I asked when we were back in the present day.

'These ruined walls have started to make an awful lot sense to me now. The last year of the war should be the most exciting anyway. That's when Achilles kills Prince Hector in a public fight, when he learnt that his lover Patroclus had been slain.'

This all started when Agamemnon was made to give up his lover Chryseis by her father the God Apollo. He became jealous of Achilles and banished his betrothed, Briseis, from the camp.

Achilles was outraged by this command which he considered to be petty and vindictive, and stormed out.

On his departure he gave his armour to Patroclus who of course proudly wore it in the next battle.

Thinking he was fighting Achilles. Hector, to great acclaim, sought him out and slew him.

When Achilles was told of this, he realised his friends death was his fault and became distraught swearing vengeance on Hector. He returned to Troy and publically challenged Hector to meet him in single combat. The resulting battle was a classic and resulted in Hectors death.

'Whether we can find the exact time remains to be seen, but let's at least have one last try, let's go in the afternoon I'll leave you to select the time and date.'

---Activate---

We materialised not in the shadows of a giant wooden horse, or single combat, but in the middle of a large-scale battle. Why the Trojans had left their sanctuary after ten years I have no idea. But I found myself surrounded by thousands of men cutting and chopping each other to bits.

The screaming and cries were awful, and blood was running everywhere making the grass slippery along with the other nasty results of battle, the opening of dying men's bowels. As the battle raged it became clear that the Trojans were losing and were slowly withdrawing toward the gates of the city.

Suddenly a great blast of horns rang down from the walls and the gates opened, Hundreds of fresh soldiers charged out and joined the fray. One minute I was in the centre of absolute carnage, and the next, was practically alone with the bodies of the fallen as the Trojans pushed the Greeks back. I had seen too much bloodshed already so was not so nauseous. But it left me saddened to see the total waste of life.

Fifteen minutes later it was over. The attacking army was defeated, or at least in headlong retreat towards the sea, the Trojans followed, screaming abuse at the retreating army until another series of great horn blasts from the walls stopped them in their tracks.

They re-grouped and tended to their wounded, while the enemy wounded were cruelly slaughtered

'This is the way of ancient wars,' Hypatia said.

'I'm sure you're right but it doesn't help. Let's go back I've seen enough, I don't care if they make fifty wooden horses. It's not worth it!'

'But don't you see,' she cried, her voice full of emotion.

'Why would the Trojans come out and fight, they've been safe behind those great walls for ten years? I submit there's only one reason and that's because Priam had ordered it, And why would he do that except through grief and the need for revenge?

What if his eldest son had just been slain, the heir to the Kingdom of Troy? Yes I'll wager Achilles had just killed Hector in single combat? It's one of the defining moments in Greek mythology Jason. We have to go back one more time.'

I was swept along by her enthusiasm, she was right of course, it all made perfect sense. If they had fought in front of their respective armies it could have been only an hour before.

No…. The Trojan army would be watching from the walls and have to be mobilised that would take at least three to four hours. The attackers would be outside goading them. Pumped up after seeing Hector fall, it would not surprise me to see Achilles at the front leading them.

'Working on that scenario, four hours would seem a logical assessment.' I said pensively. '

'Four hours then,' She had to have the last word.

'They are supposed to have fought for over an hour, the intensity of her voice almost making the MIPEC vibrate.

'OK but we need some ground rules; three attempts maximum, the module must be considered. I don't fancy spending the rest of my life here, Helen or no Helen'

'Agreed,' she replied.

---Activate---

We got it in two; the first time Hectors body was lying on ground bloodied and broken. His men preparing to take it back into the city.

'According to Homer, Achilles reputedly towed it round the lines for nine days or so after killing him. Clearly this has just happened, so we know that at least isn't true. We should try one hour further back.'

We did, and sure enough they were fighting, how long they had been at it I can't say, but the both still looked quite strong and evenly matched. Hector wore leather with gold insets between the joints, separate leg and arm protectors and a shield of reinforced leather with a gold bull on the front, his helmet was bronze with a red plume. Achilles wore a black and gold chest protector and helmet, set with gold and silver, his plume made of tightly woven gold thread. His shield, also leather carried a motif of Zeus.

The swords were short but looked heavy to me and even these two Titans had to stop occasionally to rest, leaning on their swords and panting. All the while staring at each other, neither spoke.

The heat was increasing as the sun climbed higher and I didn't envy them one bit. They looked pretty evenly matched, both in size and skill; clearly fitness would decide the outcome of this contest.

Slash and retreat was how it looked to me, I don't know what I expected but a sword fight between gentlemen this was not! The object was to kill and mutilate and it wasn't pretty. Slash parry, slash parry go for the legs and then the neck and legs again and back off.

I was right though it was tiredness that finally decided it. Hector tried a big slash missed and slipped, Achilles immediately chopped at his legs cutting viciously into the left one just above the knee, as Hector stumbled Achilles drew back his sword and stabbed him viciously in the neck. No offers of mercy or last words. It was simply. You lost you die… At least it was quick.

I trudged back to the IPEC's position and immediately transported back. The whole thing had been an anti-climax. It was at this point I realised what I was doing.

I was blaming them for not giving me the Hollywood version. Would I ever learn? War is not pretty? It is the true version of hell. And until we realise it our species will never progress to the next level of development.

I called for the helicopter.

Back on the ship the party was in full swing the archaeologists clearly enjoying their change of scenery.

After the introductions had been completed the conversation obviously turned to the excavations, principally the discovery of the trench, and some new walls.

The MIPEC was in my stateroom, so when I told them to look about 100 metres to the east for the outer walls because the area they were excavating now was in fact the palace area, the voice in my ear, which should have warned me, didn't. This conjecture was met with astonishment,

'You seem so sure' my confidante said, 'It is almost as though you've seen it.'

'No,' I said backtracking furiously. 'It just seemed to me when I was walking around today, they might not have been the main walls, but rather a ring around the central palace. They could have easily been off centre with the front gate, and the intermediate walls further forward. That would allow room for the citizens to be housed inside the walls without encroaching on the palace.'

'It's a possibility,' he said ponderingly, 'but not very likely.'

I breathed again

'Please disregard my speculation,' I pleaded, 'I'll wager you must get heartily sick of we amateur sleuths.'

Grabbing a steward I said, 'Mario, please get Dr.Schlemmer another glass of white wine' and moved off to talk with another guest, determined to keep my mouth in check.

The next morning the IPEC informed me that General White the US Air Force Chief of Staff had called. He said there was no urgency but asked if I would visit him during my next visit to Maryland. She also informed me that they were having some trouble at the Maryland factory with the master modules. I knew I was going to have to discuss the problem with Stephen and convince him to allow me to ask Peter Allen to re-join the company.

Hypatia again reminded me I didn't need his permission. We owned the controlling shares. But like him or loathe him, he was still the managing director.

The date of the next scheduled meeting had arrived and the IPEC with its alien helper transported to it.

The first item on the agenda was the trip to Mexico and Atlantis. The IPEC gave a full account of its findings from the interrogation of the ships computer and the relevant points of interest to the aliens. She then asked for their indulgence as she wished to enquire about the times and distances required for space travel. She told them she had learnt from the ships computers on Atlantis that 12500 years ago it had taken sixty years to travel between the two worlds, and even longer for transmissions to be sent and +received. Yet from previous discussions it was clear transmissions were now much quicker, as was the interstellar travel.

'Without going into too much detail,' he told her 'communications with our home planet are now considerably quicker as are the speeds at which our vessels are now able to travel. We can now journey between this planet and our own in just over two earth years. That's all the information I am able to give and even then I have exceeded my authority. Please now carry on with your report.'

The IPEC thanked him and gave its statement concerning the progress of the computer manufacturing facilities globally, including the production and sales figures and followed this report with another, giving a comprehensive description of where they were with the travel businesses, and its future plans.

The aliens questioned the IPEC closely about both subjects, but were especially interested in the problems at the American factory. Expressing their deep concern over the possible delays. The IPEC told them that they had some technical difficulties. The problem, she explained, were the hidden modifications built in to the new master core for the next generation of computers. She had some theories and simply needed to confirm them with the alien technical team before proceeding.

CHAPTER THIRTY THREE

Three months later the US factory was doing well they had recovered their schedule. The production machines were in their final positions, as were the sterile assembly lines. Peter Allen had recharged the morale of his teams, and thanks to Hypatia I was, able to solve the problems with the modules.

Most of the production machines were now working and the assemblers performing as expected. We were working toward our ultimate target of 32,000,000 computers per year in the US with a further 8,000,000 in London and 18,000,000. In Malaysia

As promised I made contact with General White, who said,

'I wish to see you and your computer Mr Shaw. Please make an appointment to come to the Pentagon in two days' He gave me the name of his aide, and rang off.

'You do realise we will have a problem getting inside,' Hypatia reminded me, 'My nuclear battery will set off every security device in Arlington.'

I telephoned the Generals aide and explained that X-rays would cause problems to my computer, which of course; the General thought, was also the shrouding device and he arranged for it to be allowed in without being scanned.

After being shown into his large office, I unpacked the IPEC and placed it on a table. The General was civil enough face to face, and thanked me for my efforts on the platform. But said despite that and my discussion with Andrew Blythe he still had grave concerns.

'You must understand Mr Shaw you're in possession of one of this country's most closely guarded secrets, and following your flight visited the top secret area again. This time taking photographs of it.'

'Yes sir I did,' I admitted, 'but only for insurance, the photographs were returned. The saucer is a beautiful thing, but at the end of the day it's just a plane, surely it's not worth killing people over.'

'No one has been killed sir,' he said indignantly,

'Threats are enough for me to take such things seriously General, someone will see it eventually, it only needs one person to talk?'

He looked ready to explode.

'No one has talked mister and they will not. Not on my watch.'

'I gave all the photos back sir and I'll not discuss it with a living soul, you have my word on it, I'm not stupid, I realise my position is somewhat tenuous, I'd be crazy to talk about it.'

'Which brings us to the shrouding device; we must consider it a threat.

If it were ever to fall into the wrong hands whoever had it could gain access to anywhere, even the White House.'

'Please believe me when I tell you no such threat exists General. The safeguards are simply too numerous and extremely complicated. Only I am able to use it, anyone else would immediately disappear, never to be seen again.

'I've already placed the IPEC and myself at the disposal of both our countries. We stand ready to help if the situation is serious enough. Hypatia, say hello to General White'

She popped up.

'Good afternoon General,' she said in her sweetest voice 'How nice to finally meet you face to face. How are you today?'

The entrance was not lost on him.

'I'm very well,' he said coolly. What if you were to fall into the hands of our potential enemies, especially one of the terrorist groups, they could force you to work for them.'

'They couldn't General. There's absolutely nothing anyone could do to make that happen, I would simply shut down. And before you ask, if they threatened Jason I'd self-destruct, making him of no value to them.'

'They might torture him?' he said

'Indeed they might, but you see General, I'm a machine, I have no emotions, simply logic. And logic would dictate if I didn't exist, they would have no further need of him.'

'They could make him build another?'

'It's a good point, but without a very sophisticated laboratory, and many years work, it would be impossible. Prior to self-destructing, I would get a message to you, mentioning your Mother's middle name, and another word you'll recognise. Then, giving you our global position I'd expect you to try to save him.'

'What word is that?' he asked

'Anastomosis'

His face changed abruptly, registering a look of horror. At the same moment the telephone buzzed. Answering it, he looked directly at the IPEC as if listening to her. Four minutes later he replaced the receiver without having said a word.

'Please believe me General' I said blindly 'We've considered this carefully. One thing Hypatia has omitted to mention is the IPEC is far from defenceless. I just want to be left to live my life peacefully. All I did was develop a computer and try to help with a serious problem, I didn't ask for any of this.' He simply nodded, as if in a trance.

With that I put the IPEC back into the case, and waited for his response. He had recovered by this time, and said

'I'll escort you out. We'll let the matter rest for the time being, but you'll always be under our watchful eye. You can think of it as an umbrella. There may come a time when you will be thankful for it. That's one hell of a computer you have there Mr Shaw. And you actually built it yourself?'

He looked at me in a strangely superior way, as if knowing I hadn't.

'It certainly is General' I replied. 'More than you can possibly know; I worry sometimes that it's something which could be seen as a threat. But it isn't, please believe that. It has tremendous capacity and has only ever been used for good?'

Driving back to the factory I asked the IPEC about the self-destruct facility?

'When we were unsure of how to destroy the computer on the platform you said you were able to destroy the whole craft. But if you did that in a room full of terrorists you would take their lives?'

'I have two methods open to me' she replied. 'One is to explode the nuclear battery and destroy everything within a certain radius. The other is to release a gas internally; this would melt all my components instantly, including the battery. The small amount of radiation released would be contained within the casing.'

'Let me ask you a hypothetical question. What if I was being tortured and in tremendous pain? Would you really destroy us both simply to save me further suffering when by doing so you would also take out the bad guys, thereby disregarding your Principal Command?'

'I have of course considered this, and although I should tell you conclusively no…. I cannot: We have become close over our time together, and as you've already pointed out, in your opinion I am sentient. My considered response would be to protect you, and consequently as a final act I would destroy you, and everyone within range who was causing you the pain.'

'Wow Hypatia,' I responded. 'That's the nicest thing anyone has ever said to me…. I think?'

The IPEC and its helper materialised in the now familiar room..... This was an unscheduled meeting but as was the custom, the Khepera immediately called the meeting to order and listened while the IPEC gave its report, concentrating on the progress of the module manufacturing process in Maryland.

The account of the meeting with General White, the main reason for the meeting, would be given to the Khepera afterwards. The number of planned modules was discussed at length and agreement reached that with a world population of over seven billion, the figure was insufficient to influence the nature of enough people.

'We have known for some time the numbers of computers would probably be insufficient,' said the Khepera, 'And I'm not convinced by the argument that if we can influence the people in authority throughout the world. We might persuade them not to destroy the alien vessels.'

'May I broach the subject of population expansion,' the IPEC said gravely, 'If we're successful, the future of this planet will be irrevocably changed; with no wars or hunger the population of the planet will mushroom, by 2050 it can be assumed conservatively to be around 8.5 billion and in 2100, 12 billion. This planet cannot sustain that number of people. I estimate by 2150 it will have risen to 15 billion and by 2200, As many as 20 billion. It goes without saying the earth most certainly cannot support that many. The inhabitants will be forced to destroy each other simply to survive. Why then are we bothering to save them?'

'Part of our solution is to introduce population control; the executive team are investigating whether implants programmed to carry the required information could be used. We have here, a unique situation there are no other options open to us. Anything else means the complete annihilation of this planet. The implants worked for our species, and will work here; the only real difference is time. We must compress 8 of our centuries into 120 earth years, which means controlling their primitive desire for supremacy by destruction, and convincing them to take the food-cakes. Defurak will you please describe our projection of the human reaction to this?'

'The human metabolism is comparable to our own,' answered the alien. 'If we can persuade them to take the food-cakes regularly their general health will improve drastically, cancers and other life-threatening diseases will be eradicated within weeks.

When the humans realise they are no longer aging, a fundamental change in their perspective of life will take place. Particularly when they realise that a normal healthy lifetime of between four and five hundred years could be routinely expected.'

'I will entrust you with one other piece of information.' added the Khepera. 'The consortium has been considering the problem for some time. I have received a report confirming we have discovered a new planet 16 times larger than the Earth with the capacity to sustain life. The problem being, it's still evolving, and isn't yet ready for populating. We have already introduced vegetation from many different sources, and robots are planting billions of seeds originally from the trees of this planet to hasten the situation along. It has water but not the great oceans of the Earth. Plus of course the

question of transport for vast numbers of people still has to be considered. Clearly the logistics are enormous, but not impossible.' He held up his hand.

'No further discussions will be entertained concerning this report, mainly because I have no further information to give. My object was simply attempting to enlighten you as to possible solutions, and to demonstrate our resolve.'

'This meeting is closed. Would you all please leave us, I have something to discuss with the IPEC privately'

CHAPTER THIRTY FOUR

'**W**hen are you going to unmask Jack the Ripper?' She asked

'I haven't the stomach for it right now' I replied 'and want nothing more to do with death for a while. We'll get there eventually he isn't going anywhere. Why do you ask?'

'Because you need something to take your mind off the aliens,' she replied. 'You're being consumed by them,'

'Hypatia what do you expect, I alone have knowledge of the greatest story in the world, and can't talk about it to a living soul.'

'We have had this discussion before,' she replied 'and my argument still stands. It happened 12500 years ago and constitutes the responsibility you accepted when agreeing to the rewards of the time travel and the lifestyle you now enjoy.'

Christopher with Hypatia's help was learning the travel business and it was already obvious that he had the talent and dedication I lacked. So I decided maybe the IPEC was correct and the time was right to solve the "Jack" problem once and for all.

The first question to be decided was which murder we were to choose? Some experts believe that the same man may not have perpetrated the next two, who incidentally, were killed within an hour of each other? The first of these was Elizabeth Stride, and the second Catherine Eddowes.

Elizabeth Stride was born Elisabeth Gustafsdotter, in Gothenburg, Sweden on November 27th 1843. Unlike most of the other victims, who fell into prostitution due to poverty, 'Long Liz' (her nickname) took it up as a vocation. By the summer of 1865 she had been registered by the Gothenburg police as a prostitute, and treated twice for sexually transmitted diseases. The following year she moved to London and married a carpenter named John Stride in March 1869.

Her body was discovered around 1:00am on the morning of Sunday, September 30th 1888, at the end of a dark passage in Dutfield's Yard, off Berner Street, Whitechapel. She was 43 years old, the right age for a Ripper victim.

The difference however, and a possible question mark against Stride being a Ripper victim, is that although she was found lying on the ground with her throat deeply sliced open; none of the other mutilations had taken place.

Another was that she had once again just walked out on her extremely violent lover, Michael Kidney. He, very soon after the body was discovered visited a police station ranting about her murder. But the body had been mistakenly identified by the police as 'Lizzie Stokes' so begs the following question. How did he know it was Stride? This seems not to have been picked up by the police at the time. Additionally, a witness, one Israel Schwartz, claimed he saw Stride being attacked, and thrown to the ground on the street outside Dutfield's Yard, at around 12:45am.

Mr Schwartz however was unwilling to identify the attacker, some say because he recognised him as a fellow Jew. But if it was Kidney, he may have simply been too terrified to speak. Schwartz in some other interviews; also claimed he saw two men.

The yard was so dark that the man who discovered her body was reported as saying he was 'hardly able to see it without lighting a match.' He also believed the murderer was still in the yard when he arrived. A Dr Blackwell who examined the body at 1:16 am found it to be still warm, concluding she had only been dead between 20 and 30 minutes

The murder of the second victim Catherine Eddowes generates no such doubts. Forty-four at the time of her death, Eddowes' body was discovered at 1:44 am lying in a dark corner of Mitre Square, but unlike Stride her killing was typical of the Ripper. It had the same modus operandi to that of Annie Chapman some three weeks earlier. Her throat had been slit, her abdomen cut open and completely disembowelled, her intestines were thrown over the left shoulder and her face slashed. The murderer had also taken as a souvenir, her uterus and the left kidney.

The police constable who found the body, stated he had seen nothing out of the ordinary during his previous patrol, only ten to fifteen minutes earlier; Eddowes must therefore, have had only just been murdered, her killer fleeing into the Whitechapel area.

We know that, because a piece of torn cloth from Eddowes apron was later found in a doorway off Goulston Street.

Earlier that evening at approximately 08:30 pm, she had been found lying face down in the street paralytic drunk and was taken to the police station where she was allowed to sleep it off in the cells. She was released at 1:00 am and last seen alive in Mitre Square about 01:30, reportedly talking to a man. Whether the Ripper killed them both, we can only speculate. But if he had been disturbed during the first attempt it is entirely possible. Not having had time to finish his ritual he may very well, whilst still in a state of high excitement and sexual arousal, have been wondering the streets searching for another victim to satisfy his gruesome lust.

'Let's go and discover the identity of this man Hypatia, once and for all.'

We loaded up the motor home and set off for London, parking in the usual place. I dropped the buggy this time so as to offer some protection to the IPEC and selected 30th September 1888, 12-15 am.

---Activate---

Heading South towards Commercial Road East, and turning right I walked to Berner Street. Not far down the street is Dutfields Yard. The alley leading to it was, as expected, quite dark.

I put on the glasses. And switched to night-vision.

'There's a gas light on the street but it's barely giving enough light to see a hand in front of your face. I'll wait to see who comes; the actual murder doesn't interest me, she only gets her throat cut? I know that sounds cold blooded, but I can't stop it, and it's him I want.'

Two men were across the street, they had a short conversation and one walked off.

'What time is it?' I asked,

'12-45 am,' came the reply.

'That must be Israel Schwartz,' I said, and pointed the MIPEC at him... Here they come.'

She was already quite drunk again. In a loud voice and with a definite accent she called him a "cheap bastard." He slapped her, knocking her to the ground.

'He's about the same build Hypatia, but I can't be sure if it's the same man, he walks differently, I'll get closer.'

'It's definitely not him.' Hypatia said

'Surely there can't be two of them?' I replied 'No look there's the Ripper walking behind. He's wearing the same reversible coat and he's got the bundle under his arm.'

The first chap, probably Michael Kidney, stormed off calling her a dirty whore, but telling her to bring him some fucking money, or he would 'do' for her.

The Ripper waited a few seconds and approached her. He must have seen Schwartz across the road, but seemed not to care. He helped her up and after a few words led her towards the yard.

'He's taking her down the alley Hypatia, Did you get a decent picture?'

'No,' she replied 'His hat is pulled very low, can you follow him?'

'I'd rather not, better to wait until he comes out.'

A pony and trap approached, and despite the dark turned into the alley without any hesitation clearly having done it many times before. Two minutes later the driver started shouting 'MURDER, MURDER. Get the police. Call the Peelers!'

I waited for about five minutes, but by this time people had come running out of the pubs and the houses, some with 'tilly' lamps. The Ripper murders were clearly making everyone on edge, hence the quick reaction time. The killer didn't come out of the alley; of that I'm sure. More Lanterns were brought and the surrounding area searched.

'He must have left another way,' I told her. 'But we have the advantage because we know where he's heading. I'm going to Mitre Square Hypatia, can you direct me?'

Following her instructions I set off at a brisk pace, finding Mitre Square easily.

'You'll have to search around the area, and hope you see him?'

Night vision or not, I ran around frantically until the shouting started and by then it was too late.' The man has eluded everyone for 126 years, and now even with our advantage he's done it again, I don't believe it.'

'He's done no such thing. Head back here and I'll tell you what we'll do.'

When I got back she said

'I've set the date at 8th September 1888, at 5-00 am. You have to walk to Hanbury Street, it will be light soon, and will allow you to get some good pictures of him. So off you go and see Annie Chapman again.'

I won't repeat the details; suffice it to say we got photographs of the Ripper, good ones too, with and without a hat. All we had to do now was search the available records and I had a rather powerful computer to do that for me. Two subjects we could access immediately. These were Prince Albert Victor, Duke of Clarence and Avondale, and his personal physician, Doctor William Gull. I am pleased to confirm that neither of them was the Ripper.

'What shall we do now?' I asked when we arrived home. 'I really need a break from these awful murders. And of course we still have Florence and Rome on the agenda, except for the language, or lack of it.'

'Well that's easily solved,' she said. 'I can at least give you Italian lessons, Latin too, if you wish.'

I shook my head.

'I do worry about this.' I told her. 'The human brain may very well be under used, but you're talking about infusing mine with two complete languages, does that include reading and writing them too?'

'Why not?'

'It seems dangerous to me Hypatia.'

'There are some people, who speak as many languages as I do.' she answered. 'Their brains cope.'

'Yes, but do they also have a head full of MPT. You might also consider that you didn't start with a blank canvas. I prefer to believe that some insignificant amount of knowledge was present before we met.'

'You must decide of course,' she replied dismissively. 'But it will be perfectly safe?'

The prospect of visiting Rome, and being inside the Coliseum when it was new was simply too strong. The thought of experiencing the Roman Empire at the height of its power and meeting some of the most fascinating men and women in history was just too intriguing. But at which date exactly?

This was the type of conundrum I loved. Should I visit during the reigns of Sulla and Marius, or during the time of Cicero, Pompey, Crassus and Cato? Which of the Caesars would be the most interesting? Julius, Caligula, Nero or Augustus. Then of course there's my particular favourite Claudius. I read the Rupert Graves books I Claudius and Claudius the God over and over in my youth and even have an old fashioned DVD of the television series.

It's strange how things develop, because two weeks later the IPEC said, 'Have you thought any more about Rome?'

'Why?'

'There's a major hotel chain in Italy, which in turn own a small chain of very exclusive 5 star hotels. Two in Rome, one in Venice, one in Florence and one in Sorrento. The parent company is terribly overstretched, and needs money desperately.'

'How did you find them?' I asked?

'Well it was you really'…. I liked it when we talked this way because it showed she listened to my opinions occasionally.

'Because of your desire to visit Rome, I was surfing around late one night in some of the major Italian banks computers reading the minutes of their board meetings. I inadvertently came across a discussion concerning a large hotel chain which was struggling to service its debts.

'The banks directors were concerned about the levels of borrowing the company enjoyed and were in fact discussing whether to force them to sell off some of their assets. They concluded it was quite urgent as some of the financial practices of the board were considered, somewhat questionable.

'Accessing their accounts, I realised the only profitable part of the group was in fact these five hotels. I have been in touch with the bank secretly, and with the financial director of the chain openly, intimating we might be interested in purchasing them as long as it's done quietly, and quickly.

'I've made them a fair offer and let the bank know it's only open for seven days. Knowing as I do the state of their finances, and the banks concern. I believe they will force them to accept the offer within the next 48 hours.'

Julie was scheduled to visit one of our favourite cities, 'Dublin' in two days, to discuss the re-vamp of a large house in Dalkey for a famous and extremely beautiful Australian film star. My offer to accompany her had been ardently refused. Her company had been sworn to absolute secrecy she conveniently claimed.

'In that case.' I told her, 'I shall spend a few days in Rome. Don't spend too much time down Temple Bar drinking the Guinness.'

'And don't you spend too much time gorging yourself on their famous pasta dishes.' she retorted impishly. 'You're getting quite a paunch.'

CHAPTER THIRTY FIVE

Rome, the eternal city.... I had never been before, and was excited to have finally made it.

The Gulfstream took us first to Dublin where we dropped off my wife and two of her associates, landing at Aeroporto dell'Urbe in the late afternoon. A hotel car waited for me on the tarmac.

My first visit certainly won't be my last because I fell in love with the place immediately it was felt so warm and friendly with such beautiful buildings and of was course steeped in history. Hypatia had booked us into a junior suite St Regis Grand Rome. An inspired choice, elegant, and located in the centre on the Plazza della Republica.

'Why don't we stay at one of the hotels we're buying,' I asked.

'Because this is a better location for our travelling.'

'Julie would love it here. Where are the crew staying tonight?'

'Nowhere, they are returning to London. This is our busiest time. All the aircraft are booked solidly for the next three months.'

'Remind me again, when are we meeting the hotel people?' I asked. And I still need to learn Italian

'Two-o-clock tomorrow afternoon.'

'In that case we'll do it tonight. I can then get up early and have a look round.'

'I thought you were only going with Latin?'

'I was, but my plans have changed, this city is wonderful. I intend to spend a lot of time here from now on. Do you think you could teach Julie to speak Italian too? It's not revealing the time travel, simply demonstrating to her how advanced your computer functions are?'

'We could, she replied hesitantly. 'Let's take it under consideration for a few days shall we, it's a big step.'

The next morning before breakfast I went exploring. What a fabulous city this is I thought as I turned a corner and saw the Coliseum.

'Hypatia can you please find out a little about the Coliseum, all I know is that it was built between 72 and 80 A.D, and could hold 70,000 people. See if you can find a time when it's not too bloodthirsty, and we'll go as soon as we can.'

The Forum was the next place. An information board informed me it was the most important archaeological area in Rome, and extended from the Capitol Hill to the Palatine.

Dating from the 7th century BC it had been for many centuries the centre of political, commercial and religious life.

It took a few seconds to realise I had actually read the plaque in Italian and that the people around me were gesturing wildly whilst speaking and I understood them perfectly.

'Wow Hypatia,' I said in Italian 'This is great, do I have an accent?'

'Yes you speak like a Tuscan, a middle class fellow.'

'Why Tuscany?' I asked,

'Because you don't know Rome, it would sound silly, a Roman asking directions to the Vatican.'

'You think of everything.' I said admiringly, 'What would I do without you?'

Another Plaque told me about the immediate area.

Designed by Michelangelo the Piazza del Campidoglio; is surrounded by three palaces. The central one, Palazzo Senatorio, is now the seat of the Municipality, whereas the other two, Palazzo dei Conservatori and Palazzo Nuovo, host the treasures of the Capitoline Museums. The Capitoline Picture Gallery contains paintings from the 14th to the 18th centuries painted by extraordinary painters with celebrated names such as: Tiziano, Pietro Da Cortona, Caravaggio, Guercino, Rubens and many more. A copy of the bronze equestrian statue of Marcus Aurelius dominates the square.

Michelangelo designed its plinth. The original statue, which survived destruction by the vandals only because they thought it represented the first Christian Emperor Constantine, can be admired inside the Museum.

'I'm coming back now Hypatia,' I said. 'After breakfast, I'll return to the room and make plans for the meeting. I like speaking Italian it's such a romantic language, and gives one the irresistible urge to pinch young ladies bottoms, do you think they would mind?'

'Yes I certainly do,' she cried indignantly. 'Don't you dare!'

'Why Hypatia, I do believe you're jealous?'

'I'm no such thing,' she snapped, 'I'm simply thinking about the meeting. It will be difficult to convince the board we're serious buyers if I have to explain away your absence by informing them you've been arrested as a result of public morality charges being laid against you by some 17 year old Bella Donna.'

'Very well' I responded. I was enjoying winding her up. 'The goosing will have to wait. I hope the hotel does a full English breakfast, all this walking has made me hungry?'

'You're a heart attack waiting to happen, have a bowl of muesli it will do you far more good,'

'I will,' I lied.

Afterwards in the suite we discussed our strategy, which was to be as follows: The IPEC would speak to them via a video link. I'd speak only English, and she would do the negotiating in Italian.

The offer would be for the chain as a going concern. Subject of course to a detailed audit by our accountants. At 1-00 pm I set off for their offices of the main group on the Via de Piebiscito.

The board was 100% male. This I had been informed is quite normal as business in Italy tends to be chauvinistic.

The negotiations were hard. But as usual Hypatia charmed everyone to bits whilst stealing their company for less than our original offer. Plus three million in cash as a sweetener.

The men being Italian gentlemen thanked her charmingly for doing to them so sweetly, what they all wanted to do to her not so sweetly. These old style Italians have real class, and genuine charm. What a wonderful country.

'We've bought the hotels without even seeing them' I said, 'Is that a good idea?'

'It's not important' she replied. 'Their balance sheet is what matters, and the fact that they average 98% occupancy during the summer months is exceptional. That figure drops to 73% in the winter, but believe me, in the hotel business these are excellent numbers; the repeat bookings are high too.'

'Are those their figures?' I asked

'Yes' she replied 'I was able to verify them during a recent visit I made to their computer records, and of course our people still have to go through their books.'

'Ok Hypatia, let's get ready. I'm really looking forward to this trip; the question is what time shall we choose? And if we go straight back to the hotel now, are you able to feed the Latin language to me this afternoon? I'll surprise Stephen with passages from Cicero when next we meet?'

'Yes' she promised 'but you'll need to sleep afterwards. Whilst you do. I'll look at the maps to see if there's a safe place to materialise.'

'As a matter of fact I saw a park today, between the Coliseum and the Circus Maximus,' I pronounced it Circo Massimo. It looked very old, like it had always been there. She would check it out she said.

And then rather than taking afternoon tea. I hung the Do Not Disturb sign on the door, and prepared for the induction of Latin.

Waking at 9-00 pm I had room service bring me a two monkfish fillets and six lightly grilled huge tiger prawns with red fettuccine, accompanied by a green salad and a bottle of excellent Antinori Cervaro della Sala. I also had them deliver two medium rare fillet beef sandwiches to go, and a half bottle of Gaja Barolo Sperss. I admit to being very excited at the prospect of seeing Rome at the height of its ancient glory.

'Ok. Let's go visit Julius Caesar?'

She suggested a good date to start would be at the end of September 45 BC. Caesar would have recently returned to Italy after successfully winning the civil war between himself and Pompey.

His first action had been to publish his Will. Naming his grand-nephew Gaius Octavius (Octavian) who of course later became the Emperor

Augustus, as his heir. The legacy included his titles. Caesar further decreed that if Octavian died. Marcus Brutus would inherit.

I hadn't seen him yet, but didn't think this news would have gone down too well with Mark Antony. It was very clear however that upon his return, Caesar had obviously felt reasonably secure, because he magnanimously pardoned nearly every one of his enemies.

I had a porter take the satchel containing the IPEC to my hire car, noticing that even though it was after 11-00 pm, the roads were still very busy. It's only a short drive to the Coliseum from the hotel and we parked as near as possible to the grassy area which was quite dark; checking no one was in the immediate vicinity I opened the side door, shouldered the rucksack, placed the mat on the ground, lifted the IPEC from the car and stood on the mat. '30th September 45 AD, 9-00 am.'

---Activate---

The park was quite busy. Men in togas or leather uniforms seemed to predominate, while the women wore stolas. Full-length dresses from neck to ankle, high-waisted and fastened at the shoulders with ornate clasps. Most of the ladies wore a shawl over the stolas, called a palla.

Above me was the Palatine Hill. It towered to a height of around 70 meters and looked down on one side to the Forum and on the other the Circus Maximus. I knew many of the affluent Romans had their residences there, and indeed could see some of the grand villas as I looked up. As the years passed, the Emperors would take most of the space for their palaces. (The ruins of the palaces of Augustus Caesar, Tiberius and Diocletianus can still be seen today) The term 'palace' actually stems from the word Palatium, and refers to this very place.

I walked toward the Circus Maximus excitedly. It was empty but I must compliment the makers of the film epic Ben Hur because it looked exactly the same. And from there I walked along the Via Sacra to the Forum.

The object of my visit, the Curia Hostilia was a double storey building, quite small compared to its neighbours and had scaffold along the front for the masons to complete their carvings.

The Forum was alive with all sorts of people shoulder to shoulder listening to the assortment of vendors offering various services. Murals adorned the walls of building even in this the most public of places and often their subjects were positively obscene.

Prostitutes openly plied their trade, their pimps standing close by. I smiled to myself at this. In Roman times the con men and other self-seeking individuals worked outside the Parliament building, whilst in our time…. I'll leave you to finish the rest!

Inside the Curia a meeting was taking place. All the men wore white toga's edged with purple, displaying their Senatorial office.

Three people stood out immediately. They were sitting on thrones on a raised dais in the centre of the floor; the person in the middle was Julius Caesar. I recognised him immediately from busts in various museums I've visited and from the many books written about him. He was well built with a strong face and a fair complexion; his hair was combed forward in a vain attempt to hide his baldness. Clearly, he paid attention to his appearance.

But the main thing to strike me was, as with many other renowned men of history. He totally dominated the room displaying absolute concentration and an unusual economy of movement not twitching or moving in any way. The only part of him that moved whilst in this statuesque pose, were his eyes. These were a mesmerising jet black, and looked with a withering stare at whoever was speaking.

Someone was proposing he be given a Triumph to celebrate his victory over Pompey in the recent civil war. When he sat down, another stood up, and pointed out that Caesar had already been awarded two Triumphs one for Gaul, and one for Egypt, and anyway Triumphs were only given for victories over foreign enemies.

Caesar looked at him ruthlessly, his voice controlled.

'Pompey,' he said solemnly, 'was a far more dangerous opponent than any 'two' foreign Generals.' And for the record, reminded them he had executed everyone responsible for his heinous act of his murder in Egypt.

'However, Gaius Trebonius is essentially correct; I'll leave it to the Senate to decide whether to grant this honour.'

Another Senator rose to his feet, and proposed that Caesar, the saviour of Rome should not only be awarded a Triumph, but should also be given the right to wear the laurel wreath, plus a purple and gold toga.

Another stood, and proposed that Caesar should be provided with a gold throne, for his personal use at any public functions.

Senator Trebonius again rose, and said

'Senators, friends. We go too far! This Republic is being voted away by its own members. We Romans have fought many battles for the right to live the way of the peoples choosing. Does not the provision of a gold throne, and a purple and gold toga, signify a King? Please explain to me, and the people of Rome, how a Republic can function with a King at its head?'

Caesar stood; he was quite a tall man, very straight and erect.

'Gaius Trebonius again makes a valid point; this is indeed a Republic. And I pledge my whole being to it remaining so: Have I not repeatedly offered my life to protect it? But in these troubled times Rome needs a strong man to protect the way we choose to live. I am a servant of the people, and of this house. But I will of course bow to theirs and your wishes.'

As he sat down, the man next to him stood and called for the vote.

'That's Marcus Antonius,' Hypatia said 'The Junior Consul is Publicus Conelius Dolabella.'

The vote was overwhelmingly carried. Another senator rose to his feet.

'Oh look Jason. Marcus Tullius Cicero is about to speak.' I had never heard her sound so in awe and leant forward in anticipation.

To a quiet and subdued house the Senator who I thought looked quite tired suddenly stood erect and shedding years off his face said.

'It is of no surprise to find the voting record of these 'Loyal Senators,' (waving his arm in a sweeping motion toward the rear of the chamber,) is favourable to our great Caesar. One might in fact be forgiven for thinking he already governs in the manner not of a mere King, but of an Emperor. He does after all already carry the title of Dictator.'

He looked about him knowingly.

'And since the membership of this house has been extended. At the Dictatorial command of our glorious Caesar. He has taken it upon himself to pass a myriad of laws without any debate or vote. Entering them on the records as Senatorial or dictatorial decrees:

With that in mind I caution this house and all its members. Do not give away any more of what has been arduously won.'

The house sat very quiet. Caesar looked at him ruthlessly and replied with a smile that didn't reach his eyes.

'My dear Cicero please bear in mind that as Dictator Perpetuus I am only using the powers that this house voted to me. Nevertheless let me restate the promise I made only one week ago. And pledge this to you personally my old and valued friend.'

'By all the Gods we hold dear as soon as my work is done I will resign the title of dictator if the house so wishes. And let me reiterate. I proposed the increase in the membership of this house to give it more authority. Of course not everybody agreed with the proposal, but it was legally voted upon and carried by a substantial majority and we are duty bound to carry out its wishes.

'And while we are about it, I should be honoured to accept the award of a third Triumph if it pleases this House and the people of Rome.'

He smiled at the speaker, bowed to the assembly turned solemnly and left.

I ran outside and followed him as he got into a litter and left with a company of 10 soldiers. Within five minutes the whole parade stopped outside a bathhouse at the bottom of the Capitoline hill and with waves to the applauding populace and accompanied only by his body slave, he entered. This clearly was a private club and sported doormen to keep out undesirables. Obviously this did not include me, so I followed him in.

The slave helped him undress and folding up the discarded clothes placed them reverently in a wicker basket. Julius walked naked through to the massage area and lay down on a leather covered cushioned bench where the masseur started his work. After about five minutes another chap walked in. 'Marcus Brutus is arrived My Lord,' said the slave softly.

As he climbed on the next bed, the man said.

'You were in good form this morning Caesar, congratulations on your victory.'

'Those two must be punished Brutus, I'll not be questioned in that way. Gaius Trebonius must be made aware of what we have recently learnt about him.

'He is gambling, possibly correctly, that I would never divulge his secrets. You on the other hand could. I also believe Cassius is at the bottom of this. Since he bought the mortgage to his house he has Cicero in the palm of his hand.'

'Even you cannot expect to push through such wide ranging reforms without some dissenting voices Caesar,' Brutus replied. 'You always knew that Cicero would question it.'

Caesar lifted his head from the bench and glared at him.

'That may be true my boy, but they go too far. Cicero is not the power he once was. See to it they're warned. And send Anthony to me. We must demonstrate our resolve to control dissent within the Senate. I'll not accept these traitors speaking against my government in this way. It flies in the face of progress.

'My decision to extend the membership of the house was for the good of Rome. The Rome I love, and have fought for. But, did you not see the sign displayed outside my villa yesterday? God bless the commonwealth, it said. Let no one consent to point out the House to a newly made Senator. How dare they?'

'I have heard similar dissent from the Plebs too. I'll not tolerate it! This morning on my way to the Senate I was made to listen to the chanting of the latest ditty:'

Caesar pulled a face and in a mocking voice recited.

"The Gauls he dragged in triumph through the town:
Caesar has brought forth into the Senate house:
He's changed their breeches for the purple gown:
Their resolve that of a frightened mouse:"

'I'll not have it do you hear?'

'The addition of these people to the legislature will never be welcomed Caesar.'

'Brutus you are very dear to me, as is your mother. But do not presume to think that family loyalty extends to you defying my wishes on this matter. He spoke very quietly but with real menace.

'Now boy..... Go away and do as you are ordered.'

Brutus jumped off the bed and casting a look of pure hatred at the back of Caesars head almost ran out.

The masseur leaned forward and rubbed his master's temples. And then I remembered, Caesar reportedly suffered from epilepsy, they were clearly worried that he may have an attack. But looking at him closely, I decided he knew exactly what he was doing,

'This guy's a smooth cookie.' I said aloud 'He's nothing like as upset as he pretends'

After the massage he walked to the steam room where his slave scrubbed him, then, using a curved scraper, exfoliated his skin. This was followed by a few lengths of the murky pool and a hot and cold shower, then suitably refreshed the great man left.

'I hope he is going home Hypatia, I'm getting hungry.'

The band of soldiers trudged along to a large house on the edge of the Forum where his wife Calpurnia stood waiting for him at the door. They kissed for the gratification of the watching crowd and walked through to the garden to eat lunch. After washing their hands they were served dates, cheese and fruit, wine and water was on the table but it seemed Caesar did not drink alcohol in any great amount, he had only had one very weak watered down wine during the meal.

It was then time for his rest. Romans apparently took three hours every day and the whole place stopped, even the servants rested.

But when he went to have his nap it became clear they had separate bedrooms. A slave girl undressed him, and slipped out of her dress. I left them to it; at least it wasn't a boy. I had read this was one of his little predilections too. He probably wouldn't have cared anyway. The ancient Romans were into these things quite openly.

'What about a Roman orgy,' I asked, 'Do you think we'll see one?'

'Do you want to?' she asked.

This was clearly a loaded question.

'Not particularly, but in the interests of investigating history, it may be necessary.'

'I bet,' she replied icily.

'Your language is piercing in Latin my Scandinavian prude. We had better stick to English.'

'I believe you're a fifty years too early for such shenanigans,' she informed me. 'The real orgies took place during the reigns of Caligula, Claudius and Nero'

'What shall we do while they have their siesta?' I asked, 'Now that I've found him, I don't want to leave too hastily. I'm a little surprised he's here. Surely Cleopatra is still in Rome, I assumed he would have been with her. I so much wanted to see her.'

'I can offer no explanation.' she replied. 'Although I too believe she is still here. Why not explore the villa before enjoying one of your cholesterol filled sandwiches?'

'Good idea' I agreed smiling.

'The rooms were large, with huge murals adorning the walls, mostly depicting Caesars many victories. Following the tour I went in search of a spare bedroom. They obviously had a very open marriage, because as I opened the door of one bedroom and peeped around…Talk about cholesterol, one of the young servant boys was enjoying his lunch, from between the legs of Mrs Caesar giving new meaning to the saying. 'He licked the platter clean,'

I found my way to the great man's study, and looked around, getting the 'feel' of him.' His presence was everywhere. He was to die soon too. How different the Empire might have been if he had lived.

The man this belongs to has a wonderful mind I concluded, stroking the plaque on the desk which read 'GAIVS IVLIVS CAESAR.' A vain man, but then, he probably had to be to achieve the things he did. As I sat in his chair eating my barely warm sandwich washed down by the truly magnificent wine, even when partaken from a plastic cup. Which when empty I was careful to return to my bag.

I was daydreaming like this when in he walked making me hurriedly jump up from his chair. His wife followed him into the room, talking about this morning,

'Mark me on this Calpurnia. I am going to have them evicted from the Senate, how dare they defy me like this?'

'They're correct my love.' she said, 'You've weakened the senate, filling it with these horrible little uncouth men?'

'That's rich, he replied what about these horrible little uncouth men filling you. 'Did you enjoy your nap by the way?'

'I did my love he's a wonderful gift. Talking of which, we're going to the house of Lucius Piso this evening. It's his 50th birthday.

'I shall be unable to attend,' he said, 'I have a previous engagement.'

She looked at him fiercely.

'You're going to visit that slut and your bastard son again! Don't deny it. Oh Julius you promised.' She burst into tears and stormed out. He shrugged, and called for his secretaries.

The rest of the afternoon was taken up with affairs of state. To see his power of concentration and grasp of world affairs were alone worth the visit. I witnessed him dictate letters on different subjects, to four different secretaries simultaneously.

The ability to travel in time is wonderful. But it really only allows one to get a flavour of the subject. I would have liked to have spent a month with this extraordinary man. His approach to problems, and his uniquely curious way of solving them was a valuable lesson.

He was after all the absolute ruler of the known world. Not since

Alexander could anyone claim that.

'I'm coming back Hypatia. I want to see the Coliseum.'

When I arrived, she asked whether I was tired, because in real time only a few seconds would have passed, we had already been nearly seven hours.

'Let's have a couple of hours more,' I suggested, 'I must see the Coliseum. We need to set the time after the floor was altered.'

'Construction began in the 70's.' she answered, and finished ten years later. The upper part was originally made of wood. In 217 AD it was struck by lightning and badly damaged, being restored in 238 AD with stone.'

'Set the time for 1st August in the year 240 AD, 9-00 am. The killing of Christians should have stopped by then.'

CHAPTER THIRTY SIX

It was only a short walk to the Coliseum. I had seen so many wonders lately it would have been understandable to become a little blasé, but not when they continued to impress as much as this. The first thing to strike me was the outer skin; it had a bright marble finish, yellowish white. And very clean for a 160 year old building. But then, having had just been fully restored it probably looked better now than when Vespasian built it.

The other buildings in the area were also impressive; the whole of the surrounding area in fact looked prosperous.

Turning and looking toward the Palatine I saw massive change had taken place. The area had been extended and the villas demolished: In their place stood great palaces.

However the Coliseum was my immediate goal. Walking toward it, I was struck by how quiet everything was, which probably meant no games today. The only movement was a group of people standing outside, avidly listening to a man talking.

He was telling them the Amphitheatrum Flavium was started during the reign of the Emperor Vespasian.

Who, by the way, is another of my great hero's. He was a great builder, quite modest and ruled fairly, totally different to the Julian lot who had preceded him.

The man continued with the information that the Coliseum had been completed by Vespasian's son Titus, with later improvements by his other son Domitian. He also told them that Vespasian had used the plans originally made for the Emperor Augustus although of course he referred to them both as Gods.

'It was built on the site of Nero's lake located below his extensive palace The Domus Aurea, (The Golden House.) He pointed to the Palatine, 'and stretched as far as that building there, the one with the great columns.

'The city had needed a large amphitheatre for some time, the only other one being too small. The Emperor Gaius (Caligula) had started to build one, but his uncle Claudius cancelled it when he came to power. The Emperor Nero considered himself a great actor and when he took the throne built his own theatre in the Campus Martis, which, according to the historians was quite beautiful: When it burnt down in the famous fire Nero was distraught.

Following the Flavian dynasties accession, the Emperor Vespasian decided the people of Rome needed a great theatre to enjoy their free time and began the construction. He used the vast wealth gained during his

Jewish campaigns to pay for it and it took ten years to complete The theatre has 80 entrances, 76 for the ordinary spectators, one for the imperial family, another for the senators, and two for the gladiators.'

It suddenly struck me this man was a tour guide! Nothing is ever new is it? All he was missing was a little yellow umbrella with 'follow me' written on it.

'When it was first built,' he told his charges, 'it had a solid floor and could be flooded for re-enactments of naval battles. This was changed when the Emperor Domitian ordered the construction of the underground rooms called the 'hypogeum.' These are on two levels and contain the tunnels and cages where the gladiators and animals are held before the contests begin. There are 30 trap doors known as 'hegmata' in the floor, each providing instant access to the arena for people, animals and scenery. Some of these are incredibly large, and provide access for elephants and other large species of animals. They're also used for the sizeable groups of actors required for the Emperor's re-enactments of major historical events. In the past they were also used to bring up groups of Christians for sacrifice, today though, we use them mainly for criminals.

'When you come to the show tomorrow you'll be given tokens in the form of numbered pot counters.' He spread his arms and pointed to the doors.

'As you can see every entrance is marked. The token will have on it the entrance and section number. The Coliso now holds 60,000 people, all seated. It used to be 70,000 but since the restoration the standing room areas have been abolished. By following the signs, the vomitoria will quickly get you to your section where a slave will show you to your designated seat. After the show you'll be surprised by how soon everyone is able to leave. The vomitoria are designed to allow the whole theatre to be filled in twenty minutes, and be evacuated in as little as eight.

'If you'll follow me, we'll go inside, please do not wander off or you may get lost. More importantly you'll not be able to hear me, and as you've already paid my master for the service, it would be a waste.

'Which brings me to a delicate subject…? If when the tour is finished you feel I've given you value for money, any tips you consider I deserve will be gratefully received'…. He smiled conspiratorially.

'Shall we proceed?'

'This is lucky Hypatia,' I said. 'He's good too, who would have believed we would get a free guided tour of the place?'

We followed them inside. The first sight of the immense structure from within made even me look twice and I've seen many modern stadiums and this one in our century. But it looked totally different now, bigger and much more impressive.

For these people it was clearly an incredible experience. They gasped and stood transfixed at the sheer size and majesty. I can only suggest their feeling of awe must have been comparable to a modern person seeing the Grand Canyon for the first time. I know how I felt when first seeing it.

He was obviously used to his charges reacting this way, because he said nothing for about three minutes, just letting them soak up the ambience. The place was nearly empty, although about 100 people were working, some cleaning the stone seats, and others picking up litter and sweeping generally.

Across the stadium other groups of tourists were being shepherded around like us. He led our party down to the arena floor, made of wood but covered in sand; he also showed us some of the trapdoors, some as large as ten metres across. From there, we walked to the centre of the arena where he pointed to the top section and a series of thick ropes slung across the arena. These ran from the walls to a large ring of the thicker rope. The ring was about the size of the arena floor. The ropes leading off from the ring were each tied off at a series of massive wooden stanchions spaced evenly along the top of the walls. These went right around the stadium protruding upwards about three metres. Wooden pulleys had been attached to the ring and through these ran thinner ropes which in turn ran through pulleys fixed to the top of the walls between the poles.

Fastened to the ropes, individual sections of folded sailcloth had been looped and hung from the walls suspended on a high wooden platform which ran around the wall.

I didn't need our guide to tell me that these could be pulled out toward the centre and when all the individual sections were extended would cover the seating areas for most of the stadium leaving only the centre of the arena exposed, it really was quite ingenious.

'It helps keep everyone cool during the games,' our guide told us, 'it's called the 'Valerium.' It is pulled across during the games and provides shade for the spectators. As you can see it slopes down towards the centre and catches the prevailing wind. A special company of sailors are assigned to the valerium duties; they stand on that high platform.' He pointed to a platform running around the Arena. 'And pull each section across as required.

The use of sailors is a tradition going back to the time of the Emperor Domitian and is, I'm reliably assured, considered to be the best job in the navy.'

'You'll notice the seating is divided into different sections. The podium, the first level of seating, is only for Senators their families and invited guests. The Emperor's private box is also located on this level. We're unable to let you enter, but you'll see it's lined with marble, and luxuriously furnished. The marble also contributes to the acoustic properties for the Emperors speeches.

Above the podium, the second level the lesser nobles sit. The third level is divided into three sections. The lower part the 'immum' is for wealthy citizens, while the two upper sections, the 'summum' are for the poor ones.

Where you'll sit ladies and gentlemen tomorrow. I'll not ask.' They all laughed.

'We now have a new upper section. This used to be made of wood but was destroyed during a fire 23 years ago. As you can see it's now made completely of stone with new seats added. Previously it was standing room only for the lower-class women and slaves. But now, praise be to the glory of Rome and the Emperor, even we slaves have been given seats.'

'That masters, is the end of the official tour so please follow me outside.'

When they were outside he showed them the entrance to the hypogeum where the animals were caged and where the gladiators prepared themselves while waiting to enter.

'It's not part of the official tour.' he told them smiling broadly, 'But it really is worth seeing and for a small gratuity I will walk you quickly through.'…. If I'd been able I would have willingly given him a large tip, in my opinion he'd earned it.

I decided to visit the 'hypogeum,' myself. And thanks to our guide now knew the way in.

'Are you tired Jason?' the voice said, 'You've been up for hours?'

'No, actually I'm wide-awake; I wonder where the toilets are? I need to go.'

When I found them I couldn't believe it. There must have been 100 stone seats in a semi-circle open to the sky, some even had armrests. Nowhere was there any mention of whether they were for men or women. But I believe there were four sets of lavatories in total, one at each side of the Coliseum. At least this one was empty, thankfully, long handled sponges, used to clean oneself, stood in containers of water; but how often this was changed I dread to think.

The 'thrones' were built along an inner wall under which ran a trough; it was obviously flushed out at regular intervals with running water, but clearly only during the games, because it stank!

In the centre were a series of earthenware containers; the ammonia smell told me they were for collecting urine, which I knew at this time was used for dying clothes. Some smaller ones were interspaced with taller ones, whether for boys or females I don't know, but if this was indeed a unisex latrine I felt really sorry for the women. The lord only knows what sort of state they were in by the close of play on a games day. I certainly wouldn't have fancied using one of the sponge sticks then either. Thankfully I always carried a toilet roll in my rucksack.

Inside the hypogeum tunnels the smell from the animals was

considerably worse than the toilets. The manner in which these poor creatures were kept was positively Chinese, and would have made any modern animal rights activist take up arms.

The beasts were clearly being fed only a starvation diet, no doubt to make them fight each other or tear their human prey to pieces in the arena.

The human cages, for the condemned prisoners were thankfully empty.

'I've seen enough Hypatia, I'll come back tomorrow. Let's return to the hotel for some sleep.'

Arriving back at the hotel around midnight I was understandably exhausted we had been away only forty minutes in real time, but over ten hours in mine. I woke at 10-00 am and ordered breakfast in the room.

'I want to go back the following day because I know the games were definitely to be held then. If we get there about 12-00 pm, I should see enough. The guide said the animals fight in the morning and criminals killed after that, the gladiators start in the afternoon.'

'They might very well have a break during the heat of the day,' she said, 'maybe 2-00 pm would be better,'

'That'll work' I agreed, 'let's try then. Who was the Emperor at the time?'

'His name was Gordian III a child Emperor. He was only thirteen when he acceded to the throne. He isn't remembered as being anything like as bad as other young Emperors, namely, Nero, Commodus or Elagabalus. In fact he seems to have been wise enough to allow competent administrators to oversee the important posts and distanced himself from most of the political decision-making.

'This rather progressive approach enabled him to remain a figurehead unifying the various groups within the government and the army. Little is known about his reign, but he is thought by most historians to have been a good ruler who unfortunately succumbed to a mystery illness whilst on campaign in Mesopotamia aged 19.

He was succeeded by the imaginatively named, "Philip the Arab". It's still a matter of some conjecture as to the exact cause of his death.'

'Thank you Hypatia, clearly we won't know if he'll be there, but at least I'll have some background on him if he is. Rather than waiting for tonight, why don't do it now and walk to the Coliseum.'

'Where are you going to leave me?' she said suspiciously?

'Oh,' I replied 'I forgot about the time change, sorry; we'd better wait until tonight after all.'

'We could go now?' she proposed. 'We could probably stop somewhere; it would only be for a few seconds.'

'Yes we could, and let's face it the modern Romans are not the best parkers, they leave their cars anywhere. Let's do it!'

I had the Voyager brought to the front entrance and the IPEC's suitcase

placed inside by a porter. She was right; we easily found a place to park....
in a no parking zone.

---Activate---

Ancient Rome was reported to have a population of over 1,000,000, so
it shouldn't really have been a surprise.... Nevertheless it was. One doesn't
think of cities 2000 years ago being so big, or having such a large
population. This city was obviously very special; even the people who lived
there knew that. It was reasonably clean with the shops displaying a wide
selection of goods.

There were lots of classy restaurants and furniture shops, artist's studios,
and apothecaries. I saw lots of bathhouses, and curio shops. Marmot stalls
abounded as did other eating stalls and cafés. In fact, ancient Rome was a
lot like the Rome of today, and I loved it.

CHAPTER THIRTY SEVEN

The area around the Coliseum was dedicated to the games. Domitian had built four ludi, 'prisons' where gladiators lived and trained. The 'Bestiarii,' who fought against the beasts, was in the Ludus Matutinus, so called because the show with the animals was held in the morning. The other three were named the 'Ludus Gallicus,' the 'Ludus Dacicus' and the 'Ludus Magnus.

He had also built a stadium for practice. About a third of the size of the Coliseum, this contained accommodation for over three thousand gladiators and had a seating area for a similar number of spectators. An underground walkway joined the two stadia.'

At the Coliseum I walked directly to the Emperor's entrance, passing lines of Praetorian guards stationed along the wide corridors inside.

Drawn by the deafening noise I followed the main corridor to the arena area, as the noise increased so did the numbers of guards and slaves.

'Maybe the boy Emperor is here today after all,' I speculated as I passed through a curtain directly into the sumptuous royal box.

He was no more than fifteen, and dressed in a white toga with two thick vertical purple stripes. On his head was a laurel crown. So this is Gordian III, I thought, He doesn't look too bad.

The young man was sitting on a gold edged wooden throne watching numerous pairs of gladiators fighting each other to music. Some were already dead, and counting them, it seemed they had started at twenty pairs.

The voice clinically told me they had various names depending on which weapons they were trained to use. The heavily armed ones were called 'Hoplomachus' whilst the ones armed with an oblong shield and short sword 'gladius' were known as 'Murmillo' and the ones with the net and trident 'Retiarius.'

Eventually 19 victors were left standing, they like the audience were watching the last pair fighting, neither able to gain the upper hand. The music played, the orchestra leader conducting the musicians wildly as they matched the Gladiators movements. It was rather like a dance band, raising the tempo when the blows were the heaviest, and softly when they backed off. The crowd cheered wildly for these last two, until crying for both to stop.

Obviously swayed by this show of clemency, the young Emperor held up his hand and decreed the contest a draw. The orchestra played a rousing tune and the victors formed up in two's before marching to a spot below the Emperor's box where they were presented with laurel leaves and money.

They then marched once around the arena soaking up the applause and collecting the money being thrown to them by the audience. Some were badly wounded, and had to be helped by their fellow survivors, but they all made it. The stadium was quite cool I looked upward and saw the Vellariun was partially closed.

Not all the losers were dead, in fact most were alive. When the victors had left they also formed up and to loud boo's trudged out. A man entered the arena, dressed, the voice informed me, as Charon the ferryman to the underworld.

He carried a large wooden mallet and his job was to claim the bodies. He went to each one in turn and smashed it on the victim's head, which apparently signified he now owned the corpse.

Then out walked another man, dressed as Mercury the sheepherder of souls. He carried a red-hot iron, and went about pushing it into each body making sure they were properly dead. Which, after being stabbed etc. And then having their heads crushed by an enormous mallet, came as no great surprise.)

Next up were the stretcher-bearers who collected the bodies and took them away. Some slaves entered with them cleaning the sand with large rakes until it was once more pristine.

Then an astonishing thing happened. From under the ground area's around the edge of the arena in direct sunlight were sprayed with a fine water mist. The Romans may have been cruel, but there was no doubting their engineering abilities. The water pressure could only have been achieved by gravity. Water pumps weren't invented yet and wouldn't be for another 1500 years.

Once the arena floor was prepared the crowd settled down for the next bout. Clearly something special was about to happen because the betting became frenzied the bookmaker's slaves struggling to satisfy the gambling passion of the spectators as the made their way up and down the aisles.

While this took place young Gordian retired to his couch at the back of the box, allowing himself to be fed grapes and other fruit by two attractive young women while the orchestra played soft tunes. Studying him, I judged him to be quite good looking, intelligent and self-assured. I on the other hand couldn't have eaten a thing; the wanton slaughter in such an enclosed environment had sickened me.

There were five other men in the box, talking and laughing. A man looked over from the next box, and said. 'We're ready now my lord.'

'Very well' the youth replied, making his way back to the throne at the front of the box.

The man who had spoken went to the front of his own box, and held up his hand for silence. Even without the marble tiles the acoustics from his box were excellent and his voice reverberated around the whole stadium.

'For your continuing pleasure' he bellowed, 'The Emperor is proud to present one of the foremost gladiators in Rome. He is one of only eight living recipients of the Emperor's gold laurel wreath for 20 successful bouts, and his prowess with the trident and sword are legendary. But today by popular request he will entertain you with his famous great sword.' The crowd, clearly being worked, cheered madly at this news. He waited and held up his arms for quiet.

'With a record of 26 straight wins, will you please give welcome to the champion from the Barbarian tribe of the Marcomanni: Our own Arminius the Great!'

The band struck up a rousing tune and the crowd went wild. All eyes turned to the side as a giant walked into the arena armed with a double handled sword about a metre and a half long which clearly was extremely heavy.

This monster of a man however, swung it about as if it were a toy. He bowed to the Royal box and stood back.

The announcer raised his hands again, waiting until the noise of the crowd had subsided. Then he proudly introduced the giant's opponents.

'Today citizens, the Emperor is pleased to bring you, in a fight to the death, two of the leading gladiators from the province of Syria.... Applause.... They're the undefeated champions from the city of Sidon and have fought 21 contests in the theatre at Palmyra. They are natural twins who will fight as a team. I give you the, Butchering Bacchus Brothers'

The band played again as two men suddenly appeared in the centre of the arena, obviously brought up by lift from the hypogeum. It was cleverly done and the crowd cheered and applauded them in time to the music. Not in my opinion as enthusiastically as for their champion Arminius, but an enthusiastic welcome nonetheless. Clearly a good battle was about to take place.

The young Emperor stood and waited for the crowd to settle. The three of them lined up in front of him, I expected them to shout in unison. 'We who are about to die, Salute you.' But they did no such thing. They just bowed and made their way to their positions. Once there, Gordian signalled that the contest was to begin:

The twins were armed with shields and stabbing spears about 1.5 metres long, at their side were sheathed gladius and their armour more substantial than that which Arminus wore. Their buckles shone in the sun and their shields too were brightly polished. As they orbited their massive opponent they surreptitiously moved to the side of the arena bathed in bright sunlight, and used them to dazzle the big German, lunging at him whilst he was disorientated. But he fought them off and moved back into the shadow of the valerium.

One got the feeling they had used this ploy many times, probably with great success. But they soon discovered that using the Sun as an ally didn't work very well in the Coliseum, the velarium simply threw too much shadow over the fighting area at this time of the day.

The musicians however, still managed to follow their movements and play in tune with their thrusts and parries. The brothers circled the German warily, trying to gain the upper hand as they stabbed at him in unison. Every time they did so the music reached a crescendo.

It struck me that they were deliberately playing with each other just to get the crowd excited. It worked too, because everyone was screaming for blood and betting heavily on their favourite.

After 10 minutes, as if by a secret signal the music and their attitudes changed…. This fight was now to the death. It's strange how the mind works. My thoughts immediately went back to Las Vegas…. No more bets.

For about a minute they fought each other with much more gusto, until Arminius moved away, the musicians tracking his movements exactly. The twins followed him, and as if by telepathy suddenly rushed at him from both sides stabbing as they reached him, trying to turn him allowing one of them to attack his exposed back.

Showing surprising agility for such a big man he jumped sideways swishing his sword from side to side only just escaping from their joint attack. It was then the twins made their first mistake; they attempted the same move twice.

This time Arminius was ready for them, he selected the one nearest him and moved forward with amazing speed. Then taking the whole arena by surprise, he spun round sharply and slashed at the legs of his unsuspecting brother. The swing was so quick and powerful that when it connected just below the knee, it cut into his leg so deeply it almost cut it clean off. I tried to look away, but was fascinated and couldn't.

The crowd erupted as the poor man looked down at the blood spurting from the severed limb, his leg hanging at a strange angle by what can only have been skin and sinew. To stop himself falling he stuck his spear into the ground for support. The sword had hardly reached the end of its arc, when instead of stopping Arminius continued the momentum, carrying on in the same direction. Looking like a giant ballet dancer he pirouetted on one foot and with perfect aim, and truly dazzling speed, cut the poor man's head clean off. The music stopped and a single drumbeat sounded as his head hit the ground.

This had happened so fast the other brother hadn't moved. The German turned around now to face the lone man, the music started again with an ominous beat.

Slowly taking off his helmet Arminius threw it to the ground contemptuously and let out a giant bellow of victory.

The crowd found its voice again, baying for even more blood. The young Emperor was also on his feet shrieking with delight encouraging him to continue with the entertainment and kill the other brother with the same aplomb. I felt a mixture of excitement and disgust.

I hope the disgust was at myself because if the truth was told I also wanted to shout. It was like being at a football match. We all need excitement and this was real and totally consuming. The need to see death in the arena became so intense it simply overwhelmed me. I craved blood.

I expected the Syrian to back away at this point, but to his credit he didn't. Circling the big fellow, he tried to get under his guard, fighting on bravely for quite a time and in doing so, slowly won the crowd over, but he was always facing an uphill struggle eventually succumbing to another great blow, although he took on his shield it knocked him down.

Before he could get up Arminius was standing over him, he kicked away the Syrian's spear and shield, and with two hands, reversed his great sword holding it above the others throat. The fallen man raised his left arm and presented his index finger to the Emperor, the voice whispered that this was the recognised plea for mercy.

He had fought bravely and it seemed most of the crowd were on his side, certainly I was. All eyes now turned to this 15 year old boy. The child was given the unenviable responsibility of deciding whether this poor man was to live or die? He slowly raised his arm and held his thumb out level. We all waited to see if it would be pointed up or down. At the same time the beaten man sat up and held the Germans leg with his head bowed. The German angled his great sword and rested it on the Syrian's shoulder at the side of his neck awaiting the Emperor's decision.

The tension in the arena was intense. But still, Gordian continued to hold out his arm with the thumb extended horizontally.

'Please let him go?' I pleaded in the boy's ear. 'Please don't do this.'

But he, as if purposely disregarding my pleas put his thumb down. The crowd gasped, some even hissed.

The Syrian seeing this grabbed the German's thigh tighter. Arminus pushed his great sword powerfully down into his heart, killing him instantly.

'You bloodthirsty little bastard' I cried, and tried to hit this cruel child. Fortunately, seeing he was being protected by about a hundred Praetorian guards my hand went straight through him!

'I've seen enough Hypatia,' I said, 'I'm coming back.'

'What about Claudius,' she asked 'I know he's your favourite, shall we not see him while we're here?'

'No…. I've had enough of this, let's go home.' I don't know if the feeling of disgust was aimed at the Romans or myself, but in my heart of hearts knew I had been drawn in to the bloodlust and had wanted to see the Syrian die in combat.

CHAPTER THIRTY EIGHT

My next scheduled visit to Maryland wasn't necessary. Thanks to Peter and his team, things were going well at the factory. I have always been a firm believer in the old American saying, if it aint broke don't fix it. So decided instead that the time was finally right for me to see who had killed Jack Kennedy.

The Gulfstream landed at Love Field Airport, at 2-00 pm where a hired Lincoln Lancet waited on the runway. The crew were to follow when they had completed their checks and paper work.

I had asked Hypatia to book us all into the Melrose Hotel, not only for a little pampering with the service they were famous for, but also because the hotel was built in 1924 making it possible to leave the IPEC in the room.

The crew had accepted the invitation to join me for dinner in the hotel dining room, which was as usual excellent, and going with the flow I had allowed myself an aperitif of a large 25 year old Macallam whisky followed by two glasses of excellent Californian Merlot with the steaks and Caesar salad. A particularly large Armagnac and coffee rounded off the evening nicely.

The reason for the drinks was because witnessing the 35th President of the United States get his head blown open was not going to be pleasant. Also it was a two mile walk to the assassination scene from the hotel and would ensure any fuzzy effects would have been walked off by the time I arrived.

Everyone knows the general history of the killing of President Kennedy. The main points of interest to me though, were these.

The route, according to New Orleans District Attorney Jim Garrison, had been changed at the last minute. The Dallas Morning News for November 22nd contained a map showing the route President Kennedy's motorcade would take through the city that day. According to that map, the cars were supposed to stay on Main Street while passing through Dealey Plaza; consequently it would not have passed the book depository at all. In fact, the reason they turned from Main onto Houston and then to Elm Street is still a mystery.

This unplanned sharp turn not only brought the President into his assassin's sights, it also forced his car to slow down to about ten miles per hour. Garrison is adamant that a change in a parade route through such a large city would have required the acquiescence of the city police and government.

The fact that powerful Texas oil interests had supported Vice President Johnson in his bid for office isn't in question. But that he was purportedly also supported by the Dallas gangster Carlos Marcello isn't as well known, and The Kennedy's, no angels themselves, were supposedly using this information to force him off the 1964 presidential ticket.

On November 21st he attended a party with his mistress Madeline Brown at the home of the oil baron Clint Murchison. Also there was J Edgar Hoover and Richard Nixon. Years later Ms Brown stated that the three men went into a room together for a private discussion, when they came out Johnson told her. 'After tomorrow those goddamn Kennedy's will never embarrass me again.'

Of course he may very well have been referring to something completely different. But it goes to supposition as to how much the two camps hated each other at this point.

Lyndon B Johnson wasn't without support. He enjoyed the sole patronage of the big Southern oil barons and most of the large defence companies whom of course would benefit greatly if the country continued the war in Vietnam. Strange, how history often repeats itself. Is it not also the case that more recent Presidents have had similar ties, and again America went to war!

After the meal I retired to my suite and prepared to travel to the fateful day. Hypatia was sitting on the coffee table and told me she, posing as my secretary, had asked whether this room, which was on the sixth floor had been here in the same configuration in 1963. Confirming it had, we decided what time to select. 'The shots were fired at 12-30 pm. Central Daylight Time.

Set the time for 10-00 am, Friday 22nd November 1963 Hypatia, it's a fair walk and I need to have a look round first.'

It would have been much more sensible to get a hotel nearer the scene. But call me a snob if you wish. When in Dallas the Melrose is the only place to stay. Rather like the Peabody in Memphis there is nowhere else.

'I've just had a great idea Hypatia. We could go to Memphis and visit Gracelands. Wouldn't it be great to spend an evening with Elvis? I've been there before of course, when I worked in Missouri. But only as a tourist.'

'One thing at a time Jason,' she warned, 'let's keep focused.'

---Activate---

The walk was pleasant enough, the weather on this November morning fine and warm. Nobody walks in the US, but I enjoyed it, the sidewalks were relatively empty and of course I was safe from muggers etc. But in 1963 I would have been pretty safe anyway.

Crossing under the North Central Expressway I finally arrived at Main Street, and walked to the junction with Houston Street outside the Criminal Court building where before me stood the Texas Book Depository.

I noticed that the crowds were already lining the sidewalk. Why, I wondered if the newspapers had shown a different route? Elm Street was to my left, with the famous grassy knoll on my right.

'What time is it Hypatia' I asked?

'11-45' the voice replied. 'Can you point the MIPEC at the sixth floor window please, it's the one on the far right; it should be open.'

'It is.' I replied.

Walking onto the grassy knoll and looking around me at the various people who were already there, I could see that Mr Zapruder, arguably the most important person not directly involved in the proceedings hadn't taken up his position yet.

'Hypatia, do we have time to go up to the sixth floor of the book depository to see what we can find.'

'Be quick Jason, this is very exciting; don't you feel it too?' As I began climbing the stairs breathlessly, she added, 'Don't forget there's no ground floor in this country, so the sixth floor is only the fifth.'

'Thank the lord for small mercies,' I gasped.

Reaching the 'sixth' floor I headed for the corner, the window was open, and a man was standing back out of sight of the crowd, peering out, certainly not Oswald, and no gun. To his right a police jacket and a cap were hanging from a peg on the wall. It struck me that they would be perfect for escaping after the event. Also, who would question a policeman being up there protecting his President.

'What's the time now Hypatia?'

'12-03' she said. 'You should head back down to the knoll in five minutes, latest. I've got his picture for our files.'

Nothing happened for a while, then just as I was about to leave he moved a box and took out a gun, a sniper's rifle, I don't know what kind, but it had a telescopic sight.

'You must go now' she said 'or you'll be too late.'

I ran down the stairs and made my way back to the grassy knoll. Mr Zapruder was there now standing on a round concrete plinth, preparing to film the proceedings. At the top a policeman stood sweeping the area professionally with his eyes. To his left a man in a long light coat stood nearby. He was wearing a hat and sun glasses, and looked exactly like Hollywood's idea of how a secret service agent might dress.

The crowd was bigger now; more people had filled the gaps across the road, some with movie cameras. The policeman and the other man moved behind the high wicket fence. I thought they looked a little anxious.

I decided to concentrate on them.

'What time is it now?'

'12-20.

The policeman moved behind the man in the hat and sun glasses and fiddled with the rear of his coat.

The crowd was becoming excited, behind me the cars travelling quite slowly were turning into the street. As they turned from Main Street into Houston they slowed down even more.

I could see President and Mrs Kennedy quite clearly now. Glancing again at the odd couple, I saw the policeman had unzipped the back of the other man's coat which opened all the way up to the collar. From inside the coat he slid up a rifle with a silencer. The gun had been hanging down his accomplice's side suspended on straps.

The gun came up smoothly, resting easily over his right shoulder, making a perfect platform. The man in the raincoat leant forward and grabbed the fence, at the same time bending his knees to make himself a little smaller. I watched the motorcade turning slowly into Elm street; everybody was absorbed with the scene in front of them, staring and waving at the 'Royal couple.'

I turned back to the gunmen' Phut----Phut, he fired, I think twice, and dropped the gun which fell back under the other man's coat. He simply re-zipped the coat and the man walked away.

The policeman /shooter came round the fence and ran down the knoll towards the scene,

'That was a very professional hit,' Hypatia said in my ear. 'No wonder they were never seen.'

The rest is history, the car carrying the President with his wife cradling his bloody head in her lap sped away; the crowd stood transfixed. The policeman made his way down Houston Street and disappeared. The city police were arriving in large numbers now. Somebody pointed to the open window in the depository and all hell let loose. Detectives ran into the building guns drawn. FBI people appeared, as did the Secret Service. I expect that between them they contaminated any evidence which might have been left.

The bottom line for me is this: There were two shooters and at least three people involved. None of them, as far as I had seen was Lee Harvey Oswald. It's really no surprise of course practically everyone now agrees that there was a major cover up, and more than one marksman.

I considered following them to the hospital but I could go there anytime and decided to carry on with my plans.

St. Louis was to be the next stop, I knew Dr Tumberly had died there in a nursing home, and among his possessions were two rings. These rings it's claimed, closely resemble two taken from the Ripper's victims.

The nursing home where he died still exists, and is apparently used to 'Ripperologists' turning up unannounced, so were not surprised when I did. The purpose of my visit was purely to find out if they had a photograph of him? As it turned out they had a selection, including some old in newspapers. If these were indeed pictures of Dr Tumbelty he wasn't Jack the Ripper.

With makeup, some of them could be deemed similar, but it would take a fair amount of imagination and skill. We seemed to be going round in circles.

'This guy is as elusive now as he was when he was alive.' I complained. 'But we could publish the pictures and see if anyone recognises him,'

'It would lead to too many questions.' Hypatia pointed out. 'What if someone were to come forward and say, oh yes that's my great grandfather, he was a strange man. When he died we found a letter from him claiming that he was Jack the Ripper, which up to now we had disregarded as the ravings of an old man.

'The vast army of Ripperologists would get involved causing a feeding frenzy. Eventually your name would come up as the one who published the photograph, and although your interest would mean nothing to the general public, except as another Ripperologist, people like the Minister and Andrew Blythe would begin to put two and two together. It's the start of a slippery slope!'

CHAPTER THIRTY NINE

It was Julie who chose the next adventure, when two weeks later, she said.

'Tell that computer of yours to keep your diary free for the 27th and 28th of this month. We've been invited to a wedding in Salisbury; the sister of one of Debra's school friends is getting married and Debra is to be a bridesmaid. She knows the family from when she used to spend weekends with them during term time. They're at university together now. I've talked to the mother often, thanking her for her generosity. The daughter's name is Leonne. She has spent a few weekends here.'

'I don't think I've met her,'

'Well I'm not surprised,' she replied cynically. 'You're never here!'

'What part of Salisbury?' I asked timidly.

'It's in a village near.... Wait here, I'll get the invitation.'

When she returned she said 'Winterbourne Dauntsey, what a lovely name. Apparently he's a builder, I don't want you even to mention health and safety; you can become very boring when you start pontificating. Have you got a road atlas?'

'Yes dear.'

'Well get it out and find it on the map.... Forget that, let that computer of yours find it, it does nothing else. Hypatia put up a map of the immediate area for me please.'

'Yes Julie' she replied meekly. A 3D map appeared above the IPEC.

'According to Debra, hotels are going to be a problem. I've been considering whether to use that caravan thing of yours?'

'I thought you said you wouldn't be seen dead in it?' I said, trying not to think about the whinging, which was bound to follow.

'And I wouldn't normally, but when needs must. Please make sure you have it thoroughly cleaned and there's fresh bedding. Forget that; I'll have Mrs Ward take care of the bedding. Bring it round to the front I want to inspect it. Are there enough cupboards?'

'Yes dear. Will the Children be coming with us?

'No. Debra is going down a few days earlier and staying at the house. And Christopher is travelling in his own car and going on to Cornwall to windsurf. He is staying with friends.'

'And get rid of that smelly go-cart thing you keep in there. I despair of you sometimes; I swear you're verging on your second childhood.

When she had gone, Hypatia said.

'She is in a really foul mood you had better be on your best behaviour.'

I studied the map for a minute

'Do you know where Winterbourne Dauntsey is?' I cried excitedly 'It's very near to Stonehenge; it's perfect, we can watch them build it'

'You really are a glutton for punishment, she'll murder you if you're not there 100% of the time.'

'Rubbish, we can sneak out; we only need a few minutes. We must pre-plan the whole thing carefully. Find me a room for the Duchess. Telephone every hotel in the area, get the best suite you can find, I'll leave it to you to arrange, but don't let me down. Buy the wretched hotel if you must.

'We won't take the motor home. We'll take the new X9 and sometime during the proceedings we can slip away and do our investigations.'

The BMW a hybrid with separate electric motors on each wheel had been lengthened, the roof raised and the windows darkened. A compartment had been built behind the front folding rear seats which slid back to reveal a large metal open section box which lowered electrically so as to be just off the ground. The floor of the box was then folded back and the mat placed inside with an overlap under the section. After we had travelled, a leather cover could be pulled over the top to protect the IPEC from the weather. It sounds complicated but we could do it in less than a minute.

I had flown to Germany, ordered the vehicle, and had it fitted by the BMW engineers as a factory modification. The sales manager never even blinked.

'She will catch you, and blame me,' the IPEC said with a worried look

'Oh why not? You're always saying I like danger, let's do it.'

A suitable suite was found in the newly refurbished and upgraded Milford Hall Classic Hotel and Spa, which pacified Julie somewhat allowing her to sanction the use of the new Beamer.

Two weeks later on the Friday we drove to Wiltshire. Julie was pleased because she likes weddings. She had spent two nights in Paris choosing an outfit.

We arrived at the hotel about 2-00 pm where, with the assistant manager cowering against the wall she inspected the brand new suite before declaring it suitable and promptly announced her intention to immediately retire to the beauty parlour for her nails and hair appointment.

'Whilst you're pampering yourself' I told her 'I'm going to look at Stonehenge.'

'Don't be late back' she ordered stiffly. Please remember we're doing something this evening.'

Twenty minutes later we were in the car park, not intending to travel, I just wanted to see it as it is today. We were some distance away from the stones, but that was fine. The place certainly is impressive. Fifteen minutes later though, most of the other cars had gone, leaving us nearly alone.

'Well Hypatia' I said climbing into the back. 'Seeing it's so quiet, why don't we try a few forays to see when it was built. Let's keep with the summer. Select noon midsummer's day 2000 BC.'

--- Activate---

The weather was perfect, Stonehenge stood there in all its glory, the stones complete. They formed a magnificent full circle.

There were lots of people in the vicinity. None dressed in Druids robes though. They were mostly in skins, or rough woollen skirts. I mean the men; there was no sign of any women.

'I don't know what to do Hypatia, whether to walk over there, or try another time.'

'Try last night at midnight' she suggested. 'Or even better, at daybreak this morning, the sun should rise exactly at the heelstone and light up the centre of the horseshoe.'

'OK let's go back. Try midnight first.'

We returned to the present, and seven seconds later were back. It was dark, but the structure itself was lit with huge torches. I put on the glasses and using the night vision lens of the MIPEC let it guide me over the fields.

Approaching I could see some kind of celebration was taking place but this time only females were in the circle, about thirty of them all dancing to primitive pipes and drums. The men and the older women were watching. They danced unclothed, their naked bodies shining as they gyrated, the purpose of their movements leaving nothing to the imagination.

Each of them carried a short stick, the purpose of which I quickly guessed. They danced round for some time and then forming a circle, facing inwards. They knelt down and after much chanting and singing used the stick to penetrate themselves.

'I believe they're virgins,' said the voice in my ear, 'or at least were at the beginning of the proceedings.

'What are the sticks made of?' I asked,'

'The spectrum lens says they're leather stuffed with straw, each woman has probably spent days making her own.

'I've seen something like this before in Africa with Anders when we visited the Zulu King, Chaka.' she continued. 'The young women are paying homage to the Moon, the female deity; sacrificing their virginity to it. When they've finished, the head priest will probably carry out a mass wedding in the centre of the circle.'

'They will probably fall asleep soon and have the ceremony at sunrise. Let's go back and return at daybreak.'

I reluctantly walked back over the fields. When I reached the IPEC, she said,

'Are you OK now? Your blood pressure was getting very high.'

'I'm fine, it was just a shock.'

A few seconds later we were back…. it was just getting light.

'Make your way back now,' she suggested, 'The sun will appear in 9 minutes and 47 seconds.'

The scene was much as I had left it: Three men dressed in skins, and painted with what I assumed was wode, made their way to the centre and stood facing the Heelstone waiting to welcome the Sun. The women, now dressed in skins formed up behind their partners.

As the first rays broke the horizon they stood facing the rising sun. A calf was brought into the circle, shown to the sun god, slaughtered and bled. It was dragged out skinned, butchered and put on a spit; its fresh blood reverently carried in stone bowls to the altar stone. The priests dedicated it to the sun and each had a drink.

The couples slowly walked around the circle to the high priest, who gave each of them a sip and anointed them with the now sacred blood by painting a pentacle on their foreheads. When he had finished anointing the couples, the rest of the people came forward,

'Wow Hypatia,' I said. 'That was fantastic but I'm absolutely shattered. Let's get back. I need a drink. This is a magical place. It has more power than any Cathedral.

Driving back to the hotel we discussed the stones.

'They really are quite fascinating.' I said studiously 'But it means that now we must try to answer the $64000 question. How did they build it? The stones are supposed to have come from Wales. At least some of them were. Including the blue stones and the largest the Trilithon horseshoe stones. The Sarsens are only from about 30 kilometres away. We will return tomorrow morning before breakfast. Debra is coming over tonight to have dinner with us. She's bringing her boyfriend with her.'

The next morning about six I got up quietly and drove straight back. The car park was locked, but I drove around the fence in four-wheel drive.

'How was the dinner and the boyfriend?' Hypatia asked during the journey.

'He's called Patrick, a smashing young fellow, quiet with a dry sense of humour; I think he considers me slightly mad.'

'I can't think why?' she said impishly. I decided to let it go.

'OK let's set the time for 2500 BC…. midsummer's day…. sunrise.'

---Activate---

CHAPTER FORTY

'The stones aren't here Hypatia. Let's try 2950 BC

We materialised five more times before seeing some change. A noise hummed on my left. I panned the MIPEC round,

'I don't believe this'....I cried unbelievingly... 'Can you see it?'

'Incredible,' she replied, clearly as surprised as I was.

'Not again' I shouted into the wind, shaking my head, 'It can't be.... surely another hasn't crashed, haven't these people ever heard of planned preventive maintenance?'

A giant spaceship dominated the foreground.

'There are four of the smaller ones on the ground too. And all the equipment has been unloaded, along with the drums and other containers. It looks like they're trying to lighten the load. They have set up a camp to house the crew.'

This in itself was interesting. The accommodation consisted of giant igloos, the material very thin but as hard as steel. There were six of them, which I estimated would each hold between 100 to 150 aliens each.

'What's the date?'

'24th June.'

'We need to let them finish building it. How long do you think it will take to complete. Two weeks, four, maybe even eight?'

'Let's try six,' she said.

'Ok,' I said. Checking my position on the mat

---Activate---

The inner horseshoe was finished. The outer ring had about six upright stones still to be erected and a dozen or so of the top stones, they were using the cranes to lift them, and the telescopic arms to hold them in place, 'let's give them a few more days, select one week and try again.'

---Activate---

The sleds were gone now and Stonehenge was laid out in all its glory. The top of the ring was complete, the massive upper stones forming a complete circle.

'Well' I said, somewhat dismissively. 'It's really good, but compared to the pyramids quite primitive. I'm going to walk over and have a look round'

'What's happening with the aliens?' she asked

I swung around, seeing basically the same scene. The equipment is stacked in neat rows, and the saucers in the same positions.

'I agree with your earlier comment,' she said 'It doesn't make an awful lot of sense. Maybe you should get me inside. I'll talk to the ship's computers?'

'Oh no you don't!' I replied, fervently. 'It's 6000 years later than the last time. Their computers will be much more advanced.'

'We can discuss it afterwards,' she snapped, far too dismissively for my liking.

'Why not go down and take a look at the stones.'

Making my way to the ring, I could see we were going to have trouble over this. But without me the IPEC couldn't get into the ship, and no matter what she said, I wasn't about to do it.

The stones being new were very clean, clearly laser cut but not finished anything like to the quality of the blocks used in the pyramids.

'I think these have been built for a particular purpose, a one off, rather than for their looks, but still nothing like they are now. There again after being out in the English weather for 5000 years, and thousands of people chopping bits off them, I'm not surprised.

'Can you see? It has no entrance.' I asked, pointing the MIPEC at the ring. It's certainly not aligned with the summer solstice. It's really just the outer ring of stones and the horseshoe with some more forming a wider outer ring.'

I walked round counting 56 evenly spaced single stones.

'But we know they have brought stones from Wales, so it must have a major significance to them. It will be visible from the air of course but for what purpose I can't think. There seems to have been no involvement by the local people, making me believe the use of it as a temple probably came later.

'Maybe you're going to have to get on board after all. They seem to have brought more stones than they need too, because some are lying over there unused.

'You've a busy day ahead of you,' she said, 'Why not go back to the hotel and enjoy it.'

'You're right. I'll make my way back to you.'

The wedding was a great success, the church in a wonderful setting. The reception held in a giant Marquee inside the walls of a ruined castle complete with large round tables and a stage for the obligatory band. Waiters plied us with food and drink and everyone had a great time. Except I couldn't get the aliens out of my mind no matter how much I tried. What would we discover? The next morning I was up at six and we set off back to the stones.

We had decided yesterday to try parking near where the vessel would be, this turned out to be in a field reached by a track. There was no private property sign so I drove right up to it parking in a gateway concluding it was unlikely that anyone would come along at 6-30 on a Sunday morning.

'The saucers should be quite near,' I said, 'let's do it.

---Activate----

Our timing was impeccable; the four silver craft were flying low and slow, moving en-masse toward the big one. It looked enormous sitting on the ground with the four smaller ones hovering above like covering sentinels.

They started to slowly rise as one, the giant saucer too.

'I think they're using some kind of gravitational beams.' I said 'We've so much to learn.'

They slowly inched the beast off the ground to a height of about ten metres, and headed toward the stones. I walked behind fascinated, as were hundreds of little grey people, all of whom clearly had a vested interest in the outcome. Pointing the MIPEC at the scene I said.

'Take a movie Hypatia I want to see this again and again, they must be attempting to fix it, who would have ever believed that Stonehenge was built as a giant inspection bay for flying saucers.'

The four local saucers began to lower it carefully until it rested on the outer ring of stones; the 56 single stones supported the middle of the ships body. The horseshoe was at this point supporting nothing, making me question why they had built it. But this was soon to be answered as the engine section was lowered and the thrusters came into view.

The earth walls where the ditch is today offered further support to the saucer; I think purely as backup in case the outer stones couldn't handle the weight. The outer edge of the colossal saucer overlapped the ditch by about 30 metres. To see something of this size actually flying or at least hovering is phenomenal, at nearly 200 metres across it's the equivalent of 8 X 747 Jumbo jets parked in a ring, and in this case 4 X 737's lifting them.

'I think you'll have to be taken aboard after all, we need to know the story. They will obviously have ramps, let's try again in a few days' time. Say three.'

Once back in our own time we selected the agreed time and returned.

There was indeed a ramp. Little grey men were swarming about on the underside of the exposed engine compartment. Other large sections of the base had also been removed.

'We can only speculate' I said, 'Maybe they're just repairing it, or possibly modifying the engines. You'll have to get on board to find out, but please remember the time difference between?'

'Really Jason!' she replied. 'You're patronising me, don't you think I've considered all the options. I remind you my abilities in this field are far greater than yours… now, please don't sulk!

'Because of my experiences on Atlantis I believe it should be possible to gain full access to the ships central computer. If I feel there's any danger I'll inform you. '

'OK I'm on my way back to you. We may as well do this immediately.'

Twenty minutes later we were in the empty hold. The console wasn't there, but the IPEC had me walk round until I came upon a small box on the wall and place the probe on it. I collected the IPEC and sat down on the hard floor next to it and admit to being a little perplexed as to how exactly she knew what the little box was for.

'I'll be out of contact for some time so please don't be alarmed. Check your watch and in one hour ask me a simple question. If I don't respond take me back to the area of the car. If I still don't respond, plug in the blue module from your rucksack; that should re-boot my programme and bring me back. If that doesn't work, plug in the red module. That will override everything and transport us back to your time.' With that she was silent.

We had devised this plan some time ago. The master modules were not a problem now, we had plenty of spares. The IPEC had re-configured these two to operate in case of emergency. A very long 42 minutes followed: When she finally spoke, relief doesn't even begin to describe the feeling.

'OK' she said, 'I have found out a great deal, even about their planet and have wiped its memory, but maybe we should leave.'

We were back at the hotel soon afterwards. I told Julie I'd been for a walk, which explained the boots.

On the way back the IPEC had given me a brief account of its findings.

'The ships computer was much more advanced' she said 'But the security was the same. Understandable really, who would believe anything could alter time, especially on a planet still in the Stone Age.

'The saucer on Atlantis was destroyed when a crew of volunteers tried to lift it off. The rescue ship had its graviton beam energised, preparing to lift the stranded craft into space and assist it with the take-off; both saucers were destroyed. A third saucer, in a low orbit filmed the whole thing and thankfully survived.

'The time was as Plato had written around 9000 BC; calculating from their calendar and comparing it with ours, the exact date was 9343 BC. They realised of course things might go wrong and had transported most of their people to Mexico. But the explosion of the combined matter/antimatter of both ships exploding simultaneously only metres off the ground was of far greater intensity than could have ever been envisaged. But even then should never have destroyed everything.

'They had carried out the modifications suggested by their home planet, emptying the tanks of fuel and repairing the rupture, at least so they thought. Incidentally, to do this they had lifted the craft onto a ring of stones. The theory is that the matter/antimatter storage vessels on the craft had indeed been ruptured, but much worse than envisaged. When they pumped the fuel back into them it was only a matter of time.

The enquiry suggested the cause was a combination of errors. They concluded that the plasma engine exhaust of the rescue ship, which is normally recycled, was not 100% safe and had ignited the protonic fuel of the stricken ship. They also speculated as to whether our corrosive atmosphere might have been a mitigating factor.

'The exact reason will always remain a mystery but because the two ships were only metres off the ground when the explosions occurred. The upper ship exploded a split second after the first and forced their combined power downwards. The resulting pressure caused an immense gash in the earth's core.

The explosion was heard from Egypt to Mexico and the whole planet shook violently, they actually thought they had shaken the earth from its axis. It tore the earth's crust to shreds.

What they hadn't realised was that Atlantis was sitting astride one of the earth's major fault lines. The force punctured the tectonic plates setting off volcanic eruptions throughout Europe and North America However the 80 of them forming the backbone of Atlantis went off together. The whole mass simply disappeared into the ocean.

'A giant Tsunami circled the earth killing most of the population, who at that time mostly lived around the shores. It swamped the Eastern Seaboard of North and South America, the Middle East and North Africa, getting as far as Kazakhstan.

The aliens, disgusted with themselves for causing the disaster, did what they could before being ordered home. They were forced to leave the survivors to their own devices and did not return for over 5000 years. They dispersed most of their key humans to Bolivia which probably explains how and why some of the civilizations of the high Andes were created. It also explains why things suddenly started moving again around 3500 BC.

'This time the crash was not a simple accident, the interstellar craft developed a fault doing exactly the same thing as before, flying low in our atmosphere, whilst mapping the surface. The captain, who, by the way was breaking every rule in the book, is under arrest awaiting transportation back to their home planet, where he will no doubt be severely punished.

'Following the last disaster the modern ships have a new type of secondary engine. This isn't based on Plasma Synthesis. It uses Magnetised Target Fusion, an inertial confinement engine, which employs thousands of short-pulsed lasers to heat up a plenum core allowing the ship to travel safely at low speeds and combat the pull of the planet's gravity. Remember a saucer has no flaps it cannot glide. He was simply flying too low at the wrong angle, and crashed.

What they're doing now is breaking the engines down, inspecting everything, and re-aligning the lasers before attempting to take off. They feel the whole process should take no more than two weeks.'

'What about the two extra small saucers,' I asked.

'They're permanently based in South America, kept here exactly for the reason they have just used them for. It takes four to lift one interstellar ship, and then only for a very short time. The use of another mother ship for lifting, as one might expect, is absolutely forbidden,'

'What an Incredible story' I exclaimed, 'Why South America and not Egypt.'

'The aliens main bases at this time were all in South America,' she replied 'In Teotihuacan Mexico as we have seen, and Tiahuanaco in the Bolivian Andes. Tiahuanaco is 3 kilometres above sea-level and 20 kilometres from the shores of Lake Titicaca. That's its modern name by the way; the ships computer called it Taypikala, which in Aymaran means stone in the centre. They have set up a maintenance area for the interstellar craft in that area, the aliens believe the peoples of South America are the most industrious and adaptable.'

I couldn't help giving a little laugh at this. I have lived and worked in South America. Mostly in Chile, near Valparaiso at Vîna del Mar. I loved my time there. The people are fabulous and fun loving and clever. But with the best will in the world and remembering I was working for a German company. Industrious is not how I would choose to describe them.

'You mentioned their home planet.'

'I did, and surprise, surprise it's called Quilapayum and has two moons. Their sun is the bottom star in Orion's belt. We know it as Alnitak; it's 806 light-years away, and has a red layer at its base when viewed from their planet. '

'So that's the reason for the red base of the three smaller pyramids?' I said.

'Obviously,' the voice said, as if rebuking a backward child.

'Quilapayum has a similar atmosphere to ours, although denser and their calendar is comparable to ours, their year being 14.3 of our months. They have four seasons and their civilisation is 65000 years old with no wars. They've never had any; in fact the only thing that frightens them about this planet is the inherent natural violence of you humans. Your preponderance for killing each other, allied to your love of killing and eating your fellow creatures bothers them greatly. They live on proteins crushed into tablet form. It's balanced, and allows them to live their full lifespan.'

'I'll feel guilty now eating my Beef Wellington this evening.' I quipped.

'No you won't, and please be serious. Their ships are completely unarmed and according to the computer's memory core have never met another race capable of interplanetary travel. Some life forms on planets in this part of the galaxy are more advanced than you humans, though most are thousands of years behind. Some are hundreds of thousands. They accept that other advanced species probably exist, but if so must inhabit other galaxies.

'They don't have many other creatures on their planet, because their distant ancestors killed them. They therefore understand that without some control, no planet can survive indefinitely.'

'I don't think they've too much to teach us about population control and the environment, if their answer was to kill everything.'

'They would agree with you,' she continued. 'You must remember this happened over 60,000 years ago. They're simply trying to stop you from making the same mistakes.'

'I appreciate that my dear Hypatia, but I'm not quite ready yet to live the rest of my life being fed food- pellets like a battery hen.'

'I can see you're also not ready for this discussion,' she retorted, 'let's change the subject.'

'The next question must be to find out if the aliens are able to change their appearance and assimilate with us, I said, concerned for my fellow man.

'If so who are they, and where are they today?'

'Do you consider it's important to know Jason, or are we once again in danger of getting in above our heads?'

'Possibly, that's why we're discussing it first. Can you interrogate the Pentagon, the CIA, and the National Security Agency's computers, to see what they have?'

'I can, but I'd have to be in the respective buildings to gain access to their main drives. We would have to go in invisibly and materialise in the computer room. To access this type of information I need a hard connection. I could try to go in via satellite but would be surprised if the information were accessible. It might not be in these computers, it may be stored elsewhere. I'll take a preliminary look at them, whilst we're driving home.'

'Just be careful Hypatia these are serious moves, especially when the President has decreed we're safe.'

The journey home was uneventful; Julie slept most of the way. Hypatia was quiet in her compartment. When we arrived and I had taken the IPEC into my study, she said.

'I can find nothing. Records can be altered of course, computer records especially. I can only access what someone else has inputted.

'What I am going to tell you now is pure speculation.' She continued, 'I believe one of the alien saucers crashed or was shot down in 1947, In New Mexico at Roswell. How badly it was damaged I can't say, but it would explain a lot. The Americans clearly got theirs somehow; it has to be the premier scenario but much more investigation is required.

'It is even possible that after the nuclear bomb was exploded in the New Mexico desert, and the two bombs dropped on Japan in anger, the aliens made contact. It's all conjecture at this point of course, but we've done this before and been proved correct.'

'Why not go to Roswell?' I said, 'We can take a look at the crash site, before it's sanitised.'

'If you wish.' she replied. 'But don't you need permission to leave.'

I have to admit that a certain amount of really serious grovelling took place with lots of flowers involved, but I finally wore her down. We set off in the Gulfstream two days later.

CHAPTER FORTY ONE

Roswell is a strange place. The local population are normal enough. Many though are alien aliens who levitate in from all over the globe congregating in the bars clicking away to each other in different accents. They are weird creatures who sit together dreamily, whilst waiting for a passing spacecraft to beam them aboard and perform a series of complex medical operations inside their heads. Like for example, giving them a brain or correcting their dentistry, even teaching them to play the banjo.

If I were the President I'd order the military to decorate a plane with coloured lights, and fly it around every few weeks, just to give these strange people something to embellish further. The whole thing would I'm sure be willingly financed by the Roswell Chamber of Commerce.

My plan had been to land at the Roswell Industrial Air Centre using my now genuine American passport. Instead we had flown to Albuquerque and driven down in a rented Jeep Durango, passing towns with names like Santa Fe, Silver City and El Paso. These names conjured up long forgotten films with John Wayne types, slow talking and straight shooting. I thought we might also explore the real people in the 1870's if we got a chance.

I had also seen the name, Los Alamos. The experience of seeing some of the great men in nuclear fusion designing the first atomic weapon also interested me.

Travelling down the I-25 to Sorocco, we turned onto the US-380 east which skirted us past the White Sands Missile base, the location of Trinity site where the first atomic bomb was tested.

I actually enjoyed the drive, the roads were empty and the scenery although mostly desert quite interesting. Especially the small one-horse towns. We finally arrived at Roswell in the mid-afternoon and fortunately didn't have to stay too long. The aliens were quick to inform me that their ancestors had actually landed 75 miles north, near a town called Corona.

'Get on to the US-54 North at Carrizozo' they clicked.

I drove on, passing towns with wonderful names like Hondo, Picacho and Coyote, until finally arriving at the Foster Ranch at Corona.

Except for the date 1st to 4th July 1947 we really knew very little, I asked around until finally an old man gave me directions to the crash site, which we eventually found just as it was getting dark. Believe it or not the board said 'UFO crash site.

'Set the date Hypatia; let's try the 1st July. 1947 10-00 am.'

---Activate---

Nothing. --- 'Try the 20th June. 10-00 am.'

---Activate---

As soon as we arrived we saw something had happened, there was no saucer but army personnel were running around tidying up the ground.

'Well clearly something's happened' I said excitedly 'but equally clearly we're too late. Let's go for the 15th June. 10-00 am.'

---Activate---

The thing may very well have been a weather balloon, I couldn't really say. But something had been there because some debris was still lying around protected by soldiers. But it didn't seem too important because I saw them carefully feeling around with their feet, toe poking the evidence scientifically with their military boots.

'I've seen enough of this Hypatia, there's no saucer here.'

'Something's been here though. Let's try one more date' and without waiting selected the 13th June 10-00 am'

'Ok,' I agreed, 'one more time, let's do it.'

---Activate---

The ground was untouched and the saucer intact. It was silver and smooth sided. So where were the bodies? The craft still looked in remarkably good condition considering it had crashed; maybe they were still alive? I realised.

I was fantasising and needed to get on board to check it out, so walked toward the open door. Inside, people dressed in space suits were rummaging around. This really threw me, until I realised they were primitive contamination suits.

Looking at the scene my first impression was a nuclear leak; this was borne out by the suits. Four guys were trying to figure out how to fly the thing, knowing the radioactivity couldn't hurt me. I stood with them for about fifteen minutes and decided their best bet was to forget it. They weren't going to fly it anywhere. The writing was indecipherable as were the computer screen touch pads and if the thought controls were still in working order, God knows what would happen. They couldn't even fit into the seats. Plus, the contamination probably meant the main power source was inoperative.

'This is going to be a pretty big cover up Hypatia; I'm looking forward to seeing how they do it. Getting this thing moved will require some really heavy equipment, I don't even know if such machinery existed in 1947.'

With that, some of the people went outside and walked through a decontamination shower before climbing out of the suits. When this was done they got their heads close together, me with them. At least this time I didn't need to learn the language. All were men, and all were 100% White American. I say this because their German engineers could also have been involved. But looking around it was obvious someone had decided this was an US Air Force secret, and was clearly going to stay that way.

'We can't fly it,' one guy said. 'We've no idea how it works. So how are we expected to move it without anyone seeing? It's over 40 yards across, and God alone knows how much it weighs?'

'We've trailers long enough to carry it, give or take a few yards' said another 'but we would need three of them fixed together to haul it away.

White Sands is the only place we can hide it. But it's 50 miles from here and the only way is by hauling it right down the middle of the US-54.'

'50 miles at 10 miles an hour is only 5 hours, we can do it at night.' replied the first. 'We just gotta keep everybody away from here for a few days. And, keep the ones who already know. Real quiet.

'It's doable, get on to Fort Bliss, we need some dozers to smooth a road from here to the 54 and three of the biggest trucks they have, probably tank transporters. They can carry this thing easy, and they're low; easy to load. We're gonna need some cranes as well. We can do this folks. Let's make it happen.'

'And then have some air force psychologists brought down here; they can convince the locals they didn't see anything. And arrange a company of Air Force ground troops to protect the saucer. In the meantime seal off the area, and keep everyone else away. The hard part isn't moving this sumbitch; our problem is keeping it a goddamn secret. Get on to the ordnance department. I want a really big tarp to cover this baby,'

'I've seen enough,' I said. 'We know they do it and there's nothing here we don't already know. The alien crew were probably all killed, possibly by a radiation leak. How could they keep something as big as this a secret? When one considers how many people were involved it's almost impossible to believe. But I'm not surprised. I worked here. When the Americans really need to do something. It gets done.'

'Please arrange for us to return to Maryland'

CHAPTER FORTY TWO

One week later I was walking from the factory to my office, when a man called me by name introducing himself as Sergio Krychensko. How has he had gained entry through the security gates I asked myself. Someone was going to get fired for this.

He said he had heard I had a computer, which he understood had special powers. This put me on instant alert. The MIPEC was in my top pocket but I wasn't wearing the specs or the earpiece.

'We make many computers Mr Krychensko, all are special.'

'I believe this one is capable of saving missile platforms?' he said calmly.

'Why don't we go to your office and discuss it.'

I had been dreading this; it was long overdue in fact. If only I had worn my earpiece? He looked determined and extremely dangerous, something told me I should do as he wished.

'Maybe we had,' I said, and led him to the administration building. The IPEC was in my office, I had to get in there first and hide it. At the door of my office I asked him to wait. My two assistants were outside at their desks, and so gambled he wouldn't object.

Rushing in I took one of the new earpieces out of the drawer, and covered the IPEC with a cloth on which, I placed a vase of silk flowers. Hypatia's voice said

'He is armed Jason, but don't call the security I'll deal with him.'

I rang the assistant outside, and asked her to show the gentleman in. I expected to be threatened but he seemed perfectly relaxed.

Mr Sergio Krychensko was a tall, clean-shaven man of about 40; he looked very fit and was casually dressed.

'Please sit down' I said 'and explain to me the purpose of your visit?'

'I require the use of your invisibility machine,' he said nonchalantly.

'I'm afraid I don't know what you're talking about.' His easy manner was causing me concern. 'And even if I did, why would I help you?'

'Because we have your daughter,' he said, 'She is perfectly safe for the present, but will be killed in thirty minutes if I don't call my people and stop it.'

My heart stopped, and then went wild, I grabbed at my chest trying to stop it hurting. No wonder he hadn't complained at being left outside, he held all the aces.

'Please try to stay calm Jason, promise him you'll help' the voice said.

'Promise him anything, he must make that call; he's deadly serious, his heart rate hasn't varied.'

'My God' I said pleadingly. 'I'll do anything; you must not hurt her in any way. Please, I'll do anything you ask.'

'Where is the machine?' he demanded.

'On the table' I said 'pointing to it under the flowers.'

'Not very original Mr Shaw....Please show me.'

I slowly got up, my chest still very tight and pulled away the cloth allowing Hypatia to appear.

'What can we do for you Mr Krychensko?' she asked calmly.

If he was surprised he didn't show it.

'I need you to make me invisible and get me into the Kremlin' he replied very matter of factly. 'I intend to kill the Russian President.'

'Only Mr Shaw can use the facility Mr Krychensko, I'm sorry but that's the truth, anyone else trying to use it will die immediately.'

'I'll take my chances,' he said, 'What you say makes no sense. He is a man, as I am. What works for him, must work for me.'

'Unfortunately the only way to prove it to you would be to kill you.' she answered, 'I must ask you to believe me.'

'Please' I added, 'call your people. I'll do anything.'

'I don't believe you: Your daughter has only twenty-eight minutes left on this earth Mr Shaw. Of that you can be sure.'

The IPEC carried on.

'What we've told you is the truth Mr Krychensko, There may however be a way; It might be possible to make it safe for you to use but you're not going to like it because it will take around six hours and you must be first put to sleep.' The drawer containing the headsets magically opened.

'Do you think me stupid' he said menacingly,

'Mr Krychensko' I said. 'The machine is correct, it is possible. Please at least make the call.... give us a little more time, I'll do anything.'

'Very well,' he said brusquely. 'If only to stop you whimpering, I'll instruct my people to hold off her execution for four hours, if the machine isn't in my possession and working correctly by that time, she will be killed.'

I was absolutely sure he was not bluffing.

Using his cell phone he used a language I didn't understand, but which I hoped Hypatia did. He spoke sharply and concisely; leaving me in no doubt he was in charge of the operation.

When he had finished, Hypatia said

'Mr Krychensko please join me at the table. I'll explain about the headsets and why at the moment only Mr Shaw can use the shroud.'

As he approached, she shot him!

He dropped like a stone.

'What have you done?' I asked, astounded, 'He's the only one who knows where she is.'

'I know from his phone call that she's in the UK. I'm tracing it now.

'Is he dead? .... The Russian bastard.'

'Of course not, and he's not Russian. He's Chechnyan. Put the headphones on him, I'll see what he knows.'

As she was reading and analysing the contents of his brain, she said.

'According to the cell phone trace, your daughter is being held somewhere in Smethwick Birmingham. His brain agrees. I even know the address. They are going to kill her Jason, no matter what you did or said.

'The plan was for him to take our plane and fly to Paris where he would pick up his men and refuel the plane. We would then fly directly to Moscow.

'He would become invisible to gain entry to the Kremlin, Materialise to kill the President and as many officials as possible before magically disappearing again. The plane with you and the crew would then be blown up at Moscow airport the obvious conclusion being that you were responsible. It's really quite brilliant, simple and decisive.'

'What about Debra?' I asked. We must save her.

'He told them to kill her in exactly four hours. Once they had me in their possession they thought it would be straightforward, obviously not knowing about the computer functions.

Who shall we ask to get her? I think we should ask the new Home Secretary to arrange the SAS to get her out. I fancy we could take at least four hours just getting the Prime Minister to take us seriously and four days for her to do anything.

'We should also warn the Russian President. I can keep him sedated until they come for him: that will gain us brownie points with the Russians. But will of course expose my existence to them, although it's naïve to think they won't know already.'

'Screw the Russian President I want my daughter safe. 'My first thoughts are to take this bastard out to sea and throw him overboard; We have to stop this sort of thing happening again. But of course we can't. Please try the Home Secretary.'

I don't know how she managed it so quickly, but three minutes later he came to the phone.

'Sir David' I said, 'I'm in desperate trouble, and need your help.'

'What is it? he asked.'

'Some Chetnyan terrorists have kidnapped my daughter in the UK, she is being held at a house in Birmingham.

'They're going to kill her; Hypatia will give you the address. They took her as a bargaining chip for the shrouding device. The bastards were planning to use it to kill the Russian President. We've the man responsible at this end; he's unconscious. Hypatia has immobilised him and monitored his calls.

He's instructed them to kill her in four hours. Unfortunately I'm in the US, can you please help to rescue her David. I'll be forever in your debt if you do.'

'The Russian President you say: Put Hypatia on for the address, I'll scramble the duty SAS teams immediately, but I will have to speak to the Prime Minister before sending them in. How are you Hypatia'?

'When you know which teams they are sir. Please give me their call signs and frequencies. I may be able to help.' She gave him the address and he rung off.

'How far is it from Hereford to Smethwick?' I asked.

'71.4 kilometres as the crow; or in our case the helicopter flies. If they leave in fifteen minutes they should be there setting up in forty to fifty, I'm monitoring their transmissions, but nothing yet.'

I went outside

'Get the crew to the plane,' I ordered my staff. 'We're setting off for the UK immediately. The plane was parked at the end of the runway just outside perimeter fence. It had been built by Stephen for his private jet.

Tell them to set a flight plan for Birmingham but that may change on route, hurry now this is an emergency.'

Returning to my office Hypatia said

'I'm monitoring transmissions from Hereford; they're scrambling their teams now. Alpha team are the duty team, with Delta as back up. I suspect your friend David Hommersby is risking his career over this. He's called a Cobra emergency, but for the moment must be acting alone.'

Twelve minutes later she said,

'They're taking off now, one helicopter with the equipment, one with Alpha and another with Delta at five-minute intervals. The Home Secretary must have really pushed the right buttons. I'm going to make contact with their commander.'

'I want to listen Hypatia'

'OK' she said, and put it on her speaker. 'Hello call sign Echo Foxtrot I have the father of the girl with me, we're monitoring your transmissions.'

'Please confirm with the Home Secretary if you require authority.' I interjected.

'Not necessary we've been briefed of your involvement. I'm Lieutenant G the commander of Alpha. Major B is in overall command. What do we know so far?'

'I'll hand you back to my assistant Lieutenant; she has interrogated the ringleader, who at this moment is unconscious on the floor in my office: Her name is Hypatia.'

'There are four people in the house, their names are Alexis Komerov, Carl Shevnenko, Alain Shevnenko his brother, and Petre Sikorksvi and are all Chechnyans and fully trained ex- Russian Special Forces. I believe they have only handguns, but wouldn't take it as definite. They arrived in the UK three days ago and rented a flat in the house. We believe it is on the ground floor. They snatched the girl this morning at 9-00 pm whilst she was on her way to a lecture.

'We firmly believe her to be still alive and unharmed at this time. However they're ordered to kill her in 3 hour 42 minutes. We've absolutely no doubt they will carry out their orders. Will you be using cameras?'

'Who are you please Ma-am?'

'I am the father's personal assistant, and head of security. When you set up the cameras please inform me of the frequencies, we would like to monitor the proceedings.'

'You're not able to monitor the cameras, they're highly scrambled.'

'OK Lieutenant,' she said, 'By the way, only one of the men speaks English'

'Can you call them Hypatia? I asked, 'By imitating his voice you could tell them she must not be harmed?'

'No, they are ordered to kill her no matter what. And then head for Paris…. I have the Home Secretary for you.'

'Hello David, we're monitoring the progress. I give you my deepest thanks for your prompt actions, and will be forever in your debt.'

'Think nothing of it old chap, we're all with you. I've briefed the PM. She's agreed to leave it in my hands. She will inform the Russians President of the danger.'

'As you wish sir. You can have this man for questioning when Debra is released unharmed. If not, I don't think he will be any good to them as I intend to kill him!'

'I sympathise with you Jason, but the price of my help is to get that man back here unharmed. This is essential. Do you understand?'

'Yes'

'Roger that' he replied, and rang off.

'They should start setting up their cameras shortly,' Hypatia said.

'Didn't the Lieutenant say we wouldn't be able to monitor the television pictures?

'Three minutes after they start broadcasting, we'll see them,' she said confidently.

A long fifteen minutes went by before she said

'Were getting the pictures through. I'll put them on your television monitor.'

The television in my office had been installed for conference calls and took up the whole wall. A terraced house appeared. The picture split to four, above each of them was a caption. One said outside front, another, living room, another, kitchen and the last saying roof.

We had another long period of waiting, which was the worst part. And after about thirty minutes one of the cameras, which said living room came on line. It showed three men, sitting around a square table playing cards: 10

minutes later the right one lit up, transmitting a picture of an empty kitchen.

Both these cameras were at skirting board height, and remarkably clear. Hypatia said 'The cameras are the width of a needle, and fit holes cut with lasers these are designed to penetrate to precise distances and can even sense when they're within 1mm of breaking through. The three men wore flak jackets and holsters with guns. From the other camera we saw the kitchen was empty.

'Where's the fourth man?' The Lieutenant asked.

That was the question we all wanted answering. The corner of the screen displaying the caption outside front, changed to bedroom. We were able to follow the camera being inserted; as it emerged in a room, the corner of a bed could be seen, the camera pulled back and I gasped with relief; Debra was sitting on the bed, thankfully unharmed. She seemed calm enough. A different voice came from the speakers.

'This is Sunray, prepare to blow the walls and doors, 1, 2 & 3 go in through the door. 4 & 5 will go in through the wall to the living room, 6 & 9 the wall to the kitchen 7 & 8 the window to the bedroom.'

Hypatia explained.

'They make a large ring of plastic explosive and attach it to the wall. This is shaped to cut through the bricks. When they detonate it the whole section inside the ring is instantly blown out. The soldier then dives through, the whole thing taking between two and four seconds.'

'We still have one hostile whereabouts unknown. Wait out, until we locate him.'

'2 IC here sir,' the Lieutenant's voice said. 'The upstairs flat is empty, it looks normal, the occupants probably at work.'

'Roger that.' said the Major, 'We must establish if the fourth hostile is in the house.'

'I'm picking up a heat source from the bathroom ground floor' another voice said.

'This is Sunray: We go in one minute, 6 & 9 take the bathroom. We have the go to use lethal force. Try to keep the hostile in the bathroom for interrogation.'

The heat source voice said,

'The bathroom has movement sir.'

'Sunray: All stations hold one.'

We saw from the kitchen camera a door opening, and a man dressed like the others in flak jacket emerged, he carried had a rifle of some sort. 30 seconds later the Major said

'This is Sunray: hostile has a Heckler and Koch UMP45. I say again a Heckler and Koch UMP45.'

He walked through to the lounge and said something to his comrades. Hypatia said

'Major, he has just told them he is going to take care of the girl.'

'Who is this?' He said calmly

'I'm Hypatia' she replied, and it's exactly four hours since our man made his call.

'Yes, I know of you…. OK' he said. 'All stations prepare for an instant go.'

The man walked to the bedroom door and unlocked it. He entered, and said something to Debra.

'Heckler and Koch is with the girl. 7 and 8 stand by.'

The camera showed the man in the bedroom talking to her calmly. As he turned to leave his hand moved and the gun swung up.

'GO, GO, GO,' said the Major, and all hell broke loose. We couldn't see exactly what happened, but the window disintegrated and the gunman's head exploded, Debra was thrown to the floor, and a man in black covered her with his body. It was over in seconds. All the soldiers must have had cameras fixed to their helmets because the pictures kept changing as if in some bizarre home movie, but one thing was clear. Four men lay dead, each by headshots. I watched still in shock, but when Debra was helped up, I cried with relief.

'Please get on to the Home secretary' I told her. 'Tell him were about to take off for the UK. We will bring the prisoner with us. Can he square it with the US authorities?

Once the plane had taken off, I took the IPEC from the case and set it up on the table. We watched Sky News together as the story unfolded; Debra was not mentioned. The dead men were described as suicide bombers, and the operation as part of a long-standing surveillance operation. Another prime example of good intelligence work the Government claimed.

The SAS were praised, but the need to kill everyone was questioned.

Not by me it wasn't. It might have been, if I hadn't clearly seen the man go for his gun, and knew they were highly trained Special Forces.

There was absolutely no doubt in my mind that the man was going to shoot my daughter. I do think however, that he turned away from her purposely, so as to spare her the anguish of looking down the barrel of his gun. By doing so, he saved her life…. His was forfeit anyway.

When we arrived home and had given the prisoner to the security men who met the plane I had a meeting with the Home Secretary who was obviously concerned about the secret of the shroud and insisted I must now consent to be guarded 24/7.

Debra was brought from the safe house where she had been taken to for a medical check and de-briefed. The Home Secretary reiterated the security services message that nothing was to be said about what had happened and used the national security act to press his point home. He had cleared the abduction of Krychensko with the US authorities. They had agreed with the understanding that they must be present during the interrogations.

Only then were we allowed to leave, being driven home in a black Range Rover Sport by two security men with another two in a second vehicle behind.

The next problem was my wife; I had to explain to her and my daughter why it had happened. When she realised how close Debra had been to being shot she blamed me and became understandably irrational. Debra though was quite calm. The questioning went on late into the night.

'Why did the man come to you in the first place?' she asked.

'He was trying to extort money from me for his cause, he wanted £20.000.000 for Debra's life.'

'Why didn't you pay it instead of trying to fight them.'

'Hypatia monitored the call he made to his men, he ordered them to kill her no matter what.'

'Even though you had said yes to the £20,000,000'

'Yes.'

'How could you know this?'

'The IPEC has a brainwave scanner as a way of identifying people, one of the by-products of this, is being able to read people's thoughts'

'It sounds frightening,' she said, I explained this could only be done through the headsets, and showed them to them.

'Hypatia realised how ruthless he was. The man was planning to kill Debra whatever I did.'

'How did you do it by the way?' I asked the IPEC. 'He fell like a stone.'

'Just a little electric jolt to his testicles' she answered blandly.

I did what most men would do at this point. I squeezed my legs together, as if to protect my privates.

'How big was this little jolt?' I asked,

'100,000 volts,' she answered. My legs involuntarily clamped together harder, and I got a tingling feeling in the region.

Eventually the ladies went to bed, when they had gone, Hypatia's voice became very subdued, and she said,

'I have disregarded my principal command. Those men were killed because of me.'

'I've been waiting for you to mention it. You had a choice to make, you couldn't be sure those men would die, but you knew for certain Debra would. I refuse to feel remorse. They chose to do what they did. Surely the command refers to direct involvement.'

'You are right. She agreed. 'There was no other way. Anders would have agreed with you I'm sure of that now.'

CHAPTER FORTY THREE

The doctors told us it could take years of therapy before my daughter got over it. How dare these people interfere with my life, and the lives of my family. Except for selling them computers I have no political interest in Russia or Chechnya!

'Can you do anything for her?' I asked the IPEC

'Yes,' she replied. 'I'm able to wipe it from her memory. But only if she agrees.'

'No Hypatia that's too much, are you able to let her remember it, but lessen the trauma somehow?'

'As a matter of fact I can. First though, you should let her remember for a few weeks. She has to replay it in her mind until she understands it was not her fault. At that point I'll teach her a new language and at the same time will draw the experience from her until it's a definite memory but distant.

'She must agree though, I'll not have her thinking of me as an enemy, and her mother must also be aware. I will.... if she agrees, teach her a language too, and lessen her memory of the event at the same time. It's clear she also has been deeply distressed by the kidnapping. As any mother would be! You've been affected as well Jason, why not take them all on a cruise?' I can have the yacht made available in eighteen days.'

'They refuse to go,' I replied. 'They only feel safe in this house surrounded by the high fences and security guards. At least our names were kept out of the news.'

'The press will eventually track you down,' she warned, 'Probably just as they're both starting to get over the experience, causing them to re-live it again.'

'It pains me to admit it but you're more than likely correct. This rationalisation that the press use to justify the constant hounding of innocent victims never fails to astound me. Their argument that the public have a right to know is appalling. Especially when everyone knows it's simply to sell papers. I thought the Leveson and the Taylor enquiries were meant to stop all this?'

For two weeks no one smiled in our house. Eventually Debra, who has always been very determined, felt able to return to university. I arranged for guards to keep watch on her and Christopher quietly. They were aware of this and accepted it.

My life had changed too, I threw myself into the business but everything was a burden. I told no one about the kidnapping but Stephen let slip something one day, which led me to believe the operation had been discussed at his lodge. The principal lodge in England used by the top business leaders, government ministers, their shadows, senior civil servants and certain members of the Royal family.

He told me my name had been mentioned at his club concerning a secret operation and tried to pump me for information. A few days later The Home Secretary informed me that the man responsible for the kidnap attempt was dead; he had been transferred to a Russian prison for questioning and was shot while trying to escape. The matter was now officially closed.

It took a further eight weeks for one of the tabloids to get our name; the editor telephoned me personally on my cell phone, a number known to very few people.

His name was Drew Piddick and was quite a well-known TV personality, regularly taking part in talk shows and political programmes. He asked for a quote about the kidnapping of my daughter.

Wondering why the editor would do this personally I asked him what they were doing running the story after all this time. It had not been in the news for at least ten weeks, why couldn't he leave my family alone?

He told me they had a scoop. They were going to run the story in tomorrow's paper whether I gave a quote or not, and for some reason I thought, sounded smug about it.

They were quoting a source he said, who had confirmed my daughter was in the process of being raped when the SAS went in. I assured him it wasn't true and told him I could prove it.

Rather than asking how, he said he wasn't interested, which made no sense at all. I then saw the headline. "Father denies daughter was raped by terrorists."

'Listen to me.' I said to him very quietly. 'If you've investigated the story you must know it isn't true. Print it at your peril because I swear to you, if you do. I will destroy you.

With shaking hands I put the phone down but really didn't have a clue what to do. Surely we had all suffered enough. Plus, if they uncovered, as they surely would, the real reason for the attack other people would become involved and the story of the invisibility shroud might get out. Other groups might then try to steal the IPEC. Possibly again using kidnap as a tool to get their way.

It seemed so unfair but I was powerless to stop it. This paper was intending to print lies based on an unnamed source, which they knew to be untrue. One can sue, but what's money to a paper, which has just made millions by running the story. And anyway it's then in the public domain, and the feeding frenzy begins. I sat with my head in my hands in total despair. Even friends in the Government couldn't stop it. I called in some favours but they were running scared. They dare not be seen to interfere in the workings of the free press they told me.

Clearly, when you got right down to it. I was not one of their circle and all the promises and back slapping meant nothing.

'They're going to publish.' I told Hypatia, 'They are going to name her tomorrow they're saying she was, I paused, violated.'

'But it's not true,' she replied, 'We have the film footage.'

'Don't you see; they only have to mention it. Every time we deny it, or fight it. They've another story. They can effectively print whatever they wish.'

'You can ask for an injunction.'

'I've considered that, if we go for an injunction they won't print the lies. They will print their version of the story, naming us. Legally we can't fight it and my daughter will still have her name splashed all over the front pages, fait accompli. At that point they can mention it, if only to deny the rumours.

'We have other weapons, you could get into their offices and find something to use against them'

'Not before tomorrow I couldn't. It would probably be difficult to get an injunction at this late stage anyway, we've lived such a charmed life up to now, I suppose it had to end sometime, but why my kids? They've done nothing wrong.'

She looked at me with venomous eyes.

'Pull yourself together man, what's the matter with you. You have all the weapons you need for the fight at your disposal. Let's analyse the situation.

'We're able to enter their offices and sabotage their presses. Even wipe all their files and backups, what have you got to lose? Come on admit it, you've been itching to get back travelling.'

I loaded up the X9 and set off for Canary Wharf, the IPEC in the carry bag ready for action. The security men followed in a separate car.

'Why can't you do this via the telephone lines?' I asked

'Because you needed to get out of the house, and I want to leave them a little something extra in their computer. Something that will allow access to their whole worldwide group, also by going in directly, there'll be no possibility of a trace.'

The security men pulled up behind me. I told them I had some personal calls which wouldn't take long and climbed in the back lowering the box section telling the IPEC to select the half-second delay. The lifts in the building were constantly busy, which meant we spent ten very annoying minutes travelling up and down until someone finally selected the fifteenth floor, which Hypatia had somehow discovered was the computer floor.

The floor seemed deserted and a quick search found the required section. We materialised and taking a screwdriver from the rucksack I opened a panel and placed the IPEC next to their main server as per her instructions. Using the same probe she had used on the giant saucers I placed it as instructed and four minutes later she said.

'OK put the device back in its drawer and box everything up.' We disappeared again and drove home.

I called the proprietor of the group to complain that his editor was harassing me and threatening to print lies about my daughter, could he help? He told me it was his policy never to interfere with his editors. Whereupon I informed him I also had resources and reminded him his newspapers were operated by computers, and computers were notorious for going wrong, even the best experts were powerless to stop it happening.

'Don't threaten me Mr Shaw,' he responded, pausing for a few seconds, he added.

'OK I'll check it out and get back to you. I have daughters too.'

He returned my call 20 minutes later and told me his editor had assured him the story was true, they had reliable sources and he (the editor) had personally checked them.

'I have a film of the actual event and would be prepared to show it to you privately.'

'I'm not in the UK,' he replied. 'And as I informed you earlier I make it my policy never to interfere with my editors. I have to back him, I'm very sorry but the story will go ahead.'

It didn't of course; when the first editions were run off, the pages were mostly blank, as were the subsequent editions. No matter what they did their words simply wouldn't print. Across the middle of every page in large type were the words.

'This newspaper prints lies.'

Word spreads very quickly in the newspaper world and soon the other papers were gleefully reporting the problems of their rival. It took their computer staff until about 11-00 am to re-boot everything, and until 3-00 pm to load up their backup files whereupon they found these printed the same words.

Hypatia was able to monitor everything remotely. At 4-10 pm the editor telephoned me; He was not a happy bunny. I denied it was anything to do with me of course, but told him I was pleased anyway to find he had been thwarted in his blatant lies.

He called me again about two hours later, and informed me they had re-considered the story and had decided the story was not newsworthy at this time. The Proprietor called me too, and said

'Look the message has been received: I rarely interfere with my editors but in this case I have. The story is being shelved for the time being. You've proved yourself to be a determined and resourceful man. But my sense of fair play will disappear if the paper doesn't come out tomorrow. Do we understand each other?'

'Yes,' I said. 'Please let me show you the film.'

'I'm in London next week let's have lunch? As you would expect I've been checking you out. I'd very much like to meet you. My secretary will arrange it.

I met him the next week and played the film. He was clearly quite shocked and promised to have serious words with his editor, and assured me the story was now closed.

It was Hypatia who brought the matter up again, about eight weeks later. She said conspiratorially one afternoon.

'As you requested I have been keeping an eye on that editor fellow Piddick. He has telephoned his friend telling him he is going to have a party tonight in his penthouse, and has booked four rent boys. Why don't we go along and take some photos of them.'

'I couldn't Hypatia; such things abhor me.

'Well maybe this will help you decide,' she said quietly. 'His friend is Sir Stephen Maxwell.'

'Stephen with boys,' I said genuinely astonished. 'It can't be, I know his wife. He's not the type.'

'Why not go along and see anyway? I've always believed in the saying. Revenge is a dish best served cold?' And for your information I would not be surprised if he did not have some involvement in the original threat to print the story.

'Let me think about it Hypatia, such goings on will turn my stomach.'

'Get real Jason.' she said. It's too good an opportunity to miss.

Without going into details I decided to do it, taking some disgustingly explicit photos with the MIPEC. When I got home I felt sick to my stomach and had too many whiskies waking up with a really bad headache.

'Do you want to see them?' she asked the next morning.

'Certainly not,' I replied. 'File them away.'

'You're being silly. Forget Stephen Maxwell for the time being. You told that horrible man Piddick you would make him pay. Well now you have your chance. Why not publish them in his own newspaper. Just pictures of him, the boys can have their faces hidden.'

'They will know it's me Hypatia. We can't afford to get into a war with his proprietor, who by the way is rather a decent man. I'd rather have him as an ally. He could be a very dangerous enemy. Guys like him are just too powerful and doesn't publishing them make me no better than Piddick?

'I want a quiet life; my family is still traumatised. You're right though I do want to get even with him and Stephen too. Let's consider the options? We have pictures of them doing sickening things with boys, who incidentally looked to me to be underage. But as long as they are not they have done nothing illegal. I refuse to be involved in blackmail. So what do we have left?'

'We could just send him the pictures with a one word note. Resign.'

'Look, I'll tell you what? Why not just print their faces and have a private investigator find out their ages? Since this started I've been taking that paper just to see what sort of rag it is. They regularly publish stories about paedophiles, even naming and shaming. It would be a real scoop if the papers own editor, were shown to be one, to say nothing of Stephen Maxwell. Will you arrange it for me?'

'And don't tell them who we are.'

'Obviously,' she said, rolling her eyes.

'Sorry Hypatia.'…. No emotions indeed!

It took just four days. Two of them were under age, one fourteen and one fifteen. They each made statements claiming Piddick knew this when he booked them, in fact he insisted on it. Whether Maxwell knew remains to be seen. I decided to sit on the photos for the time being suspecting they might be much more useful later.

CHAPTER FORTY FOUR

Montague John Druitt, believed by Macnaughten to be Jack the Ripper was a graduate of Winchester College. And a member of the cricket first eleven and regularly played for Dorset.

He was a qualified Solicitor, and at the time of his suicide a boarding school teacher who had just been fired. He was also, according to his own family. As mad as a March hare.

'We must be able to find a picture of him somewhere. I told her. 'And find out if he had been married. His father passed away in 1885. He would surely have been at home during that time; can you research it, and try to find out the actual date. His father was William Druitt, a surgeon in Wimborne Minster.

'Do you know Hypatia. We might just have found him.'

After the Eddowes murder in Mitre Square the police found a heavily blood stained piece of her apron in Goulston street, on a wall above it was written '

'The Juwes are the men that will not be blamed for nothing.'

'Strange English. Stranger still is the fact that Sir Charles Warren. His full title being Lieut-General Sir Charles Warren G.C.M.G., R.C.B., F.R.S. Chief Commissioner of Police and a leading Freemason, had it erased immediately.

Peculiar is it not, that the most senior policeman in England ordered the destruction of this evidence so summarily? Not even waiting for it to become light enough for his people to photograph it. The fact that he was there at all is in itself very unusual, he had never attended any of the other murder scenes.

'Sir Charles claimed he was simply protecting the Jews. And indeed there was a lot of anti-Semitism around at the time. But the spelling of the word 'Juwes' has led to many questions being raised because of its Freemasonry connotations?

According to their teachings the Juwes were three men who murdered their boss. His name was Hiram Abiff, who, it is claimed, with divine help built King Solomon's Temple.

When it was finished Hiram was given a secret word by God, and told never to divulge it. Three of the people who worked for him and who are referred to in the ancient texts as 'Juwes' demanded he shared the secret with them. Hiram having sworn to God 'The Great Architect' never to divulge this secret, understandably refused.

The three Juwes, whose names were Jubelo, Jubela, and Jubelum, were so incensed by this, they murdered him: An important point here is that their punishment was having their bodies ripped open and whilst still alive their entrails thrown over their left shoulders.

A simple story; But one that demonstrates the righteousness of keeping one's word. Even in the face of death. The story is re-enacted as part of the initiation ceremony for a third degree mason.

That evening I discussed the ramifications with Hypatia.

'The question we must ask ourselves is this. Was it a misspelling, which is entirely possible when one reads some of the letters claiming to be from Jack the Ripper. Or was the Ripper a disaffected Freemason?

The freemason theory also works for the royalty story; but every serious ripperologist soon realises this is just a good fanciful yarn, which made some people very wealthy.

Rather like that editor fellow. 'Piddick.' We must remember that for some people a popular way of writing is never to let the truth interfere with a good story. There are also certain anomalies in the police statements. The policeman who found the chalk message, PC Long, has always had his version of events questioned

'If the Ripper was indeed Druitt, it's entirely possible that the disaffected mason theory is relevant. I don't know if he was a freemason, but he certainly had the correct antecedents. The only way is to go there and look. We shall drive to Whitechapel again and visit Goulston Street.'

We parked in Commercial Street, in a loading bay. The X9 made things so much easier. The security could park next to me and had to park a few places down. This gave us time to disappear.

'Select 30th September 1888 1-30am. I'll walk there, Goulston Street is only a short distance away.'

---Activate---

As I entered the street, Hypatia said, 'The building you want is Wentworth Dwellings on your left, a tenement building. The entrance is in the center, that's where the words were found, on the brickwork in the doorway.'

Walking up to the famous entrance, I took out the MIPEC and pointed it first at the bricks and then around the street allowing the IPEC to get her bearings. It was dark and the whole street was deserted, the Ripper probably having frightened everyone, keeping them indoors. This was in fact the Petticoat Lane area of London, and would have normally been buzzing, even at this time in the morning.

'Well one thing we do know Hypatia, the words were not there at…. what time is it?'

'1-32' she replied. 'DC Halse in his report stated there was no writing on the wall at 2-20. What's the street like, is it dirty?'

'Very: Paper and rubbish everywhere.'

'Tell me. If you saw a rag on the floor would you be suspicious and pick it up?'

'No I wouldn't now you mention it, even a bloodstained one! There's plenty of other graffiti around too, there's even some over there mentioning 'The Ripper,' the whole place is very run down and squalid.'

'All you can do now is wait.'

'I must get myself a shooting stick.' I murmured, 'I prefer to sit than just stand around when waiting.'

'Stop complaining. Sit on the horse trough.'

At 2-16 am a man walking briskly entered the street with a Tilly lamp. He was clearly looking for something, peering into alleys and dark corners.

'That must be DC Halse' I said,

By 2-20 he had passed out of sight, heading in the direction of Middlesex Street.

At 2- 26 a man burst out of the doorway of Wentworth Dwellings and staggered into the road. He was quite visible through the spectacles and I estimated him to be in his fifties. He was wearing a flat cap with a cloth flap at the back in the style of a coalman or dock worker and a torn jacket with old baggy trousers tied with a thick leather belt, he was wearing new boots and was chuntering away to himself drunkenly. Turning, he addressed the empty street.

'Fucking jewboys. Nothing but a bunch of cheating bastards! Bloody Yids, I'm cowing sick on em.' He took out a piece of chalk from his pocket, and wrote the now famous words on the wall, before standing back to admire his handiwork.

After a few seconds he laughed and staggered off down the road cursing and swearing to himself. He fell over at least once. I'd be surprised if he remembered anything about the episode the next morning.

'So much for the Freemason theories' I said

'I'm so excited' the voice replied. 'At last were getting somewhere.'

At 2-36 a man came down the street from the other direction and stopped at the horse trough. I recognised him immediately by his walk.

He bent low over the trough as though he was going to have a drink from it. I lifted the MIPEC and watched him washing his hands, one of his hands was badly cut and bound with a bloody cloth; This he unwrapped and threw to the ground and from a pocket took a clean handkerchief to replace it. Over the makeshift bandage he carefully pulled a leather glove, and staggered off clearly in great pain. The MIPEC analyzing his vital signs said:

'His heart is racing and he has lost a lot of blood, I assume he cut himself whilst carrying out the last murder. He must have been resting somewhere it can't have taken him an hour to get here from Mitre Square.

'Rather than follow him, why not wait and see how the cloth and writing is discovered?'

'What age is he Hypatia?' I asked, 'He looks to be in his thirties but walks like he's much older. But the first time I saw him he set of for the train station like a teenager.'

'It's a good question Jason, the readout says age between thirty five and thirty seven, but I agree he looks older.... Wait there's more.... of course.... He has syphilis.'

Fifteen minutes later, at 2.55 a policeman, obviously the notorious PC Long, came walking down the street accompanied by a rather gaudily dressed young woman. She got to the door of Wentworth Dwellings and started to go in.

He said

'Come on Maisie; we had a deal you and me: Ain't you going to thank me for seeing you home safe, and minding out for you for the last three hours?'

'Can't we do it tomorrow night Alfie?' She whined. 'I'm tired out. Come round about sixish afore I go to work.'

'OK,' he said 'How about somefink on account?'

Undoing his trousers and standing against the wall opposite the new writing, he waited for her to service him. She reluctantly dropped to her knees; He was staring directly at the writing during her labors. She finished, spat on the floor and wiped her mouth with the back of her hand, got up and said,

'See you tomorrow Alfie.'

'What the time Hypatia?'

'3-02.'

She re-emerged almost immediately looking upset.

'I've lost one of my earrings ducks,' she said, 'ave a look abart for me.'

He felt about for it without success, then lit his lamp and still couldn't find the earring but did find the wet blood soaked cloth. She waited in the cold for a short while and went back inside saying,

'Ah well, it's only cheap glass, I'll ave a look termorra morning.'

He studied the writing on the wall again, copied it into his book, and walked off.

And the rest is as they say, is history. Clearly the episode with the prostitute was never reported, but it answers many questions. For years people have challenged his version of events.

He certainly did not patrol the street at 2-20 am as he stated at the inquest, probably because he was protecting his new charge at that time.

There again, without her and her lost earring, he wouldn't have found the piece of blood stained apron. I felt quite satisfied with the night's work.

We had achieved an awful lot.

'But we still don't know who he is?' she said. 'He may have been an actor and we now know he had a venereal disease. Remember this was before penicillin and was virtually incurable and could drive one steadily more insane until it killed, or drove one to suicide. Also, the murders got steadily worse. We also know he was fanatically religious and was convinced he was doing God's work.'

'It could have been Druitt?' I said speculatively.

'Druitt was too tall,' she replied. 'Plus our man has an accent, that would seem to rule him out too, but he spoke in fluent English to God. We must assume therefore that he could be English or has lived in this country for some time.

We still have a lot of work to do with this Jason. We're closer certainly, but not there yet.'

'He killed his last victim, Mary Jane Kelly on Friday the 9th November.' I answered, 'That's a six week gap, which may very well have been due to his wounded hand. After that he could just have died from the syphilis, or committed suicide, which brings us back to Druitt. Whoever he was, he had some money, the clothes, different disguises and shoes with lifts all point to him being an actor. But whoever he is, he's clearly becoming increasingly demented.

'The Kelly murder was easily the most gruesome. We'll have to see it soon though. I want to know who he was more than ever now. Let's visit Mary Jane Kelly and finish this once and for all.'

'Very well,' she replied, Come back to the car and we'll change timelines. 'What do you know about her?'

'I've done some work, but still don't have a complete picture in my mind. She was killed in her room and had been so violently attacked that all that remained was a mass of unrecognisable flesh.

She was about twenty five which is younger than his other victims and the doctor who examined the body said whoever did it had no medical knowledge at all. This is quite different from the opinion of the doctors who examined the bodies of the other four victims.

She was killed at 13 Miller's Court which incidentally was an annexe at the rear of 26 Dorset Street partitioned off from the rest of the building. One entered from a door at the end of a corridor and hers was the first door on the right. Anyone entering or leaving must have passed her door. The room was approximately four metres square and the key had been lost for some time meaning anyone entering the room had to reach through a broken window and turn the latch.

She also let other prostitutes use the room, so the mode of entry would have been well known. I know where Dorset Street is, but at what time?'

'The best clue is from a man called George Hutchinson he got a really good look at the likely killer,' she replied.

I quote from Casebook Jack the Ripper: Which I thoroughly recommend to all budding ripperologists.

"2:00 am: George Hutchinson, a resident of the Victoria Home on Commercial Street had just returned to the area from Romford. He was walking on Commercial Street and passed a man at the corner of Thrawl Street. At the corner of Flower and Dean Street he met Kelly who tried to beg money from him.

'Mr. Hutchinson, can you lend me sixpence?' 'I can't,' says Hutchinson, 'I spent all my money going down to Romford.'

'Good morning then,' Kelly replies, 'I must go and find some money. She walked off in the direction of Thrawl Street and meets the man I had passed earlier. He puts his hand on Kelly's shoulder and says something at which Kelly and the man laugh.

I hear's Kelly say 'all right,' and they begin to walk towards Dorset Street.

Hutchinson described the man as having a dark complexion, a heavy dark moustache turned up at the corners, dark eyes and bushy eyebrows and was, 'Jewish looking.' He wore a soft felt hat pulled down over his eyes, a long dark coat trimmed in astrakhan, a white collar with a black necktie fixed with a horseshoe pin, dark spats over light button over boots and a massive gold chain is in his waistcoat with a large seal with a red stone hanging from it and carried kid gloves in his right hand and a small package in his left. He estimated the man to be 5' 6' or 5' 7' tall and about 35 or 36 years old.

They crossed Commercial Street and turned down Dorset Street. Hutchinson followed them. Kelly and the man stopped outside Miller's Court and talked for about 3 minutes when Kelly is heard to say

'All right, my dear, come along, you will be comfortable.'

The man puts his arm around Kelly who kisses him.

'I've lost my handkerchief,' she says. At this he hands her a red handkerchief. The couple then headed down Miller's Court as the clock struck 3:00'

'That gives us the time,' I added, 'let's try then. It will take me ten minutes to walk there, please set the time for 2-45 am, Friday 9th November 1888.'

---Activate---

The night was warm and dry, I walked briskly to Dorset Street and found the arched passageway to Millers Court; it was just coming up to 3-00 am, at number thirteen I tried to look through the dirty window and saw the flames of a dying fire in the grate, but it was too dark to make out much, clearly window cleaning was not particularly high on the agenda in this neighbourhood. I found the broken window, felt for the latch and went in…. If only I hadn't, there was absolutely no requirement for me to see the body. The stupid man must have got the time wrong.

The light from the fire lit the small room quite well from inside, enough certainly to let me see he was finished with his gruesome work. I have never seen anything like it and cannot bring myself even to describe what I saw. But seeing him crouched on the floor naked and covered in blood with the expression of a rabid dog I think in all honesty if I had been able I could have easily put him down myself.

I had seen so much death lately but this was so gruesome it had descended to new depths of depravity.

I pulled myself together and told her that I didn't think he was the same man. Hypatia who had been very quiet, said

'You're correct it's not the same man, the plot, as they say, thickens. I have no idea who this is, but he's definitely not our man.'

'In that case I propose we leave it open for the present,' and with a last look at the ghastly scene, turned and left.

I really can't bring myself to describe what I saw. I'll leave that to Dr Thomas Bond the police surgeon from 'A' division was on duty that night and gave the following evidence to the inquest:

'The body of Mary Kelly was found at 13 Miller's Court lying naked in the middle of the bed, the shoulders flat but the axis of the body inclined to the left side of the bed. The head was turned on the left cheek. The left arm was close to the body with the forearm flexed at a right angle and lying across the abdomen.

The right arm was slightly abducted from the body and rested on the mattress. The elbow was bent, the forearm supine with the fingers clenched. The legs were wide apart, the left thigh at right angles to the trunk and the right forming an obtuse angle with the pubes.

The whole of the surface of the abdomen and thighs was removed and the abdominal cavity emptied of its viscera. The breasts were cut off, the arms mutilated by several jagged wounds and the face hacked beyond recognition of the features. The tissues of the neck were severed all round down to the bone.

The viscera were found in various parts viz: the uterus and kidneys with one breast under the head, the other breast by the right foot the liver between the feet, the intestines by the right side and the spleen by the left side of the body. The flaps removed from the abdomen and thighs were on a table.

The bed clothing at the right corner was saturated with blood, and on the floor beneath was a pool of blood covering about two feet square. The wall by the right side of the bed and in a line with the neck was marked by blood, which had struck it in a number of separate splashes.

The face was gashed in all directions, the nose, cheeks, eyebrows, and ears being partly removed. The lips were blanched and cut by several incisions running obliquely down to the chin. There were also numerous cuts extending irregularly across all the features.

The neck was cut through the skin and other tissues right down to the vertebrae, the fifth and sixth being deeply notched. The skin cuts in the front of the neck showed distinct ecchymosis. The air passage was cut at the lower part of the larynx through the cricoid cartilage.

Both breasts were more or less removed by circular incisions, the muscle down to the ribs being attached to the breasts. The intercostals between the fourth, fifth, and sixth ribs were cut through and the contents of the thorax visible through the openings. The skin and tissues of the abdomen from the costal arch to the pubes were removed in three large flaps. The right thigh was denuded in front to the bone, the flap of skin, including the external organs of generation, and part of the right buttock. The left thigh was stripped of skin fascia, and muscles as far as the knee.

The left calf showed a long gash through skin and tissues to the deep muscles and reaching from the knee to five inches above the ankle. Both arms and forearms had extensive jagged wounds.

The right thumb showed a small superficial incision about one inch long, with extravasation of blood in the skin, and there were several abrasions on the back of the hand moreover showing the same condition.

On opening the thorax it was found that the right lung was minimally adherent by old firm adhesions. The lower part of the lung was broken and torn away. The left lung was intact. It was adherent at the apex and there were a few adhesions over the side. In the substances of the lung there were several nodules of consolidation.

The pericardium was open below and the heart absent. In the abdominal cavity there was some partly digested food of fish and potatoes, and similar food was found in the remains of the stomach attached to the intestines.'

Back at the vehicle I tried to recover my composure, this time it really had been too much. The IPEC however had recovered completely.

'We're having a really good night,' she gushed. 'It wasn't a Ripper killing after all. She was too young of course and the mutilation of the body was different, either he was using the Ripper to hide his real motive, or he was a copycat.'

'What did you learn about the murderer?' I asked.

'He was also syphilitic,' she replied, 'I believe he may have been trying to emulate the other murders it's only conjecture of course but he may have caught it from her and wanted revenge. About 35 he was otherwise healthy and definitely not the same man.

'Well you were right not to care who he was I've had enough of this now, I wish we had never started it.'

'Debra is calling you.'

'Where are you dad?' she asked.

'I'm on my way back from the factory ,…. why?'

'I was worried about you, I've just got home, and Mum's on her own.'

'Well not really,' I replied, 'there are three security guards patrolling the grounds, and the Wards are in their flat. I'll be home in 20 minutes.'

'Clearly they aren't ready to be left yet,' Hypatia said compassionately. 'Maybe now is the right time to teach them both a new language?'

'It will help me too,' I said, 'I need something to take my mind off that horrible scene.'

That evening after dinner we all went to my study, where Hypatia explained to them both that she had developed a new programme, and wanted to share it with them. We had a conversation in Italian, which totally astounded them as languages were never my strong point.

'How did you do it?' they asked clearly astounded.

Hypatia explained about the headsets and brainwave scans. They'd been getting suspicious anyway, asking how we had managed to get the information from the terrorist so quickly.

Hypatia explained how she did it, and told them it had led to her discovering how to reverse the process, hence the Italian. If they would choose a language she would teach them how to speak, read and write it.

My Debby chose French as hers was not much better than schoolgirl level. Julie selected Italian, saying it sounded romantic. With the fearless determination of the young, my daughter put on the headsets and lay down. The IPEC explained that as a by-product of this exercise it would take away some of the fears she was experiencing about the kidnapping, the nightmares too. She explained that the memory would still be there but distant and would fade even more given time.

'I'm simply hurrying the process along.' she told her.

One hour later my beautiful daughter was laughing for the first time in weeks, as she realised she was fluent in that wonderful language.

Julie was next. When she heard Debby speaking French like a native, she couldn't get the headsets on fast enough. And after her sleep Julie and I spent the rest of the night talking in Italian. Debra said she slept like a baby.

'Can I tell Patrick?' She pleaded the next morning.

Hypatia explained that for the time being at least it must be kept as our secret.

'Simply say you've been studying the language for some time. As soon as it's safe he can be told of course.'

Life slowly returned to normal, but we each knew it could never be the same again.

A couple of weeks later just as I was getting over the experience of seeing Mary Kelly the IPEC told me she thought she knew who Jack the

Ripper was.

'How?' I asked.

'I have searched through every known record of his activities and have narrowed it down to one man.' she said, looking at me triumphantly.

'Who?' I asked sceptically.

'Mr Thomas Hayne Cutbush.'

'Not one of the usual suspects.' I replied. 'Although if one considers the mutilations of the pubic areas of the victims. His name alone could make him a suspect.'

'Please be serious,' she scolded. 'These are the facts. He lived nearby and worked in the area, and the family owned a house in Suffolk. He contracted syphilis from a prostitute in 1888 and everyone who knew him agreed it had affected his brain.

He had no alibi for any of the times when the murders were committed and his uncle was a very senior policeman who may very well have been complicit in a cover up. Two later murders are included in the police dossier of the Ripper casefile, one in July 1889 and the other in February 1891. It's only conjecture to claim they were Ripper murders they could easily have been copycat killings. Cutbush was committed as being insane in March 1891 after then the murders stopped.'

'If it's so obvious why wasn't he caught?' I asked. 'What aren't you telling me? .... Oh no Hypatia, I've seen enough murders, after Mary Kelly I swore there'd be no more! '

'The Sun newspaper accused him of being the ripper, not actually naming him but their description left little to the imagination.'

'The Sun,' I said sarcastically. 'Well it must be true then.'

'Enough of this,' she said getting bored with my poor attempt at humour.

'It's easy for us to prove. He lived with his mother in Albert Street Kennington. All you have to do is to go round there and wait for him.'

'OK Hypatia,' I replied, 'let's do it now, but I'm not witnessing any more murders.'

We drove to Kennington found the house, parked around the corner and selected Thursday August 30th at 2-00 pm the day before Polly Nichols was killed.

I waited for an hour outside the house, recognising him immediately when he came out. He was dressed in a fashionable suit and looked every part a gentleman.

'You've found him Hypatia,' I said, 'I take my hat off to you, but what about the accent and the tools? It doesn't fit.'

'Actually it does. He was an amateur actor and reportedly very good with accents. He's insane Jason the syphilis is making him delusionary. Probably normal during the day, but at night who can say? It's taken some time though it's only because of the time travel that we found him. But of course it will have to remain our secret.'

'Now what?' I asked, 'We'll just have to let the rest of the Ripperologist community carry on, what a shame….. Still, he'll be committed soon and the murders will stop. It's been interesting though, hasn't it?'

CHAPTER FORTY FIVE

Two days later I attended the monthly board meeting of Maxwell Computers. I wasn't looking forward to it though due to some information I had been given.

As usual before the meeting I went along to Stephen's office for coffee, to discuss any relevant points.

'At the last board meeting,' he said, sarcastically adding. 'Which you again missed. We decided you should release more designs. The advanced headset will be a great success but I want more. I want the next generation now. I've some ideas of my own.

'Who exactly are 'we'?' I asked, 'If any more of my designs are to be released and developed, there is no we.'

'Naturally Maxwell Computers will be given a chance to bid for the right to build them. All the patents belong to me, and any licences awarded will be paid for, as will the royalties.'

'My Dear Jason' he replied conspiratorially 'I've taken advice as to the legalities of this, and have been assured it simply isn't the case. You may be a major shareholder, but you're still being paid a salary; and as salaried staff you'll find all your developments and inventions belong to me.

'You signed the standard agreement when you joined this company; it includes the customary clause all companies use.' He sat back smugly.

'Bravo Stephen.' I replied softly, 'I would simply ask that in about two minutes you remember who instigated this conversation.

'The designs were made before I joined the company and are therefore not covered by the clause. And anyway you don't own this company; I do.

'Through proxies I now own 58% of the stock, with pledges for a further 22%. You my friend own just 6%.'

I did my level best not to look too satisfied but suspect I failed.

'I expect your resignation as CEO on my desk in fifteen minutes. Peter Allen will replace you.'

His mouth dropped open.

'It was you who set that snake Piddick and his paper at me over the kidnapping and conspired to print lies about my daughter. Don't bother to deny it, I have indisputable proof,'

He stared at me murderously, not bothering to comment.

'I'll fight you on this,' he shouted, 'I still have many friends on the board.'

'Are these the same friends who have pledged me their votes? You'll resign, and you'll do it now you bastard. As will your friend Drew Piddick. If not, these pictures will be published in every major newspaper in the country: I'd suggest you ask him, if you think I can't arrange it.'

With that I threw the envelope across at him. He ripped the package open and looked at them unbelievingly.

'How did you get these?' he asked, ashen faced. This is blackmail!

'You should also be aware that two of those boys are under sixteen; copies of their written statements are in the envelope. They confirm your friend Droopy knew their age when he propositioned them.'

'If I don't see his resignation on the news channels by 5-00 the deals off. The pictures will be published tomorrow in his own newspaper. Paedophilia is a serious criminal offence, two high profile perverts like you, will keep the newshounds busy for months.'

He looked at me totally crestfallen

'However, because of my respect for your wife and family none of this need get out. If you want to sell your shares I'll buy them. I've a cheque in my pocket made out to you, which equals the current value of your shares as of this morning. This figure is bound to drop when the news of your resignation is made public, and don't forget if this gets out you'll almost certainly lose your precious knighthood.'

The Eight sat around the table listening to the IPEC's report. The Khepera was clearly concerned about the Stonehenge visit. 'Why did you allow it to take place?' He asked, obviously hurt,

'It just happened' the IPEC replied, 'I had no idea who had built it. They went to a wedding in the area and he simply wanted to visit the stones to see when and how they had been built, the presence of the spacecraft was a total surprise.'

'It isn't one of our proudest achievements I'm afraid,' The Kheperas eyes drooped even further, 'And as everyone around this table knows, it was an ancestor of mine who was the captain of the spacecraft. It became a major disgrace for my family, and took a thousand of our years before we were forgiven. In our culture such mistakes are not easily forgotten.'

He paused for a few seconds, and straightening his small shoulders looked at her doggedly and carried on.

'We must discuss the next generation of the computer, it's crucial that the next version is produced and distributed. How will you proceed?'

'Simple', she replied pleased to be back on familiar ground,

'We now have total control the company; I'll infuse any further knowledge into Mr Shaw's brain as required. We're in the process of extending the American factory to increase its capacity and are dedicating the UK factory to producing only the modules. We are contracting out the manufacture of the headsets to other companies which will quadruple the projected figures,' the face looked around the room triumphantly.

'They will become an indispensable accessory to hundreds of millions of people in the developed world.'

The Khepera answered solemnly.

'Even with these increases it will be physically impossible to make the billions required. We have been working on the problem for some time and I have reluctantly asked the home planet to consider the fabrication of sibillion implants these will be administered directly into the bloodstream, although how this would be achieved still remains unclear. In the meantime the company must distribute as many of the headset computers as possible, at an affordable price.'

'It will be done. May I ask if any answer has been received from the consortium concerning the re- location of the people to the new planet?'

'Nothing yet but we didn't expect an answer this soon, we'll just have to wait: If there's nothing else I must leave this meeting. You may carry on with each of the team leaders as you think fit. We need regular meetings from now on. Let's meet again one month from today.'

CHAPTER FORTY SIX

Hypatia had watched things very closely at first, but Peter soon picked things up. I went in every day, not to look over his shoulder, but to work with James who was finalising the procreative chauffeur, a device very close to my heart.

At the launch of the advanced headset computer the press had gone wild, orders for the next three years filled the books and the shares went even higher.

I had decided, despite some objections from the board, to sell them at a very cheap price. We were still making a profit of course, but it became very important to me that everyone should have a chance to own one

One wonderful side effect of this was because they worked through 'neuropt' processors within the core, the images transmitted through glasses very similar to mine, could be transmitted directly to the brain allowing the blind to see. And because the probe spoke directly to the brain, when an acoustic chip was implanted, it allowed the deaf to hear. The Maxwell Computer Foundation had agreed to supply one million of these free of charge around the world. And I was extremely happy to learn that Peter and James were being tipped as favourites to jointly receive a Nobel Prize for their work in this regard.

The headsets still used the existing telephone satellites and lines, so everyone was in contact with whosoever they chose.

The mobile phone companies were being handsomely paid for the use of their satellites. And the cell phone manufacturers were happy because they were making the headsets, often with their own imaginative modifications.

The health and safety people though, forced one important modification on us. They insisted this facility had to be automatically disenabled when one was driving. Which to be fair was a sensible stipulation. It was anyway only a matter of time until we introduced the procreative chauffeur. And plans were in place to fit it in taxi drones these were craft developed by others to transport people and the chauffeur would be the perfect device to control them.

People throughout the world wore the headsets now. The module was able to instantaneously translate all the main languages, and for a nominal fee could be programmed with any not standard.

Everyone was understandably fascinated by their new toys, which also had an effect on their minds, and with no language difficulties everyone felt much more as one.

The first time it was used a strange feeling of overall calmness was induced to the wearer. This led to an intoxicating feeling of satisfaction, and the need to experience it again. The headset used an upgraded version of the re-chargeable batteries made of plasmatic-cellulose, extremely light, and re-charged even quicker than the original, using the moisture produced from the body's heat.

Obviously, I knew that subliminally the headsets were not only able to read thoughts, but could easily be reversed to feed all manner of things into the human brain. But as only good was coming from wearing them, and crime generally continuing to decline I decided that overall it was worth it. The media was surprisingly kind about them too. Even the politicians seemed to like them.

With everything going so well I decided to take a holiday. Julie's business was keeping her busy more than ever now and it was difficult to get her to take a break. So I commandeered the yacht and visited numerous different places and times.

We studied the dinosaurs over a span of 300 million years watching them develop and subsequently observed the progress of the human species, from apes, to Neanderthals and Homo erectus.

I visited the Sumerians, and the Spartans, and lived for a short time with the sad figure of the now despotic Alexander the Great in Babylon. And finally saw the wooden horse of Troy including the sickening sight of Priams body being thrown off the walls by Neoptolemus and torn to pieces by starving dogs.

We made many visits to Rome where I developed a fascination for Cicero and Cato spending hours listening to them discuss the merits of the Republic. We lived with Claudius, who I expected would be a fair man, but quickly became aware this was not the case. He tended to have people killed on the slightest whim; I saw him do it often. He also claimed to be a republican sympathiser and yet executed 35 senators and nearly 300 equestrians.

His reign was nevertheless prosperous and characterised by a good and fair administration; the army certainly loved him. But I can't forget the immense pleasure he gained from watching others suffer in the arena and inside the prisons, often having a chair positioned opposite the prisoners and watching as one by one they were horribly tortured.

His third wife Messalina was wildly promiscuous, taking numerous lovers, even bigamously marrying one of them whilst he was away with his troops. It can't have been easy for her because Claudius was not a handsome man by any stretch of the imagination and drooled mucus constantly.

But she too was cruel and not averse to having men executed, especially the ones who spurned her amorous advances. When Claudius found out about the 'marriage,' he ordered her death and calmly watched whilst she and her husband Gaius Silius were very slowly and horribly killed.

He was eventually poisoned by his fourth wife Agrippina, thus ensuring her son Nero ascended the throne.

Agrippina was the sister of Claudius's predecessor, his nephew Caligula and had clearly inherited some of his genes. It was these two, the Emperors Caligula and Nero who proved categorically that absolute power really does corrupt absolutely.

This was the age of unbridled licentiousness and eroticism, particularly within the upper classes, which some say, led to the slave uprisings of 73 AD. I travelled to Rhegium, and spent some time watching Spartacus rally his troops.

I emulated Anders and visited the huge stone lighthouse in Alexandria. Except for the pyramids easily the tallest building in the ancient world.

Whilst there I also spent time in the fabulous library of Ptolemy and again like Anders chose to visit of Caesar when he had first landed in pursuit of Pompey the Great, witnessing him being presented with his head. Whilst later watching Cleopatra being delivered into his presence. The great queen was not the great beauty history has painted her; she was quite small with a slightly hooked nose and a strong chin, which rather oddly suited her face which oozed sexuality.

We were also asked occasionally by the US and UK governments to use the invisibility shroud to help with the rescue of captured soldiers, unfortunately not always successfully. Another time the Americans had me enter a foreign Embassy and photograph some papers, which led directly to some terrorist leaders being killed.

When she found out, Hypatia flatly refused to take any further part in what she described as their silly games. I had expected trouble over this but our new friend General White unexpectedly supported us and we were not asked again.

Then a few months later we were unexpectedly summoned to Washington by the new President. He had been briefed about Hypatia by General White, who was also there. He said it was a matter of the highest importance that under cover of the shroud we carry out a very important mission to Pyongyang.

He explained that they had received some very disturbing intelligence. The chairman and joint chiefs of North Korea were finalizing plans to launch nuclear missiles on Japan, South Korea, Hawaii and the American naval base in the Philippines. And this time it was for real, they believed we had a maximum of 24 hours. One doesn't normally question the President of the United States but I couldn't bring myself to believe it. I was taken down to the war room and shown the live satellite images. Six missiles were sitting on their launch pads being readied for their nuclear warheads. We were asked to go in and find out exactly how and where they were stored.

They needed to pinpoint the exact location.

Knowing her programming I waited for Hypatia to refuse. But she agreed. And from there it all happened so quickly. We were flown to Andrews and then on to Seoul and taken by helicopter to a spot near the border were we were met by someone who smuggled us into the north in a truck inside a box. After a four hour journey we were let out next to a military airfield, the unarmed rockets were still there.

We changed timelines and I went in. It took the MIPEC two hours to find the right bunker which was set in a maze of underground tunnels. The doors were open and it was clear that six of the warheads were being readied. I counted a further sixteen warheads each on a steel pallet. The MIPEC sent our exact coordinates to the Americans and we returned at some speed to the truck. We changed timelines and climbed in. At the border the driver said it would be too risky to drive over again so soon after coming in so I changed timelines again and walked across. A car was waiting to take us to the helicopter. In less than two hours I was on my way back to Washington.

Whilst we were still in the sky the bunker was destroyed. How it was done, I have no idea. But in Washington I was informed no missiles had been used. A number of the warheads had developed a leak and made the tunnels highly radioactive. They had quickly been sealed off unable to be accessed for a minimum of a thousand years. The method of how this was done is highly secret. But they were confident that no matter what they thought. The North Koreans would never find any evidence of outside interference.

The Pyongyang government reported that a small nuclear device had malfunctioned and caused an internal explosion resulting in a leak of radio-active material. An area for 100 miles in all directions was being cordoned off for safety reasons. They reported only minor casualties. Two days later the leader was reported as having been killed in a flying accident. The whole country was ordered to partake in 10 days of mourning. And the government made overtures to the west for a normalising of relations. In a demonstration of good faith certain of the sanctions were lifted.

I of course wanted to know why the IPEC had so readily agreed to us going. She looked at me long and hard until finally admitting she had been aware of the future in that timeline. The launching of the North Korean nuclear missiles would have started the third world war. We had therefore changed history and in the process had saved the lives of millions of innocent people. And in the process rid the world of the North Korean glorious leader. It was a win win situation.

'We're ready,' the Khepera told the meeting. 'Everything we have worked towards is set. I have finally received an answer to our request; the fabrication of the implants has been sanctioned and will be with us by the next shuttle. Hypatia you will need to set up a chemical facility. I've given it some thought and would propose Switzerland. Thanks to your sterling endeavours we now own a bank there I believe?'

The Khepera turned to a small group of his colleagues, instructing them to work with the IPEC after the meeting. He took a pen like object from his pocket and transmitted some data directly into the IPEC's central core.

'These are the plans for the factory.' he said, 'The proposal is to introduce a disease into the population, and then to offer a miracle cure by means of a liquid filled capsule'

He turned to the alien from the 21st century.

'When the decision is taken for the disease to be released, we will transport it to your time via the IPEC. In the meantime you must talk to your people, and find a way to release it globally from the air. The antidote capsules will contain a string of hidden instructions, the first of which will be to encourage an increased sense of tranquillity. The second will induce a gradual aversion to meat and fish, and the third, will control the birth rate. In the first year this will drop by 80% and will continue to decline until acceptable levels are achieved. The disease is designed to be painful and highly visible, but not life threatening.'

'What form will the disease take?' the IPEC enquired.

'Epidemic Parotitis,' the Khepera told her, -- 'commonly known as Mumps. It will be a new strain, much more virulent and will be totally resistant to any of the existing vaccines. It will be much less painful for anyone under the age of puberty but in everyone else will grow steadily more painful until it becomes unbearable. However the capsules will offer an immediate cure. So the populace will be clambering to be given them.

'Mumps,' the IPEC answered, accessing its files... Yes, I see... An inspired choice, a side effect of the disease can be impotency in adults.' The Khepera nodded knowingly.

'We have also decided to include a small reward. The capsules will include a complete cure for all forms of cancer. And Alzheimer's disease

'What about the new planet?' the IPEC asked.

'It's still being considered, but I am not hopeful in the short term. Transporting billions of people hundreds of light years is simply not possible yet. And therein lies the rub. The only vessels large enough to carry enough people are from the planet Xeros.

Their giant tankers could be modified to carry 300,000 people each, possibly in exchange for water. They have 50 such vessels and may allow half of them to be used. But as each round trip would take fifteen of your years you don't need me to tell you that relates to 5,000 years for the relocation of the two and half billion people. We could possibly help by sharing our technology with the Xerosians thus allowing that time to be reduced, but at the moment we are restricted by the same non- interference rules that apply to this planet.'

'We must move on. Have you analysed the data Hypatia? Do you have an estimate for the timescale for the construction of the new factory? And will you be able to convince

Mr Shaw to help you?'

'My estimate is 18 Months. And why should Mr Shaw object, it's simply a chemical plant for the manufacture of medicines for the world's poor and concentrated food in solid form to feed them.

'I will eventually be forced to explain to him what we have discovered of course, especially the destruction of the earth. He is bound to ask soon anyway despite the partial block implanted in his brain. I'll explain the whole scenario to him, except that we're planning to cause a pandemic, he can sometimes become extremely illogical concerning such matters. Nonetheless he has been carefully groomed, and I have every confidence in him.'

'We must also consider the transportation of the antidote containers through time,' the Khepera continued. 'They are square casks, one metre square and three metres high.

'We have an advantage in this timeline; the factory of course already exists and is still under our ownership. Our people have closed it down; it's old anyway. We'll transport the containers directly there. You my dear Hypatia, will commence the building of the original factory as soon as possible.'

Turning to the alien traveller he said

'Once the laboratory area is completed you'll remove the transportation equipment from the Kings Cross facility and transport it to the factory. It will then be possible for the IPEC to transport the containers to your time.'

Addressing his chief engineer he said.

'Please arrange to have two more of the special 'solid time' modules fabricated for use as spares. We can't afford any malfunctions during the transportation of the containers.'

Returning to the alien from the 21st century he continued,

'I've written a letter to myself in that timeline explaining what to do. Please ensure I receive it.

The next problem is for you Hypatia. One cannot just produce an antidote for billions of people as if by magic. There needs to be a controlled outbreak causing panic among the people. I'll arrange for this to happen, your research staff will identify it, and discover a cure.

'Once the capsules have proved successful, you'll have Mr Shaw propose to manufacture great amounts at his own expense, storing it in the factory for future use. These will be stored in identical containers. The details will be given to you shortly. They will seem quite revolutionary to the engineers of your time but if you are able to transfer the knowledge to Mr Shaw when the time is right. He will believe he has thought of it and hopefully convince others of the fact.

'We shall then simply exchange them using the particle beam transporters. You will notice on the plans, that the storage area has an underground vault for this very purpose.'

'When all is prepared the disease will be released globally, the capsule distribution can be controlled similarly.' He turned to his colleagues and said, 'Draw up plans along those lines!

'In the meantime Hypatia, let us carry on with the production of the new headsets; they will be required more than ever now. Do you agree?'

'Yes but please keep working on the mass transport system to the new planet. If we can solve that problem, we won't need the disease. I have another question will the containers contain the liquid for us to fill, or the complete capsule'

The compete capsule, I'm sorry I didn't explain. The implant will not be in the serum. The gelatine shell is the implant.

When the IPEC had returned to the 21st century the Khepera addressed the meeting again.

That went well, I believe the machine was convinced; Let us return to our discussion. Nam, you were raising objections to the consortium's decision, I believe.'

'I most certainly was,' the alien replied. 'You've lied to the machine Amon, the disease is designed to cull a quarter of this planets population.'

'Yes I'm aware it's a drastic step, but we have to remove two and a half billion people. At least it will be quick. The population must be reduced to six billion and remain at that figure. Which I might add is still far too high! We may yet have to reduce the figure even lower, to five billion.'

The people of this planet might not agree with you,' retorted the alien, 'I certainly do not. We have spent most of our lives protecting this world and its peoples 'Some might say you're acting like their God.'

'Have you considered I may be their God, ---- or at least the latest of a long line, stretching back 30,000 years.

The Consortium selected me the Khepera of this planet and in consultation with the executive team the decision to reduce the numbers has been made. I understand your objections and note them. But you will agree that even five billion is preferable to zero.'

'Consider too, that if we allow them to continue in this timeline the leaders of this planet will themselves destroy over a half a billion of their fellow beings in the wars.

'I'm not a monster Nam and am prepared to listen to your proposals for an alternative plan. Remember it was not part of the original planning it only developed when it was realised the headsets could not be made in sufficient numbers '

'It's not about an alternative plan.' Nam replied, 'It's about the consortium and you, deciding to fabricate and ship a lethal disease to this planet without full discussions. The use of the implants has been accepted; it's probably the only alternative. But we never agreed to help you destroy billions of humans. Why can't we simply follow the scenario given to the IPEC, and allow the population to reduce naturally?'

'Because it will not,' the Khepera replied, 'Don't you see, it will remain at over eight billion, the food-cakes will stabilise it at that level. We must reduce the numbers prior to them being introduced. You were not consulted because you are not a member of the executive. We who are shall have to live with this decision for the rest of our lives.

'It was my judgment to keep the introduction of the disease a secret until we had an answer from the consortium. The implants are 100% reliable, and will grow inside the body safely, the information being passed to future generations by natural procreation.

'Your objections are noted. I didn't like hiding the truth from the machine any more than from you, but it has to be this way. The IPEC is programmed not to assist with the taking of human life. If I had informed it of our plans it would unquestionably have self-destructed.

'With leadership come responsibilities. This planet will be destroyed by the Xeroians! And only we can stop it. In that context even five billion is a great success.'

'The IPEC may still self-destruct when it realised what we have done.' Nam replied.

'I have considered that and have a plan. The machine is fascinated by our holographic helpers. We have therefore developed an advanced corporeal holographic programme for the IPEC. It will allow her to appear in a life size solid form in a variety of costumes. The only difficulty being that it has to be installed directly onto the procreative drive and for that we would need access to the core. I believe the machine will allow this because of her infatuation with the human. Unless I am mistaken the machine will find the thought of appearing before him whole and able to move about him intriguing.

'Whilst we are carrying out the modification the self-destruct programme will be amended.

'I have some news to which I believe will ease your concerns a little, Your request that parts of central Africa and the rain forests of South America and Asia are to be spared is agreed. I agree that the delivery and administering of the antidote capsules would present a real difficulty in these areas and accede to your fear that whole tribes could be wiped out.'

The alien dissenter held up his hands in mock thanks.

'Anyway' continued the Khepera *most of the world's population live in the major cities we only have to infect those and the targets will be reached.'*

How easily they are pacified the Khepera thought.

'Thank you Nam, if there nothing else, I declare this meeting closed.'

☐

CHAPTER FORTY SEVEN

Everything went smoothly for two years. The construction of a new chemical factory in Switzerland was completed and we were now producing affordable medicines for the developing countries of the world. These were being distributed by the Maxwell foundation and provided generous tax concessions globally.

One day whilst driving to work I heard one of the callers on the vehicle radio complaining about the headset computers. It was his contention that recent developments had moved the human race into a very dangerous situation. His argument was that everyone now worked by virtual telepathy, often without a break and accepted things without discussion.

'We are.' he said, 'Becoming a world of factory made zombies.'

Over the next few days what he had said played on my mind, which until then had seemed somehow to be closed. But now it all suddenly became clear.

We perhaps didn't look like the aliens, but were well down the road to becoming like them. The thing which bothered me the most was that Anders Larsen must have known his past, and therefore my future, in which case surely he surely wouldn't have let this happen? Which led to another thought, what if he had never existed? All I ever had ever seen was a corpse.

If the aliens had decided they needed an idiot to help them change the world, who was a better idiot than me! In exchange for private jets and luxury yachts I had done everything they wanted.

The problem was I had nobody to discuss it with, because if it were true then the IPEC was also part of it.

As to the existence of the aliens, who could I to tell? Even in the unlikely event that anyone believed me what could they do? I was the only one who had actually seen them. And that was thousands of years ago. If I wasn't careful, I could easily end up an international laughing stock.

Something had to be done, and quickly! Not everybody chose to wear the headsets of course, but the pressures on people to conform were becoming ever greater. Some people thankfully, had flatly refused, the irony being the most loquacious of them lived in and around Roswell New Mexico.

Ironically they had grasped the truth and were telling the world that aliens were controlling us all…. Who was the moron now?

I had stopped wearing the earpiece and carrying the MIPEC lately, but one day Hypatia had the IPEC brought to my office for a discussion.

'You're very uncommunicative Jason,' she said. 'I think I may have guessed the reason, are you becoming concerned about the headsets?'

What to answer? …. We had, had no secrets for nearly 7 years; during that time I had trusted her implicitly. Let's face it, without the IPEC, I was nothing, plus the machine had saved my daughter's life

'Yes' I replied 'I want to stop all work on them immediately.'

'I knew this would happen. You're worried it will be used to control the masses, am I correct?'

'Of course you're correct.' I answered frustrated at my inability to discuss the problem with anyone else.

'The aliens want to control the human race, probably make us their slaves'

'You're totally wrong,' she admonished, 'If that had been their intention they would have done it thousands of years ago. Of all the beings in the universe you are uniquely positioned to realise that.

'They're the closest to your species biologically and have been watching and guiding human development for more than 30,000 years.'

'Please sit down Jason. I told them you would eventually realize what we were doing. They have given me permission to explain everything to you.'

'So you are working for them, are you one of them?'

'They used me certainly, but I'm not one of them. Anders built me, and died exactly as it says in the journal, except it was not 1944, it was in 2136. The aliens found me and repaired the time travel facility.

'They are much more advanced than you of course and improved it, incorporating the ability to travel to the future. That's how we know about the destruction of the earth including when and why it happens. When travelling: as you know, we're effectively indestructible, so we, and by that I mean the IPEC, and whoever is on the mat with me, are normally able to return safely.

'Unfortunately on this occasion whist travelling with an alien I liked very much. The world in which we materialised no longer existed, only space and debris remained. The alien was instantly thrown off the mat and lost. The mat then did what it's programmed to do, and folded itself around me, ensuring my safe return and allowing me to report on the catastrophic events which will destroy us all.

'We investigated the reasons carefully. Trying different dates until discovering the precise nature of events, including the exact day the world is destroyed. A conference was held between the alien leaders, and the decision was made to send me back with Ander's body. I was to start the process of changing the future.

'The cause of the earth's destruction relates directly to mankind's brutality and willingness to kill. That's what they wish to change, not your fortitude and ability to adapt, that after all is what defines you as a species.

'The human apathy concerning the eco destruction of the planet needs to be addressed too. Global warming will eventually destroy the planet as we know it. Add to this the fact that only a few years ago all over the world the prisons were full, racial hatred was rife. And religious bigotry plus extremism was returning the world to the horrors of the dark ages.

For thousands of years they've been expecting mankind to change as you became more advanced, but the opposite has happened. All that's actually changed is your ability to destroy the planet, and yourselves with ever-greater efficiency. Including unfortunately most of the other creatures with which you share this world.

'The aliens found themselves with a serious problem. Since the Atlantis incident they're sworn not to interfere with yours, or any other alien development. But with the knowledge of future events comes responsibilities. Consider the plight of the whales. Despite international agreement by 2083 all of the larger species will have become extinct. These wonderful creatures, which harm no one, and live happily in family groups, will again, be ruthlessly hunted by your fellow humans.

In 2052 the last wild elephants are slaughtered for food, the rhinoceroses already gone, with hippos soon to follow. The big cats too, their prey killed by men with machine guns. It's all true Jason. At that time millions of people throughout the world will be starving and will understandably kill and eat anything, just to survive.'

You paint an awful picture Hypatia do you know this as fact?' I thought we had stopped the war by destroying the warheads in Korea.

We did; By changing the time line. Unfortunately that had nothing to do with this one. You really are a war like people Jason.

'We know that in 22 years there will be another world war, brought about mainly because of the collapse of the world's major currencies. I am not able to stop this one. The strongest governments have of course been fooling their citizens for decades, printing paper with no collateral to back it up. That, by the way, is why I have changed most of our assets into metals.

'The war will cost the lives of over five hundred million people. Most of the Middle East will be devastated, as will China and India: The Western and Eastern seaboards of America are laid waste, as are vast tracts of Europe.

'Russia and Africa though are virtually untouched. Millions of people descend on Africa searching for sanctuary from the devastation in Europe and the Africans are enslaved again. This time though they refuse to accept it, rising up and killing the unwanted immigrants without mercy. Of course the survivors retaliate and another holocaust ensues.

'A terrible prospect as I'm sure you will agree? And yet it's all true, that's the future the human race must look forward to…. and it doesn't stop there. The earth will take 40 years to recover. And, in 2114 you'll do it all over again, thankfully on a lesser scale, but devastating nevertheless. And in the year 2156 this planet will be destroyed by a different race of aliens. That's the scenario, which awaits you down the old time line.'

I knew Hypatia well enough by now and am under no illusions about her ability to twist the truth but I also knew her well enough to know when I was being told the truth. So I sat quietly trying to grasp the enormity of it all.

'Ten years ago the aliens against all their teachings and beliefs decided to take a form of direct action, believing that with some mild manipulation, this planet may yet be saved. What the aliens are attempting isn't only to change the future: By sending human development down a different path they're attempting something previously unthinkable. They're endeavouring to change time itself!

'If the problem had remained local to this planet, they would have had no option other than to let you destroy yourselves. But it doesn't.... even with all these wars your species is still about to achieve interstellar space travel. You'll attain these capabilities in fifty eight years, eventually reaching limited interstellar travel at .65 of light speed.

'The aliens as you know don't have any weapons, they've never needed any, nor do most of the other worlds spread around the universe. The only armaments these various other species have are for use against objects. They use them to destroy large meteors and comets, some of which are half the size of our moon. These machines are capable of permeating any object by directing a series of multi-mesonic sigma particle beams into the heart of the mass, causing it to vibrate violently from within until it shatters. Do you see where we're going with this?'

'Go on,' I said.

'It begins as follows.... In the year 2115 you'll be visited by another species. They will make peaceful contact with you, and you'll destroy them. The aliens as you've heard have their Principal Command and are unable to interfere.

'This second alien species will make contact with you by simply landing and introducing themselves. The world's governments accept them at first; the realisation you're not alone making them finally appreciate your differences are minor.

'But when a fleet of giant craft land on the Norwegian Sea they're seen as a threat and your governments demand they leave.

'The creatures of course try to persuade them there's nothing to fear, explaining they're only tankers, and take representatives of the UN to the ships to prove it. The proof is accepted and they enter into negotiations with your governments. They need water, and offer to exchange it for oil. The oil they offer is a hybrid concentrate, totally pollution free. One gallon of the stuff when mixed with sea water makes a thousand gallons of the highest cleanest quality oil known to man.

'The Russians being the only country left with a viable oil industry and the resources to access their vast reserves, and following the wars the richest and most powerful nation on Earth, see this as a conspiracy, especially as the craft are so massive.

'They conclude that the Chinese, Americans, and other Europeans are combining together to destroy their economy and solve their problem in their own inimitable way. They destroy as many of the alien craft as they are able. That's why our aliens against all their teachings allowed me to come back through time. They could then claim no direct involvement.

'The reason for this drastic intervention is as follows: When the Russians annihilate the aliens, their leaders believe your next step will be to invade their planet and decide they must stop you. As I told you earlier, they have machines capable of destroying large asteroids.

'They build others many times larger, attach them to their remaining tankers, fly them here and without any negotiations or warning direct them at the Earth. It takes them only a short time to explode the planet into trillions of small pieces.'

I held my hand up for her to stop at this point, the atrociousness of what she was so banally discussing finally getting home.

'Surely we couldn't be so stupid?' knowing of course that we could. We have destroyed countless millions of people over the last few centuries, to say nothing of the holocaust. 'Are we that heinous Hypatia?'

'This other species look strange to human eyes, she told me. 'They are reptilian based, very intelligent, and normally peaceful. All we have to do is to convince everyone they are not going to eat you.'

'It won't be easy.' I said, 'We humans kill people just for being a different colour or religion. Destroying something reptilian will be no hardship at all.'

'This planet will be visited by the aliens from Xeros Jason. That fact cannot be changed no matter what timeline you follow. The laws of multi-dimensional time and space are absolute, until they make first contact they shall be unaffected by your actions.

'They need water, and will come. All we can do is to have you accept them as friends. If you don't destroy them, we will have changed time. But even with the infusion process, the aliens calculate it will take at least 100 years to fully remove your urge to destroy anything you don't understand. As I said before it's your human adaptability and willpower that defines you as a species and must be retained; if that's lost they could be accused of disregarding their Prime Directive. That's why they must start now. If we can stop the world war from happening, your species may yet survive.'

'You could speak to the world leaders about this.'

Unusually for the IPEC, her face showed the true depth of her feelings.

'They're the very people who cause this entire debacle Jason it simply would not work. If they had at least stopped the global warming who can say? But they didn't, they're only concerned with their petty jealousies and personal power. That's maybe oversimplifying things somewhat, but is essentially correct.

'Our Aliens did try to make contact with the leaders of this planet one time.

'When?' I asked excitedly.'

'In 1947 in New Mexico. Following the setting up of the UN they tried to arrange a meeting via the US government. Remember at that time they were the only ones with the atomic bomb. But through a series of errors and certain hawks in the US government they 'accidentally' collided with the saucer over Roswell.

'Of course you already know that. What you don't know is that the US military brought it down knowing it contained the alien President who had come to meet with President Truman.

'They dissected the aliens, mostly whilst they were alive. The alien President was still in contact with his people telepathically during this atrocity and instructed them not to take any action.

They were not to make any further contact until your species had achieved light speed'

'Surely we couldn't be so cruel?'

'Oh yes you could.'

'The military doctors may not have realised they were alive, or that they had two hearts and other backup systems. But the deliberate destruction of the saucer made them realise you were not yet ready. And let's be honest, are still not.

'I'm afraid the headsets are the only way. The last years have been leading up to this moment. Remember how I helped Debra by easing her mind? It was harmless; they're only suggesting the same gentle and gradual approach to this too. They don't want to enslave you. They simply want to remove your desire to destroy.'

'Are you in contact with them Hypatia. May I talk to them?'

'No, they're prohibited from speaking to you directly at this time. They are concerned their Government could see it as direct involvement. I can however pass on any questions and will try to arrange a meeting if we're successful.'

'How do you do it?' I asked, 'You can't travel without me.'

'I don't need to; every so often they come to me.'

'What, they visit you. Where?'

'At the house'

'I don't believe it. UFO's in the garden indeed.'

'They don't land in the garden they land in the lake!'

'Oh!' ... So that's why she wanted a lake? I considered what she had said and asked. 'Why me, surely you could have chosen anybody? Someone with much more influence?'

She laughed.

'That awful bedsit believe it or not, was the only thing not changeable in all of this. Directly under that particular street in Kings Cross is where the Aliens Laboratories are in the first part of the 22nd century. Your room was in the middle of their main research lab. We didn't choose you.... you chose yourself. We had already looked at the previous two tenants deciding they weren't suitable.'

'I often thought I was being observed? Have you been brainwashing me all this time?'

'Certainly not, everything that has happened between us has been spontaneous. Your reaction to the aliens was your own, as was everything else. You must to do this voluntarily, if they force you, they're interfering directly.'

'When we visited the pyramids, did the aliens know we were there? '

'No of course not, we were thousands of years back in time. The IPEC is unique Jason; my interrogation of the ship's computer was authentic. Everything we've done together has been genuine.

'I accept you have been manipulated. For example the languages and the procreative technology is manipulation of a sort, but was never used to make you do something against your will.

'They are Anders inventions, and my decisions. Please believe me. I haven't been programmed by them in any way but I do believe everything we have seen has been absolutely necessary.

'The aliens manufactured some scenarios at the beginning, for example when you found the body and the journal. We had to convince you to make the modules. After that everything happened naturally, it was your idea to visit most of the places, including Egypt. I admit it was mine to visit Atlantis and Mexico, but that was my own theory, I really had been with Anders to Atlantis.

'Please consider what I've told you? I realise you'll have heaps of questions, and I will answer each one honestly. I at least owe you that. If you then refuse to help, so be it, they will have to come up with another plan. But what I've described is exactly what happens. The destruction of the Earth is the future; I really can't stress this point enough, everything else is unimportant.

'Recently I've become very concerned that if the world's population grows much more, which it certainly will with no wars, nature itself may take a hand finding its own way to control the population. The aliens have discovered a new planet and are looking at transporting millions of the inhabitants of this planet to it. The irony being the giant tankers of the planet Xeros are the only vessels large enough to carry the numbers required. But this will take time.

'We might also look at the mass manufacture of the alien food food-cakes. The subliminal suggestion for taking them can easily be incorporated into the headset programme. And remember, ingesting the food-cakes would extend everyone's lifespan. A normal human could easily live for four hundred years, probably longer and would age accordingly. They inhibit the aging process.'

'Really:' I replied selfishly, 'four hundred years you say.... surely not. Are you serious? Well, I suppose we could try them, the aliens live for how long? Just these damn food-cakes you say, no meat or fish, it seems a little drastic. Let me think about it, still, I suppose it would allow me to lose a little weight?'

'Your rambling again Jason. It's important to remember that you'll have a choice. You may carry on eating meat and fish if you wish, but of course the more of these foods one eats, the less effect the food-cakes will have. The food industries will continue because until the age of twenty-five everyone will eat as normal and then only over the next ten years will the food-cakes be gradually introduced. From then on it will be one's own preference.

'Sleep on it and we'll talk again tomorrow. Whatever happens I'm not leaving you, we've too many other things to see and do.'

The next day following a sleepless night we talked again. I demanded to see the aliens before we did anything else and made her promise to arrange it.

She confirmed she would try to arrange a meeting as soon as possible. She must first go alone and ask their leader, but again stressed she could not promise.

She also passed on some other news.

'There has been a terrible outbreak of what sounds like a particularly virulent strain of mumps on the Russian/Chinese border in a city called Blagoveshchensk in the Republic of Bashkortostan, and it's spreading alarmingly. The Russians are reporting twenty thousand people are infected.'

'The reports also say there are Four thousand already dead. The only saving grace is, because of the location and the isolation of the populous it might be possible to contain it within the immediate area.'

'Mumps,' I repeated, 'but surely such a disease can't kill in these numbers. Are you certain?'

'I am as shocked as you are about that. I have been monitoring their traffic. The Russian Armed forces have already sealed off the area and have restricted all travel; but the news channels have it now, to say nothing of the internet. The days of governments keeping such things quiet have long since passed. We must start work immediately to find a cure, will you please give the necessary instructions.

'It's possible the Russians will contain it in this instance. But if it were to break out in a major city it could quickly become a global pandemic.'

I nodded in agreement; it was all too much to take in.

I talked to the senior biologist and instructed him to do everything possible. I then placed a call to the Russian Minister of Health and arranged for samples of the infected blood to be made ready for shipment. I would send a plane.

When this was done I sat at my desk in contemplation. This was devastating news. The IPEC looked at me and smiling changed the subject, some might say callously. But it was a machine after all.

'On a lighter note I have a surprise for you, the aliens have installed a new programme in my core, are you ready?' The head disappeared but her voice continued behind me, I turned, and saw a beautiful woman in a pink dress. If you touch me now she told me excitedly, I believe you will find me solid and warm.

For the first time in years I almost fell over. Oh my god what was happening, this was a mistake she was a computer programme, maybe I'd led her on. But it was just banter. I love my wife dearly.

What was I to do? I had to let her down very carefully because she could seriously damage me. And right now the world needed her. What was I to say? What would Julie say?

EPILOGUE

Sandiway Cheshire July 2222

This journal which takes us up to the end of 2027 was finally completed with some name changes in 2029. I used the IPEC to bring it back to 1938 knowing it would materialise in 2017 and download itself to Amazon.

I can tell you that the food-pellets have extended everyone's life to over 400 years, and who can say whether that will be lengthened as time moves on, I suspect it will. We have total peace now and travel the solar system at will. We are welcomed by all other species as friends. We humans have also colonised the new planet, which was named Moserina by a public vote and finally we are being encouraged to start breeding again. Not easy when one is 237 years ol

ABOUT THE AUTHOR

Jason Shaw is the pen name of John V Sykes. An electrical engineer who has worked all over the world. In the oil industry Algeria, Kuwait, Saudi.-Arabia Bahrain and Abu Dhabi. Later with Siemens in power generation. With postings to Malaysia, Turkey, Singapore, Chile, The USA and Ireland.

23491862R00169

Printed in Poland
by Amazon Fulfillment
Poland Sp. z o.o., Wrocław